**Praise for *New York Times* bestselling author
Diana Palmer**

"Palmer knows how to make the sparks fly!"
—*Publishers Weekly*

"Diana Palmer is a mesmerizing storyteller who
captures the essence of what a romance should be."
—*Affaire de Coeur*

"The popular Palmer has penned another winning
novel, a perfect blend of romance and suspense."
—*Booklist* on *Lawman*

**Praise for *New York Times* bestselling author
Maisey Yates**

"The out-of-control temptation and pent-up desires
will keep readers eagerly turning the pages."
—*RT Book Reviews* on *Take Me, Cowboy*

"Fans of Robyn Carr and RaeAnne Thayne will
enjoy [Yates's] small-town romance."
—*Booklist* on *Part Time Cowboy*

**Diana Palmer** is a multiple *New York Times* bestselling author of over one hundred books and one of the top ten romance writers in America. She has a gift for telling even the most sensual tales with charm and humor. Diana lives with her family in Cornelia, Georgia. Visit her website at dianapalmer.com.

*New York Times* bestselling author **Maisey Yates** lives in rural Oregon with her three children and her husband, whose chiseled jaw and arresting features continue to make her swoon. She feels the epic trek she takes several times a day from her office to her coffeemaker is a true example of her pioneer spirit.

*New York Times* **Bestselling Author**

# DIANA PALMER

# MAN IN CONTROL

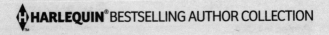

**HARLEQUIN**®BESTSELLING AUTHOR COLLECTION

ISBN-13: 978-1-335-46819-2

Man in Control

Copyright © 2017 by Harlequin Books S.A.

The publisher acknowledges the copyright holder of the individual works as follows:

Man in Control
© 2003 by Diana Palmer

Take Me, Cowboy
© 2016 by Maisey Yates

Recycling programs for this product may not exist in your area.

**HARLEQUIN**®

www.Harlequin.com

**Printed in U.S.A.**

# CONTENTS

For a complete listing of books by Diana Palmer,
please visit dianapalmer.com.

# MAN IN CONTROL

## Diana Palmer

In loving memory of Diana Galloway

# Prologue

Alexander Tyrell Cobb glared at his desk in the Houston Drug Enforcement Administration office with barely contained frustration. There was a photograph of a lovely woman in a ball gown in an expensive frame, the only visible sign of any emotional connections. Like the conservative clothes he wore to work, the photograph gave away little of the private man.

The photograph was misleading. The woman in it wasn't a close friend. She was a casual date, when he was between assignments. The frame had been given to him with the photo in it. He'd never put a woman's photo in a frame. Well, except for Jodie Clayburn. She and his sister, Margie, were best friends from years past. Most of the family photos he had included Jodie. She wasn't really family, of course. But there was no other Cobb family left, just as there was no other Clayburn family left. The three survivors of the two families were a forced mixture of different lifestyles.

Jodie was in love with Alexander. He knew it, and tried not to acknowledge it. She was totally wrong for him. He had no desire to marry and have a family. On the other hand, if he'd been seriously interested in children and a home life, Jodie would have been at the top of his list of potential mates. She had wonderful qualities. He wasn't about to tell her so. She'd been hung up on him in the past to a disturbing degree. He'd managed to keep her at arm's length, and he had no plans to lessen the space between them. He was married to his job.

Jodie, on the other hand, was an employee at a local oil corporation which was being used in an international drug smuggling operation. Alexander was almost certain of it. But he couldn't prove it. He was going to have to find some way to investigate one of Jodie's acquaintances without letting anyone realize they were being watched.

In the meantime, there was a party planned at the Cobb ranch in Jacobsville, Texas, on Saturday. He dreaded it already. He hated parties. Margie had already invited Jodie, probably because their housekeeper, Jessie, refused to work that weekend. Jodie cooked with a masterful hand, and she could make canapés. Kirry had been invited, too, because Margie was a budding dress designer who needed a friend in the business. Kirry was senior buyer for the department store where she worked. She was pretty and capable, but Alexander found her good company and not much more. Their relationship had always been lukewarm and even now, it was slowly fizzling out. She was demanding. He had enough demands on the job.

He put the picture facedown on his desk and pulled a file folder closer, opening it to the photograph of a suspected drug smuggler who was working out of Houston. He had his work cut out for him. He wished he could avoid going home for the party, but Margie would never forgive him. If he didn't show up, neither would Kirry, and Alexander would never hear the end of it. He put the weekend to the back of his mind and concentrated on the job at hand.

# Chapter 1

There was no way out of it. Margie Cobb had invited her to a party on the family ranch in Jacobsville, Texas. Jodie Clayburn had gone through her entire repertoire of excuses. Her favorite was that, given the right incentive, Margie's big brother, Alexander Tyrell Cobb, would feed her to his cattle. Not even that one had worked.

"He hates me, Margie," she groaned over the phone from her apartment in Houston, Texas. "You know he does. He'd be perfectly happy if I stayed away from him for the rest of my natural life and he never had to see me again."

"That's not true," Margie defended. "Lex really likes you, I know he does," she added with forced conviction, using the nickname that only a handful of people on earth were allowed to use. Jodie wasn't one of them.

"Right. He just hides his affection for me in bouts of bad temper laced with sarcasm," came the dry reply.

"Sure," Margie replied with failing humor.

Jodie lay back on her sofa with the freedom phone at her ear and pushed back her long blond hair. It was getting too long. She really needed to have it cut, but she liked the feel of it. Her gray eyes smiled as she remembered how much Brody Vance liked long hair. He worked at the Ritter Oil Corporation branch office in Houston with her, and was on the management fast track. As Jody was. She was administrative assistant to Brody, and if Brody had his way, she'd take his job as Human Resources generalist when he moved up to Human Resources manager. He liked her. She liked him, too. Of course he had a knockout girlfriend who was a Marketing Division manager in Houston, but she was always on the road somewhere. He was lonely. So he had lunch frequently with Jodie. She was trying very hard to develop a crush on him. He was beginning to notice her. Alexander had accused her of trying to sleep her way to the executive washroom…

"I was not!" she exclaimed, remembering his unexpected visit to her office with an executive of the company who was a personal friend. It had played havoc with her nerves and her heart. Seeing Alexander unexpectedly melted her from the neck down, despite her best efforts not to let him affect her.

"Excuse me?" Margie replied, aghast.

Jodie sat up quickly. "Nothing!" she said. "Sorry. I was just thinking. Did you know that Alexander has a friend who works for my company?"

There was a long pause. "He does?"

"Jasper Duncan, the Human Resources manager for our division."

"Oh. Yes. Jasper!" There was another pause. "How do you know about that?"

"Because Mr. Duncan brought him right to my desk while I was talking to a…well, to a good friend of mine, my boss."

"Right, the one he thinks you're sleeping with."

"Margie!" she exploded.

There was an embarrassed laugh. "Sorry. I know there's nothing going on. Alexander always thinks the worst of people. You know about Rachel."

"Everybody knows about Rachel," she muttered. "It was six years ago and he still throws her up to us."

"We did introduce him," Margie said defensively.

"Well, how were we to know she was a female gigolo who was only interested in marrying a rich man? She should have had better sense than to think Alexander would play that sort of game, anyway!"

"You do know him pretty well, don't you?" Margie murmured.

"We all grew up together in Jacobsville, Texas," Jodie reminded her. "Sort of," she added pensively. "Alexander was eight years ahead of us in school, and then he moved to Houston to work for the DEA when he got out of college."

"He's still eight years ahead of us," Margie chuckled. "Come on. You know you'll hate yourself if you miss this party. We're having a houseful of people. Derek will be there," she added sweetly, trying to inject a lure.

Derek was Margie's distant cousin, a dream of a

man with some peculiar habits and a really weird sense of humor.

"You know what happened the last time Derek and I were together," Jodie said with a sense of foreboding.

"Oh, I'm sure Alexander has forgotten about *that* by now," she was assured.

"He has a long memory. And Derek can talk me into anything," Jodie added worriedly.

"I'll hang out with both of you and protect you from dangerous impulses. Come on. Say yes. I've got an opportunity to show my designs. It depends on this party going smoothly. And I've made up this marvelous dress pattern I want to try out on you. For someone with the body of a clotheshorse, you have no sense of style at all!"

"You have enough for both of us. You're a budding fashion designer. I'm a lady executive. I have to dress the part."

"Baloney. When was the last time your boss wore a black dress to a party?"

Jodie was remembering a commercial she'd seen on television with men in black dresses. She howled, thinking of Alexander's hairy legs in a short skirt. Then she tried to imagine where he'd keep his sidearm in a short skirt, and she really howled.

She told Margie what she was thinking, and they both collapsed into laughter.

"Okay," she capitulated at last. "I'll come. But if I break a tree limb over your brother's thick skull, you can't say you weren't forewarned."

"I swear, I won't say a word."

"Then I'll see you Friday afternoon about four,"

Jodie said with resignation. "I'll rent a car and drive over."

"Uh, Jodie…"

She groaned. "All right, Margie, all right, I'll fly to the Jacobsville airport and you can pick me up there."

"Great!"

"Just because I had two little bitty fender benders," she muttered.

"You totaled two cars, Jodie, and Alexander had to bail you out of jail after the last one…"

"Well, that stupid thickheaded barbarian deserved to be hit! He called me a…well, never mind, but he asked for a punch in the mouth!" Jodie fumed.

Margie was trying not to laugh. Again.

"Anyway, it was only a small fine and the judge took my side when he heard the whole story," she said, ignoring Margie's quick reminder that Alexander had talked to the judge first. "Not that your brother ever let me forget it! Just because he works for the Justice Department is no reason for him to lecture me on law!"

"We just want you to arrive alive, darling," Margie drawled. "Now throw a few things into a suitcase, tell your boss you have a sick cousin you have to take care of before rush hour, and we'll…*I'll*…meet you at the airport Friday afternoon. You phone and tell me your flight number, okay?"

"Okay," Jodie replied, missing the slip.

"See you then! We're going to have a ball."

"Sure we are," Jodie told her. But when she hung up, she was calling herself all sorts of names for being such a weakling. Alexander was going to cut her up, she just knew it. He didn't like her. He never had. He'd gotten more antagonistic since she moved to Houston, where he worked, too. Further, it would probably mean a lot of work for Jodie, because she usually had to prepare meals if she showed up. The family cook, Jessie, hated being around Alexander when he was home, so she ran for the hills. Margie couldn't cook at all, so Jodie usually ended up with KP. Not that she minded. It was just that she felt used from time to time.

And despite Margie's assurances, she knew she was in for the fight of her life once she set foot on the Cobb ranch. At least Margie hadn't said anything about inviting Alexander's sometimes girlfriend, Kirry Dane. A weekend with the elegant buyer for an exclusive Houston department store would be too much.

The thing was, she had to go when Margie asked her. She owed the Cobbs so much. When her parents, small Jacobsville ranchers, had been drowned in a riptide during a modest Florida vacation at the beach, it had been Alexander who flew down to take care of all the arrangements and comfort a devastated seventeen-year-old Jodie. When she entered business college, Alexander had gone with her to register and paid the fees himself. She spent every holiday with Margie. Since the death of the Cobbs' father, and their inheritance of the Jacobsville ranch property, she'd spent her vacation every summer there with Margie. Her life was so intertwined with that of the Cobbs that she couldn't even imagine life without them.

But Alexander had a very ambiguous relationship with Jodie. From time to time he was affectionate, in his gruff way. But he also seemed to resent her presence and he picked at her constantly. He had for the past year.

She got up and went to pack, putting the antagonism

to the back of her mind. It did no good to dwell on her confrontations with Alexander. He was like a force of nature which had to be accepted, since it couldn't be controlled.

The Jacobsville Airport was crowded for a Friday afternoon. It was a tiny airport compared to those in larger cities, but a lot of people in south Texas used it for commuter flights to San Antonio and Houston. There was a restaurant and two concourses, and the halls were lined with beautiful paintings of traditional Texas scenery.

Jodie almost bowed under the weight of her oversize handbag and the unruly carry-on bag whose wheels didn't quite work. She looked around for Margie. The brunette wouldn't be hard to spot because she was tall for a woman, and always wore something striking— usually one of her own flamboyant designs.

But she didn't see any tall brunettes. What she did see, and what stopped her dead in her tracks, was a tall and striking dark-haired man in a gray vested business suit. A man with broad shoulders and narrow hips and big feet in hand-tooled leather boots. He turned, looking around, and spotted her. Even at the distance, those deep-set, cold green eyes were formidable. So was he. He looked absolutely furious.

She stood very still, like a woman confronted with a spitting cobra, and waited while he approached her with the long, quick stride she remembered from years of painful confrontations. Her chin lifted and her eyes narrowed. She drew in a quick breath, and geared up for combat.

Alexander Tyrell Cobb was thirty-three. He was a

senior agent for the Drug Enforcement Administration. Usually, he worked out of Houston, but he was on vacation for a week. That meant he was at the family ranch in Jacobsville. He'd grown up there, with Margie, but their mother had taken them from their father after the divorce and had them live with her in Houston. It hadn't been until her death that they'd finally been allowed to return home to their father's ranch. The old man had loved them dearly. It had broken his heart when he'd lost them to their mother.

Alexander lived on the ranch sporadically even now, when he wasn't away on business. He also had an apartment in Houston. Margie lived at the ranch all the time, and kept things running smoothly while her big brother was out shutting down drug smugglers.

He looked like a man who could do that single-handed. He had big fists, like his big feet, and Jodie had seen him use them once on a man who slapped Margie. He rarely smiled. He had a temper like a scalded snake, and he was all business when he tucked that big .45 automatic into its hand-tooled leather holster and went out looking for trouble.

In the past two years, he'd been helping to shut down an international drug lord, Manuel Lopez, who'd died mysteriously in an explosion in the Bahamas. Now he was after the dead drug lord's latest successor, a Central American national who was reputed to have business connections in the port city of Houston.

She'd developed a feverish crush on him when she was in her teens. She'd written him a love poem. Alexander, with typical efficiency, had circled the grammatical and spelling errors and bought her a supplemental English book to help her correct the mistakes. Her self-

esteem had taken a serious nosedive, and after that, she
kept her deepest feelings carefully hidden.

She'd seen him only a few times since her move to
Houston when she began attending business college.
When she visited Margie these days, Alexander never
seemed to be around except at Christmas. It was as if
he'd been avoiding her. Then, just a couple of weeks
ago, he'd dropped by her office to see Jasper. It had
been a shock to see him unexpectedly, and her hands
had trembled on her file folders, despite her best efforts
to play it cool. She wanted to think she'd outgrown her
flaming crush on him. Sadly, it had only gotten worse.
It was easier on her nerves when she didn't have to see
him. Fortunately it was a big city and they didn't travel
in the same circles. But she didn't know where Alexander's office or apartment were, and she didn't ask.

In fact, her nerves were already on edge right now,
just from the level, intent stare of those green eyes
across a crowded concourse. She clutched the handle
of her wheeled suitcase with a taut grip. Alexander
made her knees weak.

He strode toward her. He never looked right or left.
His gaze was right on her the whole way. She wondered
if he was like that on the job, so intent on what he was
doing that he seemed relentless.

He was a sexy beast, too. There was a tightly controlled sensuality in every movement of those long,
powerful legs, in the way he carried himself. He was
elegant, arrogant. Jodie couldn't remember a time in
her life when she hadn't been fascinated by him. She
hoped it didn't show. She worked hard at pretending
to be his enemy.

He stopped in front of her and looked down his nose

into her wide eyes. His were green, clear as water, with dark rims that made them seem even more piercing. He had thick black eyelashes and black eyebrows that were as black as his neatly cut, thick, straight hair.

"You're late," he said in his deep, gravelly voice, throwing down the gauntlet at once. He looked annoyed, half out of humor and wanting someone to bite.

"I can't fly the plane," she replied sarcastically. "I had to depend on *men* for that."

He gave her a speaking glance and turned. "The car's in the parking lot. Let's go."

"Margie was supposed to meet me," she muttered, dragging her case behind her.

"Margie knew I had to be here anyway, so she had me wait for you," he said enigmatically. "I never knew a woman who could keep an appointment, anyway."

The carry-on bag fell over for the tenth time. She muttered and finally just picked the heavy thing up. "You might offer to help me," she said, glowering at her companion.

His eyebrows arched. "Help a woman carry a heavy load? My God, I'd be stripped, lashed to a rail and carried through Houston by torchlight!"

She gave him a seething glance. "Manners don't go out of style!"

"Pity I never had any to begin with." He watched her struggle with the luggage, green eyes dancing with pure venom.

She was sweating already. "I hate you," she said through her teeth as she followed along with him.

"That's a change," he said with a shrug, pushing back his jacket as he dug into his slacks pocket for his car keys.

A security guard spotted the pistol on his belt and came forward menacingly. With meticulous patience, and very carefully, Alexander reached into the inside pocket of his suit coat and produced his badge and ID. He had it out before the guard reached them.

The man took it. "Wait a minute," he said, and moved aside to check it out over the radio.

"Maybe you're on a wanted list somewhere," Jodie said enthusiastically. "Maybe they'll put you in jail while they check out your ID!"

"If they do," he replied nonchalantly, "rent-a-cop over there will be looking for another job by morning."

He didn't smile as he said it, and Jodie knew he meant what he was saying. Alexander had a vindictive streak a mile wide. There was a saying among law enforcement people that Cobb would follow you all the way to hell to get you if you crossed him. From their years of uneasy acquaintance, she knew it was more than myth.

The security guard came back and handed Alexander his ID. "Sorry, sir, but it's my job to check out suspicious people."

Alexander glared at him. "Then why haven't you checked out the gentleman in the silk suit over there with the bulge in his hatband? He's terrified that you're going to notice him."

The security guard frowned and glanced toward the elegant man, who tugged at his collar. "Thanks for the tip," he murmured, and started toward the man.

"You might have offered to lend him your gun," she told Alexander.

"He's got one. Of a sort," he added with disgust

at the pearl-handled sidearm the security guard was carrying.

"Men have to have their weapons, don't they?" she chided.

He gave her a quick glance. "With a mouth like yours, you don't need a weapon. Careful you don't cut your chin with that tongue."

She aimed a kick at his shin and missed, almost losing her balance.

"Assault on a law enforcement officer is a felony," he pointed out without even breaking stride.

She recovered her balance and went out the door after him without another word. If they ever suspended the rules for one day, she knew who she was going after!

Once they reached his car, an elegant white Jaguar S-type, he did put her bags in the trunk—but he left her to open her own door and get in. It wasn't surprising to find him driving such a car, on a federal agent's salary, because he and Margie were independently wealthy. Their late mother had left them both well-off, but unlike Margie, who loved the social life, Alexander refused to live on an inheritance. He enjoyed working for his living. It was one of many things Jodie admired about him.

The admiration didn't last long. He threw down the gauntlet again without hesitation. "How's your boyfriend?" he asked as he pulled out into traffic.

"I don't have a boyfriend!" she snapped, still wiping away sweat. It was hot for August, even in south Texas.

"No? You'd like to have one, though, wouldn't you?"

He adjusted the rearview mirror as he stopped at a traffic light.

"He's my boss. That's all."

"Pity. You could hardly take your eyes off him, that day I stopped by your office."

"*He's* handsome," she said with deliberate emphasis.

His eyebrow jerked. "Looks don't get you promoted in the Drug Enforcement Administration," he told her.

"You'd know. You've worked for it half your life."

"Not quite half. I'm only thirty-three."

"One foot in the grave…"

He glanced at her. "You're twenty-five, I believe? And never been engaged?"

He knew that would hurt. She averted her gaze to the window. Until a few months ago, she'd been about fifty pounds overweight and not very careful about her clothing or makeup. She was still clueless about how to dress. She dressed like an overweight woman, with loose clothing that showed nothing of her pretty figure. She folded her arms over her breasts defensively.

"I can't go through with this," she said through her teeth. "Three days of you will put me in therapy!"

He actually smiled. "That would be worth putting up with three days of you to see."

She crossed her legs under her full skirt and concentrated on the road. Her eyes caressed the silky brown bird's-eye maple that graced the car's dash and steering wheel.

"Margie promised she'd meet me," she muttered, repeating herself.

"She told me you'd be thrilled if I did," he replied with a searing glance. "You're still hung up on me, aren't you?" he asked with faint sarcasm.

Her jaw fell. "She lied! I did not say I'd be thrilled for you to meet me!" she raged. "I only came because she promised that she'd be here when I landed. I wanted to rent a car and drive!"

His green eyes narrowed on her flushed face. "That would have been suicide," he murmured. "Or homicide, depending on your point of view."

"I can drive!"

"You and the demolition derby guys," he agreed. He accelerated around a slow-moving car and the powerful Jaguar growled like the big cat it was named for. She glanced at him and saw the pure joy of the car's performance in his face as he slid effortlessly back into the lane ahead of the slow car. He enjoyed fast cars and, gossip said, faster women. But that side of his life had always been concealed from Jodie. It was as if he'd placed her permanently off-limits and planned to keep her there.

"At least I don't humiliate other drivers by streaking past them at jet fighter speed!" she raged. She was all but babbling, and after only ten minutes of his company. Seething inwardly, she turned toward the window so that she wouldn't have to look at him.

"I wasn't streaking. I'm doing the speed limit," he said. He glanced at the speedometer, smiled faintly and eased up on the accelerator. His eyes slid over Jodie curiously. "You've lost so much weight, I hardly recognized you when I stopped by to talk to Jasper."

"Right. I looked different when I was fat."

"You were never fat," he shot back angrily. "You were voluptuous. There's a difference."

She glanced at him. "I was terribly overweight."

"And you think men like to run their hands over bones, do you?"

She shifted in her seat. "I wouldn't know."

"You had a low self-image. You still have it. There's nothing wrong with you. Except for that sharp tongue," he added.

"Look who's complaining!"

"If I don't yell, nobody listens."

"You never yell," she corrected. "You can look at people and make them run for cover."

He smiled without malice. "I practice in my bathroom mirror."

She couldn't believe she'd heard that.

"You need to start thinking about a Halloween costume," he murmured as he made a turn.

"For what? Are you going to hire me out for parties?" she muttered.

"For our annual Halloween party next month," he said with muted disgust. "Margie's invited half of Jacobsville to come over in silly clothes and masks to eat candy apples."

"What are you coming as?"

He gave her a careless glance. "A Drug Enforcement Agency field agent."

She rolled her eyes toward the ceiling of the car.

"I make a convincing DEA field agent," he persisted.

"I wouldn't argue with that," she had to agree. "I hear that Manuel Lopez mysteriously blew up in the Bahamas the year before last, and nobody's replaced him yet," she added. "Did you have anything to do with his sudden demise?"

"DEA agents don't blow up drug lords. Not even one as bad as Lopez."

"Somebody did."

He glanced at her with a faint smile. "In a manner of speaking."

"One of the former mercs from Jacobsville, I heard."

"Micah Steele was somewhere around when it happened. He's never been actually connected with Lopez's death."

"He moved back here and married Callie Kirby, didn't he? They have a little girl now."

He nodded. "He's practicing medicine at Jacobsville General as a resident, hoping to go into private practice when he finishes his last semester of study."

"Lucky Callie," she murmured absently, staring out the window. "She always wanted to get married and have kids, and she was crazy about Micah most of her life."

He watched her curiously. "Didn't you want to get married, too?"

She didn't answer. "So now that Lopez is out of the way, and nobody's replaced him, you don't have a lot to do, do you?"

He laughed shortly. "Lopez has a new successor, a Peruvian national living in Mexico on an open-ended visa. He's got colleagues in Houston helping him smuggle his product into the United States."

"Do you know who they are?" she asked excitedly.

He gave her a cold glare. "Oh, sure, I'm going to tell you their names right now."

"You don't have to be sarcastic, Cobb," she said icily.

One thick eyebrow jerked. "You're the only person

I know, outside work, who uses my last name as if it were my first name."

"You don't use my real name, either."

"Don't I?" He seemed surprised. He glanced at her. "You don't look like a Jordana."

"I never thought I looked like a Jordana, either," she said with a sigh. "My mother loved odd names. She even gave them to the cats."

Remembering her mother made her sad. She'd lost both parents in a freak accident during a modest vacation in Florida after her high school graduation. Her parents had gone swimming in the ocean, having no idea that the pretty red flags on the beach warned of treacherous riptides that could drown even experienced swimmers. Which her mother and father were not. She could still remember the horror of it. Alexander had come to take care of the details, and to get her back home. Odd how many tragedies and crises he'd seen her through over the years.

"Your mother was a sweet woman," he recalled. "I'm sorry you lost her. And your father."

"He was a sweet man, too," she recalled. It had been eight years ago, and she could remember happy times now, but it still made her sad to think of them.

"Strange, isn't it, that you don't take after either of them?" he asked caustically. "No man in his right mind could call you 'sweet.'"

"Stop right there, Cobb," she threatened, using his last name again. It was much more comfortable than getting personal with the nickname Margie used for him. "I could say things about you, too."

"What? That I'm dashing and intelligent and the answer to a maiden's prayer?" He pursed his lips and glanced her way as he pulled into the road that led to the ranch. "Which brings up another question. Are you sleeping with that airheaded boss of yours at work yet?"

"He is not airheaded!" she exclaimed, offended.

"He eats tofu and quiche, he drives a red convertible of uncertain age, he plays tennis and he doesn't know how to program a computer without crashing the system."

That was far too knowledgeable to have come from a dossier. Her eyes narrowed. "You've had him checked out!" she accused with certainty.

He only smiled. It wasn't a nice smile.

## Chapter 2

"You can't go around snooping into people's private lives like that," Jodie exclaimed heatedly. "It's not right!"

"I'm looking for a high-level divisional manager who works for the new drug lord in his Houston territory," he replied calmly. "I check out everybody who might have an inkling of what's going on." He turned his head slightly. "I even checked you out."

"Me?" she exclaimed.

He gave her a speaking look. "I should have known better. If I had a social life like yours, I'd join a convent."

"I can see you now, in long skirts…"

"It was a figure of speech," he said curtly. "You haven't been on a date in two years. Amazing, considering how many eligible bachelors there are in your building alone, much less the whole of Houston." He gave her a penetrating stare. "Are you sure you aren't still stuck on me?"

She drew in a short breath. "Oh, sure, I am," she muttered. "I only come down here so that I can sit and moon over you and think of ways to poison all your girlfriends."

He chuckled in spite of himself. "Okay. I get the idea."

"Who in my building do you suspect, exactly?" she persisted.

He hesitated. His dark brows drew together in a frown as the ranch house came into view down the long, dusty road. "I can't tell you that," he said. "Right now it's only a suspicion."

"I could help you trap him," she volunteered. "If I get a gun, that is. I won't help you if I have to be unarmed."

He chuckled again. "You shoot like you drive, Jodie."

She made an angry sound in her throat. "I could shoot just fine if I got enough practice. Is it my fault that my landlord doesn't like us busting targets in my apartment building?"

"Have Margie invite you down just to shoot. She can teach you as well as I can."

It was an unpleasant reminder that he wasn't keen on being with her.

"I don't remember asking you to teach me anything," she returned.

He pulled up in front of the house. "Well, not lately, at least," he had to agree.

Margie heard the car drive up and came barreling

out onto the porch. She was tall, like Alexander, and she had green eyes, too, but her dark hair had faint undertones of auburn. She was pretty, unlike poor Jodie, and she wore anything with flair. She designed and made her own clothes, and they were beautiful.

She ran to Jodie and hugged her, laughing. "I'm so glad you came!"

"I thought you were going to pick me up at the airport, Margie," came the droll reply.

Margie looked blank for an instant. "Oh, gosh, I was, wasn't I? I got busy with a design and just lost all track of time. Besides, Lex had already gone to the airport to pick up Kirry, but she couldn't get his cell phone, so she phoned me and said she was delayed until tomorrow afternoon. He was right there already, so I just phoned him and had him bring you home."

Kirry was Alexander's current girlfriend. The fashion buyer had just returned home recently from a buying trip to Paris. It didn't occur to Margie that it would have been pure torture to have to ride to the ranch with Alexander and his girlfriend. But, then, Margie didn't think things through. And to give her credit, she didn't realize that Jodie was still crazy about Alexander Cobb.

"She's coming down tomorrow to look at some of my new designs," Margie continued, unabashed, "and, of course, for the party in her honor that we're giving here. She leads a very busy life."

Jodie felt her heart crashing at her feet, and she didn't dare show it. A weekend with Kirry Dane drooling over Alexander, and vice versa. Why hadn't she argued harder and stayed home?

Alexander checked his watch. "I've got to make a

few phone calls, then I'm going to drive into town and see about that fencing I ordered."

"That's what we have a foreman for," Margie informed him.

"Chayce went home to Georgia for the weekend. His father's in the hospital."

"You didn't tell me that!"

"Did you need to know?" he shot right back.

Margie shook her head, exasperated, as he just walked away without a backward glance. "I do live here, too," she muttered, but it was too late. He'd already gone into the house.

"I'm going to be in the way if the party's for Kirry," Jodie said worriedly. "Honestly, Margie, you shouldn't have invited me. No wonder Alexander's so angry!"

"It's my house, too, and I can invite who I like," Margie replied curtly, intimating that she and Alexander had argued about Jodie's inclusion at the party. That hurt even more. "You're my best friend, Jodie, and I need an ego boost," Margie continued unabashed. "Kirry is so worldly and sophisticated. She hates it here and she makes me feel insecure. But I need her help to get my designs shown at the store where she works. So, you're my security blanket." She linked her arm with Jodie's. "Besides, Kirry and Lex together get on my nerves."

What about my nerves? Jodie was wondering. And my heart, having to see Alexander with Kirry all weekend? But she only smiled and pretended that it didn't matter. She was Margie's friend, and she owed her a lot. Even if it was going to mean eating her heart out watching the man she loved hang on to that beautiful woman, Kirry Dane.

Margie stopped just before they went into the house. She looked worried. "You have gotten over that crush you had on my brother…?" she asked quickly.

"You and your brother!" Jodie gasped. "Honestly, I'm too old for schoolgirl crushes," she lied through her teeth, "and besides, there's this wonderful guy at the office that I like a lot. It's just that he's going with someone."

Margie grimaced. "You poor kid. It's always like that with you, isn't it?"

"Go right ahead and step on my ego, don't mind me," Jodie retorted.

Margie flushed. "I'm a pig," she said. "Sorry, Jodie. I don't know what's the matter with me. Yes, I do," she added at once. "Cousin Derek arrived unexpectedly this morning. Jessie's already threatened to cook him up with a pan of eggs, and one of the cowboys ran a tractor through a fence trying to get away from him. In fact, Jessie remembered that she could have a weekend off whenever she wanted, so she's gone to Dallas for the weekend to see her brother. And here I am with no cook and a party tomorrow night!"

"Except me?" Jodie ventured, and her heart sank again when she saw Margie's face. No wonder she'd been insistent. There wouldn't be any food without someone to cook it, and Margie couldn't cook.

"You don't mind, do you, dear?" Margie asked quickly. "After all, you do make the most scrumptious little canapés, and you're a great cook. Even Jessie asks you for recipes."

"No," Jodie lied. "I don't mind."

"And you can help me keep Derek out of Alexander's way."

"Derek." Jodie's eyes lit up. She loved the Cobbs' renegade cousin from Oklahoma. He was a rodeo cowboy who won belts at every competition, six foot two of pure lithe muscle, with a handsome face and a modest demeanor—when he wasn't up to some horrible devilment. He drove housekeepers and cowboys crazy with his antics, and Alexander barely tolerated him. He was Margie's favorite of their few cousins. Not that he was really a cousin. He was only related by marriage. Of course, Margie didn't know that. Derek had told Jodie once, but asked her not to tell. She wondered why.

"Don't even think about helping him do anything crazy while you're here," Margie cautioned. "Lex doesn't know he's here yet. I, uh, haven't told him."

"Margie!" came a thunderous roar from the general direction of Alexander's office.

Margie groaned. "Oh, dear, Lex does seem to know about Derek."

"My suitcase," Jodie said, halting, hoping to get out of the line of fire in time.

"Lex will bring it in, dear, come along." She almost dragged her best friend into the house.

Derek was leaning against the staircase banister, handsome as a devil, with dancing brown eyes and a lean, good-looking face under jet-black hair. In front of him, Alexander was holding up a rubber chicken by the neck.

"I thought you liked chicken," Derek drawled.

"Cooked," Alexander replied tersely. "Not in my desk chair pretending to be a cushion!"

"You could cook that, but the fumes would clear out the kitchen for sure," Derek chuckled.

Cobb threw it at the man, turned, went back into his

office and slammed the door. Muttered curses came right through two inches of solid mahogany.

"Derek, how could you?" Margie wailed.

He tossed her the chicken and came forward to lift her up and kiss her saucily on the nose. "Now, now, you can't expect me to be dignified. It isn't in my nature. Hi, sprout!" he added, putting Margie down only to pick up Jodie and swing her around in a bear hug. "How's my best girl?"

"I'm just fine, Derek," she replied, kissing his cheek. "You look great."

"So do you." He let her dangle from his hands and his keen dark eyes scanned her flushed face. "Has Cobb been picking on you all the way home?" he asked lazily.

"Why can't you two call him Lex, like I do?" Margie wanted to know.

"He doesn't look like a Lex," Derek replied.

"He always picks on me," Jodie said heavily as Derek let her slide back onto her feet. "If he had a list of people he doesn't like, I'd lead it."

"We'd tie for that spot, I reckon," Derek replied. He gave Margie a slow, steady appraisal. "New duds? I like that skirt."

Margie grinned up at him. "I made it."

"Good for you. When are you going to have a show of all those pretty things you make?"

"That's what I'm working on. Lex's girlfriend Kirry is trying to get her store to let me do a parade of my designs."

"Kirry." Derek wrinkled his straight nose. "Talk about slow poison. And he thought Rachel was bad!"

"Don't mention Rachel!" Margie cautioned quickly.

"Kirry makes her look like a church mouse," Derek said flatly. "She's a social climber with dollar signs for eyes. Mark my words, it isn't his body she's after."

"He likes her," Margie replied.

"He likes liver and onions, too," Derek said, and made a horrible face.

Jodie laughed at the byplay.

Derek glanced at her. "Why doesn't he ever look at you, sprout? You'd be perfect for him."

"Don't be silly," Jodie said with a forced smile. "I'm not his type at all."

"You're not mercenary. You're a sucker for anyone in trouble. You like cats and dogs and children, and you don't like nightlife. You're perfect."

"He likes opera and theater," she returned.

"And you don't?" Derek asked.

Margie grabbed him by the arm. "Come on and let's have coffee while you tell us about your latest rodeo triumph."

"How do you know it was?" he teased.

"When have you ever lost a belt?" she replied with a grin.

Jodie followed along behind them, already uneasy about the weekend. She had a feeling that it wasn't going to be the best one of her life.

Later, Jodie escaped from the banter between Margie and her cousin and went out to the corral near the barn to look at the new calves. One of the older ranch hands, Johnny, came out to join her. He was missing a tooth in front from a bull's hooves and a finger from a too-tight rope that slipped. His chaps and hat and boots were worn and dirty from hard work. But he had a heart of pure gold, and Jodie loved him. He reminded her of her late father.

"Hey, Johnny!" she greeted, standing on the top rung of the wooden fence in old jeans, boots, and a long-sleeved blue checked shirt. Her hair was up in a ponytail. She looked about twelve.

He grinned back. "Hey, Jodie! Come to see my babies?"

"Sure have!"

"Ain't they purty?" he drawled, joining her at the fence, where she was feeding her eyes on the pretty little white-faced, red-coated calves.

"Yes, they are," she agreed with a sigh. "I miss this up in Houston. The closest I get to cattle is the rodeo when it comes to town."

He winced. "You poor kid," he said. "You lost everything at once, all them years ago."

That was true. She'd lost her parents and her home, all at once. If Alexander hadn't gotten her into business college, where she could live on campus, she'd have been homeless.

She smiled down at him. "Time heals even the worst wounds, Johnny. Besides, I still get to come down here and visit once in a while."

He looked irritated. "Wish you came more than that Dane woman," he said under his breath. "Can't stand cattle and dust, don't like cowboys, looks at us like we'd get her dirty just by speaking to her."

She reached over and patted him gently on the shoulder. "We all have our burdens to bear."

He sighed. "I reckon so. Why don't you move back down here?" he added. "Plenty of jobs going in Jacobsville right now. I hear tell the police chief needs a new secretary."

She chuckled. "I'm not going to work for Cash Grier," she assured him. "They said his last secretary emptied the trash can over his head, and it was full of half-empty coffee cups and coffee grounds."

"Well, some folks don't take to police work," he said, but he chuckled.

"Nothing to do, Johnny?" came a deep, terse voice from behind Jodie.

Johnny straightened immediately. "Just started mucking out the stable, boss. I only came over to say howdy to Miss Jodie."

"Good to see you again, Johnny," she said.

"Same here, miss."

He tipped his hat and went slowly back into the barn.

"Don't divert the hired help," Alexander said curtly.

She got down from the fence. It was a long way up to his eyes in her flat shoes. "He was a friend of my father's," she reminded him. "I was being polite."

She turned and started back to the house.

"Running away?"

She stopped and faced him. "I'm not going to be your whipping boy," she said.

His eyebrows arched. "Wrong gender."

"You know what I mean. You're furious that Derek's here, and Kirry's not, and you want somebody to take it out on."

He moved restlessly at the accusation. His scowl was suddenly darker. "Don't do that."

She knew what he meant. She could always see through his bad temper to the reason for it, something his own sister had never been able to do.

"Derek will leave in the morning and Kirry will be here by afternoon," she said. "Derek can't do that much damage in a night. Besides, you know how close he and Margie are."

"He's too flighty for her, distant relation or not," he muttered.

She sighed, looking up at him with quiet, soft eyes full of memories. "Like me," she said under her breath.

He frowned. "What?"

"That's always been your main argument against me—that I'm too flighty. That's why you didn't like it when Derek was trying to get me to go out with him three years ago," she reminded him.

He stared at her for a few seconds, still scowling. "Did I say that?"

She nodded then turned away. "I've got to go help Margie organize the food and drinks," she added. "Left to her own devices, we'll be eating turkey and bacon roll-ups and drinking spring water."

"What did you have in mind?" he asked amusedly.

"A nice baked chicken with garlic-and-chives mashed potatoes, fruit salad, homemade rolls and biscuits, gravy, fresh asparagus and a chocolate pound cake for dessert," she said absently.

"You can cook?" he asked, astonished.

She glared at him over one shoulder. "You didn't notice? Margie hasn't cooked a meal any time I've been down here for the weekend, except for one barbecue that the cowboys roasted a side of beef for."

He didn't say another word, but he looked unusually thoughtful.

The meal came out beautifully. By the time she had it on the table, Jodie was flushed from the heat of the kitchen and her hair was disheveled, but she'd produced a perfect meal.

Margie enthused over the results with every dish she tasted, and so did Derek. Alexander was unusually quiet. He finished his chocolate pound cake and a second cup of coffee before he gave his sister a dark look.

"You told me you'd been doing all the cooking when Jessie wasn't here and Jodie was," he said flatly.

Margie actually flushed. She dropped her fork and couldn't meet Jodie's surprised glance.

"You always made such a fuss of extra company when Jessie was gone," she protested without realizing she was only making things worse.

Alexander's teeth ground together when he saw the look on Jodie's face. He threw down his napkin and got noisily to his feet. "You're as insensitive as a cactus plant, Margie," he said angrily.

"You're better?" she retorted, with her eyebrows reaching for her hairline. "You're the one who always complains when I invite Jodie, even though she hasn't got any family except us…oh, dear."

Jodie had already gotten to her own feet and was collecting dirty dishes. She didn't respond to the bickering. She felt it, though. It hurt to know that Alexander barely tolerated her; almost as much as it hurt to know Margie had taken credit for her cooking all these years.

"I'll help you clear, darlin'," Derek offered with a meaningful look at the Cobbs. "Both of you could use some sensitivity training. You just step all over Jodie's feelings without the least notice. Some 'second family' you turned out to be!"

He propelled Jodie ahead of him into the kitchen and closed the door. For once, he looked angry.

She smiled at him. "Don't take it so personally, Derek," she said. "Insults just bounce off me. I'm so used to Alexander by now that I hardly listen."

He tilted her chin up and read the pain in her soft eyes. "He walks on your heart every time he speaks to you," he said bluntly. "He doesn't even know how you feel, when a blind man could see it."

She patted his cheek. "You're a nice man, Derek."

He shrugged. "I've always been a nice man, for all the good it does me. Women flock to hang all over Cobb while he glowers and insults them."

"Someday a nice, sweet woman will come along and take you in hand, and thank God every day for you," she told him.

He chuckled. "Want to take me on?"

She wrinkled her nose at him. "You're very sweet, but I've got my eye on a rather nice man at my office. He's sweet, too, and his girlfriend treats him like dirt. He deserves someone better."

"He'd be lucky to get you," Derek said.

She smiled.

They were frozen in that affectionate tableau when the door opened and Alexander exploded into the room. He stopped short, obviously unsettled by what he thought he was seeing. Especially when Jodie jerked her hand down from Derek's cheek, and he let go of her chin.

"Something you forgot to say about Jodie's unwanted presence in your life?" Derek drawled, and for an instant, the smiling, gentle man Jodie knew became a threatening presence.

Alexander scowled. "Margie didn't mean that the way it sounded," he returned.

"Margie never means things the way they sound," Derek said coldly, "but she never stops to think how much words can hurt, either. She walks around in a perpetual Margie-haze of self-absorption. Even now, Jodie's only here because she can make canapés for the party tomorrow night—or didn't you know?" he added with absolute venom.

Margie came into the room behind her brother, downcast and quiet. She winced as she met Derek's accusing eyes.

"I'm a pig," she confessed. "I really don't mean to hurt people. I love Jodie. She knows it, even if you don't."

"You have a great way of showing it, honey," Derek replied, a little less antagonistic to her than to her brother. "Inviting Jodie down just to cook for a party is pretty thoughtless."

Margie's eyes fell. "You can go home if you want to, Jodie, and I'm really sorry," she offered.

"Oh, for heaven's sake, I don't mind cooking!" Jodie went to Margie and hugged her hard. "I could always say no if I didn't want to do it! Derek's just being kind, that's all."

Margie glared at her cousin. "Kind."

Derek glared back. "Sure I am. It runs in the family. Glad you could come, Jodie, want to wash and wax my car when you finish doing the dishes?" he added sarcastically.

"You stop that!" Margie raged at him.

"Then get in here and help her do the dishes," Derek drawled. "Or do your hands melt in hot water?"

"We do have a dishwasher," Alexander said tersely.

"Gosh! You've actually seen it, then?" Derek exclaimed.

Alexander said a nasty word and stormed out of the kitchen.

"One down," Derek said with twinkling eyes and looking at Margie. "One to go."

"Quit that, or she'll toss you out and I'll be stuck here with them and Kirry all weekend," Jodie said softly.

"Kirry?" He gaped at Margie. "You invited Kirry?"

Margie ground her teeth together and clenched her small hands. "She's the guest of honor!"

"Lord, give me a bus ticket!" He moved toward the door. "Sorry, honey, I'm not into masochism, and a night of unadulterated Kirry would put me in a mental ward. I'm leaving."

"But you just got here!" Margie wailed.

He turned at the door. "You should have told me who was coming to the party. I'd still be in San Antonio. Want to come with me, Jodie?" he offered. "I'll take you to a fiesta!"

Margie looked murderous. "She's my friend."

"She's not, or you wouldn't have forced her down here to suffer Kirry all weekend," he added.

"Give me a minute to get out of the line of fire, will you?" Jodie held up her hands and went back to the dining room to scoop up dirty dishes, forcibly smiling.

Derek glanced at the closed door, and moved closer to Margie. "Don't try to convince me that you don't know how Jodie feels about your brother."

"She got over that old crush years ago, she said so!" Margie returned.

"She lied," he said shortly. "She's as much in love

with him as she ever was, not that either of you ever notice! It's killing her just to be around him, and you stick her with Kirry. How do you think she's going to feel, watching Kirry slither all over Cobb for a whole night?"

Margie bit her lower lip and looked hunted. "She said…"

"Oh, sure, she's going to tell you that she's in love with Cobb." He nodded. "Great instincts, Marge."

"Don't call me Marge!"

He bent and brushed an insolent kiss across her parted lips, making her gasp. His dark eyes narrowed as he assayed the unwilling response. "Never thought of me like that, either, huh?" he drawled.

"You're…my…cousin," she choked.

"I'm no close relation to you at all, despite Cobb's antagonism. One day I'm going to walk out the door with you over my shoulder, and Cobb can do his worst." He winked at her. "See you, sweetheart."

He turned and ambled out the door. Margie was still staring after him helplessly and holding her hand to her lips when Jodie came in with another stack of dishes.

"What's wrong with you?" Jodie asked.

"Derek kissed me," she said in a husky tone.

"He's always kissing you."

Margie swallowed hard. "Not like this."

Jodie's eyebrows went up and she grinned. "I thought it was about time."

"What?"

"Nothing," Jodie said at once. "Here, can you open the dishwasher for me? My hands are full."

Margie broke out of her trance and went to help, shell-shocked and quiet.

"Don't let Derek upset you," Jodie said gently. "He thinks he's doing me a favor, but he's not. I don't mind helping out, in any way I can. I owe you and Cobb so much…"

"You don't owe us a thing," Margie said at once. "Oh, Jodie, you shouldn't let me make use of you like this. You should speak up for yourself. You don't do that enough."

"I know. It's why I haven't advanced in the company," she had to admit. "I just don't like confrontations."

"You had enough of them as a kid, didn't you?" Margie asked.

Jodie flushed. "I loved my parents. I really did."

"But they fought, too. Just like ours. Our mother hated our father, even after he was dead. She drank and drank, trying to forget him, just the same. She soured my brother on women, you know. She picked on him from the time he was six, and every year it got worse. He had a roaring inferiority complex when he was in high school."

"Yes? Well, he's obviously got over it now," Jodie said waspishly.

Margie shook her head. "Not really. If he had, he'd know he could do better than Kirry."

"I thought you liked her!"

Margie looked shamefaced. "I do, sort of. Well, she's got an important job and she could really help me get my foot in the door at Weston's, the exclusive department store where she works."

"Oh, Margie," Jodie said wearily, shaking her head.

"I use people," Margie admitted. "But," she added

brightly, "I try to do it in a nice way, and I always send flowers or presents or something afterward, don't I?"

Jodie laughed helplessly. "Yes, you do," she admitted. "Here, help me load up the dishes, and then you can tell me what sort of canapés you want me to make for tomorrow."

She didn't add that she knew she'd spend the whole day tomorrow making them, because the party was for almost forty people, and lunch had to be provided, as well. It was a logistical nightmare. But she could cope. She'd done it before. And Margie was her best friend.

# Chapter 3

Jodie was up at dawn making biscuits and dough for the canapés. She'd only just taken up breakfast when Alexander came into the kitchen, wearing jeans and boots and a long-sleeved chambray shirt. He looked freshly showered and clean-shaven, his dark hair still damp.

"I've got breakfast," Jodie offered without looking too closely at him. He was overpowering in tight jeans and a shirt unbuttoned to his collarbone, where thick curling black hair peeked out. She had to fight not to throw herself at him.

"Coffee?" he murmured.

"In the pot."

He poured himself a cup, watching the deft motions of her hands as she buttered biscuits and scooped eggs onto a platter already brimming over with bacon and sausages.

"Aren't you eating?" he asked as he seated himself at the table.

"Haven't time," she said, arranging a layer of canapés on a baking sheet. "Most of your guests are coming in time for lunch, so these have to be done now, before I get too busy."

His sensuous lips made a thin line. "I can't stand him, but Derek is right about one thing. You do let Margie use you."

"You and Margie were there when I had nobody else," she said without seeing the flinch of his eyelids. "I consider that she's entitled to anything I can ever do for her."

"You sell yourself short."

"I appreciate it when people do things for me without being asked," she replied. She put the canapés in the oven and set the timer, pushing back sweaty hair that had escaped from her bun.

His eyes went over her figure in baggy pants and an oversize T-shirt. "You dress like a bag lady," he muttered.

She glanced at him, surprised. "I dress very nicely at work."

"Like a dowager bag lady," he corrected. "You wear the same sort of clothes you favored when you were overweight. You're not anymore. Why don't you wear things that fit?"

It was surprising that he noticed her enough to even know what she was wearing. "Margie's the fashion model, not me," she reminded him. "Besides, I'm not the type for trendy stuff. I'm just ordinary."

He frowned. She had a real ego problem. He and Margie hadn't done much for it, either. She accepted anything that was thrown at her, as if she deserved it. He was surprised how much it bothered him, to see her so undervalued even by herself. Not that he was interested in her, he added silently. She wasn't his type at all.

"Kirry's coming this morning," he added. "I have to pick her up at the airport at noon."

Jodie only smiled. "Margie's hoping she'll help her with a market for her designs."

"I think she'll try," he said conservatively. "Eat breakfast," he said. "You can't go all day without food."

"I don't have time," she repeated, starting on another batch of canapés. "Unless you want to sacrifice yourself in a bowl of dough?" she offered, extending the bowl with a mischievous smile.

His green eyes twinkled affectionately in spite of himself. "No, thanks."

"I didn't think so."

He watched her work while he ate, nebulous thoughts racing through his mind. Jodie was so much a part of his life that he never felt discomfort when they were together. He had a hard time with strangers. He appeared to be stoic and aloof, but in fact he was an introvert who didn't quite know how to mix with people who weren't in law enforcement. Like Jodie herself, he considered. She was almost painfully shy around people she didn't know—and tonight, she was going to be thrown in headfirst with a crowd she probably wouldn't even like.

Kirry's friends were social climbers, high society. Alexander himself wasn't comfortable with them, and Jodie certainly wouldn't be. They were into expensive cars, European vacations, diamonds, investments, and they traveled in circles that included some of the most famous people alive, from movie stars to Formula 1 race car drivers, to financial geniuses, playwrights and authors. They classified their friends by wealth and status, not by character. In their world, right and wrong didn't even exist.

"You're not going to like this crowd," he said aloud.

She glanced at him. "I'll be in the kitchen most of the time," she said easily, "or helping serve."

He looked outraged. "You're a guest, not the kitchen help!"

"Don't be absurd," she murmured absently, "I haven't even got the right clothes to wear to Kirry's sort of party. I'd be an embarrassment."

He set his coffee cup down with muted force. "Then why the hell did you come in the first place?" he asked.

"Margie asked me to," she said simply.

He got up and went out without another word. Jodie was going to regret this visit. He was sorry Margie had insisted that she come.

The party was in full swing. Alexander had picked up Kirry at the airport and lugged her suitcases up to the second guest room, down the hall from Jodie's. Kirry, blonde and svelte and from a wealthy background, was like the Cobbs, old money and family ties. She looked at Jodie without seeing her, and talked only to Margie and Alexander during lunch. Fortunately there were plenty of other people there who didn't mind talking to Jodie, especially an elderly couple apparently rolling in wealth to judge by the diamonds the matron was decked out in.

After lunch, Kirry had Alexander drive her into

town and Jodie silently excused herself and escaped to the kitchen.

She had a nice little black dress, off the rack at a local department store, and high heels to match, which she wore to the party. But it was hidden under the big apron she wore most of the evening, heating and arranging canapés and washing dishes and crystal glasses in between uses.

It was almost ten o'clock before she was able to join Margie and her friends. But by then, Margie was hanging on to Kirry like a bat, with Alexander nearby, and Jodie couldn't get near her.

She stood in a corner by herself, wishing that Derek hadn't run from this weekend, so that she'd at least have someone to talk to. But that wasn't happening. She started talking to the elderly matron she'd sat beside at lunch, but another couple joined them and mentioned their week in Paris, and a mutual friend, and Jodie was out of her depth. She moved to another circle, but they were discussing annuities and investments, and she knew nothing to contribute to that discussion, either.

Alexander noticed, seething, that she was alone most of the evening. He started to get up, but Kirry moved closer and clung to his sleeve while Margie talked about her latest collection and offered to show it to Kirry in the morning. Kirry was very possessive. They weren't involved, as he'd been with other women. Perhaps that was why she was reluctant to let him move away. She hated the very thought of any other woman looking at him. That possessiveness was wearing thin. She was beautiful and she carried herself well, but she had an attitude he didn't like, and she was positively rude to any of his colleagues that spoke to him when they were together. Not that she had any idea what Alexander actually did for a living. He was independently wealthy and people in his and Margie's circle of friends assumed that the ranch was his full-time occupation. He'd taught Jodie and Margie never to mention that he worked in Drug Enforcement. They could say that he dabbled in security work, if they liked, but nothing more. When he'd started out with the DEA, he'd done a lot of undercover work. It wasn't politic to let people know that.

Jodie, meanwhile, had discovered champagne. She'd never let herself drink at any of the Cobb parties in the past, but she was feeling particularly isolated tonight, and it was painful. She liked the bubbles, the fragrance of flowers that clung to the exquisite beverage and the delicious taste. So she had three glasses, one after the other, and pretty soon she didn't mind at all that Margie and Alexander's guests were treating her like a barmaid who'd tried to insert herself into their exalted circles.

She noticed that she'd had too much to drink when she walked toward a doorway and ran headfirst into the door facing. She began to giggle softly. Her hair was coming down from its high coiffure, but she didn't care. She took out the circular comb that had held it in place and shook her head, letting the thick, waving wealth of hair fall to her shoulders.

The action caught the eye of a man nearby, a bored race car driver who'd been dragged to this hick party by his wife. He sized up Jodie, and despite the dress that did absolutely nothing for her, he was intrigued.

He moved close, leaning against the door facing she'd hit so unexpectedly.

"Hurt yourself?" he asked in a pleasant deep drawl, faintly accented.

Jodie looked up at the newcomer curiously and managed a lopsided grin. He was a dish, with curly black hair and dancing black eyes, an olive complexion and the body of an athlete.

"Only my hard head," she replied with a chuckle. "Who are you?"

"Francisco," he replied lazily. He lifted his glass to her in a toast. "You're the first person tonight who even asked." He leaned down so that he was eye to eye with her. "I'm a foreigner, you see."

"Are you, really?"

He was enchanted. He laughed, and it wasn't a polite social laugh at all. "I'm from Madrid," he said. "Didn't you notice my accent?"

"I don't speak any foreign languages," she confessed sadly, sipping what was left of her champagne. "I don't understand high finance or read popular novels or know any movie stars, and I've never been on a holiday abroad. So I thought I'd go sit in the kitchen."

He laughed again. "May I join you, then?" he asked.

She looked pointedly at his left hand. There was no ring.

He took a ring out of his slacks pocket and dangled it in front of her. "We don't advertise our commitment at parties. My wife likes it that way. That's my wife," he added with pure disdain, nodding toward a blonde woman in a skintight red dress that looked sprayed on. She was leaning against a very handsome blond man.

"She's beautiful," she remarked.

"She's anybody's," he returned coldly. "The man she's stalking is a rising motion picture star. He's poor. She's rich. She's financing his career in return for the occasional loan of his body."

Her eyes almost popped out of her eyelids.

He shook his head. "You're not worldly, are you?" he mused. "I have an open marriage. She does what she pleases. So do I."

"Don't you love her?" she asked curiously.

"One marries for love, you think." He sighed. "What a child you are. I married her because her father owned the company. As his son-in-law, I get to drive the car in competition."

"You're the race car driver!" she exclaimed softly. "Kirry mentioned you were coming."

"Kirry." His lips curled distastefully and he glanced across the room into a pair of cold, angry green eyes above the head of Kirry Dane. "She was last year's diversion," he murmured. "She wanted to be seen at Monaco."

Jodie was surprised by his lack of inhibition. She wondered if Alexander knew about this relationship, or if he cared. She'd never thought whether he bothered asking about his date's previous entanglements.

"Her boyfriend doesn't like me," he murmured absently, and smiled icily, lifting his glass.

Jodie looked behind her. Kirry had turned away, but Alexander was suddenly making a beeline across the room toward them.

Francisco made a face. "There's one man you don't want to make an enemy of," he confided. "Are you a relation of his, by any chance?"

Jodie laughed a little too loudly. "Good Lord, no." She chuckled. "I'm the cook!"

"I beg your pardon?" he asked.

By that time, Alexander was facing her. He took

the crystal champagne flute from her hands and put it gingerly on a nearby table.

"I wasn't going to break it, Alexander," she muttered. "I do know it's Waterford crystal!"

"How many glasses have you had?" he demanded.

"I don't like your tone," she retorted, moving clumsily, so that Francisco had to grab her arm to keep her upright. "I had three glasses. It's not that strong, and I'm not drunk!"

"And ducks don't have feathers," Alexander replied tersely. He caught her other arm and pulled her none too gently from Francisco's grasp. "I'll take care of Jodie. Hadn't you better reacquire your wife?" he added pointedly to the younger man.

Francisco sighed, with a long, wistful appraisal of Jodie. "It seems so," he replied. "Nice to have met you—Jodie, is it?"

Jodie grinned woozily. "It's Jordana, actually, but most people call me Jodie. And I was glad to meet you, too, Francisco! I never met a real race car driver before!"

He started to speak, but it was too late, because Alexander was already marching her out of the room and down the hall.

"Will you stop dragging me around?" she demanded, stumbling on her high heels.

He pulled her into the dark-paneled library and closed the door with a muted thud. He let go of her arm and glared down at her. "Will you stop trying to seduce married men?" he shot back. "Gomez and his wife are on the cover of half the tabloids in Texas right now," he added bluntly.

"Why?"

"Her father just died and she inherited the car company. She's trying to sell it and her husband is fighting her in court, tooth and nail."

"And they're still married?"

"Apparently, in name, at least. She's pregnant, I hear, with another man's child."

She looked up at him coldly. "Some circles you and Margie travel in," she said with contempt.

"Circles you'd never fit into," he agreed.

"Not hardly," she drawled ungrammatically. "And I wouldn't want to. In my world, people get married and have kids and build a home together." She nodded her head toward the closed door. "Those people in there wouldn't know what a home was if you drew it for them!"

His green eyes narrowed on her face. "You're smashed. Why don't you go to bed?"

She lifted her chin and smiled mistily. "Why don't you come with me?" she purred.

The look on his face would have amused her, if she'd been sober. He just stared, shocked.

She arched her shoulders and made a husky little sound in her throat. She parted her lips and ran her tongue slowly around them, the way she'd read in a magazine article that said men were turned on by it.

Apparently they were. Alexander was staring at her mouth with an odd expression. His chest was rising and falling very quickly. She could see the motion of it through his white shirt and dinner jacket.

She moved closer, draping herself against him as she'd seen that slinky blonde woman in the red dress do it. She moved her leg against his and felt his whole body stiffen abruptly.

Her hands went to the front of his shirt under the jacket. She drew her fingers down it, feeling the ripple of muscle. His big hands caught her shoulders, but he wasn't pushing.

"You look at me, but you never see me," she murmured. Her lips brushed against his throat. He smelled of expensive cologne and soap. "I'm not pretty. I'm not sexy. But I would die for you…!"

His hard mouth cut off the words. He curled her into his body with a rigid arm at her back, and his mouth opened against her moist, full, parted lips with the fury of a summer storm.

It wasn't premeditated. The feel of her against him had triggered a raging arousal in his muscular body. He went in headfirst, without thinking of the consequences.

If he was helpless, so was she. As he enveloped her against him, her arms slid around his warm body under the jacket and her mouth answered the hunger of his. She made a husky little moan that apparently made matters worse. His mouth became suddenly insistent, as if he heard the need in her soft cry and was doing his best to satisfy the hunger it betrayed.

Her hands lifted to the back of his head and her fingers dug into his scalp as she arched her body upward in a hopeless plea.

He whispered something that she couldn't understand before he bent and lifted her, with her mouth still trapped under his demanding lips, and carried her to the sofa.

He spread her body onto the cold leather and slid over it, one powerful leg inserting itself between both of hers in a frantic, furious exchange of passion. He'd never known such raging need, not only in himself, but in Jodie. She was liquid in his embrace, yielding to everything he asked without a word being spoken.

He moved slightly, just enough to get his hand in between them. It smoothed over her collarbone and down into the soft dip of her dress, over the lacy bra she was wearing underneath. He felt the hard little nipple in his palm as he increased the insistent pressure of the caress and heard her cry of delight go into his open mouth.

Her hands were on the buttons of his shirt. It was dangerous. It was reckless. She'd incited him to madness, and he couldn't stop. When he felt the buttons give, and her hands speared into the thick hair over his chest, he groaned harshly. His body shivered with desire.

His mouth ground into hers as his leg moved between hers. One lean hand went under her hips and gathered her up against the fierce arousal of his body, moving her against him in a blatant physical statement of intent.

Jodie's head was spinning. All her dreams of love were coming true. Alexander wanted her! She could feel the insistent pressure of his body over hers. He was kissing her as if he'd die to have her, and she gloried in the fury of his hunger. She relaxed with a husky little laugh and kissed him back languidly, feeling her body melt under him, melt into him. She was on fire, burning with unfamiliar needs, drowning in unfamiliar sensations that made her whole body tingle with pleasure. She lifted her hips against his and gasped at the blatant contact.

Alexander lifted his head and looked at her. His face was a rigid mask. Only his green eyes were alive in it, glittering down at her in a rasping, unsteady silence of merged breathing.

"Don't stop," she whispered, moving her hips again.

He was tempted. It showed. But that iron control wouldn't let him slip into carelessness. She'd been drinking. In fact, she was smashed. He had his own suspicions about her innocence, and they wouldn't shut up. His body was begging him to forget her lack of experience and give it relief. But his will was too strong. He was the man in control. It was his responsibility to protect her, even from himself.

"You're drunk, Jodie," he said. His voice was faintly unsteady, but it was terse and firm.

"Does it matter?" she asked lazily.

"Don't be ridiculous."

He moved away, getting to his feet. He looked down at her sprawled body in its disheveled dress and he ached all the way to his toes. But he couldn't do this. Not when she was so vulnerable.

She sighed and closed her eyes. It had been so sweet, lying in his arms. She smiled dreamily. Was she dreaming?

"Get up, for God's sake!" he snapped.

When her eyes opened, he was standing her firmly on her feet. "You're going to bed, right now, before you make an utter fool of yourself!"

She blinked, staring up at him. "I can't go to bed. Who'll do the dishes?"

"Jodie!"

She giggled, trying to lean against him. He thrust her away and took her arm, moving her toward the door. "I told Francisco I was the cook. That's me," she drawled cheerfully. "Cook, bottle-washer, best friend and household slave." She laughed louder.

He propelled her out the door, back down the hall toward the staircase, and urged her up it. She was still giggling a little too loudly for comfort, but the noise of the music from the living room covered it nicely.

He got her to the guest room she was occupying and put her inside. "Go to bed," he said through his teeth.

She leaned against the door facing, totally at sea. "You could come inside," she murmured wickedly. "There's a bed."

"You need one," he agreed tersely. "Go get in it."

"Always bossing me around," she sighed. "Don't you like kissing me, Alexander?"

"You're going to hate yourself in the morning," he assured her.

She yawned, her mind going around in circles, like the room. "I think I'll go to bed now."

"Great idea."

He started to walk out.

"Could you send Francisco up, please?" she taunted. "I'd like to lie down and discuss race cars with him."

"In your dreams!" he said coldly.

He actually slammed the door, totally out of patience, self-control and tact. He waited a minute, to make sure she didn't try to come back out. But there was only the sound of slow progress toward the bed and a sudden loud whoosh. When he opened the door again and peeked in, she was lying facedown in her dress on the covers, sound asleep. He closed the door again, determined not to get close to her a second time. He went back to the party, feeling as if he'd had his stomach punched. He couldn't imagine what had possessed him to let Jodie tempt him into indiscretion. His lack of control worried him so much that he was twice as attentive to Kirry as he usually was.

When he saw her up to her room, after the party was over, he kissed her with intent. She was perfectly willing, but his body let him down. He couldn't manage any interest at all.

"You're just tired," she assured him with a worldly smile. "We have all the time in the world. Sleep tight."

"Sure. You, too."

He left her and went back downstairs. He was restless, angry at his attack of impotence with the one woman who was capable of curing it. Or, at least, he imagined she was. He and Kirry had never been lovers, although they'd come close at one time. Now she was a pleasant companion from time to time, a bauble to show off, to take around town. It infuriated him that he could be whole with Jodie, who was almost certainly a virgin, and he couldn't even function with a sophisticated woman like Kirry. Maybe it was his age.

The rattle of plates caught his attention. He moved toward the sound and found a distressed Margie in the kitchen trying to put dishes in the dishwasher.

"That doesn't look right," he commented with a frown when he noticed the lack of conformity in the way she was tossing plates and bowls and cups and crystal all together. "You'll break the crystal."

She glared at him. "Well, what do I know about washing dishes?" she exclaimed. "That's why we have Jessie!"

He cocked his head. "You're out of sorts."

She pushed back her red-tinged dark hair angrily. "Yes, I'm out of sorts! Kirry said she doesn't think I'm ready to show my collection yet. She said her store had shows booked for the rest of the year, and she couldn't help me!"

"All that buttering up and dragging Jodie down here to work, for nothing," he said sarcastically.

"Where is Jodie?" she demanded. "I haven't seen her for two hours, and here's all this work that isn't getting done except by me!"

He leaned back against the half-open door and stared at his sister. "She's passed out on her bed, dead drunk," he said distastefully. "After trying to seduce the world's number one race car driver, and then me."

Margie stood up and stared back. "You?"

"I wish I could impress on you how tired I am of finding Jodie underfoot every time I walk into my own house," he said coldly. "We can't have a party without her, we can't have a holiday without her. My own birthday means an invitation! Why can't you just hire a cook when you need one instead of landing me with your erstwhile best friend?"

"I thought you liked Jodie, a little," Margie stammered.

"She's blue collar, Margie," he persisted, still smarting under his loss of control and furious that Jodie was responsible for it. "She'll never fit in our circles, no matter how much you try to force her into them. She was telling people tonight that she was the cook, and it's not far wrong. She's a social disaster with legs. She knows nothing about our sort of lifestyle, she can't carry on a decent conversation and she dresses like a homeless person. It's an embarrassment to have her here!"

Margie sighed miserably. "I hope you haven't said

things like that to her, Lex," she worried. "She may not be an upper class sort of person, but she's sweet and kind, and she doesn't gossip. She's the only real friend I've ever had. Not that I've behaved much like one," she added sadly.

"You should have friends in your own class," he said coldly. "I don't want Jodie invited down here again," he added firmly, holding up a hand when Margie tried to speak. "I mean it. You find some excuse, but you keep her away from here. I'm not going to be stalked by your bag lady of a friend. I don't want her underfoot at any more holidays, and God forbid, at my birthday party! If you want to see her, drive to Houston, fly to Houston, stay in Houston! But don't bring her here anymore."

"Did she really try to seduce you?" Margie wondered aloud.

"I don't want to talk about it," he said flatly. "It was embarrassing."

"She'll probably be horrified when she wakes up and remembers what happened. Whatever did," Margie added, fishing.

"I'll be horrified for months myself. Kirry is my steady girl," he added deliberately. "I'm not hitting on some other woman behind her back, and Jodie should have known it. Not that it seemed to matter to her, about me or the married racer."

"She's never had a drink, as far as I know," Margie ventured gently. "She's not like our mother, Lex."

His face closed up. Jodie's behavior had aroused painful memories of his mother, who drank often, and to excess. She was a constant embarrassment anytime people came to the house, and she delighted in embarrassing her son any way possible. Jodie's unmanageable silliness brought back nightmares.

"There's nothing in the world more disgusting than a drunk woman," he said aloud. "Nothing that makes me sicker to my stomach."

Margie closed the dishwasher and started it. There was a terrible cracking sound. The crystal! She winced. "I don't care what's broken. I'm not a cook. I can't wash dishes. I'm a dress designer!"

"Hire help for Jessie," he said.

"Okay," she said, giving in. "I won't invite Jodie back again. But how do I tell her, Lex? She's never going to understand. And it will hurt her."

He knew that. He couldn't bear to know it. His face hardened. "Just keep her away from me. I don't care how."

"I'll think of something," Margie said weakly.

Outside in the hall, a white-faced Jodie was stealthily making her way back to the staircase. She'd come down belatedly to do the dishes, still tingling hours after Alexander's feverish lovemaking. She'd been floating, delirious with hope that he might have started to see her in a different light. And then she'd heard what he said. She'd heard every single word. She disgusted him. She was such a social disaster, in fact, that he never wanted her to come to the house again. She'd embarrassed him and made a fool of herself.

He was right. She'd behaved stupidly, and now she was going to pay for it by being an outcast. The only family she had no longer wanted her.

She went back to her room, closed the door quietly, and picked up the telephone. She changed her airplane ticket for an early-morning flight.

* * *

The next morning, she went to Margie's room at daybreak. She hadn't slept a wink. She'd packed and changed her clothes, and now she was ready to go.

"Will you drive me to the airport?" she asked her sleepy friend. "Or do you want me to ask Johnny?"

Margie sat up, blinking. Then she remembered Lex's odd comments and her own shame at how she'd treated her best friend. She flushed.

"I'll drive you," Margie said at once. "But don't you want to wait until after breakfast?" She flushed again, remembering that Jodie would have had to cook it.

"I'm not hungry. There's leftover sausage and bacon in the fridge, along with some biscuits. You can just heat them up. Alexander can cook eggs to go with them," she added, almost choking on his name.

Margie felt guilty. "You're upset," she ventured.

Keeping quiet was the hardest thing Jodie had ever done. "I got drunk last night and did some…really stupid things," she summarized. "I'd just like to go home, Margie. Okay?"

Margie tried not to let her relief show. Jodie was leaving without a fuss. Lex would be pleased, and she'd be off the hook. She smiled. "Okay. I'll just get dressed, and then we'll go!"

# Chapter 4

If running away seemed the right thing to do, actually doing it became complicated the minute Jodie went down the staircase with her suitcase.

The last thing she'd expected was to find the cause of her flight standing in the hall watching her. She ground her teeth together to keep from speaking.

Alexander was leaning against the banister, and he looked both uncomfortable and concerned when he saw Jodie's pale complexion and swollen eyelids.

He stood upright, scowling. "I'm driving Kirry back to Houston this afternoon," he said at once, noting Jodie's suitcase. "You can ride with us."

Jodie forced a quiet smile. Her eyes didn't quite meet his. "Thanks for the offer, Alexander, but I have an airplane ticket."

"Then I'll drive you to the airport," he added quietly.

Her face tightened. She swallowed down her hurt. "Thanks, but Margie's already dressed and ready to go. And we have some things to talk about on the way," she added before he could offer again.

He watched her uneasily. Jodie was acting like a fugitive evading the police. She wouldn't meet his eyes, or let him near her. He'd had all night to regret his behavior, and he was still blaming her for it. He'd overreacted. He knew she'd had a crush on him at one time. He'd hurt her with his cold rejection. She'd been drinking. It hadn't been her fault, but he'd blamed her for the whole fiasco. He felt guilty because of the way she looked.

Before he could say anything else, Margie came bouncing down the steps. "Okay, I'm ready! Let's go," she told Jodie.

"I'm right behind you. So long, Alexander," she told him without looking up past his top shirt button.

He didn't reply. He stood watching until the front door closed behind her. He still didn't understand his own conflicting emotions. He'd hoped to have some time alone with Jodie while he explored this suddenly changed relationship between them. But she was clearly embarrassed about her behavior the night before, and she was running scared. Probably letting her go was the best way to handle it. After a few days, he'd go to see her at the office and smooth things over. He couldn't bear having her look that way and knowing he was responsible for it. Regardless of his burst of bad temper, he cared about Jodie. He didn't want her to be hurt.

"You look very pale, Jodie," Margie commented when she walked her best friend to the security checkpoint. "Are you sure you're all right?"

"I'm embarrassed about how I acted last night, that's all," she assured her best friend. "How did you luck out with Kirry, by the way?"

"Not too well," she replied with a sigh. "And I think I broke all the crystal by putting it in the dishwasher."

"I'm sorry I wasn't able to do that for you," Jodie apologized.

"It's not your fault. Nothing is your fault." Margie looked tormented. "I was going to ask you down to Lex's birthday party next month…"

"Margie, I can't really face Alexander right now, okay?" she interrupted gently, and saw the relief plain on the taller woman's face. "So I'm going to make myself scarce for a little while."

"That might be best," Margie had to admit.

Jodie smiled. "Thanks for asking me to the party," she managed. "I had a good time."

That was a lie, and they both knew it.

"I'll make all this up to you one day, I promise I will," Margie said unexpectedly, and hugged Jodie, hard. "I'm not much of a friend, Jodie, but I'm going to change. I am. You'll see."

"I wouldn't be much of a friend if I wanted to remake you," Jodie replied, smiling. "I'll see you around, Margie," she added enigmatically, and left before Margie could ask what she meant.

It was a short trip back to Houston. Jodie fought tears all the way. She couldn't remember anything hurting so much in all her life. Alexander couldn't bear the sight of her. He didn't want her around. She made him sick. She…disgusted him.

Most of her memories of love swirled around Alexander Cobb. She'd daydreamed about him even before she realized her feelings had deepened into love. She treasured unexpected meetings with him, she tingled just from having him smile at her. But all that had been a lie. She was a responsibility he took seriously, like his job. She meant nothing more than that to him. It was a painful realization, and it was going to take time for the hurt to lessen.

But for the moment it was too painful to bear. She drew the air carrier's magazine out of its pocket in the back of the seat ahead of her and settled back to read it. By the time she finished, the plane was landing. She walked through the Houston concourse with a new resolution. She was going to forget Alexander. It was time to put away the past and start fresh.

Alexander was alone in the library when his sister came back from the airport.

He went out into the hall to meet her. "Did she say anything to you?" he asked at once.

Surprised by the question, and his faint anxiety, she hesitated. "About what?"

He glowered down at her. "About why she was leaving abruptly. I know her ticket was for late this afternoon. She must have changed it."

"She said she was too embarrassed to face you," Margie replied.

"Anything else?" he persisted.

"Not really." She felt uneasy herself. "You know Jodie. She's painfully shy, Lex. She doesn't drink, ever. I guess whatever happened made her ashamed of herself and uncomfortable around you. She'll get over it in time."

"Do you think so?" he wondered aloud.

"What are you both doing down here?" Kirry asked petulantly with a yawn. She came down the staircase in a red silk gown and black silk robe and slippers, her long blond hair sweeping around her shoulders. "I feel as if I haven't even slept. Is breakfast ready?"

Margie started. "Well, Jessie isn't here," she began.

"Where's that little cook who was at the party last night?" she asked carelessly. "Why can't she make breakfast?"

"Jodie's not a cook," Alexander said tersely. "She's Margie's best friend."

Kirry's eyebrows arched. "She looked like a lush to me," Kirry said unkindly. "People like that should never drink. Is she too hung over to cook, then?"

"She's gone home," Margie said, resenting Kirry's remarks.

"Then who's going to make toast and coffee for me?" Kirry demanded. "I have to have breakfast."

"I can make toast," Margie said, turning. She wanted Kirry's help with her collection, but she disliked the woman intensely.

"Then I'll get dressed. Want to come up and do my zip, Lex?" Kirry drawled.

"No," he said flatly. "I'll make coffee." He went into the kitchen behind Margie.

Kirry stared after him blankly. He'd never spoken to her in such a way before, and Margie had been positively rude. They shouldn't drink, either, she was thinking as she went back upstairs to dress. Obviously it was hangovers and bad tempers all around this morning.

Two weeks later, Jodie sat in on a meeting between Brody and an employee of their information systems section who had been rude and insulting to a fellow worker. It was Brody's job as Human Resources generalist to oversee personnel matters, and he was a diplomat. It gave Jodie the chance to see what sort of duties she would be expected to perform if she moved up from administrative assistant to manager.

"Mr. Koswalski, this is Ms. Clayburn, my administrative assistant. She's here to take notes," he added.

Jodie was surprised, because she thought she was there to learn the job. But she smiled and pulled out her small pad and pen, perching it on her knee.

"You've had a complaint about me, haven't you?" Koswalski asked with a sigh.

Brody's eyebrows arched. "Well, yes…"

"One of our executives hired a systems specialist with no practical experience in oil exploration," Koswalski told him. "I was preparing an article for inclusion in our quarterly magazine and the system went down. She was sent to repair it. She saw my article and made some comments about the terms I used, and how unprofessional they sounded. Obviously she didn't understand the difference between a rigger and a roughneck. When I tried to explain, she accused me of talking down to her and walked out." He threw up his hands. "Sir, I wasn't rude, and I wasn't uncooperative. I was trying to teach her the language of the industry."

Brody looked as if he meant to say something, but he glanced at Jodie and cleared his throat instead. "You didn't call her names, Mr. Koswalski?"

"No, sir, I did not," the young man replied courteously. "But she did call me several. Besides that, quite frankly, she had a glazed look in her eyes and a red nose." His face tautened. "Mr. Vance, I've seen too many people who use drugs to mistake signs of drug use. She didn't repair the system, she made matters worse. I had to call in another specialist to undo her damage. I have his name, and his assignment," he added, producing a slip of paper, which he handed to Brody. "I'm sorry to make a countercharge of incompetence against another employee, but my integrity is at stake."

Brody took the slip of paper and read the name. He looked at the younger man again. "I know this technician. He's the best we have. He'll confirm what you just told me?"

"He will, Mr. Vance."

Brody nodded. "I'll check with him and make some investigation of your charges. You'll be notified when we have a resolution. Thank you, Mr. Koswalski."

"Thank you, Mr. Vance," the young man replied, standing. "I enjoy my job very much. If I lose it, it should be on merit, not lies."

"I quite agree," Brody replied. "Good day."

"Good day." Koswalski left, very dignified.

Brody turned to Jodie. "How would you characterize our Mr. Koswalski?"

"He seems sincere, honest, and hardworking."

He nodded. "He's here on time every morning, never takes longer than he has for lunch, does any task he's given willingly and without protest, even if it means working late hours."

He picked up a file folder. "On the other hand, the systems specialist, a Ms. Burgen, has been late four out of five mornings she's worked here. She misses work on Mondays every other week. She complains if she's

asked to do overtime, and her work is unsatisfactory."
He looked up. "Your course of action, in my place?"

"I would fire her," she said.

He smiled slowly. "She has an invalid mother and
a two-year-old son," he said surprisingly. "She was
fired from her last job. If she loses this one, she faces
an uncertain future."

She bit her lower lip. It was one thing to condone
firing an incompetent employee, but given the woman's
home life the decision was uncomfortable.

"If you take my place, you'll be required to make
such recommendations. In fact, you'll be required to
make them to me," he added. "You can't wear your
heart on your sleeve. You work for a business that depends on its income. Incompetent employees will cost
us time, money, and possibly even clients. No business
can exist that way for long."

She looked up at him with sad eyes. "It's not a nice
job, Brody."

He nodded. "It's like gardening. You have to separate the weeds from the vegetables. Too many weeds,
no more vegetables."

"I understand." She looked at her pad. "So what will
you recommend?" she added.

"That our security section make a thorough investigation of her job performance," he said. "If she has
a drug problem that relates to it, she'll be given the
choice of counseling and treatment or separation. Unless she's caught using drugs on the job, of course," he
added coolly. "In that case, she'll be arrested."

She knew she was growing cold inside. What had
sounded like a wonderful position was weighing on
her like a rock.

"Jodie, is this really what you want to do?" he asked gently, smiling. "Forgive me, but you're not a hard-hearted person, and you're forever making excuses for people. It isn't the mark of a manager."

"I'm beginning to realize that," she said quietly. She searched his eyes. "Doesn't it bother you, recommending that people lose their jobs?"

"No," he said simply. "I'm sorry for them, but not sorry enough to risk my paycheck and yours keeping them on a job they're not qualified to perform. That's business, Jodie."

"I suppose so." She toyed with her pad. "I was a whiz with computers in business college," she mused. "I didn't want to be a systems specialist because I'm not mechanically-minded, but I could do anything with software." She glanced at him. "Maybe I'm in the wrong job to begin with. Maybe I should have been a software specialist."

He grinned. "If you decide, eventually, that you'd like to do that, write a job description, give it to your Human Resources manager, and apply for the job," he counseled.

"You're kidding!"

"I'm not. It's how I got my job," he confided.

"Well!"

"You don't have to fire software," he reminded her. "And if it doesn't work, it won't worry your conscience to toss it out. But all this is premature. You don't have to decide right now what you want to do. Besides," he added with a sigh, "I may not even get that promotion I'm hoping for."

"You'll get it," she assured him. "You're terrific at what you do, Brody."

"Do you really think so?" he asked, and seemed to care about her reply.

"I certainly do."

He smiled. "Thanks. Cara doesn't think much of my abilities, I'm afraid. I suppose it's because she's so good at marketing. She gets promotions all the time. And the travel...! She's out of town more than she's in, but she loves it. She was in Mexico last week and in Peru the week before that. Imagine! I'd love to go to Mexico and see Chichen Itza." He sighed.

"So would I. You like archaeology?" she fished.

He grinned. "Love it. You?"

"Oh, yes!"

"There's a museum exhibit of Mayan pottery at the art museum," he said enthusiastically. "Cara hates that sort of thing. I don't suppose you'd like to go with me to see it next Saturday?"

Next Saturday. Alexander's birthday. She'd mourned for the past two weeks since she'd come back from the Cobbs' party, miserable and hurting. But she wouldn't be invited to his birthday party, and she wouldn't go even if she was.

"I'd love to," she said with a beaming smile. "But... won't your girlfriend mind?"

He frowned. "I don't know." He looked down at her. "We, uh, don't have to advertise it, do we?"

She understood. It was a little uncomfortable going out with a committed man, but it wasn't as if he were married or anything. Besides, his girlfriend treated him like dirt. She wouldn't.

"No, we don't," she agreed. "I'll look forward to it."

"Great!" He beamed, too. "I'll phone you Friday night and we'll decide where and when to meet, okay?"

"Okay!"

\* \* \*

She was on a new track, a new life, and she felt like a new person. She'd started going to a retro coffeehouse in the evenings, where they served good coffee and people read poetry onstage or played folk music with guitars. Jodie fit right in with the artsy crowd. She'd even gotten up for the first time and read one of her poems, a sad one about rejected love that Alexander had inspired. Everyone applauded, even the owner, a man named Johnny. The boost of confidence she felt made her less inhibited, and the next time she read her poetry, she wasn't afraid of the crowd. She was reborn. She was the new, improved Jodie, who could conquer the world. And now Brody wanted to date her. She was delighted.

That feeling lasted precisely two hours. She came back in after lunch to find Alexander Cobb perched on her desk, in her small cubicle, waiting for her.

She hadn't had enough time to get over her disastrous last meeting with him. She wanted to turn and run, but that wasn't going to work. He'd already spotted her.

She walked calmly to her desk—although her heart was doing cartwheels—and put her purse in her lower desk drawer.

"Hello, Alexander," she said somberly. "What can I do for you?"

Her attitude sent him reeling. Jodie had always been unsettled and full of joy when she came upon him unexpectedly. He didn't realize how much he'd enjoyed the headlong reaction until it wasn't there anymore.

He stared at her across the desk, puzzled and disturbed. "What happened wasn't anybody's fault," he said stiffly. "Don't wear yourself out regretting it."

She relaxed a little, but only a little. "I drank too much. I won't do it a second time," she assured him. "How's Margie?"

"Quiet," he said. The one word was alarming. Margie was never quiet.

"Why?" she asked.

Shrugging, he picked up a paper clip from her desk and studied it. "She can't get anywhere with her designs. She expected immediate success, and she can't even get a foot in the door."

"I'm sorry. She's really good."

He nodded and his green eyes met hers narrowly. "I need to talk to you," he said. "Can you meet me downstairs at the coffee bar when you get off from work?"

She didn't want to, and it was obvious. "Couldn't you just phone me at home?" she countered.

He scowled. "No. I can't discuss this over the phone." She was still hesitating. "Do you have other plans?" he asked.

She shook her head. "No. I don't want to miss my bus."

"I can drive you…"

"No! I mean—" she lowered her voice "—no, I won't put you to any trouble. There are two buses. The second runs an hour after the first one."

"It won't take an hour," he assured her. But he felt as if something was missing from their conversation. She didn't tease him, taunt him, antagonize him. In fact, she looked very much as if she wanted to avoid him altogether.

"All right, then," she said, sitting down at her desk. "I'll see you there about five after five."

He nodded, pausing at the opening of the cubicle to look back at her. It was a bad time to remember the taste of her full, soft mouth under his. But he couldn't help it. She was wearing a very businesslike dark suit with a pale pink blouse, her long hair up in a bun. She should have looked like a businesswoman, but she was much too vulnerable, too insecure, to give that image. She didn't have the self-confidence to rate a higher job, but he couldn't tell her that. Jodie had a massive inferiority complex. The least thing hurt her. As he'd hurt her.

The muscles in his jaw tautened. "This doesn't suit you," he said abruptly, nodding around the sterile little glass and wood cage they kept her in. "Won't they even let you have a potted plant?"

She was aghast at the comment. He never made personal remarks. She shifted restlessly in her chair. "It isn't dignified," she stammered.

He moved a step closer. "Jodie, a job shouldn't mimic jail. If you don't like what you do, where you do it, you're wasting the major part of your life."

She knew that. She tasted panic when she swallowed. But jobs were thin on the ground and she had the chance for advancement in this one. She put to the back of her mind Brody's comments on her shortcomings as a manager.

"I like my job very much," she lied.

His eyes slid over her with something like possession. "No, you don't. Pity. You have a gift for computer programming. I'll bet you haven't written a single routine since you've been here."

Her face clenched. "Don't you have something to do? Because I'm busy."

"Suit yourself. As soon after five as you can make it, please," he said, adding deliberately, "I have a dinner date."

With Kirry. Always with Kirry. She knew it. She hated Kirry. She hated him, too. But she smiled. "No problem. See you." She turned on her computer and pulled up her memo file to see what tasks were upcoming. She ignored Alexander, who gave her another long, curious appraisal before he left her alone.

She felt the sting of his presence all the way to her poor heart. He was so much a part of her life that it was like being amputated when she thought of a lifetime without his complicated presence.

For the first time, she thought about moving to another city. Ritter Oil Corporation had a headquarters office in Tulsa, Oklahoma. Perhaps she could get a transfer there…and do what, she asked herself? She was barely qualified for the predominantly clerical job she was doing now, and painfully unqualified for firing people, even if they deserved it. She'd let her pride force her into taking this job, because Alexander kept asking when she was going to start working after her graduation from business college. He probably hadn't meant that he thought she was taking advantage of his financial help—but she took it that way. So she went to work for the first company that offered her a job, just to shut him up.

In retrospect, she should have looked a little harder. She'd been under consideration for a job with the local police department, as a computer specialist. She had the skills to write programs, to restructure software.

She was a whiz at opening protected files, finding lost documents, tracking down suspicious emails and finding ways to circumvent write-protected software. Her professor had recommended her for a career in law enforcement as a cyber crime specialist, but she'd jumped at the first post-college job that came her way.

Now here she was, stuck in a dead-end job that she didn't even like, kept in a cubicle like a box of printer paper and only taken out when some higher-up needed her to take a letter or organize a schedule, or compile his notes…

She had a vision of herself as a cardboard box full of supplies and started giggling.

Another administrative assistant stuck her head in the cubicle. "Better keep it down," she advised softly. "They've had a complaint about the noise levels in here."

"I'm only laughing to myself," Jodie protested, shocked.

"They want us quiet while we're working. No personal phone calls, no talking to ourselves—and there's a new memo about the length of time people are taking in the bathroom…"

"Oh, good God!" Jodie burst out furiously.

The other woman put a feverish hand to her lips and looked around nervously. "Shhh!" she cautioned.

Jodie stood up and gave the woman her best military salute.

Sadly the vice president in charge of personnel was walking by her cubicle at the time. He stopped, eyeing both women suspiciously.

Already in trouble, and not giving a damn anymore, Jodie saluted him, too.

Surprisingly he had to suppress a smile. He wiped it off quickly. "Back to work, girls," he cautioned and kept walking.

The other woman moved closer. "Now see what you've done!" she hissed. "We'll both be on report!"

"If he tries to put me on report, I'll put him on report, as well," Jodie replied coolly. "Nobody calls me a 'girl' in a working office!"

The other woman threw up her hands and walked out.

Jodie turned her attention back to her chores and put the incident out of her mind. But it was very disturbing to realize how much authority the company had over her working life, and she didn't like it. She wondered if old man Ritter, the head of the corporation, encouraged such office politics. From what she'd heard about him, he was something of a renegade. He didn't seem to like rules and regulations very much, but, then, he couldn't be everywhere. Maybe he didn't even know the suppressive tactics his executives used to keep employees under control here.

Being cautioned never to speak was bad enough, and personalization of cubicles was strictly forbidden by company policy. But to have executives complain about the time employees spent in the bathroom made Jodie furious. She had a girlfriend who was a diabetic, and made frequent trips to the restroom in school. Some teachers had made it very difficult for her until her parents had requested a teacher conference to explain their daughter's health problem. She had a feeling no sort of conference would help at this job.

She went back to work, but the day had been disturbing in more ways than one.

* * *

At exactly five minutes past quitting time, she walked into the little coffee shop downstairs. Alexander had a table, and he was waiting for her. He'd already ordered the French Vanilla cappuccino she liked so much, along with chocolate biscotti.

She was surprised by his memory of her preferences. She draped her old coat over the empty chair at the corner table and sat down. Fortunately the shop wasn't crowded, as it was early in the evening, and there were no customers anywhere near them.

"Right on time," Alexander noted, checking his expensive wristwatch.

"I usually am," she said absently, sipping her cappuccino. "This is wonderful," she added with a tiny smile.

He seemed puzzled. "Don't you come here often?"

"Actually, it's not something I can fit into my budget," she confessed.

Now it was shock that claimed his features. "You make a good salary," he commented.

"If you want to rent someplace with good security, it costs more," she told him. "I have to dress nicely for work, and that costs, too. By the time I add in utilities and food and bus fare, there isn't a lot left. We aren't all in your income tax bracket, Alexander," she added without rancor.

He let his attention wander to his own cappuccino. He sipped it quietly.

"I never think of you as being in a different economic class," he said.

"Don't you?" She knew better, and her thoughts were bitter. She couldn't forget what she'd overheard him say to his sister, that she was only blue collar and she didn't fit in with them.

He sat up straight. "Something's worrying you," he said flatly. "You're not the same. You haven't been since the party."

Her face felt numb. She couldn't lower her pride enough to tell him what she'd overheard. It was just too much, on top of everything else that had gone haywire lately.

"Why can't you talk to me?" he persisted.

She looked up at him with buried resentments, hurt pride, and outraged sentiment plain in her cold eyes. "It would be like talking to the floor," she said. "If you're here, it's because you want something. So, what is it?"

His expression was eloquent. He sipped cappuccino carefully and then put the delicate cup in its saucer with precision.

"Why do you think I want something?"

She felt ancient. "Margie invites me to parties so that I can cook and clean up the kitchen, if Jessie isn't available," she said in a tone without inflection. "Or if she's sick and needs nursing. You come to see me if you need something typed, or a computer program tweaked, or some clue traced back to an ISP online. Neither of you ever come near me unless I'm useful."

His breath caught. "Jodie, it's not like that!"

She looked at him steadily. "Yes, it is. It always has been. I'm not complaining," she added at once. "I don't know what I would have done if it hadn't been for you and Margie. I owe you more than I can ever repay in my lifetime. It's just that since you're here, there's something you need done, and I know it. No problem. Tell me what you want me to do."

His eyes closed and opened again, on a pained expression. It was true. He and Margie had used her shamelessly, but without realizing they were so obvious. He hated the thought.

"It's a little late to develop a conscience," she added with a faint smile. "It's out of character, anyway. Come on. What is it?"

He toyed with his biscotti. "I told you that we're tracking a link to the drug cartel."

She nodded.

"In your company," he added.

"You said I couldn't help," she reminded him.

"Well, I was wrong. In fact, you're the only one who can help me with this."

A few weeks ago, she'd have joked about getting a badge or a gun. Now she just waited for answers. The days of friendly teasing were long gone.

He met her searching gaze. "I want you to pretend that we're developing a relationship," he said, "so that I have a reason to hang around your division."

She didn't react. She was proud of herself. It would have been painfully easy to dump the thick, creamy cappuccino all over his immaculate trousers and anoint him with the cream.

His eyebrow jerked. "Yes, you're right, I'm using you. It's the only way I can find to do surveillance. I can't hang around Jasper or people will think I'm keen on him!"

That thought provoked a faint smile. "His wife wouldn't like it."

He shrugged. "Will you do it?"

She hesitated.

He anticipated that. He took out a photograph and slid it across the table to her.

She picked it up. It was of two young boys, about five or six, both smiling broadly. They had thick, straight black hair and black eyes and dark complexions. They looked Latin. She looked back up at Alexander with a question in her eyes.

"Their mother was tired of having drug users in her neighborhood. They met in an abandoned house next door to her. There were frequent disputes, usually followed by running gun battles. The dealer who made the house his headquarters got ambitious. He decided to double-cross the new drug leadership that came in after Manuel Lopez's old territory was finally divided," he said carelessly. "Mama Garcia kept a close eye on what was going on and kept the police informed. She made the fatal error of telling her infrequent neighbor that his days in her neighborhood were numbered. He told his supplier.

"All this got back to the new dealer network. So when they came to take out the double-crossing dealer, they were quite particular about where they placed the shots. They knew where Mama Garcia lived, and they targeted her along with their rival. Miguel and Juan were hit almost twenty times with automatic weapon fire. They died in the firefight, along with the rebellious dealer. Their mother was wounded and will probably never walk again."

She winced as she looked at the photograph of the two little boys, so happy and smiling. Both dead, over drugs.

He saw her discomfort and nodded. "The local distributor I'm after ordered the hit. He works in this building, in this corporation, in this division." He leaned forward, and she'd never seen him look so menacing. "I'm going to take him out. So, I'll ask you one more time, Jodie. Will you help me?"

# Chapter 5

Jodie groaned inwardly. She knew as she looked one last time at the photograph that she couldn't let a child killer walk the streets, no matter what the sacrifice to herself.

She handed him back the photograph. "Yes, I'll do it," she said in a subdued tone. "When do I start?"

"Tomorrow at lunch. We'll go out to eat. You can give me the grand tour on the way."

"Okay."

"You still look reluctant," he said with narrowed eyes.

"Brody just asked me out, for the first time," she confessed, trying to sound more despondent than she actually was. It wouldn't hurt to let Alexander know that she wasn't pining over him.

His expression was not easily read. "I thought he was engaged."

She grimaced. "Well, things are cooling off," she defended herself. "His girlfriend travels all over the world. She just came back from trips to Mexico and Peru, and she doesn't pay Brody much attention even when she's here!" she muttered.

"Peru?" He seemed thoughtful. He studied her quietly for a long moment before he spoke. "They're still engaged, Jodie."

And he thought less of her because she was ignoring another woman's rights. Of course he did. She didn't like the idea, either, and she knew she wasn't going to go out with Brody a week from Saturday. Not now. Alexander made her feel too guilty.

She traced the rim of her china coffee cup. "You're right," she had to admit. "It's just that she treats him so badly," she added with a wistful smile. "He's a sweet man. He's always encouraging me in my job, telling me I can do things, believing in me."

"Which is no damned reason to have an affair with a man," he said furiously. It made him angry to think that another man was trying to uplift Jodie's ego when he'd done nothing but damage to it.

She lowered her voice. "I am not having an affair with him!"

"But you would, if he asked," he said, his eyes as cold as green glass.

She started to argue, then stopped. It would do no good to argue. Besides, it was her life, and he had no business telling her how to live it.

"How do you want me to act while we're pretending to get involved?" she countered sourly. "Do you want me to throw myself at you and start kissing you when you walk into my cubicle?"

His eyes dilated. "I beg your pardon?"

"Never mind," she said, ruffled. "I'll play it by ear."

He really did seem different, she thought, watching him hesitate uncharacteristically. He drew a USB flash drive out of his inside jacket pocket and handed it to her.

"Another chore," he added, glancing around to make sure they weren't being observed. "I want you to check out these websites, and the email addresses, without leaving footprints. I want to know if they're legitimate and who owns them. They're password protected and in code."

"No problem," she said easily. "I can get behind any firewall they put up."

"Don't leave an address they can trace back to you," he emphasized. "These people won't hesitate to kill children. They wouldn't mind wasting you."

"I get the point. I'm not sloppy." She slipped the USB flash drive into her purse and finished her coffee. "Anything else?"

"Yes. Margie said to tell you that she's sorry."

Her eyebrows arched. "For what?"

"For everything." He searched her eyes. "And for the record, you don't owe us endless favors, debt or no debt."

She got to her feet. "I know that. I'll have this information for you tomorrow by the time you get here."

He got up, too, catching the bill before she had time to grab it. "My conference, my treat," he said. He stared down at her with an intensity that was disturbing. "You're still keeping something back," he said in a deep, low tone.

"Nothing of any importance," she replied. It was disconcerting that he could read her expressions that well.

His eyes narrowed. "Do you really like working here, Jodie?"

"You're the one who said I needed to stop loafing and get a job," she accused with more bitterness than she realized. "So I got one."

He actually winced. "I said you needed to get your priorities straight," he countered. "Not that you needed to jump into a job you hate."

"I like Brody."

"Brody isn't the damned job," he replied tersely. "You're not cut out for monotony. It will kill your soul."

She knew that; she didn't want to admit it. "Don't you have a hot date?" she asked sarcastically, out of patience with his meddling.

He sighed heavily. "Yes. Why don't you?"

"Men aren't worth the trouble they cause," she lied, turning.

"Oh, you'd know?" he drawled sarcastically. "With your hectic social life?"

She turned, furious. "When Brody's free, look out," she said.

He didn't reply. But he watched her all the way down the hall.

She fumed all the way home. Alexander had such a nerve, she thought angrily. He could taunt her with his conquests, use her to do his decryption work, force her into becoming his accomplice in an investigation…!

Wait a minute, she thought suddenly, her hand resting on her purse over the USB flash drive he'd entrusted her with. He had some of the best cyber crime experts in the country on his payroll. Why was he farming out work to an amateur who didn't even work for him?

The answer came in slowly, as she recalled bits and pieces of information she'd heard during the Lopez investigation. She knew people in Jacobsville who kept in touch with her after her move to Houston. Someone had mentioned that there were suspicions of a mole in the law enforcement community, a shadowy figure who'd funneled information to Lopez so that he could escape capture.

Then Alexander's unusual request made sense. He suspected somebody in his organization of working with the drug dealers, and he wanted someone he could trust to do this investigation for him.

She felt oddly touched by his confidence, not only in her ability, but also in her character. He'd refused to let her help him before, but now he was trusting her with explosive information. He was letting her into his life, even on a limited basis. He had to care about her, a little.

Sure he did, she told herself glumly. She was a computer whiz, and he knew it. Hadn't he paid for the college education that had honed those skills? He trusted her ability to manipulate software and track criminal activity through cyberspace. That didn't amount to a declaration of love. She had to stop living in dreams. There was no hope of a future with Alexander. She wasn't even his type. He liked highly intelligent, confident women. He liked professionals. Jodie was more like a mouse. She kept in her little corner, avoiding confrontation, hiding her abilities, speaking only when spoken to, never demanding anything.

She traced the outline of the USB flash drive

through the soft leather of her purse, bought almost new at a yard sale. She pursed her lips. Well, maybe it was time she stopped being everybody's lackey and started standing up for herself. She was smart. She was capable. She could do any job she really wanted to do.

She thought about firing a woman with a dependent elderly mother and child and ground her teeth together. It was becoming obvious that she was never going to enjoy that sort of job.

On the other hand, tracking down criminals was exciting. It made her face flush as she considered how valuable she could be to Alexander in this investigation. She thought of the two little Garcia boys and their poor mother, and her eyes narrowed angrily. She was going to help Alexander catch the animal who'd ordered that depraved execution. And she was just the woman with the skills to do it.

Jodie spent most of the evening and the wee hours of the morning tracking down the information Alexander had asked her to find for him. She despaired a time or two, because she ran into one dead end after another. The drug dealers must have cyber experts of their own, and of a high caliber, if they could do this sort of thing.

She finally found a website that listed information which was, on the surface, nothing more than advisories about the best sites to find UFO information. But one of the addresses coincided with the material she'd printed out from Alexander's USB flash drive, as a possible link to the drug network. She opened site after site, but she found nothing more than double-talk about possible landing sites and dates. Most covered pages and pages of data, but the last one had only one page of information. It was oddly concise, and the sites were all in a defined area—Texas and Mexico and Peru. Strange, she thought. But, then, Peru was right next door to Colombia. And while drugs and Colombia went together like apples and pie, few people outside law enforcement would connect Peru with drug smuggling.

It was two in the morning, and she was so sleepy that she began to laugh at her own inadequacy. But as she looked at the last site she made sudden sense of the numbers and landing sites. Quickly she printed out the single page of UFO landing sites.

There was a pattern in the listings. It was so obvious that it hit her in the face. She grabbed a pencil and pad and began writing down the numbers. From there, it was a quick move to transpose them with letters. They spelled an email address.

She plugged back into her ISP and changed identities to avoid leaving digital footprints. Then she used a hacker's device to find the source of the email. It originated from a foreign server, and linked directly to a city in Peru. Moreover, a city in Peru near the border with Colombia. She copied down the information without risking leaving it in her hard drive and got out fast.

She folded the sheets of paper covered with her information—because she hadn't wanted to leave anything on her computer that could be accessed if she were online—and placed them in her purse. She smiled sleepily as she climbed into bed with a huge yawn. Alexander, she thought, was going to be impressed.

In fact, he was speechless. He went over the figures in his car in the parking lot on the way to lunch. His eyes met Jodie's and he shook his head.

"This is ingenious," he murmured.

"They did do a good job of hiding information…" she agreed.

"No! Your work," he corrected instantly. "This is quality work, Jodie. Quality work. I can't think of anyone who could have done it better."

"Thanks," she said.

"And you're taking notes for Brody Vance," he said with veiled contempt. "He should be working for you."

She chuckled at the thought of Brody with a pad and pen sitting with his legs crossed under a skirt, in front of her desk. "He wouldn't suit."

"You don't suit the job you're doing," he replied. "When this case is solved, I want you to consider switching vocations. Any law enforcement agency with a cyber crime unit would be proud to have you."

Except his, she was thinking, but she didn't say it. A compliment from Alexander was worth something. "I might do that," she said noncommittally.

"I'll put this to good use," he said, sliding the folded sheets into his inside suit pocket. "Where do you want to eat?" he added.

"I usually eat downstairs in the cafeteria. They have a blue plate special…"

"Where does your boss have lunch?"

"Brody?" She blinked. "When his girlfriend's in town, he usually goes to a Mexican restaurant, La Rancheria. It's three blocks over near the north expressway," she added.

"I know where it is. What's his girlfriend like?"

She shrugged. "Very dark, very beautiful, very chic. She's District Marketing manager for the whole southwest. She oversees our sales force for the gas and propane distribution network. We sell all over the world, of course, not just in Texas."

"But she travels to Mexico and Peru," he murmured as he turned the Jaguar into traffic.

"She has family in both places," she said disinterestedly. "Her mother was moving from a town in Peru near the Colombian border down to Mexico City, and Cara had to help organize it. That's what she told Brody." She frowned. "Odd, I thought Brody said her mother was dead. But, then, I didn't really pay attention. I've only seen her a couple of times. She leads Brody around by the nose. He's not very forceful."

"Do you like Mexican food?"

"The real thing, yes," she said with a sigh. "I usually get my chili fix from cans or TV dinners. It's not the same."

"No, it's not."

"You used to love eggs ranchero for breakfast," she commented, and then could have bitten her tongue out for admitting that she remembered his food preferences.

"Yes. You made them for me at four in the morning, the day my father died. Jessie was in tears, so was Margie. Nobody was awake. I'd come from overseas and didn't even have supper. You heard me rattling around in the kitchen trying to make a sandwich," he recalled with a strangely tender smile. "You got up and started cooking. Never said a word, either," he added. "You put the plate in front of me, poured coffee, and went away." He shrugged. "I couldn't have talked to save my life. I was too broken up at losing Dad. You knew that. I never understood how."

"Neither did I," she confessed. She looked out the

window. It was a cold day, misting rain. The city looked smoggy. That wasn't surprising. It usually did.

"What is it about Vance that attracts you?" he asked abruptly.

"Brody? Well, he's kind and encouraging, he always makes people feel good about themselves. I like being with him. He's… I don't know…comfortable."

"Comfortable." He made the word sound insulting. He turned into the parking lot of the Mexican restaurant.

"You asked," she pointed out.

He cut off the engine and glanced at her. "God forbid that a woman should ever find me comfortable!"

"That would take a miracle," she said sweetly and unfastened her seat belt.

He only laughed.

They had a quiet lunch. Brody wasn't there, but Alexander kept looking around as if he expected the man to materialize right beside the table.

"Are you looking for someone?" she asked finally.

He glanced at her over his dessert, a caramel flan. "I'm always looking for someone," he returned. "It's my job."

She didn't think about what he did for a living most of the time. Of course, the bulge under his jacket where he carried his gun was a dead giveaway, and sometimes he mentioned a case he was working on. Today, their combined efforts on the computer tracking brought it up. But she could go whole days without realizing that he put himself at risk to do the job. In his position, it was inevitable that he would make enemies. Some of them must have been dangerous, but he'd never been wounded.

"Thinking deep thoughts?" he asked her as he registered her expression.

"Not really. This flan is delicious."

"No wonder your boss frequents the place. The food is good, too."

"I really like the way they make coffee…"

"Kennedy!" Alexander called to a man just entering the restaurant, interrupting Jodie's comment.

An older man glanced his way, hesitated, and then smiled broadly as he joined them. "Cobb!" he greeted. "Good to see you!"

"I thought you were in New Orleans," Alexander commented.

"I was. Got through quicker than I thought I would. Who's this?" he added with a curious glance at Jodie.

"Jodie's my girl," Alexander said carelessly. "Jodie, this is Bert Kennedy, one of my senior agents."

They shook hands.

"Glad to meet you, Mr. Kennedy."

"Same here, Miss…?"

Alexander ignored the question. Jodie just smiled at him.

"Uh, any luck on the shipyard tip?" Kennedy asked.

Alexander shook his head. "Didn't pan out." He didn't meet the older man's eyes. "We may put a man at Thorn Oil next week," he said in a quiet tone, glancing around to make sure they weren't subject to eavesdroppers. "I'll tell you about it later."

Kennedy had been nervous, but now he relaxed and began to grin. "Great! I'd love to be in on the surveillance," he added. "Unless you have something bigger?"

"We'll talk about it later. See you."

Kennedy nodded, and walked on to a table by the window.

"Is he one of your best men?" she asked Alexander.

"Kennedy is a renegade," he murmured coolly, watching the man from a distance. "He's the bird who brought mercenaries into my drug bust in Jacobsville the year before last, without warning me first. One of their undercover guys almost got killed because we didn't know who he was."

"Eb Scott's men," she ventured.

He nodded. "I was already upset because Manuel Lopez had killed my undercover officer, Walt Monroe. He was my newest agent. I sent him to infiltrate Lopez's organization." His eyes were bleak. "I wanted Lopez. I wanted him badly. The night of the raid, I had no idea that Scott and his gang were even on the place. They were running a Mexican national undercover. If Kennedy knew, he didn't tell me. We could have killed him, or Scott, or any of his men. They weren't supposed to be there."

"I expect Mr. Kennedy lived to regret that decision."

He gave her a cool look. "Oh, he regretted it, all right."

She wasn't surprised that Mr. Kennedy was intimidated by Alexander. Most people were, herself included.

She finished her coffee. "Thanks for lunch," she said. "I really enjoyed it."

He studied her with real interest. "You have exquisite manners," he commented. "Your mother did, too."

She felt her cheeks go hot. "She was a stickler for courtesy," she replied.

"So was your father. They were good people."

"Like your own father."

"I loved him. My mother never forgave him for leaving her for a younger woman," he commented in a rare lapse. "She drank like a fish. Margie and I were stuck with her, because she put on such a good front in court that nobody believed she was a raging alcoholic. She got custody and made us pay for my father's infidelities until she finally died. By then, we were almost grown. We still loved him, though."

She hadn't known the Cobbs' mother very well. Margie had been reluctant to invite her to their home while the older woman was still alive, although Margie spent a lot of time at Jodie's home. Margie and Alexander were very fond of Mr. and Mrs. Clayburn, and they brought wonderful Christmas presents to them every year. Jodie had often wondered just how much damage his mother had done to Alexander in his younger, formative years. It might explain a lot about his behavior from time to time.

"Did you love your mother?" she asked.

He glared at her. "I hated her."

She swallowed. She thought back to the party, to her uninhibited behavior when she'd had those glasses of champagne. She'd brought back terrible memories for Alexander, of his mother, his childhood. Only now did she understand why he'd reacted so violently. No wonder she'd made him sick. He identified her behavior with his mother's. But he'd said other things, as well, things she couldn't forget. Things that hurt.

She dropped her eyes and looked at her watch. "I really have to get back," she began.

His hand went across the table to cover hers.

"Don't," he said roughly. "Don't look like that! You don't drink normally, not ever. That's why the champagne hit you so hard. I overreacted. Don't let it ruin things between us, Jodie."

She took a slow breath to calm herself. She couldn't meet his eyes. She looked at his mouth instead, and that was worse. It was a chiseled, sensuous mouth and she couldn't stop remembering how it felt to be kissed by it. He was expert. He was overwhelming. She wanted him to drag her into his arms and kiss her blind, and that would never do.

She withdrew her hand with a slow smile. "I'm not holding grudges, Alexander," she reassured him. "Listen, I really have to get back. I've got a USB flash drive full of letters to get out by quitting time."

"All right," he said. "Let's go."

Kennedy raised his hand and waved as they went out. Alexander returned the salute, sliding his hand around Jodie's waist as they left the building. But she noticed that he dropped it the minute they entered the parking lot. He was putting on an act, and she'd better remember it. She'd already been hurt once. There was no sense in inviting more pain from the same source.

He left her at the front door of her building with a curious, narrow-eyed gaze that stayed with her the rest of the day.

The phone on her desk rang early the following morning and she answered it absently while she typed.

"Do you still like symphony concerts?" came a deep voice in reply.

Alexander! Her fingers flew across the keys, making errors. "Uh, yes."

"There's a special performance of Debussy tomorrow night."

"I read about it in the entertainment section of the newspaper," she said. "They're doing 'Afternoon of a Faun' and 'La Mer,' my two favorites."

He chuckled. "I know."

"I'd love to see it," she admitted.

"I've got tickets. I'll pick you up at seven. Will you have time to eat supper by then?" he added, implying that he was asking her to the concert only, not to dinner.

"Of course," she replied.

"I have to work late, or I'd include dinner," he said softly.

"No problem. I have leftovers that have to be eaten," she said.

"Then I'll see you at seven."

"At seven." She hung up. Her hands were ice cold and shaking. She felt her insides shake. Alexander was taking her to a concert. Mentally her thoughts flew to her closet. She only had one good dress, a black one. She could pair it with her winter coat and a small strand of pearls that Margie and Alexander had given her when she graduated from college. She could put her hair up. She wouldn't look too bad.

She felt like a teenager on her first date until she realized why they were going out together. Alexander hadn't just discovered love eternal. He was putting on an act. But why put it on at a concert?

The answer came in an unexpected way. Brody stopped by her office a few minutes after Alexander's call. He came into the cubicle, looking nervous.

"Is something wrong?" she asked.

He drew in a long breath. "About next Saturday…" he began.

"I can't go," she blurted out.

His relief was patent. "I'm so glad you said that," he replied, relief making him limp. "Cara's going to be home and she wants to spend the day with me."

"Alexander's having a birthday party that day," she replied, painfully aware that she wouldn't be invited, although Alexander would surely want her coworkers to think that she was.

"I, uh, couldn't help but notice that he took you out to lunch yesterday," he said. "You've known him for a long time."

"A very long time," she confessed. "He just phoned, in fact, to invite me to a concert of Debussy…"

"Debussy?" he exclaimed.

"Well, yes…?"

"I'll see you there," he said. "Cara and I are going, too. Isn't *that* a coincidence?"

She laughed, as he did. "I can't believe it! I didn't even know you liked Debussy!"

He grimaced. "Actually, I don't," he had to confess. "Cara does."

She smiled wickedly. "I don't think Alexander's very keen on him, either, but he'll pretend to be."

He smiled back. "Forgive me, but he doesn't seem quite your type," he began slowly, flushing a little. "He's a rather tough sort of man, isn't he? And I think he was wearing a gun yesterday, too… Jodie?" he added when she burst out laughing.

"He's sort of in security work, part-time," she told him, without adding where he worked or what he did. Alexander had always made a point of keeping his exact job secret, even among his friends, for reasons Jodie was only beginning to understand.

"Oh. Oh!" He laughed with sheer relief. "And here I thought maybe you were getting involved with a mobster!"

She'd have to remember to tell Alexander that. Not that it would impress him.

"No, he's not quite that bad," she assured him. "About next Saturday, Brody, I would have canceled anyway. It didn't feel right."

"No, it didn't," he seconded. "You and I are too conventional, Jodie. Neither of us is comfortable stepping out of bounds. I'll bet you never had a speeding ticket."

"Never," she agreed. "Not that I drive very much anymore. It's so convenient to take buses," she added, without mentioning that she'd had to sell her car months ago. The repair bills, because it was an older model, were eating her alive.

"I suppose so. Uh, I did notice that your friend drives a new Jaguar."

She smiled sedately. "He and his sister are independently wealthy," she told him. "They own a ranch and breed some of the finest cattle in south Texas. That's how he can afford to run a Jaguar."

"I see." He stuck his hands in his pockets and watched her. "Debussy. Somehow I never thought of you as a classical concert-goer."

"But I am. I love ballet and theater, too. Not that I get the opportunity to see much of them these days."

"Does your friend like them, too?"

"He's the one who taught me about them," she confided. "He was forever taking me and his sister to performances when we were in our teens. He said that we needed to learn culture, because it was important. We weren't keen at the time, but we learned to love it as he did. Except for Debussy," she added on a chuckle. "And I sometimes think I like that composer just to spite him."

"It's a beautiful piece, if you like modern. I'm a Beethoven man myself."

"And I don't like Beethoven, except for the Ninth Symphony."

"That figures. Well, thanks for understanding. I, uh, I guess we'll see you at the concert tonight, then!"

"I guess so."

They exchanged smiles and then he left. She turned her attention back to her computer, curious about the coincidence.

Had Alexander known that Brody and his girlfriend Cara were going to the same performance? Or had it really been one of those inexplicable things?

Then another thought popped into her mind. What if Alexander was staking out her company because he suspected Brody of being in the drug lord's organization?

# Chapter 6

The suspicion that Alexander was after Brody kept Jodie brooding for the rest of the day. Brody was a gentle, sweet man. Surely he couldn't be involved in anything as unsavory as drug smuggling!

If someone at the corporation was under investigation, she couldn't blow Alexander's cover by mentioning anything to her boss. But, wait, hadn't Alexander told his agent, Kennedy, that they were investigating a case at Thorn Oil Corporation? Then she remembered why Alexander wanted to pretend to be interested in Jodie. Something was crazy here. Why would he lie to Kennedy?

She shook her head and put the questions away. She wasn't going to find any answers on her own.

She'd been dressed and ready for an hour when she buzzed Alexander into her apartment building. By the time he got to her room and knocked at the door, she was a nervous wreck.

She opened the door, and he gave her a not very flattering scrutiny. She thought she looked nice in her sedate black dress and high heels, with her hair in a bun. Obviously he didn't. He was dashing, though, in a dinner jacket and slacks and highly polished black shoes. His black tie was perfectly straight against the expensive white cotton of his shirt.

"You never wear your hair down," Alexander said curtly. "And you've worn that same dress to two out of three parties at our house."

She flushed. "It's the only good dress I have, Alexander," she said tightly.

He sighed angrily. "Margie would love to make you something, if you'd let her."

She turned to lock her door. Her hands were cold and numb. He couldn't let her enjoy one single evening without criticizing something about her. She felt near tears…

She gasped as he suddenly whipped her around and bent to kiss her with grinding, passionate fervor. She didn't have time to respond. It was over as soon as it had begun, despite her rubbery legs and wispy breathing. She stood looking up at him with wide, misty, shocked eyes in a pale face.

His own green eyes glittered into hers as he studied her reaction. "Stop letting me put you down," he said unexpectedly. "I know I don't do much for your ego, but you have to stand up for yourself. You're not a carpet, Jodie, stop letting people walk on you."

She was still trying to breathe and think at the same time.

"And now you look like an accident victim," he murmured. He pulled out a handkerchief, his eyes on her mouth. "I suppose I'm covered with pink lipstick," he added, pressing the handkerchief into her hand. "Clean me up."

"It…doesn't come off," she stammered.

He cocked an eyebrow and waited for an explanation.

"It's that new kind they advertise. You put it on and it lasts all day. It won't come off on coffee cups or even linen." She handed him back the handkerchief.

He put it up, but he didn't move. His hands went to the pert bun on the top of her head and before she could stop him, he loosed her hair from the circular comb that held the wealth of hair in place. It fell softly, in waves, to her shoulders.

Alexander caught his breath. "Beautiful," he whispered, the comb held absently in one hand while he ran the other through the soft strands of hair.

"It took forever…to get it put up," she protested weakly.

"I love long hair," he said gruffly. He bent, tilting her chin up, to kiss her with exquisite tenderness. "Leave it like that."

He put the comb in her hand and waited while she stuck it into her purse. Her hands shook. He saw that, too, and he smiled.

When she finished, he linked her fingers into his and they started off down the hall.

The concert hall was full. Apparently quite a few people in Houston liked Debussy, Jodie thought mischievously as they walked down the aisle to their seats.

She knew that Alexander didn't like it at all, but it was nice of him to suffer through it, considering her own affection for the pieces the orchestra was playing.

Of course, he might only be here because he was spying on Brody, she thought, and then worried about that. She couldn't believe Brody would ever deal in anything dishonest. He was too much like Jodie herself. But why would Alexander be spending so much time at her place of work if he didn't suspect Brody?

It was all very puzzling. She sat down in the reserved seat next to Alexander and waited for the curtain to go up. They'd gotten into a traffic jam on the way and had arrived just in the nick of time. The lights went out almost the minute they sat down.

In the darkness, lit comfortably by the lights from the stage where the orchestra was placed, she felt Alexander's big, warm hand curl into hers. She sighed helplessly, loving the exciting, electric contact of his touch.

He heard the soft sound, and his fingers tightened. He didn't let go until intermission.

"Want to stretch your legs?" he invited, standing.

"Yes, I think so," she agreed. She got up, still excited by his proximity, and walked out with him. He didn't hold her hand this time, she noticed, and wondered why.

When they were in the lobby, Brody spotted them and moved quickly toward them, his girlfriend in tow.

She was pretty, Jodie noted, very elegant and dark-haired and long-legged. She wished she was half as pretty. Brody's girlfriend looked Hispanic. She was certainly striking.

"Well, hello!" Brody said with genuine warmth. "Sweetheart, this is my secretary, Jodie Clayburn…

excuse me," he added quickly, with an embarrassed smile at Jodie's tight-lipped glance, "I mean, my administrative assistant. And this is Jodie's date, Mr., uh, Mr..."

"Cobb," Alexander prompted.

"Mr. Cobb," Brody parroted. "This is my girlfriend, Cara Dominguez," he introduced.

"Pleased to meet you," Cara said in a bored tone.

"Same here," Jodie replied.

"Cara's in marketing," Brody said, trying to force the conversation to ignite. "She works for Bradford Marketing Associates, down the street. They're a subsidiary of Ritter Oil Corporation. They sell drilling equipment and machine parts for oil equipment all over the United States. Cara is over the southwestern division."

"And what do you do, Mr. Cobb?" Cara asked Alexander, who was simply watching her, without commenting.

"Oh, he's in security work," Brody volunteered.

Cara's eyebrows arched. "Really!" she asked, but without much real interest.

"I work for the Drug Enforcement Administration," Alexander said with a faint smile, his eyes acknowledging Jodie's shock. "I'm undercover and out of the country a lot of the time," he added with the straightest face Jodie had ever seen. "I don't have to work at all, of course," he added with a cool smile, "but I like the cachet of law enforcement duties."

Jodie was trying not to look at him or react. It was difficult.

"How nice," Cara said after a minute, and she seemed disconcerted by his honesty. "You are working on a case now?" she fished.

One of the first things Jodie and Margie had learned from Alexander when he went with the DEA was not to mention what he did for a living, past the fact that he did "security work." She'd always assumed it had something to do with his infrequent undercover assignments. And here he was spilling all the beans!

"Sort of," Alexander said lazily. "We're investigating a company with Houston connections," he added deliberately.

Cara was all ears. "That would not be Thorn Oil Corporation?"

Alexander gave her a very nice shocked look.

She laughed. "One hears things," she mused. "Don't worry, I never tell what I know."

"Right," Brody chuckled, making a joke of it. He hadn't known what Alexander did for a living until now.

Alexander laughed, too. "I have to have the occasional diversion," he confessed. "My father was wealthy. My sister and I were his only beneficiaries."

Cara was eyeing him with increased interest. "You live in Houston, Mr. Cobb?"

He nodded.

"Are you enjoying the concert?" Brody broke in, uncomfortable at the way his girlfriend was looking at Alexander.

"It's wonderful," Jodie said.

"I understand the Houston ballet is doing *The Nutcracker* starting in November," Cara purred, smiling at Alexander. "If you like ballet, perhaps we will meet again."

"Perhaps we will," Alexander replied. "Do you live in Houston, also, Miss Dominguez?"

"Yes, but I travel a great deal," she said with careless detachment. "My contacts are far reaching."

"She's only just come back from Mexico," Brody said with a nervous laugh.

"Yes, I've been helping my mother move," Cara said tightly. "After my father…died, she lost her home and had nowhere to go."

"I'm very sorry," Jodie told her. "I lost my parents some years ago. I know how it feels."

Cara turned back to Brody. "We need to get back to our seats. Nice to have met you both," she added with a social smile as she took Brody's hand and drew him along with her. He barely had time to say goodbye.

Alexander glanced down at Jodie. "Your boss looked shocked when I told him what I did."

She shook her head. "You told me never to do that, but you told them everything!"

"I told them nothing Cara didn't know already," he said enigmatically. He slid his hand into hers and smiled secretively. "Let's go back."

"It's a very nice concert," she commented.

"Is it? I hate Debussy," he murmured unsurprisingly.

The comment kept her quiet until they were out of the theater and on their way back to her apartment in his car.

"Why did you ask me out if you don't like concerts?" she asked.

He glanced at her. "I had my reasons. What do you think of your boss's girlfriend?"

"She's nice enough. She leads Brody around like a child, though."

"Most women would," he said lazily. "He's not assertive."

"He certainly is," she defended him. "He has to fire people."

"He's not for you, Jodie, girlfriend or not," he said surprisingly. "You'd stagnate in a relationship with him."

"It's my life," she pointed out.

"So it is."

They went the rest of the way in silence. He walked her to her apartment door and stood staring down at her for a long moment. "Buy a new dress."

"Why?" she asked, surprised.

"I'll take you to see *The Nutcracker* next month. As I recall, it was one of your favorite ballets."

"Yes," she stammered.

"So I'll take you," he said. He checked his watch. "I've got a late call to make, and meetings the first of the week. But I'll take you to lunch next Wednesday."

"Okay," she replied.

He reached out suddenly and drew her against him, hard. He held her there, probing her eyes with his until her lips parted. Then he bent and kissed her hungrily, twisting his mouth against hers until she yielded and gave him what he wanted. A long, breathless moment later, he lifted his head.

"Not bad," he murmured softly. "But you could use a little practice. Sleep well."

He let her go and walked away while she tried to find her voice. He never looked back once. Jodie stood at her door watching until he stepped into the elevator and the doors closed.

She usually left at eleven-thirty to go to lunch, and Alexander knew it. But he was late the following

Wednesday. She'd chewed off three of her long fingernails by the time he showed up. She was in the lobby
where clients were met, along with several of her colleagues who were just leaving for lunch. Alexander
came in, looking windblown and half out of humor.

"I can't make it for lunch," he said at once. "I'm
sorry. Something came up."

"That's all right," she said, trying not to let her disappointment show. "Another time."

"I'll be out of town for the next couple of days," he
continued, not lowering his voice, "but don't you forget my birthday party on Saturday. Call me from the
airport and I'll pick you up. If I'm not back by then,
Margie will. All right?"

Amazing how much he sounded as if he really
wanted her to come. But she knew he was only putting
on an act for the employees who were listening to him.

"All right," she agreed. "Have a safe trip. I'll see
you Saturday."

He reached out and touched her cheek tenderly. "So
long," he said, smiling. He walked away slowly, as if he
hated to leave her, and she watched him go with equal
reluctance. There were smiling faces all around. It was
working. People believed they were involved, which
was just what he wanted.

Later, while Brody was signing the letters he'd dictated earlier, she wondered where Alexander was going
that would keep him out of town for so long.

"You look pensive," Brody said curiously. "Something worrying you?"

"Nothing, really," she lied. "I was just thinking
about Alexander's birthday party on Saturday."

He sighed as he signed the last letter. "It must be

nice to have a party," he murmured. "I stopped having them years ago."

"Cara could throw one for you," she suggested.

He grimaced. "She's not the least bit sentimental. She's all business, most of the time, and she never seems to stop working. She's on a trip to Arizona this week to try to land a new client."

"You'll miss her, I'm sure," Jodie said.

He shrugged. "I'll try to." He flushed. "Sorry, that just popped out."

She smiled. "We all have our problems, Brody."

"Yes, I noticed that your friend, Cobb, hardly touches you, except when he thinks someone is watching. He must be one cold fish," he added with disgust.

Jodie flushed then, remembering Alexander's ardor.

He cleared his throat and changed the subject, and not a minute too soon.

Jodie was doing housework in her apartment when the phone rang Saturday morning.

"Jodie?" Margie asked gently.

"Yes. How are you, Margie?" she asked, but not with her usual cheerful friendliness.

"You're still angry at me, aren't you?" She sighed. "I'm so sorry for making you do all the cooking…"

"I'm not angry," Jodie replied.

There was a long sigh. "I thought Kirry would help me arrange a showing of my designs at her department store," she confessed miserably. "But that's never going to happen. She only pretended to be my friend so that she could get to Alexander. I guess you know she's furious because he's been seen with you?"

"She has nothing to be jealous about," Jodie said

coldly. "You can tell her so, for me. Was that all you wanted?"

"Jodie, that's not why I called!" Margie exclaimed. She hesitated. "Alexander wanted me to phone you and make sure you were coming to his birthday party."

"There's no chance of that," Jodie replied firmly.

"But…but he's expecting you," Margie stammered. "He said you promised to come, but that I had to call you and make sure you showed up."

"Kirry's invited, of course?" Jodie asked.

"Well…well, yes, I assumed he'd want her to come so I invited her, too."

"I'm invited to make her jealous, I suppose."

There was a static pause. "Jodie, what's going on? You won't return my calls, you won't meet me for lunch, you don't answer notes. If you're not mad at me, what's wrong?"

Jodie looked down at the floor. It needed mopping, she thought absently. "Alexander told you that he was sick of tripping over me every time he came back to the ranch, and that you were especially not to ask me to his birthday party."

There was a terrible stillness on the end of the line for several seconds. "Oh, my God," Margie groaned. "You heard what he said that night!"

"I heard every single word, Margie," Jodie said tightly. "He thinks I'm still crazy about him, and it… disgusts him. He said I'm not in your social set and you should make friends among your own social circle." She took a deep, steadying breath. "Maybe he's right, Margie. The two of you took care of me when I had nobody else, but I've been taking advantage of it all these years, making believe that you were my family.

In a way I'm grateful that Alexander opened my eyes. I've been an idiot."

"Jodie, he didn't mean it, I know he didn't! Sometimes he just says things without thinking them through. I know he wouldn't hurt you deliberately."

"He didn't know I could hear him," she said. "I drank too much and behaved like an idiot. We both know how Alexander feels about women who get drunk. But I've come to my senses now. I'm not going to impose on your hospitality…"

"But Alexander wants you to come!" Margie argued. "He said so!"

"No, he doesn't, Margie," Jodie said wistfully. "You don't understand what's going on, but I'm helping Alexander with a case. He's using me as a blind while he's surveilling a suspect, and don't you dare let on that you know it. It's not personal between us. It couldn't be. I'm not his sort of woman and we both know it."

Margie's intake of breath was audible. "What am I going to tell him when you don't show up?"

"You won't need to tell him anything," Jodie said easily. "He isn't expecting me. It was just for show. He'll tell you all about it one day. Now I have to go, Margie. I'm working in the kitchen, and things are going to burn," she added, lying through her teeth.

"We could have lunch next week," the other woman offered.

"No. You need to find friends in your class, Margie. I'm not part of your family, and you don't owe me anything. Now, goodbye!"

She hung up and unplugged the phone in case Margie tried to call back. She felt sick. But severing ties with Margie was the right thing to do. Once Alexander was through with her, once he'd caught his criminal, he'd leave her strictly alone. She was going to get out of his life, and Margie's, right now. It was the only sensible way to get over her feelings for Alexander.

The house was full of people when Alexander went inside, carrying his bag on a shoulder strap.

Margie met him at the door. "I'll bet you're tired, but at least you got here." She chuckled, trying not to show her worry. "Leave your bag by the door and come on in. Everybody's in the dining room with the cake."

He walked beside her toward the spacious dining room, where about twenty people were waiting near a table set with china and crystal, punch and coffee and cake. He searched the crowd and began to scowl.

"I don't see Jodie," he said at once. "Where is she? Didn't you phone her?"

"Yes," she groaned, "but she wouldn't come. Please, Lex, can't we talk about it later? Look, Kirry's here!"

"Damn Kirry," he said through his teeth, glaring down at his sister. "Why didn't she come?"

She drew in a miserable breath. "Because she heard us talking the last time she was here," she replied slowly. "She said you were right about her not being in our social class, and that she heard you say that the last thing you wanted was to trip over her at your birthday party." She winced, because the look on his face was so full of pain.

"She heard me," he said, almost choking on the words. "Good God, no wonder she looked at me the way she did. No wonder she's been acting so strangely!"

"She won't go out to lunch with me, she won't come

here, she doesn't even want me to call her anymore," Margie said sadly. "I feel as if I've lost my own sister."

His own loss was much worse. He felt sick to his soul. He'd never meant for Jodie to hear those harsh, terrible words. He'd been reacting to his own helpless loss of control with her, not her hesitant ardor. It was himself he'd been angry at. Now he understood why Jodie was so reluctant to be around him lately. It was ironic that he found himself thinking about her around the clock, and she was as standoffish as a woman who found him bad company when they were alone. If only he could turn the clock back, make everything right. Jodie, so sweet and tender and loving, Jodie who had loved him once, hearing him tell Margie that Jodie disgusted him…!

"I should be shot," he ground out. "Shot!"

"Don't. It's your birthday," Margie reminded him. "Please. All these people came just to wish you well."

He didn't say another word. He simply walked into the room and let the congratulations flow over him. But he didn't feel happy. He felt as if his heart had withered and died in his chest.

That night, he slipped into his office while Kirry was talking to Margie, and he phoned Jodie. He'd had two straight malt whiskeys with no water, and he wasn't quite sober. It had taken that much to dull the sharp edge of pain.

"You didn't come," he said when she answered.

She hadn't expected him to notice. She swallowed, hard. "The invitation was all for show," she said, her voice husky. "You didn't expect me."

There was a pause. "Did you go out with Brody

after all?" he drawled sarcastically. "Is that why you didn't show up?"

"No, I didn't," she muttered. "I'm not spending another minute of my life trying to fit into your exalted social class," she added hotly. "Cheating wives, consciousless husbands, social climbing friends…that's not my idea of a party!"

He sat back in his chair. "You might not believe it, but it's not mine, either," he said flatly. "I'd rather get a fast food hamburger and talk shop with the guys."

That was surprising. But she didn't quite trust him. "That isn't Kirry's style," she pointed out.

He laughed coldly. "It would become her style in minutes if she thought it would make me propose. I'm rich. Haven't you noticed?"

"It's hard to miss," she replied.

"Kirry likes life in the fast lane. She wants to be decked out in diamonds and taken to all the most expensive places four nights a week. Five on holidays."

"I'm sure she wants you, too."

"Are you?"

"I'm folding clothes, Alexander. Was there anything else?" she added formally, trying to get him to hang up. The conversation was getting painful.

"I never knew that you heard me the night of our last party, Jodie," he said in a deep, husky, pained sort of voice. "I'm more sorry than I can say. You don't know what it was like when my mother had parties. She drank like a fish…"

So Margie had told him. It wasn't really a surprise. "I had some champagne," she interrupted. "I don't drink, so it overwhelmed me. I'm very sorry for the way I behaved."

There was another pause. "I loved it," he said gruffly.

Now she couldn't even manage a reply. She just stared at the receiver, waiting for him to say something else.

"Talk to me!" he growled.

"What do you want me to say?" she asked unsteadily. "You were right. I don't belong in your class. I never will. You said I was a nuisance, and you were ri—"

"Jodie!" Her name sounded as if it were torn from his throat. "Jodie, don't! I didn't mean what I said. You've never been a nuisance!"

"It's too late," she said heavily. "I won't come back to the ranch again, ever, Alexander, not for you or even for Margie. I'm going to live my own life, make my own way in the world."

"By pushing us out of it?" he queried.

She sighed. "I suppose so."

"But not until I solve this case," he added after a minute. "Right?"

She wanted to argue, but she kept seeing the little boys' faces in that photograph he'd shown her. "Not until then," she said.

There was a rough sound, as if he'd been holding his breath and suddenly let it out. "All right."

"Alexander, where are you?" That was Kirry's voice, very loud.

"In a minute, Kirry! I'm on the phone!"

"We're going to open the presents. Come on!"

Jodie heard the sound Alexander made, and she laughed softly in spite of herself. "I thought it was your birthday?" she mused.

"It started to be, but my best present is back in Houston folding clothes," he said vehemently.

Her heart jumped. She had to fight not to react. "I'm nobody's present, Alexander," she informed him. "And now I really do have to go. Happy birthday."

"I'm thirty-four," he said. "Margie is the only family I have. Two of my colleagues just had babies," he remarked, his voice just slightly slurred. "Their desks are full of photographs of the kids and their wives. Know what I've got in a frame on my desk, Jodie? Kirry, in a ball gown."

"I guess the married guys would switch places with you…"

"That's not what I mean! I didn't put it there, she did. Instead of a wife and kids, I've got a would-be debutante who wants to own Paris."

"That was your choice," she pointed out.

"That's what you think. She gave me the framed picture." There was a pause. "Why don't you give me a photo?"

"Sure. Why not? Who would you like a photo of, and I'll see if I can find one for you."

"You, idiot!"

"I don't have any photos of myself."

"Why not?"

"Who'd take them?" she asked. "I don't even own a camera."

"We'll have to do something about that," he murmured. "Do you like parks? We could go jogging early Monday in that one near where you live. The one with the goofy sculpture."

"It's modern art. It isn't goofy."

"You're entitled to your opinion. Do you jog?"

"Not really."

"Do you have sweats and sneakers?"

She sighed irritably. "Well, yes, but…"

"No buts. I'll see you bright and early Monday." There was a pause. "I'll even apologize."

"That would be a media event."

"I'm serious," he added quietly. "I've never regretted anything in my life more than knowing you heard what I said to Margie that night."

For an apology, it was fairly headlong. Alexander never made apologies. It was a red letter event.

"Okay," she said after a few seconds.

He sighed, hard. "We can start over," he said firmly.

"Alexander, are you coming out of there?" came Kirry's petulant voice in the background.

"Better tell Kirry first," she chided.

"I'll tell her…get the hell out of my study!" he raged abruptly, and there was the sound of something heavy hitting the wall. Then there was the sound of a door closing with a quick snap.

"What did you do?" Jodie exclaimed.

"I threw a book in her general direction. Don't worry. It wasn't a book I liked. It was something on Colombian politics."

"You could have hit her!"

"In pistol competition, I hit one hundred targets out of a hundred shots. The book hit ten feet from where she was standing."

"You shouldn't throw things at people."

"But I'm uncivilized," he reminded her. "I need someone to mellow me out."

"Kirry's already there."

"Not for long, if she opens that damned door again. I'll see you Monday. Okay?"

There was a long hesitation. But finally she said, "Okay."

She put down the receiver and stared at it blankly. Her life had just shifted ten degrees and she had no idea why. At least, not right then.

# *Chapter 7*

Jodie had just changed into her sweats and was making breakfast in her sock feet when Alexander knocked on the door.

He was wearing gray sweats, like hers, with gray running shoes. He gave her a long, thorough appraisal. "I don't like your hair in a bun," he commented.

"I can't run with it down," she told him. "It tangles."

He sniffed the air. "Breakfast?" he asked hopefully.

"Just bacon and eggs and biscuits."

"Just! I had a granola bar," he said with absolute disdain.

She laughed nervously. It was new to have him in her apartment, to have him wanting to be with her. She didn't understand his change of attitude, and she didn't really trust it. But she was too enchanted to question it too closely.

"If you'll feed me," he began, "I'll let you keep up with me while we jog."

"That sounds suspiciously like a bribe," she teased, moving toward the table. "What *would* your bosses say?"

"You're not a client," he pointed out, seating himself at the table. "Or a perpetrator. So it doesn't count."

She poured him a mug of coffee and put it next to his plate, frowning as she noted the lack of matching dishes and even silverware. The table—a prize from a yard sale—had noticeable scratches and she didn't even have a tablecloth.

"What a comedown this must be," she muttered to herself as she fetched the blackberry jam and put it on the table, along with another teaspoon that didn't match the forks.

He gave her an odd look. "I'm not making comparisons, Jodie," he said softly, and his eyes were as soft as his deep voice. "You live within your means, and you do extremely well at it. You'd be surprised how many people are mortgaged right down to the fillings in their teeth trying to put on a show for their acquaintances. Which is, incidentally, why a lot of them end up in prison, trying to make a quick buck by selling drugs."

She made a face. "I'd rather starve than live like that."

"So would I," he confessed. He bit into a biscuit and moaned softly. "If only Jessie could make these the way you do," he said.

She smiled, pleased at the compliment, because Jessie was a wonderful cook. "They're the only thing I do well."

"No, they aren't." He tasted the jam and frowned. "I didn't know they made blackberry jam," he noted.

"You can buy it, but I like to make my own and put it up," she said. "That came from blackberries I picked last summer, on the ranch. They're actually your own blackberries," she added sheepishly.

"You can have as many as you like, if you'll keep me supplied with this jam," he said, helping himself to more biscuits.

"I'm glad you like it."

They ate in a companionable silence. When she poured their second cups of strong coffee, there weren't any biscuits left.

"Now I need to jog," he teased, "to work off the weight I've just put on. Coffee's good, too, Jodie. Everything was good."

"You were just hungry."

He sat back holding his coffee and stared at her. "You've never learned how to take a compliment," he said gently. "You do a lot of things better than other people, but you're modest to the point of self-abasement."

She moved a shoulder. "I like cooking."

He sipped coffee, still watching her. She was pretty early in the morning, he mused, with her face blooming like a rose, her skin clean and free of makeup. Her lips had a natural blush, and they had a shape that was arousing. He remembered how it felt to kiss her, and he ached to do it again. But this was new territory for her. He had to take his time. If he rushed her, he was going to lose her. That thought, once indifferent, took on supreme importance now. He was only beginning to see how much a part of him Jodie already was. He could have kicked himself for what he'd said about her at the ill-fated party.

"The party was a bust," he said abruptly.

Her eyes widened. "Pardon?"

"Kirry opened the presents and commented on their value and usefulness until the guests turned to strong drink," he said with a twinkle in his green eyes. "Then she took offense when a former friend of hers turned up with her ex-boyfriend and made a scene. She left in a trail of flames by cab before we even got to the live band."

She was trying not to smile. It was hard not to be amused at Kirry's situation. The woman was trying, even to people like Margie, who wanted to be friends with her.

"I guess there went Margie's shot at fashion fame," she said sadly.

"Kirry would never have helped her," he said carelessly, and finished his coffee. "She never had any intention of risking her job on a new designer's reputation. She was stringing Margie along so that she could hang out with us. She was wearing thin even before Saturday night."

"Sorry," she said, not knowing what else to say.

"We weren't lovers," he offered blatantly.

She blushed and then caught her breath. "Alexander...!"

"I wanted you to know that, in case anything is ever said about my relationship with her," he added, very seriously. "It was never more than a surface attraction. I can't abide a woman who wears makeup to bed."

She wouldn't ask, she wouldn't ask, she wouldn't...! "How do you know she does?" she blurted out.

He grinned at her. "Margie told me. She asked Kirry why, and Kirry said you never knew when a gentleman might knock on your door after midnight." He leaned forward. "I never did."

"I wasn't going to ask!"

"Sure you were." His eyes slid over her pretty breasts, nicely but not blatantly outlined under the gray jersey top she was wearing. "You're possessive about me. You don't want to be, but you are."

She was losing ground. She got to her feet and made a big thing of checking to see that her shoelaces were tied. "Shouldn't we go?"

He got up, stretched lazily, and started to clear the table. She was shocked to watch him.

"You've never done that," she remarked.

He glanced at her. "If I get married, and I might, I think marriage should be a fifty-fifty proposition. There's nothing romantic about a man lying around the apartment in a dirty T-shirt watching football while his wife slaves in the kitchen." He frowned thoughtfully. "Come to think of it, I don't like football."

"You don't wear dirty T-shirts, either," she replied, feeling sad because he'd mentioned marrying. Maybe there was another woman in his life, besides Kirry.

He chuckled. "Not unless I'm working in the garage." He came around the table after he'd put the dishes in the sink and took her gently by the shoulders, his expression somber. "We've never discussed personal issues. I know less about you than a stranger does. Do you like children? Do you want to have them? Or is a career primary in your life right now?"

The questions were vaguely terrifying. He was

going from total indifference to intent scrutiny, and it was too soon. Her face took on a hunted look.

"Never mind," he said quickly, when he saw that. "Don't worry about the question. It isn't important."

She relaxed, but only a little. "I...love children," she faltered. "I like working, or I would if I had a challenging job. But that doesn't mean I'd want to put off having a family if I got married. My mother worked while I was growing up, but she was always there when I needed her, and she never put her job before her family. Neither would I." She searched his eyes, thinking how beautiful a shade of green they were, and about little children with them. Her expression went dreamy. "Fame and fortune may sound enticing, but they wouldn't make up for having people love you." She shrugged. "I guess that sounds corny."

"Actually, it sounds very mature." He bent and drew his mouth gently over her lips, a whisper of contact that didn't demand anything. "I feel the same way."

"You do?" She was unconsciously reaching up to him, trying to prolong the contact. It was unsettling that his lightest touch could send her reeling like this. She wanted more. She wanted him to crush her in his arms and kiss her blind.

He nibbled her upper lip slowly. "It isn't enough, is it?"

"Well...no..."

His arms drew her up, against the steely length of his body, and his mouth opened her lips to a kiss that was consuming with its heat. She moaned helplessly, clinging to him.

He lifted his mouth a breath away. His voice was

strained when he spoke. "Do you have any idea what those little noises do to me?" he groaned.

"Noises?" she asked, oblivious, as she stared at his mouth.

"Never mind." He kissed her again, devouring her soft lips. The sounds she made drugged him. He was measuring the distance from the kitchen to her bedroom when he realized how fast things were progressing.

He drew back, and held her away from him, his jaw taut with an attempt at control.

"Alexander," she whispered, her voice pleading as she looked up at him with misty soft eyes.

"I almost never get women pregnant on Monday, but this could be an exception," he said in a choked tone.

Her eyes widened like saucers as she realized what he was saying.

He burst out laughing at her expression. He moved back even more. "I only carry identification and twenty dollars on me when I jog," he confessed. "The other things I keep in my wallet are still in it, at my apartment," he added, his tone blatantly expressive.

She divined what he was intimating and she flushed. She pushed back straggly hair from her face as she searched for her composure.

"Of course, a lot of modern women keep their own supply," he drawled. "I expect you have a box full in your medicine cabinet."

She flushed even more, and now she was glaring at him.

He chuckled, amused. "Your parents were very strict," he recalled. "And deeply religious. You still have those old attitudes about premarital sex, don't you?"

She nodded, grimacing.

"Don't apologize," he said wistfully. "In ten minutes or so, the ache will ease and I can actually stand up straight... God, Jodie!" he burst out laughing at her horrified expression. "I'm kidding!"

"You're a terrible man," she moaned.

"No, I'm just normal," he replied. "I'd love nothing better than a few hours in bed with you, but I'm not enough of a scoundrel to seduce you. Besides all that—" he sighed "—your conscience would kill both of us."

"Rub it in."

He shrugged. "You'd be surprised how many women at my office abstain, and make no bones about it to eligible bachelors who want to take them out," he said, and he smiled tenderly at her. "We tend to think of them as rugged individualists with the good sense not to take chances." He leaned forward. "And there are actually a couple of the younger male agents who feel the same way!"

"You're kidding!"

He shook his head, smiling. "Maybe it's a trend. You know, back in the early twentieth century, most women and men went to their weddings chaste. A man with a bad reputation was as untouchable as a woman with one."

"I'll bet you never told a woman in your life that you were going to abstain," she murmured wickedly.

He didn't smile back. He studied her for a long moment. "I'm telling you that I am. For the foreseeable future."

She didn't know how to take that, and it showed.

"I'm not in your class as a novice," he confessed, "but I'm no rake, either. I don't find other women desirable lately. Just you." He shrugged. "Careful, it may be contagious."

She laughed. Her whole face lit up. She was beautiful.

He drew her against him and kissed her, very briefly, before he moved away again. "We should go," he said. "I have a meeting at the office at ten. Then we could have lunch."

"Okay," she said. She felt lighthearted. Overwhelmed. She started toward the door and then stopped. "Can I ask you a question?"

"Shoot."

"Are you staking out my company because you're investigating Brody for drug smuggling?"

He gave her an old, wise look. "You're sharp, Jodie. I'll have to watch what I say around you."

"That means you're not going to tell me. Right?"

He chuckled. "Right." He led the way into the hall and then waited for her to lock her door behind them.

She slipped the key into her pocket.

"No ID?" he mused as they went downstairs and started jogging down the sparsely occupied sidewalk.

"Just the key and five dollars, in case I need money for a bottle of water or something," she confessed.

He sighed, not even showing the strain as they moved quickly along. "One of our forensic reconstruction artists is always lecturing us on carrying identification. She says that it's easier to have something on you that will identify you, so that she doesn't have to take your skull and model clay to do a reconstruction of your face. She helps solve a lot of murder victims' identities, but she has plenty that she can't identify. The faces haunt her, she says."

"I watched a program about forensic reconstruction on educational television two weeks ago."

"I know the one you mean. I saw it, too. That was our artist," he said with traces of pride in his deep voice. "She's a wonder."

"I guess it wouldn't hurt to carry my driver's license around with me," she murmured.

He didn't say another word, but he grinned to himself.

The meeting was a drug task force formed of a special agent from the Houston FBI office, a Houston police detective who specialized in local gangs, a Texas Ranger from Company A, an agent from the US Customs Service and a sheriff's deputy from Harris County who headed her department's drug unit.

They sat down in a conference room in the nearest Houston police station to discuss intelligence.

"We've got a good lead on the new division chief of the Culebra cartel in Mexico," Alexander announced when it was his turn to speak. "We know that he has somebody on his payroll from Ritter Oil Corporation, and that he's funneling drugs through a warehouse where oil regulators and drilling equipment are kept before they're shipped out all over the southwest. Since the parking lot of that warehouse is locked by a key code, the division chief has to have someone on the inside."

"Do we know how it's being moved and when?" the FBI agent asked.

Alexander had suspicions, but no concrete evidence. "Waiting for final word on when. But we do have an informant, a young man who got cold feet and came to US Customs with information about the drug smuggling. I interviewed the young man, with help from Customs," he added, nodding with a smile at the petite brunette customs official at the table with them.

"That would be me," she said with a grin.

"The informant says that a shipment of processed cocaine is on the way here, one of the biggest in several years. It was shipped from the Guajira Peninsula in Colombia to Central America and transshipped by plane to an isolated landing site in rural Mexico. From there it was carried to a warehouse in Mexico City owned by a subsidiary of an oil company here in Houston. It was reboxed with legitimate oil processing equipment manufactured in Europe, in boxes with false bottoms. It was shipped legally to the oil company's district office in Galveston where it was inspected briefly and passed through customs."

"The oil company is one that's never been involved in any illegal activity," the customs representative said wistfully, "so the agent didn't look for hidden contraband."

"To continue," Alexander said, "it's going to be shipped into the Houston warehouse via the Houston Ship Canal as domestic inventory from Galveston."

"Which means, no more customs inspections," the Texas Ranger said.

"Exactly," Alexander agreed.

The brunette customs agent shook her head. "A few shipments get by our inspectors, but not many. We have contacts everywhere, too, and one of those tipped us off about the young man who was willing to inform on the perpetrators of an incoming cocaine shipment," she told the others. "So we saved our bacon."

"You had the contacts I gave you, don't forget," the blonde lieutenant of detectives from Houston reminded her with a smile, as she adjusted her collar.

"Do we even have a suspect?" the customs agent asked.

Alexander nodded. "I've got someone on the inside at Ritter Oil, and I'm watching a potential suspect. I don't have enough evidence yet to make an accusation, but I hope to get it, and soon. I'm doing this undercover, so this information is to be kept in this room. I've put it out that we have another company, Thorn Oil, under surveillance, as a cover story. Under no circumstances are any of you to discuss any of this meeting, even with another DEA agent—*especially* with another DEA agent—until further notice. That's essential."

The police lieutenant gave him a pointed look. "Can I ask why?"

"Because the oil corporation isn't the only entity that's harboring an inside informant," Alexander replied flatly. "And that's all I feel comfortable saying."

"You can count on us," the Texas Ranger assured him. "We won't blow your cover. The person you're watching, can you tell us why you're watching him?"

"In order to use that warehouse for storage purposes, the drug lord has to have access to it," Alexander explained. "I'm betting he has some sort of access to the locked gate and that he's paying the night watchman to look the other way."

"That would make sense," the customs agent agreed grimly. "These people know how little law enforcement personnel make. They can easily afford to offer a poorly paid night watchman a six figure 'donation' to just turn his head at the appropriate time."

"That much money would tempt even a law-abiding citizen," Alexander agreed. "But more than that, very often there's a need that compromises integrity. A sheriff in another state had a wife dying of cancer and no insurance. He got fifty thousand dollars for not noticing a shipment of drugs coming into his county."

"They catch him?" the policewoman asked.

"Yes. He wasn't very good at being a crook. He confessed, before he was even suspected of being involved."

"How many people in your agency know about this?" the deputy sheriff asked Alexander.

"Nobody, at the moment," he replied. "It has to stay that way, until we make the bust. I'll depend on all of you to back me up. The mules working for the new drug lord carry automatic weapons and they've killed so many people down in Mexico that they won't hesitate to waste anyone who gets in their way."

"Good thing the president of Mexico isn't intimidated by them," the customs agent said with a grin. "He's done more to attack drug trafficking than any president before him."

"He's a good egg," Alexander agreed. "Let's hope we can shut down this operation before any more kids go down."

"Amen to that," the FBI agent said solemnly.

Alexander showed up at Jodie's office feeling more optimistic than he had for weeks. He was close to an arrest, but the next few days would be critical. After their meeting, the task force had gleaned information from the informant that the drug shipment was coming into Houston the following week. He had to be alert, and he had to spend a lot of time at Jodie's office so that he didn't miss anything.

He took her out to lunch, but he was preoccupied.

"You're onto something," she guessed.

He nodded, smiling. "Something big. How would you like to be part of a surveillance?"

"Me? Wow. Can I have a gun?"

He glared at her. "No."

She shrugged. "Okay. But don't expect me to save your life without one."

"Not giving you one might save my life," he said pointedly.

She ignored the gibe. "Surveillance?" she prodded. "Of what?"

"You'll find out when we go, and not a word to anybody."

"Okay," she agreed. "How do you do surveillance?"

"We sit in a parked car and drink coffee and wish we were watching television," he said honestly. "It gets incredibly boring. Not so much if we have a companion. That's where you come in," he added with a grin. "We can sit in the car and neck and nobody will guess we're spying on them."

"In a Jaguar," she murmured. "Sure, nobody will notice us in one of those!"

He gave her a long look. "We'll be in a law enforcement vehicle, undercover."

"Right. In a car with government license plates, four antennae and those little round hubcaps..."

"Will you stop?" he groaned.

"Sorry!" She grinned at him over her coffee. "But I like the necking part."

He pursed his lips and gave her a wicked grin. "So do I."

She laughed a little self-consciously and finished her lunch.

They were on the way back to his Jaguar when his DEA agent, Kennedy, drove up. He got out of his car and approached them with a big smile.

"Hi, Cobb! How's it going?" he asked.

"Couldn't be better," Alexander told him complacently. "What's new?"

"Oh, nothing, I'm still working on that smuggling ring." He glanced at Alexander curiously. "Heard anything about a new drug task force?"

"Just rumors," Alexander assured him, and noticed a faint reaction from the other man. "Nothing definite. I'll let you know if I hear anything."

"Thanks." Kennedy shrugged. "There are always rumors."

"Do you have anybody at Thorn Oil, just in case?" Alexander asked him pointedly.

Kennedy cleared his throat and laughed. "Nobody at all. Why?"

"No reason. No reason at all. Enjoy your lunch."

"Sure. I never see you at staff meetings lately," he added. "You got something undercover going on?"

Alexander deliberately tugged Jodie close against his side and gave her a look that could have warmed coffee. "Something," he said, with a smile in Kennedy's direction. "See you."

"Yeah. See you!"

Kennedy walked on toward the restaurant, a little distracted.

Jodie waited until they were closed up in Alexander's car before she spoke. "You didn't tell him anything truthful," she remarked.

"Kennedy's got a loose tongue," he told her as he cranked the car. "You don't tell him anything you don't want repeated. Honest to God, he's worse than Margie!"

"So that's it," she said, laughing. "I just wondered. Isn't it odd that he seems to show up at places where we eat a lot?"

"Plenty of the guys eat where we do," he replied lazily. "We know where the good food is."

"You really do," she had to admit. "That steak was wonderful!"

"Glad you liked it."

"I could cook for you, sometime," she offered, and then flushed at her own boldness.

"After I wind up this case, I'll let you," he said, with a warm smile. "Meanwhile, I've got a lot of work to do."

She wondered about that statement after he left her at the office. She was still puzzling over it when she walked right into Brody when she got off the elevator at her floor.

"Oh, sorry!" she exclaimed, only then noticing that Cara was with him. "Hello," she greeted the woman as she stopped to punch her time card before entering the cubicle area.

Cara wasn't inclined to be polite. She gave Jodie a cold look and turned back to Brody. "I don't understand why you can't do me this one little favor," she muttered. "It isn't as if I ask you often for anything."

"Yes, but dear, it's an odd place to leave your car. There are garages…"

"My car is very expensive," she pointed out, her faint accent growing in intensity, like the anger in her black eyes. "All I require is for you to let me in, only that."

Jodie's ears perked up. She pretended to have trouble getting her card into the time clock, and hummed deliberately to herself, although not so loudly that she couldn't hear what the other two people were saying.

"Company rules…" he began.

"Rules, rules! You are to be an executive, are you not? Do you have to ask permission for such a small thing? Or are you not man enough to make such decisions for yourself?" she added cannily.

"Nice to see you both," Jodie said, and moved away—but not quickly. She fumbled in her purse and walked very slowly as she did. She was curious to know what Cara wanted.

"I suppose I could, just this once," Brody capitulated. "But you know, dear, a warehouse isn't as safe as a parking garage, strictly speaking."

Jodie's heart leaped.

"Yours certainly is, you have an armed guard, do you not? Besides, I work for a subsidiary of Ritter Oil. It is not as if I had no right to leave my car there when I go out of town for the company."

"All right, all right," Brody said. "Tomorrow night then. What time?"

"At six-thirty," she told him. "It will be dark, so you must flash your lights twice to let me know it is you."

They spoke at length, but Jodie was already out of earshot. She'd heard enough of the suspicious conversation to wonder about it. But she was much too cautious to phone Alexander from her work station.

She would have to wait until the end of the day, even if it drove her crazy. Meanwhile she pretended that she'd noticed nothing.

Brody came by her cubicle later that afternoon, just before quitting time, while she was finishing a letter he'd dictated.

"Can I help you?" she asked automatically, and smiled.

He smiled back and looked uncomfortable. "No, not really. I just wondered what you thought about what Cara asked me?"

She gave him a blank look. "What she asked you?" she said. "I'm sorry, I'd just come from having lunch with Alexander." She smiled and sighed and lowered her eyes demurely. "To tell you the truth, I wasn't paying attention to anything except the time clock. What did she ask you?" She opened her eyes very wide and looked blank.

"Never mind. She phoned and made a comment about your being there. It's nothing. Nothing at all."

She smiled up at him. "Did you enjoy the concert that night?"

"Yes, actually I did, despite the fact that Cara went out to the powder room and didn't show up again for an hour." He shook his head. "Honestly, that woman is so mysterious! I never know what she's thinking."

"She's very crisp, isn't she?" she mused. "I mean, she's assertive and aggressive. I guess she's a good marketer."

"She is," he sighed. "At least, I guess she is. I haven't heard much from the big boss about her work. In fact, there was some talk about letting her go a month or two ago, because she lost a contract. Funny, it was one she was supposedly out of town negotiating at the time, but the client said he'd never seen her. Mr. Ritter talked him into staying, but he had words with Cara about the affair."

"Could that have been when her mother was ill?" she asked.

"Her mother hasn't ever been ill, as far as I know," he murmured. "She did move from Peru to Mexico, but you know about that." He put his hands in his pockets. "She wants me to do something that isn't quite acceptable, and I'm nervous about it. I'm due for a promotion. I don't want to get mixed up in anything the least bit suspicious."

"Why, Brody, what does she want you to do?" she asked innocently.

He glanced at her, started to speak, and then smiled sheepishly. "Well, it's nothing, really. Just a favor." He shrugged. "I'm sure I'm making a big deal out of nothing. You never told me that your boyfriend works for the Drug Enforcement Administration."

"He doesn't advertise it," she stammered. "He does a lot of undercover work at night," she added.

Brody sighed. "I see. Well, I'll let you finish. You and Cobb seem to get along very well," he added.

"I've known him a long time."

"So you have. You've known me a long time, too, though," he added with a slow smile.

"Not really. Only three years."

"Is it? I thought it was longer." He toyed with his tie. "You and Cobb seem to spend a lot of time together."

"Not as much as we'd like," she said, seeing a chance to help Alexander and throw Cara off the track. "And I have a cousin staying with me for a few days, so we spend a lot of time in parked cars necking," she added.

Brody actually flushed. "Oh." He glanced at his watch and grimaced. "I've got a meeting with our vice president in charge of human resources at four, I'd better get going. See you later."

"See you, Brody."

She was very glad that she'd learned to keep what she knew to herself. What Brody's girlfriend had let slip was potentially explosive information, even if it was only circumstantial. She'd have a lot to tell Alexander when she saw him. Furthermore, she'd already given Alexander some cover by telling Brody about the company car, and the fact that they spent time at night necking in one. He was going to be proud of her, she just knew it!

## Chapter 8

The minute she got to her apartment, Jodie grabbed the phone and called Alexander.

"Can you come by right away?" Jodie asked him quickly.

He hesitated. "To your apartment? Why?"

She didn't know if her phone might be bugged. She couldn't risk it. She sighed theatrically. "Because I'm wearing a see-through gown with a row of prophylactics pinned to the hem...!"

"Jodie!" He sounded shocked.

"Listen, I have something to tell you," she said firmly.

He hesitated again and then he groaned. "I can't right now..."

"Who's on the phone, Alex?" came a sultry voice from somewhere in the background.

Jodie didn't need to ask who the voice belonged to.

Her heart began to race with impotent fury. "Sorry I interrupted," she said flatly. "I'm sure you and Kirry have lots to talk about."

She hung up and then unplugged the phone. So much for any feelings Alexander had for her. He was already seeing Kirry again, alone and at his apartment. No doubt he was only seeing Jodie to avert suspicion at Ritter Oil. The sweet talk was to allay any suspicion that he was using her. Why hadn't she realized that? The Cobbs were always using her, for one reason or another. She was being a fool again. Despite what he'd said, it was obvious now that Alexander had no interest in her except as a pawn.

She fought down tears and went to her computer. She might as well use some of her expertise to check out Miss Cara Dominguez and see if the woman had a rap sheet. With a silent apology to the local law enforcement departments, she hacked into criminal files and checked her out.

What she found was interesting enough to take her mind off Alexander. It seemed that Cara didn't have a lily-white past at all. In fact, she'd once been arrested for possession with intent to distribute cocaine and had managed to get the charges dropped. Besides that, she had some very odd connections internationally. It was hinted in the records of an international law enforcement agency—whose files gave way to her expertise also—that her uncle was one of the Colombian drug lords. She wondered if Alexander knew that.

Would he care? He was with Kirry. Damn Kirry! She threw a plastic coffee cup at the wall in impotent rage. Just as it hit, there was a buzz at the intercom. She glowered at it, but the caller was insistent. She pushed the button.

"Yes?" she asked angrily.

"Let me in," Alexander said tersely.

"Are you alone?" she asked with barely contained sarcasm.

"In more ways than you might realize," he replied, his voice deep and subdued. "Let me in, Jodie."

She buzzed him in with helpless reluctance and waited at her opened door for him to come out of the elevator.

He was still in his suit. He looked elegant, expensive, and very irritated. He walked into the apartment ahead of her and went straight to the kitchen.

"I was going to take you out to eat when Kirry showed up, in tears, and begged to talk to me," he said heavily, examining pots until he found one that contained a nice beef stew. He got a bowl out of the cupboard and proceeded to fill it. "Any corn bread?" he asked wistfully, having sniffed it when he entered the apartment.

"It's only just getting done," she said, reaching around him for a pot holder. She opened the oven and produced a pone of corn bread.

"I'm hungry," he said.

"You're always hungry," she accused, but she was feeling better.

He caught her by the shoulders and pulled her against him, tilting her chin up so that he could see into her mutinous eyes. "I don't want Kirry. I said that, and I meant it."

"Even if you didn't, you couldn't say so," she muttered. "You need me to help you smoke out your drug smuggler."

He scowled. "Do you really think I'm that sort of man?" he asked, and sounded wounded. "I'll admit that Margie and I don't have a good track record with you, but I'd draw the line at pretending an emotion I didn't feel, just to catch crooks."

She shifted restlessly and didn't speak.

He shook his head. "No ego," he mused, watching her. "None at all. You can't see what's right under your nose."

"My chin, and no, I can't see it…"

He chuckled, bending to kiss her briefly, fiercely. "Feed me. Then we might watch television together for a while. I'll be working most evenings during the week, but Friday night we could go see a movie or something."

Her heart skipped. "A movie?"

"Or we could go bowling. I used to like it."

Her mind was spinning. He actually wanted to be with her! But cold reality worked its way between them again. "You haven't asked why I wanted you to come over," she began as he started for the table with his bowl of stew.

"No, I haven't. Why?" he asked, pouring himself a cup of freshly brewed coffee and accepting a dish of corn bread from her.

She put coffee and corn bread at her place at the table and put butter next to it before she sat down and gave Alexander a mischievous smile. "Cara talked Brody into letting her into the warehouse parking lot after hours tomorrow—about six-thirty in the evening. She said she wanted to park her car there, but it sounded thin to me."

He caught his breath. "Jodie, you're a wonder."

"That's not all," she added, sipping coffee and adding more cream to it. "She was arrested at the age of seventeen for possession with intent to distribute cocaine, and she got off because the charges were dropped. There's an unconfirmed suspicion that her uncle is one of the top Colombian drug lords."

"Where did you get that?"

She flushed. "I can't tell you. Sorry."

"You've hacked into some poor soul's protected files, haven't you?" he asked sternly, but with twinkling eyes.

"I can't tell you," she repeated.

"Okay, I give up." He ate stew and corn bread with obvious enthusiasm. "Then I guess you and I will go on a stakeout tomorrow night."

She smiled smugly. "Yes, in your boss's borrowed security car, because my cousin is visiting and we can't neck in the apartment. I told Brody that, and he'll tell Cara that, so if we're seen near my office, they won't think a thing of it."

"Sheer genius," he mused, studying her. "Like I said, you're a natural for law enforcement work. You've got to get your expert computer certification and change professions, Jodie. You're wasted in personnel work."

"Human resources work," she reminded him.

"New label, same job."

She wrinkled her nose. "Maybe so."

They finished their supper in pleasant silence, and she produced a small loaf of pound cake for dessert, with peaches and whipped cream.

"If I ate here often, I'd get fat," he murmured.

She laughed. "Not likely. The cake was made with margarine and reduced-fat milk. I make rolls the same way, except with light olive oil in place of margarine. I don't want clogged arteries before I'm thirty," she added. "And I especially don't want to look like I used to."

He smiled at her warmly. "I like the way you used to look," he said surprisingly. "I like you any way at all, Jodie," he continued softly. "That hasn't changed."

She didn't know whether or not to trust him, and it showed in her face.

He sighed. "It's going to be a long siege," he said enigmatically.

Later, they curled up together on the couch to watch the evening news. There was a brief allusion to a drug smuggling catch by US Customs in the Gulf of Mexico, showing the helicopters they used to catch the fast little boats used in smuggling.

"Those boats go like the wind," Jodie remarked.

He yawned. "They do, indeed. The Colombian National Police busted an operation that was building a submarine for drug smuggling a couple of years ago."

"That's incredible!"

"Some of the smuggling methods are, too, like the tunnel under the Mexican border that was discovered, and having little children swallow balloons filled with cocaine to get them through customs."

"That's barbaric," she said.

He nodded. "It's a profitable business. Greed makes animals of men sometimes, and of women, too."

She cuddled close to him. "It isn't Brody you were after, is it? It's his girlfriend."

He chuckled and wrapped her up in his arms. "You're too sharp for me."

"I learned from an expert," she said, lifting her eyes to his handsome face.

He looked down at her intently for a few seconds before he bent to her mouth and began to kiss her hungrily. Her arms slid up around his neck and she held on for dear life as the kiss devoured her.

Finally he lifted his head and put her away from him, with visible effort. "No more of that tonight," he said huskily.

"Spoilsport," she muttered.

"You're the one with the conscience, honey," he drawled meaningfully. "I'm willing, but you'd never live it down."

"I probably wouldn't," she confessed, but her eyes were misty and wistful.

He pushed back her hair. "Don't look like that," he chided. "It isn't the end of the world. I like you the way you are, Jodie, hang-ups and all. Okay?"

She smiled. "Okay."

"And I'm not sleeping with Kirry!"

The smile grew larger.

He kissed the tip of her nose and got up. "I've got some preparations to make. I'll pick you up tomorrow at 6:20 sharp and we'll park at the warehouse in the undercover car." He hesitated. "It might be better if I had a female agent in the car with me..."

"No, you don't," she said firmly, getting to her feet. "This is my stakeout. You wouldn't even know where to go, or when, if it wasn't for me."

"True. But it could be very dangerous," he added grimly.

"I'm not afraid."

"All right," he said finally. "But you'll stay in the car and out of the line of fire."

"Whatever you say," she agreed at once.

The warehouse parking lot was deserted. The night watchman was visible in the doorway of the warehouse as he opened the door to look out. He did that twice.

"He's in on it," Alexander said coldly, folding Jodie closer in his arms. "He knows they're coming, and he's watching for them."

"No doubt. Ouch." She reached under her rib cage and touched a small hard object in his coat pocket. "What is that, another gun?"

"Another cell phone," he said. "I have two. I'm leaving one with you, in case you see something I don't while I'm inside," he added, indicating a cell phone he'd placed on the dash.

"You do have backup?" she worried.

"Yes. My whole team. They're well concealed, but they're in place."

"Thank goodness!"

He shifted her in his arms so that he could look to his left at the warehouse while he was apparently kissing her.

"Your heart is going very fast," she murmured under his cool lips.

"Adrenaline," he murmured. "I live on rushes of it. I could never settle for a nine-to-five desk job."

She smiled against his mouth. "I don't like it much, either."

He nuzzled her cheek with his just as a car drove

past them toward the warehouse. It hesitated for a few seconds and then sped on.

"That's Brody's car," she murmured.

"And that one, following it?" he asked, indicating a small red hardtop convertible of some expensive foreign make.

"Cara."

"Amazing that she can afford a Ferrari on thirty-five thousand a year," he mused, "and considering that her mother is poor."

"I was thinking the same thing," she murmured. "Kiss me again."

"No time, honey." He pulled out a two-way radio and spoke into it. "All units, stand by. Target in motion. Repeat, target in motion. Stand by."

Several voices took turns asserting their readiness. Alexander watched as Brody's car suddenly reappeared and he drove away. The gates of the warehouse closed behind his car. He paused near Alexander's car again, and then drove off down the road.

As soon as he was out of sight, a van came into sight. Cara appeared at the parking lot entrance, inserted a card key into the lock, opened the gate and motioned the van forward. The gate didn't close again, but remained open.

Alexander gave it time to get to a loading dock and its occupants to exit the cab and begin opening the rear doors before he took out the walkie-talkie again.

"All units, move in. I repeat, all units, move in. We are good to go!"

He took the cell phone from the dash and put it into Jodie's hands. "You sit right here, with the doors locked, and don't move until I call you on that phone and tell you it's safe. Under no circumstances are you to come into the parking lot. Okay?"

She nodded. "Okay. Don't get shot," she added.

He kissed her. "I don't plan to. See you later."

He got out of the car and went toward a building next door to the warehouse. He was joined by another figure in black. They went down an alley together, out of sight.

Jodie slid down into her seat, so that only her eyes and the top of her head were visible in the concealing darkness, barely lit by a nearby streetlight. She waited with her heart pounding in her chest for several minutes, until she heard a single gunshot. There was pandemonium in the parking lot. Dark figures ran to and fro. More shots were fired. Her heart jumped into her throat. She gritted her teeth, praying that Alexander wasn't in the line of fire.

Then, suddenly, she spotted him, with another dark figure. They had two people in custody, a man and a woman. They were standing near another loading dock, apparently conversing with the men, when Jodie spotted a solitary figure outside the gates, on the sidewalk, moving toward the open gate. The figure was slight, and it held what looked like an automatic weapon. She'd seen Alexander with one of those, a rare time when he'd been arming himself for a drug bust.

She had a single button to push to make Alexander's cell phone ring, but when she pressed in the number, nothing happened. The phone went dead in her hand.

The man with the machine gun was moving closer to where Alexander and the other man stood with their prisoners, their backs to the gate.

The key was in the car. She only saw one way to

save Alexander. She got behind the wheel, cranked the car, put it in gear and aimed it right for the armed man, who was now framed in the gate.

She ran the car at him. He whirled at the sudden noise of an approaching vehicle and started spraying it with machine gun fire.

Jodie ducked down behind the wheel, praying that the weapon didn't have bullets that would penetrate the engine block as easily as they shattered the windshield of the car she was driving. There was a loud thud.

She had to stop the car, because she couldn't see where she was going, but the windshield didn't catch any more bullets. Now she heard gunshots that didn't sound like that of the small automatic her assailant was carrying.

The door of the car was suddenly jerked open, and she looked up, wide-eyed and panicky, into Alexander's white face.

"Jodie!" he ground out. "Put the car out of gear!"

She put it into Park with trembling hands and cut off the ignition.

Alexander dragged her out of it and began going over her with his hands, feeling for blood. She was covered with little shards of glass. Her face was bleeding. So were her hands. She'd put them over her face the instant the man started firing.

Slowly she became aware that Alexander's hands had a faint tremor as they searched her body.

"I'm okay," she said in a thin voice. "Are you?"

"Yes."

But he was rattled, and it showed.

"He was going to shoot you in the back," she began.

"I told you to use the cell phone!" he raged.

"It wouldn't work!"

He reached beside her and picked it up. His eyes closed. The battery was dead.

"And you stop yelling at me," she raged back at him. "I couldn't let him kill you!"

He caught her up in his arms, bruisingly close, and kissed her furiously. Then he just held her, rocked her, riveted her to his hard body with fierce hunger. "You crazy woman," he bit off at her ear. "You brave, crazy, wonderful woman!"

She held him, too, content now, safe now. Her eyes closed. It was over, and he was alive. Thank God.

He let her go reluctantly as two other men came up, giving them curious looks.

"She's all right," he told them, moving back a little. "Just a few cuts from the broken windshield."

"That was one of the bravest things I've ever seen a woman do," one of the men, an older man with jet-black hair and eyes, murmured. "She drove right into the bullets."

"We'd be dead if she hadn't," the other man, equally dark-haired and dark-eyed, said with a grin. "Thanks!"

"You're welcome," she said with a sheepish smile as she moved closer to Alexander.

"The car's a total write-off," the older man mused.

"Like you've never totaled a car in a gun battle, Hunter," Alexander said with a chuckle.

The other man shrugged. "Maybe one or two. What the hell. The government has all that money we confiscate from drug smugglers to replace cars. You might ask your boss for that cute little Ferrari, Cobb."

"I already drive a Jaguar," he said, laughing. "With

all due respect to Ferrari, I wouldn't trade it for anything else."

"I helped make the bust," Jodie complained. "They should give it to me!"

"I wouldn't be too optimistic about that," came a droll remark from the second of the two men. "I think Cobb's boss is partial to Italian sports cars, and he can't afford a Ferrari on his salary."

"Darn," Jodie said on a sigh. "Just my luck."

"You should take her to the hospital and have her checked," Hunter told Alexander. "She's bleeding."

"She could be dead, pulling a stunt like that," Alexander said with renewed anger as he looked at her.

"That's no way to thank a person for saving your life," Jodie pointed out, still riding an adrenaline high.

"You're probably right, but you took a chance you shouldn't have," Alexander said grimly. "Come on. We'll hitch a ride with one of my men."

"Your car might still be drivable," she said, looking at it. The windshield was shattered but still clinging to the frame. She winced. "Or maybe not."

"Maybe not," Alexander agreed. "See you, Hunter. Lane. Thanks for the help."

"Any time," Hunter replied, and they walked back toward the warehouse with Alexander and Jodie. "Colby Lane was in town overnight and bored to death, so I brought him along for the fun."

"Fun!" Jodie exclaimed.

The older man chuckled. "He leads a mundane nine-to-five life. I've talked him into giving it up for international intrigue at Ritter Oil."

"I was just convinced," the man named Colby Lane said with a chuckle.

"Good. Tomorrow you can tell Ritter you'll take the job. See you, Cobb."

"Sure thing."

"Who were those two guys you were talking to?" Jodie asked when the hospital had treated her cuts and Alexander had commandeered another car to take her home in.

"Phillip Hunter and Colby Lane. You've surely heard of Hunter."

"He's a local legend," she replied with a smile, "but I didn't recognize him in that black garb. He's our security chief."

"Lane's doing the same job for the Hutton corporation, but they're moving overseas and he isn't keen on going. So Hunter's trying to get him to come down here as his second-in-command at Ritter Oil."

"Why was Mr. Lane here tonight?"

"Probably just as Phillip said—Lane just got into town, and Hunter volunteered him to help out. He and Hunter are old friends."

"He looked very dark," she commented.

"They're both Apache," he said easily. "Hunter's married to a knockout blonde geologist who works for Ritter. They have a young daughter. Lane's not married."

"They seem to know each other very well."

Alexander chuckled. "They have similar backgrounds in black ops. Highest level covert operations," he clarified. "They used to work for the 'company.'"

"Not Ritter's company," she guessed.

He chuckled. "No. Not Ritter's."

"Did you arrest Cara?"

"Our Houston policewoman made the actual arrest,

so that Cara wouldn't know I headed the operation.
Cara was arrested along with two men she swears she
doesn't know," he replied. "We had probable cause to
do a search anyway, but I had a search warrant in my
pocket, and I had to use it. We found enough cocaine
in there to get a city high, and the two men in the truck
had some on them."

"How about Cara?"

He sighed. "She was clean. Now we have to connect her." He glanced at her apologetically. "That will
mean getting your boss involved. However innocently,
he did let her into a locked parking lot."

"But wasn't the night watchman working for them?
Couldn't he have let them in?"

"He could have. But I have a feeling Cara wanted
Brody involved, so that he'd be willing to do what she
asked so that she didn't give him away for breaking a
strict company rule," he replied. He saw her expression and he smiled. "Don't worry. I won't let him be
prosecuted."

"Thanks, Alexander."

He moved closer and studied the cuts on her face
and arms. He winced. "You poor baby," he said gently.
"I wouldn't have had you hurt for the world."

"You'd have been dead if I hadn't done something,"
she said matter-of-factly. "The phone went dead and
you were too far away to hear me if I yelled. Besides,"
she added with a chuckle, "I hate going to funerals."

"Me, too." He swept her close and kissed the breath
out of her. "I have to go back to work, tie up loose ends.
You'll need to come with me to the nearest police pre-
cinct and give a statement, as well. You're a material
witness." He hesitated, frowning.

"What's wrong?" she asked.

"Cara knows who you are, and she can find out where you live," he said. "She's a vengeful witch. Chances are very good that she's going to make bond. I'm going to arrange some security for you."

"Do you think that's necessary?"

He nodded grimly. "I'm afraid it is. Would you like to know the estimated street value of the cocaine we've just confiscated?"

"Yes."

"From thirty to thirty-five million dollars."

She whistled softly. "Now I understand why they're willing to kill people. And that's just one shipment, right?"

"Just one, although it's unusually large. There's another drug smuggling investigation going on right now involving Colombian rebels, but I can't tell you about that one. It's top secret." He smoothed back her hair and looked at her as if she were a treasure trove. "Thank you for what you did," he said after a minute. "Even if it was crazy, it saved my life, not to mention Lane's and Hunter's."

She reached up a soft hand to smooth over his cheek, where it was slightly rough from a day's growth of beard. "You're welcome. But you would have done the same thing, if it had been me or Margie."

"Yes, I'm afraid I would have."

He still looked worried. She tugged his head down and kissed him warmly, her body exploding inside when he half lifted her against him and kissed her until her lips were sore.

"I could have lost you tonight," he said curtly.

"Oh, I'm a weed," she murmured into his throat. "We're very hard to uproot."

His arms tightened. "Just the same, you watch your back. If Brody asks what you know, and he will, you tell him nothing," he added. "You were with me when things started happening, you didn't even know what was going on until bullets started flying. Right?"

"Right."

He sighed heavily and kissed her one last time before he put her back onto her own feet. "I've got to go help the guys with the paperwork," he said reluctantly. "I'd much rather be with you. For tonight, lock your doors and keep your freedom phone handy. If you need me, I'm a phone call away. Tomorrow, you'll have security."

"I've got a nice, big, heavy flashlight like the one you keep in your car," she told him pertly. "If anybody tries to get in, they'll get a headache."

Unless they had guns, he added silently, but he didn't say that. "Don't be overconfident," he cautioned. "Never underestimate the enemy."

She saluted him.

He tugged her face up and kissed her, hard. "Incorrigible," he pronounced her. "But I can't imagine life without you, so be cautious!"

"I will. I promise. You have to promise, too," she added.

He gave her a warm smile. "Oh, I have my eye on the future, too," he assured her. "I don't plan to cash in my chips right now. I'll phone you tomorrow."

"Okay. Good night."

"Good night. Lock this," he added when he went out the door.

She did, loudly, and heard him chuckle as he went

down the hall. Once he was gone, she sank down into her single easy chair and shivered as she recalled the feverish events of the evening. She was alive. He was alive. But she could still hear the bullets, feel the shattering of the windshield followed by dozens of tiny, painful cuts on her skin even through the sweater she'd been wearing. It was amazing that she'd come out of a firefight with so few wounds.

She went to bed, but she didn't sleep well. Alexander phoned very early the next morning to check on her and tell her that he'd see her at lunch.

She put on her coat and went to work, prepared for some comments from her coworkers, despite the fact that she was wearing a long-sleeved, high-necked blouse. Nothing was going to hide the tiny cuts that lined her cheeks and chin. She knew better than to mention where she got them, so she made up a nasty fall down the steps at her apartment building.

It worked with everyone except Brody. He came in as soon as she'd turned on her computer, looking worried and sad.

"Are you all right?" he asked abruptly. "I was worried sick all night."

Her wide-eyed look wasn't feigned. "How did you know?" she faltered.

"I had to go and bail Cara out of jail early this morning," he said coolly. "She's been accused of drug smuggling, can you imagine it? She was only parking her car when those lunatics opened fire!"

## Chapter 9

Remembering what Alexander had cautioned her about, Jodie managed not to laugh out loud at Brody. How could a man be so naive?

"Drug smuggling?" she exclaimed, playing her part. "Cara?"

"That's what they said," he replied. "Apparently some of Ritter's security people had the warehouse staked out. When the shooting started, they returned fire, and I guess they called in the police. In fact, your friend Cobb was there when they arrested Cara."

"Yes, I know. He heard the shooting and walked right into it," she said, choosing her words carefully. "We were parked across the street..."

"I saw you when I let Cara into the parking lot," Brody said, embarrassed. "One of the gang came in with a machine gun and they say you aimed Cobb's car right at him and drove into a hail of bullets to save his life. I guess you really do care about him."

"Yes," she confessed. "I do."

"It was a courageous thing to do. Cara said you must be crazy about the guy to do that."

"Poor Cara," she replied, sidestepping the question. "I'm so sorry for the trouble she's in. Why in the world do they think she was involved? She was just in the wrong place at the wrong time."

Brody seemed to relax. "That's what Cara said. Uh, Cobb wasn't in on that bust deliberately, was he?"

"We were in a parked car outside the gate. We didn't know about any bust," she replied.

"So that's why he was there," he murmured absently, nodding. "I thought it must be something of the sort. Cara didn't know any of the others, but one was a female detective and another was a female deputy sheriff. The policewoman arrested her."

"Don't mess with Texas women," Jodie said, adding on a word to the well-known Texas motto.

He laughed. "So it seems. Uh, there was supposed to be a DEA agent there, as well. Cara has a friend who works out of the Houston office, but he's been out of town a lot lately and she hasn't been able to contact him. She says it's funny, but he seems to actually be avoiding her." He gave her an odd look. "I gather that it wasn't Cobb. But do you know anything about who the agent was?"

"No," she said straight-faced. "And Alexander didn't mention it, either. He tells me everything, so I'd know if it was him."

"I see."

She wondered if Cara's friend at the DEA was named

Kennedy, but she pretended to know nothing. "What's Cara going to do?" she asked, sounding concerned.

"Get a good lawyer, I suppose," he said heavily.

"I wish her well. I'm so sorry, Brody."

He sighed heavily. "I seem to have a knack for getting myself into tight corners, but I think Cara's easily superior to me in that respect. Well, I'd better phone the attorney whose name she gave me. You're sure you're all right?"

"I'm fine, Brody, honestly." She smiled at him.

He smiled back. "See you."

She watched him go with relief. She'd been improvising widely to make sure he didn't connect Alexander with the surveillance of the warehouse.

When Alexander phoned her, she arranged to meet him briefly at the café downstairs for coffee. He was pushed for time, having been in meetings with his drug unit most of the day planning strategy.

"You've become a local legend," he told her with a mischievous smile when they were drinking cappuccino.

"Me?" she exclaimed.

He grinned at her. "The oil clerk who drove through a hail of bullets to save her lover."

She flushed and glared at him. "Point one, I am not a clerk, I'm an administrative assistant. And point two, I am not your—!"

"I didn't say I started the rumor." He chuckled. His eyes became solemn as he studied her across the table. "But the part about being a heroine, I endorse enthusiastically. That being said, would you like to add to your legend?"

She paid attention. "Are you kidding? What do you want me to do?"

"Cara made bond this afternoon," he told her. "We've got a tail on her, but she's sure to suspect that. She'll make contact with one of her subordinates, in some public place where she thinks we won't be able to tape her. When she does, I'm going to want you to accidentally happen upon her and plant a microphone under her table."

"Wow! 'Jane Bond' stuff!"

"Jane?" he wondered.

She shrugged. "A woman named James would be a novelty."

"Point taken. Are you game?"

"Of course. But why wouldn't you let one of your own people do it?"

His face was revealing. "The last hearty professional we sent to do that little task stumbled over his own feet and pitched headfirst into the table our target was occupying. In the process he overturned a carafe of scalding coffee, also on the target, who had to be taken to the hospital for treatment."

"What if I do the same thing?" she worried.

He smiled gently. "You don't have a clumsy bone in your body, Jodie. But even if you did, Cara knows you. She might suspect me, but she won't suspect you."

"When do I start?"

"I'll let you know," he promised. "In the meantime, keep your eyes and ears open, and don't…"

Just as he spoke, there was a commotion outside the coffee shop. A young woman with long blond hair was trailing away a dark-haired little girl with a shocked face. Behind them, one of the men Jodie recognized from the drug bust—one of Alexander's friends—was waving his arms and talking loudly in a language Jodie had never heard before, his expression furious.

The trio passed out of sight, but not before Jodie finally recognized the man Alexander had called Colby Lane.

"What in the world…?" she wondered.

"It's a long story," Alexander told her. "And I'm not at liberty to repeat it. Let's just say that Colby has been rather suddenly introduced to a previously unknown member of his family."

"Was he cursing—and in what language?" she persisted.

"You can't curse in Apache," he assured her. "It's like Japanese—if you really want to tick somebody off in Japan, you say something about their mother's belly button. But giving them the finger doesn't have any meaning."

"Really?" She was fascinated.

He chuckled. "Anyway, Native Americans—whose origins are also suspected to be Asian—don't use curse words in their own language."

"Mr. Lane looked very upset. And I thought I recognized that blonde woman. She was transferred here from their Arizona office just a few weeks ago. She has a little girl, about the same age as Mr. Hunter's daughter."

"Let it lie," Alexander advised. "We have problems of our own. I meant to mention that we've located one of Cara's known associates serving as a waiter in a little coffeehouse off Alameda called The Beat…"

"I go there!" she exclaimed. "I go there a lot! You can get all sorts of fancy coffees and it's like a retro 'beatnik' joint. They play bongos and wear all black and customers get up and read their poetry." She flushed. "I actually did that myself, just last week."

He was impressed. "You, getting up in front of people to read poetry? I didn't know you still wrote poetry, Jodie."

"It's very personal stuff," she said, uneasy.

He began to look arrogant. "About me?"

She glared at him. "At the time I wrote it, you were my least favorite person on the planet," she informed him.

"Ouch!" He was thinking again. "But if they already know you there, it's even less of a stretch if you show up when Cara does—assuming she even uses the café for her purposes. We'll have to wait and see. I don't expect her to arrange a rendezvous with a colleague just to suit me."

"Nice of you," she teased.

He chuckled. He reached across the table and linked her fingers with his. His green eyes probed hers for a long moment. "Those cuts are noticeable on your face," he said quietly. "Do they hurt?"

"Not nearly as much as having you gunned down in front of me would have," she replied.

His eyes began to glitter with feeling. His fingers contracted around hers. "Which is just how I felt when I saw those bullets slamming into the windshield of my car, with you at the wheel."

Her breath caught. He'd never admitted so much in the past.

He laughed self-consciously and released her hand. "We're getting morose. A miss is as good as a mile, and I still have paperwork to finish that I haven't even started on." He glanced at his watch. "I can't promise anything, but we might see a movie this weekend."

"That would be nice," she said. "You'll let me know…?"

He frowned. "I don't like putting you in the line of fire a second time."

"I go to the coffee shop all the time," she reminded him. "I'm not risking anything." Except my heart, again, she thought.

He sighed. "I suppose so. Just the same, don't let down your guard. I hope you can tell if someone's tailing you?"

"I get goose bumps on the back of my neck," she assured him. "I'll be careful. You do the same," she added firmly.

He smiled gently. "I'll do my best."

Having settled down with a good book the following day after a sandwich and soup supper, it was a surprise to have Alexander phone her and ask her to go down to the coffee shop on the double.

"I'll meet you in the parking lot with the equipment," he said. "Get a cab and have it drop you off. I'll reimburse you. Hurry, Jodie."

"Okay. I'm on my way," she promised, lounging in pajamas and a robe.

She dashed into the bedroom, threw on a long black velvet skirt, a black sweater, loafers, and ran a quick brush through her loose hair before perching her little black beret on top of her head. She grabbed her coat and rushed out the door, barely pausing except to lock it. She was at the elevator before she remembered her purse, lying on the couch. She dashed back to get it, cursing her own lack of preparedness in an emergency.

Minutes later, she got out of the cab at the side door of The Beat coffeehouse.

Alexander waited by his company car while Jodie paid the cab. She joined him, careful to notice that she was unobserved.

He straightened at her approach. In the well-lit parking lot, she could see his eyes. They were troubled.

"I'm here," she said, just for something to say. "What do you want me to do?"

"I'm not sure I want you to do anything," he said honestly. "This is dangerous. Right now, she has no reason to suspect you. But if you bug her table for me, and she finds out that you did, your life could be in danger."

"Hey, listen, you were the one who told me about the little boys being shot by her henchmen," she reminded him. "I know the risk, Alexander. I'm willing to take it."

"Your knees are knocking," he murmured.

She laughed, a little unsteadily. "I guess they are. And my heart's pounding. But I'm still willing to do it. Now what exactly do I do?"

He opened the passenger door for her. "Get in. I'll brief you."

"Is she here?" she asked when they were inside.

"Yes. She's at the table nearest the kitchen door, at the left side of the stage. Here." He handed her a fountain pen.

"No, thanks," she said, waving it away. "I've got two in my purse..."

He opened her hand and placed the capped pen in

it. She looked at it, surprised by its heaviness. "It's a miniature receiver," he told her. He produced a small black box with an antenna, and what looked like an earplug with a tiny wire sticking out the fat end. "The box is a receiver, linked to a tape recorder. The earplug is also a receiver, which we use when we're in close quarters and don't want to attract attention. Since the box has a range of several hundred feet, I'll be able to hear what comes into the pen from my car."

"Do you want me to accidentally leave the pen on her table?"

"I want you to accidentally drop it under her table," he said. "If she sees it, the game's up. We're not the only people who deal in counterespionage."

She sucked in her breath. She was getting the picture. Cara was no dummy. "Okay. I'll lean over her table to say hello and make sure I put it where she won't feel it with her foot. How will that do?"

"Yes. But you have to make sure she doesn't see you do it."

"I'll be very careful."

He was having second thoughts. She was brave, but courage wasn't the only requirement for such an assignment. He remembered her driving through gunfire to save him. She could have died then. He'd thought about little else, and he hadn't slept well. Jodie was like a silver thread that ran through his life. In recent weeks, he'd been considering, seriously, how hard it would be to go on without her. He wasn't certain that he could.

"Why are you watching me like that?" she wanted to know, smiling curiously. "I'm not a dummy. I won't let you down, honest."

"It wasn't that." He closed her fingers around the pen. "Are you sure you want to go through with this?"

"Very sure."

"Okay." He hesitated. "What are you going to give as an excuse for being there?"

She gave him a bright smile. "I phoned Johnny—the owner—earlier, just after you phoned me and told him I had a new poem, but I was a little nervous about getting up in front of a big crowd. He said there was only a small crowd and I'd do fine."

"You improvise very well."

"I've been observing you for years," she teased. "But it's true. I do have a poem to read, which should throw Cara off the track."

He tugged her chin up and kissed her, hard. "You're going to be fine."

She smiled at him. "Which one of us are you supposed to be reassuring?"

"Both of us," he said tenderly. He kissed her again. "Go to work."

"What do I do when she leaves?"

"Get a cab back to your apartment. I'll meet you there. If anything goes wrong," he added firmly, "or if she acts suspicious, you stay in the coffeehouse and phone my cell number. Got that?" He handed her a card with his mobile phone number on it.

"I've got it."

She opened the car door and stepped out into the cool night air. With a subdued wave, she turned, pulled her coat closer around her and walked purposefully toward the coffeehouse. What she didn't tell Alexander was that her new poem was about him.

She didn't look around noticeably as she made her

way through the sparse crowd to the table where she usually sat on her evenings here. She held the pen carefully in her hand, behind a long fold of her coat. As she pulled out a chair at the table, her eyes swept the room and she spotted Cara at a table with another woman. She smiled and Cara frowned.

Uh-oh, she thought, but she pinned the smile firmly to her face and moved to Cara's table.

"I thought it was you," she said cheerily. "I didn't know you ever came here! Brody never mentioned it to me."

Cara gave her a very suspicious look. "This is not your normal evening entertainment, surely?"

"But I come here all the time," Jodie replied honestly. "Johnny's one of my fans."

"Fans." Cara turned the word over on her tongue as if she'd never heard it.

"Aficionados," Jodie persisted. "I write poetry."

"You?"

The other woman made it sound like an insult. The woman beside her, an even older woman with a face like plate steel, only looked.

Jodie felt a chill of fear and worked to hide it. Her palm sweated against the weight of the pen hidden in her hand. As she hesitated, Johnny came walking over in his apron.

"Hey, Jodie!" he greeted. "Now don't worry, there's only these two unfamiliar ladies in here, you know everybody else. You just get up there and give it your best. It'll be great!"

"Johnny, you make me feel so much better," she told the man.

"These ladies friends of yours?" he asked, noticing them—especially Cara—with interested dark eyes.

"Cara's boyfriend is my boss at work," Jodie said.

"Lucky boyfriend," Johnny murmured, his voice dropping an octave.

Cara relaxed and smiled. "I am Cara Dominguez," she introduced herself. "This is my *amiga*, Chiva."

Johnny leaned over the table to shake hands and Jodie pretended to be overbalanced by him. In the process of righting herself and accepting his apology, she managed to let the pen drop under the table where it lay unnoticed several inches from either woman's foot.

"Sorry, Jodie, meeting two such lovely ladies made me clumsy." He chuckled.

She grinned at him. "No harm done. I'm not hurt."

"Okay, then, you go get on that stage. Want your usual French Vanilla cappuccino?"

"You bet. Make it a large one, with a croissant, please."

"It'll be on the house," he informed her. "That's incentive for you."

"Gee, thanks!" she exclaimed.

"My treat. Nice to meet you ladies."

"It is for us the same," Cara purred. She glanced at Jodie, much less suspicious now. "So you write poetry. I will enjoy listening to it."

Jodie chuckled. "I'm not great, but people here are generally kind. Good to see you."

Cara shrugged. The other woman said nothing.

Jodie pulled off her coat and went up onto the stage, trying to ignore her shaking knees. Meanwhile she prayed that Alexander could hear what the two women were saying. Because the minute she pulled the microphone closer, introduced herself, and pulled out the folded sheet of paper that contained her poem, Cara leaned toward the other woman and started speaking urgently.

Probably exchanging fashion tips, or some such thing, Jodie thought dismally, but she smiled at the crowd, unfolded the paper, and began to read.

Apparently her efforts weren't too bad, because the small crowd paid attention to every line of the poem. And when she finished reading it, there was enthusiastic applause.

Cara and her friend, however, were much too intent on conversation to pay Jodie any attention. She went back to her seat, ate her croissant and drank her cappuccino with her back to the table where Cara and the other woman were sitting, just to make sure they knew she wasn't watching them.

A few minutes later, Johnny came by her table and patted her on the back. "That was some good work, girl!" he exclaimed. "I'm sorry your friend didn't seem to care enough to listen to it."

"She's not into poetry," she confided.

"I guess not. She and that odd-looking friend of hers didn't even finish their coffee."

"They're gone?" she asked without turning.

He nodded. "About five minutes ago, I guess. No great loss, if you ask me."

"Thanks for the treat, Johnny, and for the encouragement," she added.

"Um, I sure would like to have a copy of that poem."

Her eyes widened. "You would? Honestly?"

He shrugged. "It was really good. I know this guy.

He works for a small press. They publish poetry. I'd like to show it to him. If you don't mind."

"Mind!" She handed him the folded paper. "I don't mind! Thanks, Johnny!"

"No problem. I'll be in touch." He turned, and then paused, digging into his apron pocket. "Say, is this yours? I'm afraid I may have stepped on it. It was under that table where your friend was sitting."

"Yes, it's mine," she said, taking it from him. "Thanks a lot."

He winced. "If I broke it, I'll buy you a new one, okay?"

"It's just a pen," she said with determined careless-ness. "No problem."

"You wait, I'll call you a cab."

"That would be great!"

She settled back to wait, her head full of hopeful success, and not only for Alexander.

"Is it broken?" she asked Alexander when she was back at her apartment, and he was examining his lis-tening device.

"I'll have the lab guys check it out," he told her.

"Could you hear anything?"

He grinned hugely. "Not only did I hear plenty, I taped it. We've got a lead we'd never have had without you. There's just one bad thing."

"Oh?"

"Cara thinks your poetry stinks," he said with a twinkle in his eyes.

"She can think what she likes, but Johnny's show-ing it to a publisher friend of his. He thought it was wonderful."

He searched her face. "So did I, Jodie."

She felt a little nervous, but certainly he couldn't have known that he was the subject of it, so she just thanked him offhandedly.

"Now I'm sure I'm cut out for espionage," she murmured.

"You may be, but I don't know if my nerves could take it."

"You thought I'd mess up," she guessed.

He shook his head, holding her hand firmly in his. "It wasn't that. I don't like having you at risk, Jodie. I don't want you on the firing line ever again, even if you did save my skin last night."

She searched his green eyes hungrily. "I wouldn't want to live in a world that didn't contain you, too," she said. Then, backtracking out of embarrassment, she laughed and added, "I really couldn't live without the aggravation."

He laughed, as he was meant to. "Same here." He checked his watch. "I don't want to go," he said unexpectedly, "but I've got to get back to my office and go through this tape. Tomorrow, I'll be in conference with my drug unit. You pretend that nothing at all was amiss, except you saw Cara at your favorite evening haunt. Right?"

"Right," she assured him.

"I'll call you."

"That's what they all say," she said drily.

He paused at the door and looked at her. "Who?"

"Excuse me?"

"Who else is promising to call you?" he persisted.

"The president, for my advice on his foreign policy, of course," she informed him.

He laughed warmly. "Incorrigible," he said to himself, winked at her, and let himself out. "Lock it!" he called through it.

She snicked the lock audibly and heard him chuckle again. She leaned back against the door with a relieved sigh. It was over. She'd done what he asked her, and she hadn't fouled it up. Most of all, he was pleased with her.

She was amazed at the smiles she got from him in recent weeks. He'd always been reserved, taciturn, with most other people. But he enjoyed her company and it showed.

The next day, Brody seemed very preoccupied. She took dictation, which he gave haltingly, and almost absently.

"Are you okay?" she wanted to know.

He moved restively around his office. He turned to stare at her curiously. "Are you involved in some sort of top secret operation or something?"

Her eyes popped. "Pardon?"

He cleared his throat. "I know you were at a coffeehouse where Cara went last night with a friend. I wondered if you were spying on her...?"

"I go to The Beat all the time, Brody," she told him, surprised. "Alexander's idea of an evening out is a concert or the theater, but my tastes run to bad poetry and bongos. I've been going there for weeks. It's no secret. The owner knows me very well."

He relaxed suddenly and smiled. "Thank goodness! That's what Cara told me, of course, but it seemed odd that you'd be there when she was. I mean, like you and your boyfriend showed up at the restaurant where we had lunch that day, and then you were at the concert, too. And your friend does work for the DEA…"

"Coincidences," she said lazily. "That's all. Unless you think I've been following you," she added with deliberate emphasis, demurely lowering her eyes.

There was a long, shocked pause. "Why, I never thought…considered…really?"

She crossed her legs. "I think you're very nice, Brody, and Cara treats you like a pet dog," she said with appropriate indignation. She peered at him covertly. "You're too good for her."

He was obviously embarrassed, flattered, and uncertain. "My gosh… I'm sorry, but I knew about Cobb working for the DEA, and then the drug bust came so unexpectedly. Well, it seemed logical that he might be spying on Cara with your help…"

"I never dreamed that I looked like a secret agent!" she exclaimed, and then she chuckled. "As if Alexander would ever trust me with something so dangerous," she added, lowering her eyes so that he couldn't see them.

He sighed. "Forgive me. I've had these crazy theories. Cara thought I was nuts, especially after she told me the owner of that coffeehouse knew you very well and encouraged you to read…well…very bad poetry. She thought maybe he had a case on you."

"It was not bad poetry! And he had a case on Cara, not me," she replied with just the right amount of pique.

"Did he!"

"I told him she was your girlfriend, don't worry," she said, and managed to sound regretful.

"Jodie, I'm very flattered," he faltered.

She held up a hand. "Let's not talk about it, Brody, okay? You just dictate, and I'll write."

He sighed, studying her closely. After a minute, he shrugged, and began dictating. This time, he was concise and relaxed. Jodie felt like collapsing with relief, herself. It had been a close call, and not even because Cara was suspicious. It was Brody who seemed to sense problems.

# Chapter 10

It was a relief that Cara didn't suspect Jodie of spying, but it was worrying that Brody did. He was an intelligent man, and it wouldn't be easy to fool him. She'd have to mention that to Alexander when she saw him.

He came by the apartment that evening, soon after Jodie got home from work, taciturn and worried.

"Something happened," she guessed uneasily.

He nodded. "Got any coffee?"

"Sure. Come on into the kitchen."

He sat down and she poured him a cup from the potful she'd just made. He sipped it and studied her across the table. "Kennedy came back to town today. He's Cara's contact."

"Oh, dear," she murmured, sensing that something was very wrong.

He nodded. "I called him into my office and told

him I was firing him, and why. I have sworn statements from two witnesses who are willing to testify against him in return for reduced sentences." He sighed. "He said that he knew you were involved, that you'd helped me finger Cara, and that he'd tell her if I didn't back down."

"Don't feel bad about it," she said, mentally panicking while trying not to show it. "You couldn't let him stay, after what he did."

He looked at her blankly. "You're a constant surprise to me, Jodie. How did you know I wouldn't back down?"

She smiled gently. "You wouldn't be Alexander if you let people bluff you."

"Yes, baby, but he's not bluffing."

The endearment caught her off guard, made her feel warm inside, warm all over. "So what do we do now?" she asked, a little disconcerted.

He noted her warm color and smiled tenderly. "You go live with Margie for a few days, until I wrap up this case. Our cover's blown now for sure."

"Margie can shoot a gun, but she's not all that great at it, Alexander," she pointed out.

"Our foreman, Chayce, is, and so is cousin Derek," he replied. "He was involved in national security work when he was just out of college. He's a dead shot, and he'll be bringing his two brothers with him." He chuckled. "Funny. All I had to say was that Margie might be in danger along with you, and he volunteered at once."

"You don't like him," she recalled.

He shrugged. "I don't like the idea of Margie getting involved with a cousin. But Derek seemed to know that, too, and he told me something I didn't know before when I phoned him. He wasn't my uncle's son. His mother had an affair with an old beau and he was the result. It was a family secret until last night. Which means," he added, "that he's only related to us by marriage, not by blood."

"He told you himself?" she asked.

"He told me. Apparently, he told you, too. But he didn't tell Margie."

"Have you?" she wondered.

"That's for him to do," he replied. "I've interfered enough." He checked his watch. "I've got to go. I have a man watching the apartment," he added. "The one I told you about. But tomorrow, you tell Brody you're taking a few days off to look after a sick relative and you go to Margie. Got that?"

"But my job…!"

"It's your life!" he shot back, eyes blazing. "This is no game. These people will kill you as surely as they killed those children. I am not going to watch you die, Jodie. Least of all for something I got you into!"

She caught her breath. This was far more serious than she'd realized.

"I told you," he emphasized, "Cara knows you were involved. The secret's out. You leave town. Period."

She stared at him and knew she was trapped. Her job was going to be an afterthought. They'd fire her. She was even afraid to take a day off when she was sick, because the company policy in her department was so strict.

"If you lose that job, it will be a blessing," Alexander told her flatly. "You're too good to waste your life taking somebody else's dictation. When this is over, I'll help you find something better. I'll take you to classes so that you can get your expert computer certification, then I'll get an employment agency busy to find you a better job."

That was a little disappointing. Obviously he didn't have a future with her in mind, or he wouldn't be interested in getting her a job.

He leaned back in his chair, sipping coffee. "Although," he added suddenly, his gaze intent, "there might be an alternative."

"An alternative?"

"We'll talk about that later," he said. He finished his coffee. "I have to go."

She got up and walked him to the door. "You be careful, too," she chided.

He opened his jacket and indicated the .45 automatic in its hand-tooled leather holster.

"It won't shoot itself," she reminded him pertly.

He chuckled, drew her into his arms, and kissed her until her young body ached with deep, secret longings.

He lifted his head finally, and he wasn't breathing normally. She felt the intensity of his gaze all the way to her toes as he looked at her. "All these years," he murmured, "and I wasted them sniping at you."

"You seemed to enjoy it at the time," she remarked absently, watching his mouth hover over hers.

"I didn't want a marriage like my parents had. I played the field, to keep women from getting serious about me," he confessed. He traced her upper lip with his mouth, with breathless tenderness. "Especially you," he added roughly. "No one else posed the threat you did, with your old-fashioned ideals and your sterling character. But I couldn't let you see how attracted to you I was. I did a pretty good job. And then you had too much champagne at a party and did what I'd been afraid you'd do since you graduated from high school."

"You were afraid...?"

He nibbled her upper lip. "I knew that if you ever got close, I'd never be able to let you go," he whispered sensuously. "What I spouted to Margie was a lot of hot air. I ached from head to toe after what we did together. I wanted you so badly, honey. I didn't sleep all night thinking about how easy it would have been."

"I didn't sleep thinking that you hated me," she confessed.

He sighed regretfully. "I didn't know you'd overheard me, but I said enough when I left you at your bedroom. I felt guilty when I went downstairs and saw your face. You were shamed and humiliated, and it was my fault. I only wanted a chance to make amends, but you started backing away and you wouldn't stop. That was when I knew what a mistake I'd made."

She toyed with his shirt button. "And then you needed help to catch a drug smuggler," she mused.

There was a pause long enough to make her look up. "You're good, Jodie, and I did need somebody out of the agency to dig out that information for me. But..."

"But?"

He smiled sheepishly. "Houston PD owes me a favor. They'd have been glad to get the information for me. So would the Texas Rangers, or the county sheriff."

"Then why did you ask me to do it?" she exclaimed.

His hands went to frame her face. They felt warm and strong against her soft skin. "I was losing you," he whispered as he bent again to rub his lips tenderly over her mouth. "You wouldn't let me near you any other way."

His mouth was making pudding of her brain. She slid her arms up around his neck and her hands tangled in the thick hair above his nape. "But there was Kirry…"

"Window dressing. I didn't even like her, especially by the time my birthday rolled around. I gave Margie hell for inviting her to my birthday party, did she tell you?"

She shook her head, dazed.

He caught her upper lip in his mouth and toyed with it. His breathing grew unsteady. His hands on her face became insistent. "I got drunk when Margie told me you'd overheard us," he whispered. "It took two neat whiskeys for me to even phone you. Too much was riding on my ability to make an apology. And frankly, baby, I don't make a habit of giving them."

She melted into his body, hungry for closer contact. "I was so ashamed of what I'd done…"

His mouth crushed down onto hers with passionate intent. "I loved what you did," he ground out. "I wasn't kidding when I told you that. I could taste you long after I went to bed. I dreamed about it all night."

"So did I," she whispered.

His lips parted hers ardently. "I thought you were hung up on damned Brody," he murmured, "until you aimed that car at the gunman. I prayed for all I was worth until I got to you and knew that you were all right. I could have lost you forever. It haunts me!"

"I'm tougher than old cowboy boots," she whispered, elated beyond belief at what he was saying to her.

"And softer than silk, in all the right places. Come here." He moved her against the wall. His body pressed hers gently against it while he kissed her with all the pent-up longing he'd been suppressing for weeks. When she moaned, he felt his body tremble with aching need.

"You're killing me," he ground out.

"Wh…what?"

He lifted his head and looked down into soft, curious gray eyes. "You haven't got a clue," he muttered. "Can't you tell when a man's dying of lust?"

Her eyebrows arched as he rested his weight on his hands next to her ears on the wall and suddenly pressed his hips into hers, emphatically demonstrating the question.

She swallowed hard. "Alexander, I was really only kidding about having a dress with prophylactics pinned to the hem…"

He burst out laughing and forced his aching body away from hers. "I've never laughed as much in my life as I do with you," he said on a long sigh. "But I really would give half an arm to lay you down on the carpet right now, Jodie."

She flushed with more delight than fear. "One of us could run to the drugstore, I guess," she murmured drily.

"Not now," he whispered wickedly. "But hold that thought until I wind up this case."

She laughed. "Okay."

He nibbled her upper lip. "I'll pick you up at work about nine in the morning," he murmured as he lifted his head. "And I'll drive you down to Jacobsville."

"You're really worried," she realized, when she saw the somber expression.

"Yes, Jodie. I'm really worried. Keep your doors locked and don't answer the phone."

"What if it's you?" she worried.

"Do you still have the cell phone I loaned you?"

"Yes."

She produced it. He opened it, turned it on, and checked the battery. "It's fully charged. Leave it on. If I need to call you, I'll use this number. You can call me if you're afraid. Okay?"

"Okay."

He kissed her one last time, gave her a soulful, enigmatic look, and went out the door. She bolted it behind him and stood there for several long seconds, her head whirling with the changes that were suddenly upsetting her life and career. Alexander was trying to tell her something, but she couldn't quite decide what. Did he want an affair? He certainly couldn't be thinking about marriage, he hated the whole thought of it. But, what did he want? She worried the question until morning, and still had no answers.


"You're going to leave for three days, just like that?" Brody exploded at work the next morning, his face harder than Jodie had ever seen it. "How the hell am I going to manage without a secretary?" he blustered. "I can't type my own letters!"

The real man, under the facade, Jodie thought, fascinated with her first glimpse of Brody's dark side. She'd never seen him really angry.

"I'm not just a secretary," she reminded him.

"Oh, hell, you do mail and requisition forms," he said coldly. "Call it what you like, it's donkey work."

His eyes narrowed. "It's because of what you did to Cara, isn't it? You're scared, so you're running away!"

Her face flamed with temper. She stood up from her desk and gave him a look that would have melted steel. "Would you be keen to hang around if they were gunning for you? You listen to me, Brody, these drug lords don't care who dies as long as they get their money. There are two dead little children who didn't do a thing wrong, except stand between a drug dealer and their mother, who was trying to shut down drug dealing in her neighborhood. Cara is part of that sick trade, and if you defend her, so are you!"

He gaped at her. In the years they'd worked together, Jodie had never talked back to him.

She grabbed up her purse and got the few personal belongings out of her desk. "Never mind holding my job open for me. I quit!" she told him flatly. "There must be more to life than pandering to the ego of a man who thinks I'm a donkey. One more thing, Brody," she added, facing him with her arms full of her belongings. "You and your drug-dealing girlfriend can both go to hell, with my blessing!"

She turned and stalked out of her cubicle. She imagined a trail of fire behind her. Brody's incredulous gasp had been music to her ears. Alexander was right. She was wasted here. She'd find something better, she knew it.

On her way out the door, she almost collided with Phillip Hunter. He righted her, his black eyebrows arching.

"You're leaving, Miss Clayburn?" he asked.

"I'm leaving, Mr. Hunter," she said, still bristling from her encounter with Brody.

"Great. Come with me."

He motioned with his chin. She followed him, puzzled, because he'd never spoken to her before except in a cordial, impersonal way.

He led her into the boardroom and closed the door. Inside was the other dark man she'd met briefly during the drug bust at the warehouse, Colby Lane, and the owner of the corporation himself, Eugene Ritter.

"Sit down, Ms. Clayburn," Ritter said with a warm smile, his blue eyes twinkling under a lock of silver hair.

She dropped into a chair, with her sack full of possessions clutched close to her chest.

"Mr. Ritter," she began, wondering what in the world she was going to do now. "I can explain…"

"You don't have to," he said gently. "I already know everything. When this drug case is wrapped up—and Cobb assures me it will be soon—how would you like to come back and work for me in an area where your skills won't be wasted?"

She was speechless. She just stared at him over her bulging carry-all.

"Phillip wants to go home to Arizona to work in our branch office there, and Colby Lane here—" he indicated the other dark man "—is going to replace him. He knows about your computer skills and Cobb's already told him that you're a whiz with investigations. How would you like to work for Lane as a computer security consultant? It will pay well and you'll have autonomy within the corporation. The downside," he added slowly, "is that you may have to do some traveling eventually, to our various branch offices, to work with Hunter and our other troubleshooters. Is that a problem?"

She shook her head, still grasping for a hold on the situation.

"Good!" He rubbed his hands together. "Then we'll draw up a contract for you, and you can have your attorney read and approve it when you come back." He was suddenly solemn. "There are going to be a lot of changes here in the near future. I've been coasting along in our headquarters office in Oklahoma and letting the outlying divisions take care of themselves, with near-disastrous results. If Hunter hadn't been tipped off by Cobb about the warehouse being used as a drug drop, we could have been facing federal charges, with no intentional involvement whatsoever on our part, on international drug smuggling. Tell Cobb we owe him one for that."

She grinned. "I will. And, Mr. Ritter, thank you very much for the opportunity. I won't let you down."

"I know that, Ms. Clayburn," he told her, smiling back. "Hunter will walk you outside. Just in case. Not that I think you need too much protection," he added, tongue-in-cheek. "There aren't a lot of people who'll drive into gunfire to save another person."

She laughed. "If I'd had time to think about it, I probably wouldn't have done it. Just the same, I won't mind having an escort to the front entrance," she confessed, standing. "I'm getting a cab to my apartment."

"We'll talk again," Ritter assured her, standing. He was tall and very elegant in a gray business suit. "All right, come on, Lane. We'll inspect the warehouse one last time."

"Yes, sir," Lane agreed.

"I'm just stunned," Jodie murmured when they reached the street, where the cab she'd called was waiting. She'd also phoned Cobb to meet her at her apartment.

"Ritter sees more than people think he does," Hunter told her, chuckling. "He's sharp, and he doesn't miss much. Tell Cobb I owe him one, too. My wife and I have been a little preoccupied lately—we just found out that we're expecting again. My mind hasn't been as much on the job as it should have been."

"Congratulations!"

He shrugged. "I wouldn't mind another girl, but Jennifer wants a son this time, a matched set, she calls it. She wants to be near her cousin Danetta, who's also expecting a second child. She and Cabe Ritter, the old man's son, have a son but they want a daughter." He chuckled. "We'll see what we both get. Meanwhile, you go straight to your apartment with no stops," he directed, becoming solemn. He looked over the top of the cab, saw something, and nodded approvingly. "Cobb's having you tailed. No, don't look back. If anyone makes a try for you, dive for cover and let your escort handle it, okay?"

"Okay. But I'm not really nervous about it now."

"So I saw the other night," he replied. "You've got guts, Ms. Clayburn. You'll be a welcome addition to security here."

She beamed. "I'll do my best. Thanks again."

"No problem. Be safe."

He closed the door and watched the taxi pull away. Her escort, in a dark unmarked car, pulled right out behind the cab. She found herself wishing that Cara and her group would make a try for her. It wouldn't bother her one bit to have the woman land in jail for a long time.

Alexander was waiting for her at her apartment. He picked up the suitcase she'd packed and then he drove her down to the Jacobsville ranch. She didn't have time to tell him about the changes in her life. She was saving that for a surprise. She was feeling good about her own abilities, and her confidence in herself had a surprising effect on her friend Margie, who met her at the door with faint shock.

Margie hugged her, but her eyes were wary. "There's something different about you," she murmured sedately.

"I've been exercising," she assured the other woman amusedly.

"Sure she has." Alexander chuckled. "By aiming cars at men armed with automatic weapons."

"What!" Margie exclaimed, gasping.

"Well, they were shooting at Alexander," Jodie told her. "What else could I do?"

Margie and her brother exchanged a long, serious look. He nodded slowly, and then he smiled. Margie beamed.

"What's that all about?" Jodie wondered aloud.

"We're passing along mental messages," Margie told her with wicked eyes. "Never mind. You're just in time to try on the flamenco dress I made you for our Halloween party."

"Halloween party." Jodie nodded blankly.

"It's this Saturday," Margie said, exasperated. "We

always have it the weekend before Halloween, remember?"

"I didn't realize it was that far along in the month," Jodie said. "I guess I've been busier than I realized."

"She writes poetry about me," Alexander said as he went up the staircase with Jodie's bag.

"I do not write poetry about you!" Jodie called after him.

He only laughed. "And she reads it onstage in a retro beatnik coffeehouse."

"For real?" Margie asked. "Jodie, I have to come stay with you in Houston so you can take me there. I love coffeehouses and poetry!" She shook her head. "I can't imagine you reading poetry on a stage. Or driving a car into bullets, for that matter." She looked shocked. "Jodie, you've changed."

Jodie nodded. "I guess I have."

Margie hugged her impulsively. "Are we still friends?" she wondered. "I haven't been a good one, but I'm going to try. I can actually make canapés!" she added. "I took lessons. So now you can come to parties when Jessie's not here, and I won't even ask you to do any of the work!"

Jodie burst out laughing. "This I have to see."

"You can, Friday. I expect it will take all day, what with the decorating, and I'm doing all that myself, too. Derek thinks I'm improving madly," she added, and a faint flush came to her cheeks.

"Cousin Derek's here already?" she asked.

"He's not actually my cousin at all, except by marriage, although I only just found out," Margie said, drawing Jodie along with her into the living room. "He's got two brothers and they're on the way here.

One of them is a cattle rancher and the other is a divorced grizzly bear."

"A what?"

Margie looked worried. "He's a Bureau of Land Management enforcement agent," she said. "He tracks down poachers and people who deal in illegal hunting and such. He's the one whose wife left him for a car salesman. He's very bitter."

"Is Derek close to them?"

"To the rancher one," Margie said. "He doesn't see the grizzly bear too often, thank goodness."

"Thank goodness?" Jodie probed delicately.

Margie flushed. "I think Cousin Derek wants to be much more than my cousin."

"It's about time," Jodie said with a wicked smile. "He's just your type."

Margie made a face. "Come on into the kitchen and we'll see what there is to eat. I don't know about you, but I'm hungry." She stopped suddenly. "Don't take this the wrong way, but why are Derek and his brothers moving in and why are you and Alexander here in the middle of the week?"

"Oh, somebody's just going to try to kill me, that's all," Jodie said matter-of-factly. "But Alexander's more than able to handle them, with Cousin Derek's help and some hard work by the DEA and Alexander's drug unit."

"Trying to kill you." Margie nodded. "Right."

"That's no joke," Alexander said from the doorway. He came into the room and pulled Jodie to his side, bending to kiss her gently. "I have to go. Derek's on the job, and his brothers will be here within an hour or two. Nothing to worry about."

"Except you getting shot," Jodie replied worriedly.

He opened his jacket and showed her his gun.

"I know. You're indestructible. But come back in one piece, okay?" she asked softly.

He searched her eyes and smiled tenderly. "That's a deal. See you later." He winked at Margie and took one last look at Jodie before he left.

"How people change," Margie murmured drily.

But Jodie wasn't really listening. Her eyes were still on Alexander's broad back as he went out the door.


Alexander and his group met somberly that evening to compare notes and plan strategy. They knew by now where Cara Dominguez was, who her cohorts were and just how much Brody Vance knew about her operation. The security guard on the job at the Ritter warehouse was linked to the organization, as well, but thought he was home free. What he didn't know was that Alexander had a court order to wiretap his office, and the agent overseeing that job had some interesting information to impart about a drug shipment that was still concealed in Ritter's warehouse. It was one that no one knew about until the wiretap. And it was a much bigger load than the one the drug unit had just busted.

The trick was going to be catching the thieves with the merchandise. It wasn't enough to know they were connected with it. They had to have hard evidence, facts that would stand up in court. They had to have a chain of evidence that would definitively link Cara to the drug shipment.

Just when Alexander thought he was ready to spring the trap, Cara Dominguez disappeared off the face of the earth. The security guard was immediately arrested, before he could flee, but he had nothing to say under advice of counsel.

When they went to the Ritter warehouse, with Colby Lane and Phillip Hunter, to appropriate the drug shipment, they found cartons of drilling equipment parts. Even with drug-sniffing dogs, they found no trace of the missing shipment. And everybody connected with Cara Dominguez suddenly developed amnesia and couldn't remember anything about her.

The only good thing about it was that the operation had obviously changed locations, and there was no further reason for anyone to target Jodie. Where it had moved was a job for the DEA to follow up on. Alexander was sure that Kennedy had something to do with the sudden disappearance of Cara, and the shipment, but he couldn't prove a thing. The only move he had left was to prosecute Kennedy for giving secret information to a known drug dealer, and that he could prove. He had Kennedy arraigned on charges of conspiracy to distribute controlled substances, which effectively removed the man from any chance of a future job in law enforcement—even if he managed to weasel out of a long jail term for what he'd already done.

Alexander returned to the Jacobsville ranch on Friday, to find Margie and Jodie in the kitchen making canapés while Cousin Derek and two other men sat at the kitchen table. Derek was sampling the sausage rolls while a taller dark-eyed man with jet-black hair oiled his handgun and a second dark-haired man with eyes as green as Alexander's sat glaring at his two companions.

"She's gone," Alexander said heavily. "Took a powder. We can't find a trace of her, so far, and the drug shipment vanished into thin air. Needless to say, I'm relieved on your behalf," he told a radiant Jodie. "But it's not what I wanted to happen."

"Your inside man slipped up," the green-eyed stranger said in a deep bass voice.

"I didn't have an inside man, Zeke," Alexander said, dropping into a chair with the other men. "More's the pity."

"Don't mind him," the other stranger said easily. "He's perfect. He never loses a case or misses a shot. And he can cook."

Zeke glared at him. "You could do with a few lessons in marksmanship, Josiah," he returned curtly. "You can't even hit a target."

"That's a fact," Derek agreed at once, dark eyes dancing. "He tried to shoot a snake once and took the mailbox down with a shotgun."

"I can hit what I aim at when I want to," Josiah said huffily. "I hated that damned mailbox. I shot it on purpose."

His brothers almost rolled on the floor laughing. Josiah sighed and poured himself another cup of coffee. "Then I guess I'm on a plane back to Oklahoma."

"And I'm on one to Wyoming." Zeke nodded.

Derek glared at them. "And I'm booked for a rodeo in Arizona. Listen, why don't we sell up and move down here? Texas has lots of ranches. In fact, I expect we could find one near here without a lot of trouble."

"You might at that," Alexander told them as he poured his own cup of coffee, taking the opportunity to ruffle Jodie's blond hair and smile tenderly down at her. "I hear the old Jacobs place is up for sale again. That eastern dude who took it over lost his shirt in the stock market. It's just as well. He didn't know much about horses anyway."

"It's a horse farm?" Josiah asked, interested.

Alexander nodded. "A seed herd of Arabians and a couple of foals they bred from racing stock. He had pipe dreams about entering a horse in the Kentucky Derby one day."

"Why'd he give it up?"

"Well, for one thing, he didn't know anything about horses. He wouldn't ask for advice from anybody who did, but he'd read this book. He figured he could do it himself. That was before he got kicked out of the barn the first time," he added in a droll tone.

Zeke made a rough sound. "I'm not keen on horses. And I work in Wyoming."

"You're a little too late, anyway," Margie interrupted, but she was watching Derek with new intensity. "We heard that one of Cash Grier's brothers came down here to look at it. Apparently, they're interested."

"Grier has brothers?" Jodie exclaimed. "What a horrifying thought! How many?"

"Three. They've been on the outs for a long time, but they're making overtures. It seems the ranch would get them close enough to Cash to try and heal the breach."

"That's one mean hombre," Derek ventured.

"He keeps the peace," Alexander defended him. "And he makes life interesting in town. Especially just lately."

"What's going on lately?" Derek wanted to know.

Alexander, Jodie and Margie exchanged secretive smiles. "Never mind," Alexander said. "There are other properties, if you're really interested. You might stop by one of the real estate agencies and stock up on brochures."

"He'll never leave Oklahoma," Derek said, nodding toward Josiah. "And Wyoming's the only place left that's sparsely populated enough to appeal to our family grizzly." He glanced at Margie and grinned. "However, I only need a temporary base of operations since I'm on the road so much. I might buy me a little cabin nearby and come serenade Margie on weekends when I'm in town."

Margie laughed, but she was flushed with excitement. "Might you, now?"

"Of course, you're set on a designing career," he mused.

"And you're hooked on breaking bones and spraining muscles in the rodeo circuit."

"We might find some common ground one day," Derek replied.

Margie only smiled. "Are you all staying for my Halloween party?" she asked the brothers.

Zeke finished his coffee and got up. "I don't do parties. Excuse me. I have to call the airline."

"I'm right behind you," Josiah said, following his brother with an apologetic smile.

"Well, I guess it's just me," Derek said. "What do you think, Marge, how about if I borrow one of Alex's suits and come as a college professor?"

She burst out laughing.

Alexander caught Jodie by the hand and pulled her out of the kitchen with him.

"Where are we going?" she asked.

"For a walk, now that nobody's shooting at us," he said, linking her fingers into his.

He led her out the front door and around to the side of the house, by the long fences that kept the cattle in.

"When do you have to go back to work?" he asked Jodie reluctantly.

"That wasn't exactly discussed," she confessed, with a secret smile, because he didn't know which job she was returning to take. "But I suppose next week will do nicely."

"I still think Brody Vance is involved in this somehow," he said flatly, turning to her. "I can't prove it yet, but I'm certain he's not as innocent as he's pretending to be."

"That's exactly what I think," she agreed, surprising him. "By the way," she added, "I quit my job before we came down here."

"You quit…good for you!" he exclaimed, hugging her close. "I'm proud of you, Jodie!"

She laughed, holding on tight. "Don't be too proud. I'm still working for Mr. Ritter. But it's going to be in a totally different capacity."

"Doing what?" he asked flatly.

"I'm going to be working with Colby Lane as a computer security consultant," she told him.

"What about Hunter?" he asked.

"He's going back to Arizona with his wife. They're expecting a second child, and I think they want a little less excitement in their life right now," she confided with a grin. "So Colby Lane is taking over security. Mr. Ritter said I might have to do some traveling later on as a troubleshooter, but it wouldn't be often."

He was studying her with soft, quiet eyes. "As long as it's sporadic and not for too long, that's fine. You'll do well in security," he said. "Old man Ritter isn't as dense as I thought he was. I'm glad he's still keeping an eye on the company. Colby Lane will keep his security people on their toes just as well as Hunter did."

"I think Mr. Hunter is irritated that Cara managed to get into that warehouse parking lot," she ventured.

"He is. But it could have happened to anyone. Brody Vance is our wild card. He's going to need watching. And no, you can't offer to do it," he added firmly. "Let Lane set up his own surveillance. You stick to the job you're given and stop sticking your neck out."

"I like that!" she exclaimed. "And who was it who encouraged me to stick my neck out in the first place planting bugs near people in coffeehouses?"

He searched her eyes quietly. "You did a great job. I was proud of you. I always thought we might work well together."

"We did, didn't we?" she mused.

He pushed back wispy strands of loose hair from her cheek and studied her hungrily. "I have in mind another opportunity for mutual cooperation," he said, bending to her mouth.

# Chapter 11

"What sort of mutual cooperation?" she whispered against his searching lips. "Does it involve guns and bugs?"

He smiled against her soft mouth. "I was thinking more of prophylactics..."

While Jodie was trying to let the extraordinary statement filter into her brain, and trying to decide whether to slug him or kiss him back, a loud voice penetrated their oblivion.

"Jodie!" Margie yelled. "Where are you?"

Alexander lifted his head. He seemed as dazed as she felt.

"Jodie!" Margie yelled more insistently.

"On my way!" Jodie yelled back.

"Sisters are a pain," he murmured on a long sigh.

She smiled at him. "I'm sure it's a minor disaster that only I can cope with," she assured him.

He chuckled. "Go ahead. But tonight," he added in a deep, husky tone, "you're mine."

She flushed at the way he said it. She started to argue, but Margie was yelling again, so she ran toward the house instead.

Alexander stared hungrily at Jodie when she came down the stairs just before the first party guest arrived the next evening. They'd spent the day together, riding around the ranch and talking. There hadn't been any more physical encounters, but there was a new closeness between them that everyone noticed.

Jodie's blond hair was long and wavy. She was wearing a red dress with a long, ruffled hem, an elasticized neckline that was pushed off the shoulders, leaving her creamy skin visible. She was wearing high heels and more makeup than she usually put on. And she was breathtaking. He just shook his head, his eyes eating her as she came down the staircase, holding on to the banister.

"You could be dessert," he murmured when she reached him.

"So could you," she replied, adoring him with her eyes. "But you aren't even wearing a costume."

"I am so," he argued with a wry smile. "I'm disguised as a government agent."

"Alexander!" she wailed.

He chuckled and caught her fingers in his. "I look better than Derek does. He's coming as a rodeo cowboy, complete with banged-up chaps, worn-out boots, and a championship belt buckle the size of my foot."

"He'll look authentic," she replied.

He smiled. "So do I. Don't I?"

She sighed, loving the way he looked. "I suppose you do, at that. There's going to be a big crowd, Margie says."

He tilted her chin up to his eyes. "There won't be anyone here except the two of us, Jodie," he said quietly.

The way he was looking at her, she could almost believe it.

"I think Margie feels that way with Derek," she murmured absently. "Too bad his brothers wouldn't stay."

"They aren't the partying type," he said. "Neither are we, really."

She nodded. Her eyes searched his and she felt giddy all over at the shift in their relationship. It was as if all the arguments of years past were blown away like sand. She felt new, young, on top of the world. And if his expression was anything to go by, he felt the same way.

He traced her face with his eyes. "How do you feel about short engagements?" he asked out of the blue.

She was sure that it was a rhetorical question. "I suppose it depends on the people involved. If they knew each other well…"

"I've known you longer than any other woman in my life except my sister," he interrupted. His face tightened as he stared down at her with narrow, hungry eyes. "I want to marry you, Jodie."

She opened her mouth to speak and couldn't even manage words. The shock robbed her of speech.

He grimaced. "I thought it might come as a shock. You don't have to answer me this minute," he said easily, taking her hand. "You think about it for a while.

Let's go mingle with the guests as they come in and spend the night dancing. Then I'll ask you again."

She went along with him unprotesting, but she was certain she was hearing things. Alexander wasn't a marrying man. He must be temporarily out of his mind with worry over his unsolved case. But he didn't look like the product of a deranged mind, and the way he held Jodie's hand tight in his, and the way he watched her, were convincing.

Not only that, but he had eyes for her alone. Kirry didn't come, but there were plenty of other attractive women at the party. None of them attracted so much as a glance from Alexander. He danced only with Jodie, and held her so closely that people who knew both of them started to speculate openly on their changed relationship.

"People are watching us," Jodie murmured as they finished one dance only to start right into another one.

"Let them watch," he said huskily. His eyes fell to her soft mouth. "I'm glad you work in Houston, Jodie. I won't have to find excuses to commute to Jacobsville to see you."

"You never liked me before," she murmured out loud.

"I never got this close to you before," he countered. "I've lived my whole life trying to forget the way my mother was, Jodie," he confessed. "She gave me emotional scars that I still carry. I kept women at a safe distance. I actually thought I had you at a safe distance, too," he added on a chuckle. "And then I started taking you around for business reasons and got caught in my own web."

"Did you, really?" she murmured with wonder.

"Careful," he whispered. "I'm dead serious." He bent and brushed his mouth beside hers, nuzzling her cheek with his nose. "It's too late to go back, Jodie. I can't let go."

His arm contracted. She gasped softly at the increased intimacy of the contact. She could feel the hunger in him. Her own body began to vibrate faintly as she realized how susceptible she was.

"You be careful," she countered breathlessly. "I'm on fire! You could find yourself on the floor in a closet, being ravished, if you keep this up."

"If that's a promise, lead me to a closet," he said, only half joking.

She laughed. He didn't.

In fact, his arm contracted even more and he groaned softly at her ear. "Jodie," he said in a choked tone, "how do you feel about runaway marriages?"

"Excuse me?"

He lifted his head and looked down into her eyes with dark intensity. "Runaway marriage. You get in a car, run away to Mexico in the middle of somebody's Halloween party and get married." His arm brought her closer. "They're binding even in this country. We could get to the airport in about six minutes, and onto a plane in less than an hour."

"To where?" she burst out, aghast.

"Anywhere in Mexico," he groaned, his eyes biting into hers as he lifted his head. "We can be married again in Jacobsville whenever you like."

"Then why go to Mexico tonight?" she asked, flustered.

His hand slid low on her spine and pulled her hips into his with a look that made her blush.

"That is not a good reason to go to Mexico on the spur of the moment," she said, while her body told her brain to shut up.

"That's what you think." His expression was eloquent.

"But what if I said yes?" she burst out. "You could end up tied to me for life, when all you want is immediate relief! And speaking of relief, there's a bedroom right up the stairs...!"

He stopped dancing. His face was solemn. "Tell me you wouldn't mind a quick fling in my bed, Jodie," he challenged. "Tell me your conscience wouldn't bother you at all."

She sighed. "I'd like to," she began.

"But your parents didn't raise you that way," he concluded for her. "In fact, my father was like that," he added quietly. "He was old-fashioned and I'm like him. There haven't even been that many women, if you'd like to know, Jodie," he confessed. "And right now, I wish there hadn't been even one."

"That is the sweetest thing to say," she whispered, and pulled his face down so that she could kiss him.

"As it happens, I mean it." He kissed her back, very lightly. "Run away with me," he challenged. "Right now!"

It was crazy. He had to be out of his mind. But the temptation to get him to a minister before he changed his mind was all-consuming. She was suddenly caught up in the same excitement she saw in his face. "But you're so conventional!"

"I'll be very conventional again first thing tomorrow," he promised. "Tonight, I'm going for broke. Grab a coat. Don't tell anybody where we're going. I'll think up something to say to Margie."

She glanced toward the back of the room, where Margie was watching them excitedly and whispering something to Derek that made him laugh.

"All right. We're both crazy, but I'm not arguing with you. Tell her whatever you like. Make it good," she told him, and dashed up the staircase.

He was waiting for her at the front door. He looked irritated.

"What's wrong?" Jodie asked when she reached him. Her heart plummeted. "Changed your mind?"

"Not on your life!" He caught her arm and pulled her out the door, closing it quickly behind them. "Margie's too smart for her own good. Or Derek is."

"You can't put anything past Margie," she said, laughing with relief as they ran down the steps and toward the garage, where he kept his Jaguar.

"Or Derek," he murmured, chuckling.

He unlocked the door with his keyless entry and popped out the laser key with his thumb on the button. He looked down at her hesitantly. "I'm game if you are," he told her. "But you can still back out if you want to."

She shook her head, her eyes full of dreams. "You might never be in the mood again."

"That's a laugh." He put her inside and minutes later, they were en route to the airport.

Holding hands all the way during the flight, making plans, they arrived in El Paso with bated breath. Alexander rented a car at the airport and they drove across

the border, stopping at customs and looking so radiant that the guard guessed their purpose immediately.

"You're going over to get married, I'd bet," the man
said with a huge grin. *"Buena suerte,"* he added, hand-
ing back their identification. "And drive carefully!"

"You bet!" Alexander told him as he drove off.

They found a small chapel and a minister willing to
perform the ceremony after a short conversation with
a police officer near a traffic light.

Jodie borrowed a peso from the minister's wife for
luck and was handed a small bouquet of silk flowers
to hold while the words were spoken, in Spanish, that
would make them man and wife.

Alexander translated for her, his eyes soft and warm
and possessive as the minister pronounced them man
and wife at last. He drew a ring out of his pocket, a
beautiful embossed gold band, which he slid onto her
finger. It was a perfect fit. She recognized it as one
she'd sighed over years ago in a jewelry shop she'd
gone to with Margie when they were dreaming about
marriage in the distant future. She'd been back to the
shop over the years to make sure it was still there. Apparently Margie had told Alexander about it.

They signed the necessary documents, Alexander
paid the minister, and they got back into the car with
a marriage license.

Jodie stared at her ring and her new husband with
wide-eyed wonder. "We must be crazy," she commented.

He laughed. "We're not crazy. We're very sensible.
First we have an elopement, then we have a honeymoon, then we have a normal wedding with Margie and
our friends." He glanced at her with twinkling eyes.

"You said you didn't have to be back at work until next week. We'll have our honeymoon before you go back."

"Where, exactly, did you have in mind for a honeymoon?" she asked.

Three hours later, tangled with Alexander in a big king-size bed with waves pounding the shore outside the window, she lay in the shadows of the moonlit Gulf of Mexico. The hotel was first class, the food was supposed to be the best in Galveston, the beach was like sugar sand. But all she saw was Alexander's face above hers as her body throbbed in the molasses slow rhythm of his kisses on her breasts on cool, crisp sheets.

"You taste like candy," he whispered against her belly.

"You never said I was sweet before," she teased breathlessly.

"You always were. I didn't know how to say it. You gave me the shakes every time I got near you." His mouth opened on her diaphragm and pressed down, hard.

She gasped at the warm pleasure of it. Her hands tangled in his thick, dark hair. "That was mutual, too." She drew his face to her breasts and coaxed his mouth onto them. "This is very nice," she murmured unsteadily.

"It gets better." His hands found her in a new and invasive way. She started to protest, only to find his mouth crushing down over her parted lips about the same time that his movements lifted her completely off the bed in a throbbing wave of unexpected pleasure.

"Oh, you like that, do you?" he murmured against her mouth. "How about this…?"

She cried out. His lips stifled the sound and his leg moved between both of hers. He kissed her passionately while his lean hips shifted and she felt him in an intimacy they hadn't yet shared.

He felt her body jerk as she tried to reject the shock of invasion, but his mouth gentled hers, his hands soothed her, teased her, coaxed her into allowing the slow merging of their bodies.

She gasped, her hands biting into his back in mingled fear and excitement.

"It won't hurt long," he whispered reassuringly, and his tongue probed her lips as he began a slow, steady rhythm that rippled down her nerves like pure joy on a roller coaster of pleasure.

"That's it," he murmured against her eager lips. "Come up against me and find the pressure and the rhythm that you need. That's it. That's…it!"

She was amazed that he didn't mind letting her experiment, that he was willing to help her experience him. She'd heard some horror stories about wedding nights from former friends. This wasn't one. She'd found a man who wanted eager participation, not passive acceptance. She moved and shifted and he laughed roughly, his deep voice throbbing with pleasure, as her seeking body kindled waves of delight in his own.

She was on fire with power. She moved under him, invited him, challenged him, provoked him. And he went with her, every step of the way up the ladder to a mutual climax that groaned out at her ear in ripples of satiation. She clung to him, shivering in the explosive aftermath of an experience that exceeded her wildest hopes.

"And now you know," he whispered, kissing her eyelids closed.

"Now I know." She nose-dived into his damp throat and clung while they slowly settled back to earth again.

"I love you, baby," he whispered tenderly.

Joy flooded through her. "I love you, too!" she whispered breathlessly.

He curled her into his body with a long yawn and with the ocean purring like a wet kitten outside the windows, they drifted off into a warm, soft sleep.

"Hey."

She heard his voice at her ear. Then there was an aroma, a delicious smell of fresh coffee, rich and dark and delicious.

Her eyes didn't even open, but her head followed the retreat of the coffee.

"I thought that would do it. Breakfast," Alexander coaxed. "We've got your favorite, pecan waffles with bacon."

Her eyes opened. "You remembered!"

He grinned at her. "I know what you like." His lips pursed. "Especially after last night."

She laughed, dragging herself out of bed in the slip she'd worn to bed, because it was still too soon to sleep in nothing at all. She was shy with him.

He was completely dressed, right down to his shoes. He gave her an appreciative sweep of his green eyes that took in her bare feet and her disheveled hair.

"You look wonderful like that," he said. "I always knew you would."

"When was that, exactly?" she chided, taking a seat

at the table facing the window. "Before or after you accused me of being a layabout?"

"Ouch!" he groaned.

"It's okay. I forgive you," she said with a wicked glance. "I could never hold a grudge against a man who was that good in bed."

"And just think, I was very subdued last night, in deference to your first time."

She gasped. "Well!"

His eyebrows arched. "Think of the possibilities. If you aren't too delicate after last night, we could explore some of them later."

"Later?"

"I had in mind taking you around town and showing you off," he said, flipping open a napkin. "They have all sorts of interesting things to see here."

She sipped coffee, trying to ignore her body, which was making emphatic statements about what *it* wanted to do with the day.

He was watching her with covert, wise eyes. "On the other hand," he murmured as he nibbled a pancake, "if you were feeling lazy, we could just lie around in the bed and listen to the ocean, while we..."

Her hand poised over the waffle. "While we...?"

He began to smile. She laughed. The intimacy was new and secret, and exciting. She rushed through the waffle and part of the bacon, and then pushed herself away from the table and literally threw herself into his arms across the chair. He prided himself on his control, because they actually almost made it to the bed...

Two days later, worn-out, and not because of any sightseeing trip, they dragged themselves into the ranch house with a bag full of peace offerings for Margie which included seashells, baskets, a pretty ruffled sundress and some taffy.

Margie gave them a long, amused look. "There is going to have to be a wedding here," she informed them. "It won't do to run off to Mexico and get married, you have to do it in Jacobsville before anybody will believe you're really man and wife."

"I don't mind," Alexander said complacently, "but I'm not making the arrangements."

"Jodie and I can do that."

"But I have to go back to work," she told Margie, and went forward to hand her the bag and hug her. "And I haven't even told you about my new job!"

"What about your new husband?" Alexander groaned. "Are you going to desert me?"

She gave him a wicked glance. "Don't you have to talk to somebody about ranch business? Margie doesn't even know that I'm changing jobs!"

He sighed. "That's all husbands are good for," he murmured to himself. "You marry a woman, and she runs off and leaves you to gossip with a girlfriend."

"My sister-in-law, if you please," Jodie corrected him with a grin. "I'll cook you a nice apple pie for later, Alexander," she promised.

"Okay, I do take bribes," he had to confess. He grinned at her. "But now that we're married, couldn't you find something else to call me? Something a little less formal?"

She thought about it for a minute. "Darling," she said.

He looked at her with an odd expression, smiled as if he couldn't help himself, and made a noise like a tiger. He went out the back door while they were still laughing.

* * *

Jodie moved into her new job with a little apprehension, because of what she'd said to Brody Vance, but he was as genial as if no cross words had ever been spoken between them. Cara Dominguez still hadn't been heard from or seen, neither had her accomplice. There was still a shipment of drugs missing, that had to be in the warehouse somewhere, but guards and stepped-up surveillance assured that the drug dealers couldn't get near the warehouse to search for it.

One of Cara's rivals in the business was arrested in a guns-for-drugs deal in Houston that made national and international headlines. Alexander told Jodie about it just before the wire services broke the story, and assured her that Cara's organization was going to be next on the list of objectives for his department.

Meanwhile, Jodie learned the ropes of computer security and went back to school to finish her certification, with Alexander's blessing. Margie came up to see her while she was arranging a showing of her new designs with a local modeling agency and a department store that Kirry didn't work for.

Alexander kept shorter hours and did more delegating of chores, so that he could be at home when Jodie was. They bought a small house on the outskirts of Houston. Margie arranged to help Jodie with the decorating scheme. She was still amazed at the change in her best friend, who was now independent, strong-willed, hardworking and nobody's doormat.

There was still the retro coffeehouse, of course, and one night Jodie had a phone call from the owner, Johnny. She listened, exploded with delight, and ran to tell Alexander the news.

Dear Reader,

Since you are a lover of our books, your opinions are important to us... and so is your time.

That's why we made sure your **"FAST FIVE" READER SURVEY** can be completed in just a few minutes. Your answers to the five questions will help us remain at the forefront of women's fiction.

And, as a thank-you for participating, we'd like to send you **4 FREE THANK-YOU GIFTS!**

Enjoy your gifts with our appreciation,

*Pam Powers*

## To get your
## 4 FREE THANK-YOU GIFTS:

✱ Quickly complete the "Fast Five" Reader Survey
and return the insert.

## "FAST FIVE" READER SURVEY

| 1 | Do you sometimes read a book a second or third time? | ○ Yes ○ No |
| 2 | Do you often choose reading over other forms of entertainment such as television? | ○ Yes ○ No |
| 3 | When you were a child, did someone regularly read aloud to you? | ○ Yes ○ No |
| 4 | Do you sometimes take a book with you when you travel outside the home? | ○ Yes ○ No |
| 5 | In addition to books, do you regularly read newspapers and magazines? | ○ Yes ○ No |

**YES!** I have completed the above Reader Survey. Please send me my 4 FREE GIFTS (gifts worth over $20 retail). I understand that I am under no obligation to buy anything, as explained on the back of this card.

### 194/394 MDL GMVZ

FIRST NAME          LAST NAME

ADDRESS

APT.#          CITY

STATE/PROV.          ZIP/POSTAL CODE

## READER SERVICE—Here's how it works:

"The publisher wants to buy my poems!" she exclaimed. "He wants to include them in an anthology of Texas poetry! Isn't it exciting?"

"It's exciting," he agreed, bending to kiss her warmly. "Now tell the truth. They're about me, aren't they?"

She sighed. "Yes, they're about you. But I'm afraid this will be the only volume of poetry I ever create."

"Really? Why?"

She nibbled his chin. "Because misery is what makes good poetry. And just between us two," she added as her fingers went to his shirt buttons, "I'm far too happy to write good poetry ever again."

He guided her fingers down his shirt, smiling secretively. "I have plans to keep you that way, too," he murmured deeply.

And he did.

\* \* \* \* \*

## Also by Maisey Yates

### HQN Books

### Harlequin Desire

### Look for the first of a brand-new series

For more books by Maisey Yates,
visit www.maiseyyates.com.

# TAKE ME, COWBOY

Maisey Yates

To Nicole Helm, for your friendship, profane texts and love of farm animals in sweaters. My life would be boring without you.

# *Chapter 1*

**W**hen Anna Brown walked into Ace's bar, she was contemplating whether or not she could get away with murdering her older brothers.

*That's really nice that the invitation includes a plus one. You know you can't bring your socket wrench.*

She wanted to punch Daniel in his smug face for that one. She had been flattered when she'd received her invitation to the community charity event that the West family hosted every year. A lot less so when Daniel and Mark had gotten ahold of it and decided it was the funniest thing in the world to imagine her trying to get a date to the coveted fund-raiser.

Because apparently the idea of her having a date at all was the pinnacle of comedic genius.

*I can get a date, jackasses.*

*You want to make a bet?*

*Sure. It's your money.*

That exchange had seemed both enraging and empowering about an hour ago. Now she was feeling both humiliated and a little bit uncertain. The fact that she had bet on her dating prowess was…well, embarrassing didn't even begin to describe it. But on top of that, she was a little concerned that she had no prowess to speak of.

It had been longer than she wanted to admit since she'd actually had a date. In fact, it was entirely possible that she had never technically been on one. That quick roll in the literal hay with Corbin Martin hadn't exactly been a date per se.

And it hadn't led to anything, either. Since she had done a wonderful job of smashing his ego with a hammer the next day at school when she'd told her best friend, Chase, about Corbin's…limitations.

Yeah, her sexual debut had also been the final curtain.

But if men weren't such whiny babies, maybe that wouldn't have been the case. Also, maybe if Corbin had been able to prove to her that sex was worth the trouble, she would view it differently.

But he hadn't. So she didn't.

And now she needed a date.

She stalked across the room, heading toward the table that she and Chase, and often his brother, Sam, occupied on Friday nights. The lighting was dim, so she knew someone was sitting there but couldn't make out which McCormack brother it was.

She hoped it was Chase. Because as long as she'd known Sam, she still had a hard time making conversation with him.

Talking wasn't really his thing.

She moved closer, and the man at the table tilted his head up. Sam. Dammit. Drinking a beer and looking grumpy, which was pretty much par for the course with him. But Chase was nowhere to be seen.

"Hi," she said, plopping down in the chair beside him. "Bad day?"

"A day."

"Right." At least when it came to Sam, she knew the difficult-conversation thing had nothing to do with her. That was all him.

She tapped the top of her knee, looking around the bar, trying to decide if she was going to get up and order a drink or wait for someone to come to the table. She allowed her gaze to drift across the bar, and her attention was caught by the figure of a man in the corner, black cowboy hat on his head, his face shrouded by the dim light. A woman was standing in front of him looking up at his face like he was her every birthday wish come true.

For a moment the sight of the man standing there struck her completely dumb. Broad shoulders, broad chest, strong-looking hands. The kind of hands that made her wonder if she needed to investigate the potential fuss of sex again.

He leaned up against the wall, his forearm above his head. He said something and the little blonde he was talking to practically shimmered with excitement. Anna wondered what that was like. To be the focus of a man's attention like that. To have him look at you like a sex object instead of a drinking buddy.

For a moment she envied the woman standing there, who could absolutely get a date if she wanted one. Who would know what to wear and how to act if she were invited to a fancy gala whatever.

That woman would know what to do if the guy wanted to take her home after the date and get naked. She wouldn't be awkward and make jokes and laugh when he got naked because there were all these feelings that were so…so weird she didn't know how else to react.

With a man like that one…well, she doubted she would laugh. He would be all lean muscle and wicked smiles. He would look at her and she would… Okay, even in fantasy she didn't know. But she felt hot. Very, very hot.

But in a flash, that hot feeling turned into utter horror. Because the man shifted, pushing his hat back on his head and angling slightly toward Anna, a light from above catching his angular features and illuminating his face. He changed then, from a fantasy to flesh and blood. And she realized exactly who she had just been checking out.

Chase McCormack. Her best friend in the entire world. The man she had spent years training herself to never, ever have feelings below the belt for.

She blinked rapidly, squeezing her hands into fists and trying to calm the fluttering in her stomach. "I'm going to get a drink," she said, looking at Sam. *And talk to Ace about the damn lighting in here.* "Did you want something?"

He lifted his brow, and his bottle of beer. "I'm covered."

Her heart was still pounding a little heavier than usual when she reached the bar and signaled Ace, the establishment's owner, to ask for whatever pale ale he had on tap.

And her heart stopped altogether when she heard a deep voice from behind her.

"Why don't you make that two."

She whisked around and came face-to-chest with Chase. A man whose presence should be commonplace, and usually was. She was just in a weird place, thanks to high-pressure invitations and idiot brothers.

"Pale ale," she said, taking a step back and looking up at his face. A face that should also be commonplace. But it was just so very symmetrical. Square jaw, straight nose, strong brows and dark eyes that were so direct they bordered on obscene. Like they were looking straight through your clothes or something. Not that he would ever want to look through hers. Not that she would want him to. She was too smart for that.

"That's kind of an unusual order for you," she continued, more to remind herself of who he was than to actually make commentary on his beverage choice. To remind herself that she knew him better than she knew herself. To do whatever she could to put that temporary moment of insanity when she'd spotted him in the corner out of her mind.

"I'm feeling adventurous," he said, lifting one corner of his mouth, the lopsided grin disrupting the symmetry she had been admiring earlier and somehow making him look all the more compelling for it.

"Come on, McCormack. Adventurous is bungee jumping from Multnomah Falls. Adventurous is not trying a new beer."

"Says the expert in adventure?"

"I'm an expert in a couple of things. Beer and motor oil being at the top of the list."

"Then I won't challenge you."

"Probably for the best. I'm feeling a little bit blood-thirsty tonight." She pressed her hands onto the bar top and leaned forward, watching as Ace went to get their drinks. "So. Why aren't you still talking to short, blonde and stacked over there?"

He chuckled and it settled oddly inside her chest, rattling around before skittering down her spine. "Not really all that interested."

"You seemed interested to me."

"Well," he said, "I'm not."

"That's inconsistent," she said.

"Okay, I'll bite," he said, regarding her a little more closely than she would like. "Why are you in the mood to cause death and dismemberment?"

"Do I seem that feral?"

"Completely. Why?"

"The same reason I usually am," she said.

"Your brothers."

"You're fast, I like that."

Ace returned to their end of the bar and passed two pints toward them. "Do you want to open a tab?"

"Sure," she said. "On him." She gestured to Chase.

Ace smiled in return. "You look nice tonight, Anna."

"I look…the same as I always do," she said, glancing down at her worn gray T-shirt and no-fuss jeans.

He winked. "Exactly."

She looked up at Chase, who was staring at the bartender, his expression unreadable. Then she looked back at Ace.

Ace was pretty hot, really. In that bearded, flannel-wearing way. Lumbersexual, or so she had overheard some college girls saying the other night as they giggled over him. Maybe *he* would want to be her date. Of course, easy compliments and charm aside, he also had his pick of any woman who turned up in his bar. And Anna was never anyone's pick.

She let go of her fleeting Ace fantasy pretty quickly.

Chase grabbed the beer from the counter and handed one to her. She was careful not to let their fingers brush as she took it from him. That type of avoidance was second nature to her. Hazards of spending the years since adolescence feeling electricity when Chase got too close, and pretending she didn't.

"We should go back and sit with Sam," she suggested. "He looks lonely."

Chase laughed. "You and I both know he's no such thing. I think he would rather sit there alone."

"Well, if he wants to be alone, then he can stay at home and drink."

"He probably would if I didn't force him to come out. But if I didn't do that, he would fuse to the furniture and then I would have all of that to deal with."

They walked back over to the table, and gradually, her heart rate returned to normal. She was relieved that the initial weirdness she had felt upon his arrival was receding.

"Hi, Sam," Chase said, taking his seat beside his brother. Sam grunted in response. "We were just talking about the hazards of you turning into a hermit."

"Am I not a convincing hermit already?" he asked. "Do I need to make my disdain for mankind a little less subtle?"

"That might help," Chase said.

"I might just go play a game of darts instead. I'll catch up with you in a minute." Sam took a long drink of his beer and stood, leaving the bottle on the table as he made his way over to the dartboard across the bar.

Silence settled between Chase and herself. Why was this suddenly weird? Why was Anna suddenly conscious of the way his throat moved when he swallowed a sip of beer, of the shift in his forearms as he set the bottle back down on the table? Of just how masculine a sound he made when he cleared his throat?

She was suddenly even conscious of the way he breathed.

She leaned back in her chair, lifting her beer to her lips and surveying the scene around them.

It was Friday night, so most of the town of Copper Ridge, Oregon, was hanging out, drowning the last vestiges of the workweek in booze. It was not the end of the workweek for Anna. Farmers and ranchers didn't take time off, so neither did she. She had to be on hand to make repairs when necessary, especially right now, since she was just getting her own garage off the ground.

She'd just recently quit her job at Jake's in order to open her own shop specializing in heavy equipment, which really was how she found herself in the position she was in right now. Invited to the charity gala thing and embroiled in a bet on whether or not she could get a date.

"So why exactly do you want to kill your brothers today?" Chase asked, startling her out of her thoughts.

"Various reasons." She didn't know why, but something stopped her from wanting to tell him exactly what was going on. Maybe because it was humiliating. Yes, it was definitely humiliating.

"Sure. But that's every day. Why specifically do you want to kill them today?"

She took a deep breath, keeping her eyes fixed on the fishing boat that was mounted to the wall opposite her, and very determinedly not looking at Chase. "Because. They bet that I couldn't get a date to this thing I'm invited to and I bet them that I could." She thought about the woman he'd been talking to a moment ago. A woman so different from herself they might as well be different species. "And right about now I'm afraid they're right."

Chase was doing his best to process his best friend's statement. It was difficult, though. Daniel and Mark had solid asshole tendencies when it came to Anna—that much he knew—but this was pretty low even for them.

He studied Anna's profile, her dark hair pulled back into a braid, her gray T-shirt that was streaked with oil. He watched as she raised her bottle of beer to her lips. She had oil on her hands, too. Beneath her fingernails. Anna wasn't the kind of girl who attracted a lot of male attention. But he kind of figured that was her choice.

She wasn't conventionally beautiful. Mostly because of the motor oil. But that didn't mean that getting a date should be impossible for her.

"Why don't you think you can get a date?"

She snorted, looking over at him, one dark brow raised. "Um." She waved a hand up and down, indicating her body. "Because of all of this."

He took a moment to look at *all of that*. Really look. Like he was a man and she was a woman. Which they were, but not in a conventional sense. Not to each other.

He'd looked at her almost every day for the past fifteen years, so it was difficult to imagine seeing her for the first time. But just then, he tried.

She had a nice nose. And her lips were full, nicely shaped, her top lip a little fuller than her bottom lip, which was unique and sort of...not sexy, because it was Anna. But interesting.

"A little elbow grease and that cleans right off," he said. "Anyway, men are pretty simple."

She frowned. "What does that mean?"

"Exactly what it sounds like. You don't have to do much to get male attention if you want it. Give a guy what he's after..."

"Okay, that's just insulting. You're saying that I can get a guy because men just want to get laid? So it doesn't matter if I'm a wrench-toting troll?"

"You are not a wrench-toting troll. You're a wrench-toting woman who could easily bludgeon me to death, and I am aware of that. Which means I need to choose my next words a little more carefully."

Those full lips thinned into a dangerous line, her green eyes glittering dangerously. "Why don't you do that, Chase."

He cleared his throat. "I'm just saying, if you want a date, you can get one."

"By unzipping my coveralls down to my belly button?"

He tipped his beer bottle back, taking a larger swallow than he intended to, coughing as it went down wrong. He did not need to picture the visual she had just handed to him. But he was a man, so he did.

It was damned unsettling. His best friend, bare beneath a pair of coveralls unfastened so that a very generous wedge of skin was revealed all the way down…

And he was done with that. He didn't think of Anna that way. Not at all. They'd been friends since they were freshmen in high school and he'd navigated teenage boy hormones without lingering too long on thoughts of her breasts.

He was thirty years old, and he could have sex whenever he damn well pleased. Breasts were no longer mysterious to him. He wasn't going to go pondering the mysteries of *her* breasts now.

"It couldn't hurt, Anna," he said, his words containing a little more bite than he would like them to. But he was unsettled.

"Okay, I'll keep that in mind. But barring that, do you have any other suggestions? Because I think I'm going to be expected to wear something fancy, and I don't own anything fancy. And it's obvious that Mark and Daniel think I suck at being a girl."

"That's not true. And anyway, why do you care what they—or anyone else—think?"

"Because. I've got this new business…"

"And anyone who brings their heavy equipment to you for a tune-up won't care whether or not you can walk in high heels."

"But I don't want to show up at these things looking…" She sighed. "Chase, the bottom line is I've spent a long time not fitting in. And people here are nice to me. I mean, now that I'm not in school. People in school sucked. But I get that I don't fit. And I'm tired of it. Honestly, I wouldn't care about my brothers if there wasn't so much…truth to the teasing."

"They do suck. They're awful. So why does it matter what they think?"

"Because," she said. "It just does. I'm that poor Anna Brown with no mom to teach her the right way to do things and I'm just…tired of it. I don't want to be poor Anna Brown. I want to be Anna Brown, heavy equipment mechanic who can wear coveralls and walk in heels."

"Not at the same time, I wouldn't think."

She shot him a deadly glare. "I don't fail," she said, her eyes glinting in the dim bar light. "I won't fail at this."

"You're not in remote danger of failing. Now, what's the mystery event that has you thinking about high heels?" he asked.

Copper Ridge wasn't exactly a societal epicenter. Nestled between the evergreen mountains and a steel-gray sea on the Oregon Coast, there were probably more deer than people in the small town. There were only so many events in existence. And there was a good chance she was making a mountain out of a small-town molehill, and none of it would be that big of a deal.

"That charity thing that the West family has every year," she mumbled. "Gala Under the Stars or whatever."

The West family's annual fund-raising event for schools. It was a weekend event, with the town's top earners coming to a small black-tie get-together on the West property.

The McCormacks had been founding members of the community of Copper Ridge back in the 1800s. Their forge had been used by everyone in town and in the neighboring communities. But as the economy had changed, so had the success of the business.

They'd been hanging on by their fingernails when Chase's parents had been killed in an accident when he was in high school. They'd still gotten an invitation to the gala. But Chase had thrown it on top of the never-ending pile of mail and bills that he couldn't bring himself to look through and forgotten about it.

Until some woman—probably an assistant to the West family—had called him one year when he hadn't bothered to RSVP. He had been...well, he'd been less than polite.

*Dealing with a damned crisis here, so sorry I can't go to your party.*

Unsurprisingly, he hadn't gotten any invitations after that. And he hadn't really thought much about it since.

Until now.

He and Sam had managed to keep the operation and properties afloat, but he wanted more. He needed it.

The ranch had animals, but that wasn't the source of their income. The forge was the heart of the ranch, where they did premium custom metal- and leatherwork. On top of that, there were outbuildings on the property they rented out—including the shop they leased to Anna. They had built things back up since their parents had died, but it still wasn't enough, not to Chase.

He had promised his father he would take an interest in the family legacy. That he would build for the McCormacks, not just for himself. Chase had promised he wouldn't let his dad down. He'd had to make those promises at a grave site because before the accident he'd been a hotheaded jackass who'd thought he was too big for the family legacy.

But even if his father never knew, Chase had sworn it. And so he'd see it done.

In order to expand McCormack Iron Works, the heart and soul of their ranch, to bring it back to what it had been, they needed interest. Investments.

Chase had always had a good business mind, and early on he'd imagined he would go to school away from Copper Ridge. Get a degree. Find work in the city. Then everything had changed. Then it hadn't been about Chase McCormack anymore. It had been about the McCormack legacy.

School had become out of the question. Leaving had been out of the question. But now he saw where he and Sam were failing, and he could see how to turn the tide.

He'd spent a lot of late nights figuring out exactly how to expand as the demand for handmade items had gone down. Finding ways to convince people that highly customized iron details for homes and businesses, and handmade leather bridles and saddles, were worth paying more for.

Finding ways to push harder, to innovate and modernize while staying true to the family name. While actively butting up against Sam and his refusal to go out and make that happen. Sam, who was so talented he didn't have to pound horseshoe nails if he didn't want to. Sam, who could forget gates and scrollwork on staircases and be selling his artwork for a small fortune. Sam, who resisted change like it was the black plague.

He would kill for an invitation to the Wests' event. Well, not kill. But possibly engage in nefarious activities or the trading of sexual favors. And Anna had an invitation.

"You get to bring a date?" he asked.

"That's what I've been saying," she said. "Of course, it all depends on whether or not I can actually acquire one."

Anna needed a date; he wanted to have a chance to talk to Nathan West. In the grand tradition of their friendship, they both filled the gaps in each other's lives. This was—in his opinion—perfect.

"I'll be your date," he said.

She snorted. "Yeah, right. Daniel and Mark will never believe that."

She had a point. The two of them had been friends forever. And with a bet on the table her brothers would never believe that he had suddenly decided to go out with her because his feelings had randomly changed.

"Okay. Maybe that's true." That frown was back. "Not because there's something wrong with you," he continued, trying to dig himself out of the pit he'd just thrown himself into, "but because it's a little too convenient."

"Okay, that's better."

"But what if we made it clear that things had changed between us?"

"What do you mean?"

"I mean…what if…we built up the change? Showed people that our relationship was evolving."

She gave him a fierce side-eye. "I'm not your type." He thought back to the blonde he'd been talking to only twenty minutes earlier. Tight dress cut up to the tops of her thighs, long, wavy hair and the kind of smile that invited you right on in. Curves that had probably wrecked more men than windy Highway 101. She was his type.

And she wasn't Anna. Barefaced, scowling with a figure that was slightly more…subtle. He cleared his throat. "You could be. A little less grease, a little more lipstick."

Her top lip curled. "So the ninth circle of hell basically."

"What were you planning on wearing to the fundraiser?"

She shifted uncomfortably in her seat. "I have black jeans. But…I mean, I guess I could go to the mall in Tolowa and get a dress."

"That isn't going to work."

"Why not?"

"What kind of dress would you buy?" he asked.

"Something floral? Kind of…down to the knee?"

He pinched the bridge of his nose. "You're not Scarlett O'Hara," he said, knowing that with her love of old movies, Anna would appreciate the reference. "You aren't going dressed in the drapes."

Anna scowled. "Why the hell do you know so much about women's clothes?"

"Because I spend a lot of time taking them off my dates."

That shut her up. Her pale cheeks flamed and she looked away from him, and that response stirred… well, it stirred something in his gut he wished would go the hell away.

"Why do *you* want to go anyway?" she asked, still not looking at him.

"I want to talk to Nathan West and the other businessmen there about investment opportunities. I want to prove that Sam and I are the kind of people that can move in their circles. The kind of people they want to do business with."

"And you have to put on a suit and hobnob at a gala to do that?"

"The fact is, I don't get chances like this very often, Anna. I didn't get an invitation. And I need one. Plus, if you take me, you'll win your bet."

"Unless Dan and Mark tell me you don't count."

"Loophole. If they never said you couldn't recruit a date, you're fine."

"It violates the spirit of the bet."

"It doesn't have to," he insisted. "Anyway, by the time I'm through with you, you'll be able to get any date you want."

She blinked. "Are you... Are you Henry Higgins-ing me?"

He had only a vague knowledge of the old movie *My Fair Lady*, but he was pretty sure that was the reference. A man who took a grubby flower girl and turned her into the talk of the town. "Yes," he said thoughtfully. "Yes, I am. Take me up on this, Anna Brown, and I will turn you into a woman."

# Chapter 2

Anna just about laughed herself off her chair. "You're going to make me a...a...a woman?"

"Why is that funny?"

"What about it *isn't* funny?"

"I'm offering to help you."

"You're offering to help me be something that I am by birth. I mean, Chase, I get that women are kind of your thing, but that's pretty arrogant. Even with all things considered."

"Okay, obviously I'm not going to make you a woman." Something about the way he said the phrase this time hit her in an entirely different way. Made her think about *other* applications that phrase occasionally had. Things she needed to never, ever, ever, ever think about in connection with Chase.

If she valued her sanity and their friendship.

She cleared her throat, suddenly aware that it was dry and scratchy. "Obviously."

"I just meant that you need help getting a date, and I need to go to this party. And you said that you were concerned about your appearance in the community."

"Right." He wasn't wrong. The thing was, she knew that whether or not she could blend in at an event like this didn't matter at all to how well her business did. Nobody cared if their mechanic knew which shade of lipstick she should wear. But that wasn't the point.

She—her family collectively—was the town charity case. Living on the edge of the community in a run-down house, raised by a single father who was in over his head, who spent his days at the mill. Her older brothers had been in charge of taking care of her, and they had done so. But, of course, they were also older brothers. Which meant they had tormented her while feeding and clothing her. Anyway, she didn't exactly blame them.

It wasn't like the two of them had wanted to raise a sister when they would rather be out raising hell.

Especially a sister who was committed to driving them crazy.

She loved her brothers. But that didn't mean they always had an easy relationship. It didn't mean they didn't hurt her by accident when they teased her about things. She acted invulnerable, so they assumed that she was.

But now, beneath her coveralls and engine grease, she was starting to feel a little bit battered. It was difficult to walk around with a *screw you* attitude barely covering a raw wound. Because eventually that shield started to wear down. Especially when people were used to being able to lob pretty intense rocks at that shield.

That was her life. It was either pity or a kind of merciless camaraderie that had no softness to it. Her dad, her brothers, all the guy friends she had...

And she couldn't really blame them. She had never behaved in a way that would demonstrate she needed any softness. In fact, a few months ago, a few weeks ago even, the idea would have been unthinkable to her.

But there was something about this invitation. Something about imagining herself in yet another situation where she was forced to deflect good-natured comments about her appearance, about the fact that she was more like a guy than the roughest cowboys in town. Yeah, there was something about that thought that had made her want to curl into a ball and never unfurl.

Then, even if it was unintentional, her brothers had piled on. It had hurt her feelings. Which meant she had reacted in anger, naturally. So now she had a bet. A bet, and her best friend looking at her with laser focus after having just promised he would make her a woman.

"Why do you care?" He was pressing, and she wanted to hit him now.

Which kind of summed up why she was in this position in the first place.

She swallowed hard. "Maybe I just want to surprise people. Isn't that enough?"

"You came from nothing. You started your own business with no support from your father. You're a female mechanic. I would say that you're surprising as hell."

"Well, I want to add another dimension to that. Okay?"

"Okay," he said. "Multidimensional Anna. That seems like a good idea to me."

"Where do we start?"

"With you not falling off your chair laughing at me because I've offered to make you a woman."

A giggle rose in her throat again. Hysteria. She was verging on hysteria. Because this was uncomfortable and sincere. She hated both of those things. "I'm sorry. I can't. You can't say that to me and expect me not to choke."

He looked at her again, his dark eyes intense. "Is it a problem, Anna? The idea that I might make you a woman."

He purposefully made his voice deeper. Purposefully added a kind of provocative inflection to the words. She knew he was kidding. Still, it made her chest tighten. Made her heart flutter a little bit.

Wow. How *annoying*. She hadn't had a relapse of Chase Underpants Feelings this bad in a long time.

Apparently she still hadn't recovered from her earlier bit of mistaken identity. She really needed to recover. And he needed to stop being…Chase. If at all possible.

"Is it a problem for *you*?" she asked.

"What?"

"The idea that I might make you a soprano?"

He chuckled. "You probably want to hold off on threats of castration when you're at a fancy party."

"We aren't at one right now."

She was her own worst enemy. Everything that she had just been silently complaining about, she was doing right now. Throwing out barbs the moment she got un-comfortable, because it kept people from seeing what was actually happening inside of her.

*Yes, but you really need to keep Chase from seeing that you fluttered internally over something he said.*

Yes. Good point.

She noticed that he was looking past her now, and she followed his line of sight. He was looking at that blonde again. "Regrets, Chase?"

He winced, looking back at her. "No."

"So. I assume that to get a guy to come up and hit on me in a bar, I have to put on a dress that is essentially a red ACE bandage sprinkled with glitter?"

He hesitated. "It's more than that."

"What?"

"Well, for a start, there's not looking at a man like you want to dismember him."

She rolled her eyes. "I don't."

"You aren't exactly approachable, Anna."

"That isn't true." She liked to play darts, and hang out, and talk about sports. What wasn't approachable about that?

"I've seen men try to talk to you," Chase continued. "You shut them down pretty quick. For example—" he barreled on before she could interrupt him "—Ace Thompson paid you a compliment back at the bar."

"Ace Thompson compliments everything with boobs."

"And a couple of weeks ago there was a guy in here that tried to buy you a drink. You told him you could buy your own."

"I *can*," she said, "and he was a stranger."

"He was flirting with you."

She thought back on that night, that guy. *Damn.* He had been flirting. "Well, he should get better at it. I'm not going to reward mediocrity. If I can't tell you're flirting, you aren't doing a very good job."

"Part of the problem is you don't think male attention is being directed at you when it actually is."

She looked back over at the shimmery blonde. "Why would any male attention be directed at me when *that's* over there?"

Chase leaned in, his expression taking on a conspiratorial quality that did…things to her insides. "Here's the thing about a girl like that. She knows she looks good. She assumes that men are looking at her. She assumes that if a man talks to her, that means he wants her."

She took a breath, trying to ease the tightness in her chest. "And that's not…a turnoff?"

"No way." He smiled, a sort of lazy half smile. "Confidence is sexy."

He kind of proved that rule. The thought made her bristle.

"All right. So far with our lessons I've learned that I should unzip my coveralls and as long as I'm confident it will be okay."

"You forgot not looking like you want to stab someone."

"Okay. Confident, nonstabby, showing my boobs."

Chase choked on his beer. "That's a good place to start," he said, setting the bottle down. "Do you want to go play darts? I want to go play darts."

"I thought we were having female lessons."

"Rain check," he said. "How about tomorrow I come by the shop and we get started. I think I'm going to need a lesson plan."

* * *

Chase hadn't exactly excelled in school, unless it was at driving his teachers to drink. So why exactly he had decided he needed a lesson plan to teach Anna how to be a woman, he didn't know.

All he knew was that somewhere around the time they started discussing her boobs last night he had become unable to process thoughts normally. He didn't like that. He didn't like it at all. He did not like the fact that he had been forced to consider her breasts more than once in a single hour. He did not like the fact that he was facing down the possibility of thinking about them a few more times over the next few weeks.

But then, that was the game.

Not only was he teaching her how to blend in at a function like this, he was pretending to be her date.

So there was more than one level of hell to deal with. Perfect.

He cleared his throat, walking down the front porch of the farmhouse that he shared with his brother, making his way across the property toward the shop that Anna was renting and using as her business.

It was after five, so she should be knocking off by now. A good time for the two of them to meet.

He looked down at the piece of lined yellow paper in his hand. His lesson plan.

Then he pressed on, his boots crunching on the gravel as he made his way to the rustic wood building. He inhaled deeply, the last gasp of winter riding over the top of the spring air, mixing with the salt from the sea, giving it a crisp bite unique to Copper Ridge.

He relished this. The small moment of clarity before he dived right into the craziness that was his current situation.

Chase McCormack was many things, but he wasn't a coward. He was hardly going to get skittish over giving his best friend some seduction lessons.

He pushed the door open but didn't see Anna anywhere.

He looked around the room, and the dismembered tractors whose various parts weren't in any order that he could possibly define. Though he knew that it must make sense to Anna.

"Hello?"

"Just up here."

He turned, looked up and saw Anna leaning over what used to be a hayloft, looking down at him, a long dark braid hanging down.

"What exactly are you doing up there?"

"I stashed a tool up here, and now I need it. It's good storage. Of course, then I end up climbing the walls a little more often than I would like. Literally. Not figuratively."

"I figured you would be finished for the day by now."

"No. I have to get this tractor fixed for Connor Garrett. And it's been a bigger job than I thought." She disappeared from view for a moment. "But I would like a reputation as someone who makes miracles. So I better make miracles."

She planted her boot hard on the first rung of the ladder and began to climb down. She was covered from head to toe in motor oil and dust. Probably from crawling around in this space, and beneath tractors.

She jumped down past the last three rungs, brushing dirt off her thighs and leaving more behind, since her hands were coated, too. "You don't exactly look like a miracle," he said, looking her over.

She held up her hand, then displayed her middle finger. "Consider it a miracle that I don't punch you."

"Remember what we talked about? Not looking at a guy like you want to stab him? Much less threatening actual bodily harm."

"Hey, I don't think you would tell a woman you actually wanted to hook up with that she didn't look like a miracle."

"Most women I want to hook up with aren't quite this disheveled. Before we start anyway."

Much to his surprise, color flooded her cheeks.

"Well," she said, her voice betraying nothing, "I'm not most women, Chase McCormack. I thought you would've known that by now."

Then she sauntered past him, wearing those ridiculous baggy coveralls, head held high like she was queen of the dust bowl.

"Oh, I'm well aware of that," he said. "That's part of the problem."

"And now it's your problem to fix."

"That's right. And I have the lesson plan. As promised."

She whipped around to face him, one dark brow lifted. "Oh, really?"

"Yes, really." He held up the lined notepaper.

"That's very professional."

"It's as professional as you're gonna get. Now, the first order of business is to plant the seed that we're more than friends."

She looked as though he had just suggested she eat a handful of bees. "Do we really need to do that?"

"Yeah, we *really* need to do that. You won't just have a date for the charity event. You're going to have a date every so often until then."

She looked skeptical. "That seems…excessive."

"You want people to believe this. You don't want people to think I'm going because of a bet. You don't want your brothers to think for one moment that they might be right."

"Well, they're going to think it for a few moments at least."

"True. I mean, they are going to be suspicious. But we can make this look real. It isn't going to be that hard. We already hang out most weekends."

"Sure," she said, "but you go home with other girls at the end of the night."

Those words struck him down. "Yes, I guess I do."

"You won't be able to do that now," she pointed out.

"Why not?" he asked.

"Because if I were with you and you went home with another woman, I would castrate you with nothing but my car keys and a bottle of whiskey."

He had no doubt about that. "At least you'd give me some whiskey."

"Hell no. The whiskey would be for me."

"But we're not really together," he said.

"Sure, Chase, but the entire town knows that if any man were to cheat on me, I would castrate him with my car keys, because I don't take crap from anyone. So if they're going to believe that we're together, you're going to have to look like you're being faithful to me."

"That's fine." It wasn't all that fine. He didn't do

celibacy. Never had. Not from the moment he'd discovered that women were God's greatest invention.

"No booty calls," she said, her tone stern.

"Wait a second. I can't even call a woman to hook up in private?"

"No. You can't. Because then *she* would know. I have pride. I mean, right now, standing here in this garage taking lessons from you on how to conform to my own gender's beauty standards, it's definitely marginal, but I have it."

"It isn't like you really know any of the girls that I…"

"Neither do you," she said.

"This isn't about me. It's about you. Now, I got you some things. But I left them in the house. And you are going to have to…hose off before you put them on."

She blinked, her expression almost comical. "Did you buy me clothes?"

He'd taken a long lunch and gone down to Main Street, popping into one of the ridiculously expensive shops that—in his mind—were mostly for tourists, and had found her a dress he thought would work.

"Yeah, I bought you clothes. Because we both know you can't actually wear this out tonight."

"We're going out *tonight*?"

"Hell yeah. I'm taking you somewhere fancy."

"My fancy threshold is very low. If I have to go eat tiny food on a stick sometime next month, I'm going to need actual sustenance in every other meal until then."

He chuckled, trying to imagine Anna coping with miniature food. "Beaches. I'm taking you to Beaches."

She screwed up her face slightly. "We don't go there."

"No, we haven't gone there. We go to Ace's. We shoot pool, we order fried crap and we split the tab. Because we're friends. And that's what friends do. Friends don't go out to Beaches, not just the two of them. But lovers do."

She looked at him owlishly. "Right. I suppose they do."

"And when all this is finished, the entire town of Copper Ridge is going to think that we're lovers."

# Chapter 3

Anna was reeling slightly by the time she walked up the front porch and into Chase's house. The entire town was going to think that they were...*lovers*. She had never had a lover. At least, she would never characterize the guy she'd slept with as a lover. He was an unfortunate incident. But fortunately, her hymen was the only casualty. Her heart had remained intact, and she was otherwise uninjured. Or pleasured.

*Lovers.*

That word sounded...well, like it came from some old movie or something. Which under normal circumstances she was a big fan of. In this circumstance, it just made her feel...like her insides were vibrating. She didn't like it.

Chase lived in the old family home on the property. It was a large, log cabin–style house with warm, honey-colored wood and a green metal roof designed to withstand all kinds of weather. Wrought-iron details on the porch and the door were a testament to his and Sam's craftsmanship. There were people who would pay millions for a home like this. But Sam and Chase had made it this beautiful on their own.

Chase always kept the home admirably clean considering he was a bachelor. She imagined that the other house on the property, the smaller one inhabited by Sam, wasn't quite as well kept. But she also imagined that Sam didn't have the same amount of guests over that Chase did. And by *guests*, she meant female companions. Which he would be cut off from for the next few weeks.

Some small, mean part of her took a little bit of joy in that.

*Because you don't like the idea of other women touching him. It doesn't matter how long it's been going on, or how many women there are, you still don't like it.*

She sniffed, cutting off that line of thinking. She was just a crabby bitch who was enjoying the idea of him being celibate and suffering a bit. That was all.

"Okay, where are my…girlie things?"

"You aren't even going to look at them until you scrub that grease off."

"And how am I supposed to do that? Are you going to hose me off?"

He clenched his jaw. "No. You can use my shower."

She took a deep breath, trying to dispel the slight fluttering in her stomach. She had never used Chase's shower before. She assumed countless women before her had. When he brought them up here, took their clothes off them. And probably joined them.

She wasn't going to think about that.

"Okay."

She knew where his shower was, of course. Because she had been inside his bedroom casually, countless times. It had never mattered before. Before, she had never been about to get naked.

She banished that thought as she walked up the stairs and down the hall to his room. His room was… well, it was very well-appointed, but then again, obviously designed to house guests of the female variety. The bed was large and full of plush pillows. A soft-looking green throw was folded up at the foot of it. An overstuffed chair was in the corner, another blanket draped over the back.

She doubted the explosion of comfort and cozy was for Chase's benefit.

She tamped that thought down, continuing on through the bathroom door, then locking it for good measure. Not that he would walk in. And he was the only person in the house.

Still, she felt insecure without the lock flipped. She took a deep breath, stripped off her coveralls, then the clothes she had on beneath them, and started the shower. Speaking of things that were designed to be shared…

It was enclosed in glass, and she had a feeling that with the door open it was right in the line of sight from the bed. Inside was red tile, and a bench seat that… She wasn't even going to think what that could be used for.

She turned and looked in the mirror. She was grubby. More than grubby. She had grease all over her face, all up under her fingernails.

Thankfully, Chase had some orange-and-pumice

cleaner right there on his sink. So she was able to start scrubbing at her hands while the water warmed up.

Steam filled the air and she stepped inside the shower, letting the hot spray cascade over her skin.

It was a *massaging* showerhead. A nice one. She did not have a nice massaging showerhead in her little rental house down in town. Next on her list of Ways She Was Changing Her Life would be to get her own house. With one of these.

She rolled her shoulders beneath the spray and sighed. The water droplets almost felt like fingers moving over her tight muscles. And, suddenly, it was all too easy to imagine a man standing behind her, working at her muscles with his strong hands.

She closed her eyes, letting her head fall back, her mouth going slack. She didn't even have the strength to fight the fantasy, God help her. She'd been edgy and aroused for the past twenty-four hours, no denying it. So this little moment to let herself fantasize… she just needed it.

Then she realized exactly whose hands she was picturing.

Chase's. Tall and strong behind her, his hands moving over her skin, down lower to the slight dip in her spine, just above the curve of her behind…

She grabbed hold of the sponge hanging behind her and began to drag it ferociously over her skin, only belatedly realizing that this was probably what he used to wash himself.

"He uses it to wash his balls," she said into the space. Hoping that that would disgust her. It really should disgust her.

It did not disgust her.

She put the scrubber back, taking a little shower gel and squeezing it into the palm of her hand. Okay, so she would smell like a playboy for a day. It wasn't the end of the world. She started to rub the slick soap over her flesh, ignoring the images of Chase that were trying to intrude.

She was being a crazy person. She had showered at friends' houses before, and never imagined that they were in the shower stall with her.

But ever since last night in the bar, her equilibrium had been off where Chase was concerned. Her control was being sorely tested. She was decidedly unstoked about it.

She shut the water off and got out of the shower, grabbing a towel off the rack and drying her skin with more ferocity than was strictly necessary. Almost as though she was trying to punish her wicked, wicked skin for imagining what it might be like to be touched by her best friend.

But that would be crazy.

Except she felt a little crazy.

She looked around the room. And realized that her stupid friend, who had not wanted her to touch the nice clothing he had bought her, had left her without anything to wear. She couldn't put her sweaty, grease-covered clothes back on. That would negate the entire shower.

She let out an exasperated breath, not entirely certain what she should do.

"Chase?" she called.

She didn't hear anything.

"Chase?" She raised the volume this time.

Still no answer.

"Butthead," she muttered, walking over to the door and tapping the doorknob, trying to decide what her next move was.

She was being ridiculous. Just because she was having an increase of weird, borderline sexual thoughts about him, did not mean he was having them about her. She twisted the knob, undoing the lock as she did, and opened the door a crack. "Chase!"

The door to the bedroom swung open, and Chase walked in, carrying one of those plastic bags fancy dresses were stored in and a pair of shoes.

"I don't have clothes," she hissed through the crack in the door.

"Sorry," he said, looking stricken. At least, she thought he looked stricken.

She opened the door slightly wider, extending her arm outside. "Give them to me."

He crossed the room, walking over to the bathroom door. "You're going to have to open the door wider than that."

She already felt exposed. There was nothing between them. Nothing but some air and the towel she was clutching to her naked body. Well, and most of the door. But she still felt exposed.

Still, he was not going to fit that bag through the crack.

She opened the door slightly wider, then grabbed hold of the bag in his hand and jerked it back through. "I'll get the shoes later," she called through the door.

She dropped the towel and unzipped the bag, staring at the contents with no small amount of horror. There was…underwear inside of it. Underwear that Chase had purchased for her.

Which meant he had somehow managed to look at her breasts and evaluate their size. Not to mention her ass. And ass size.

She grabbed the pair of panties that were attached to a little hanger. Oh, they had no ass. So she supposed the size of hers didn't matter much.

She swallowed hard, taking hold of the soft material and rubbing her thumb over it. He would know exactly what she was wearing beneath the dress. Would know just how little that was.

*He isn't going to think about it. Because he doesn't think about you that way.*

He never had. He never would. And it was a damn good thing. Because where would they be if either of them acted on an attraction between them?

Up shit creek without a paddle or a friendship.

No, thank you. She was never going to touch him. She'd made that decision a long time ago. For a lot of reasons that were as valid today as they had been the very first time he'd ever made her stomach jump when she looked at him.

She was never going to encourage or act on the attraction that she occasionally felt for Chase. But she would take his expertise in sexual politics and use it to her advantage.

Oh, but those panties.

The bra wasn't really any less unsettling. Though at least it wasn't missing large swathes of fabric.

Still, it was very thin. And she had a feeling that a cool ocean breeze would reveal the shape of her nipples to all and sundry.

Then again, maybe it was time all and sundry got

a look at her nipples. Maybe if they had a better view, men would be a little more interested.

She scowled, wrenching the panties off the hanger and dragging them on as quickly as possible, followed closely by the bra. She was overthinking things. She was overthinking all of this. Had been from the moment Chase had walked into the barn. As evidenced by that lapse in the shower.

She had spent years honing her Chase Control. It was just this change in how they were interacting that was screwing with it. She was not letting this get inside her head, and she was not letting hot, unsettled feelings get inside her pants.

She pulled the garment bag away entirely, revealing a tight red dress slightly too reminiscent of what the woman he had been flirting with last night was wearing.

"Clearly you have a type, Chase McCormack," she muttered, beginning to remove the slinky scrap of material from the hanger.

She tugged it up over her hips, having to do a pretty intense wiggle to get it up all the way before zipping it into place. She took a deep breath, turned around. She faced her reflection in the mirror full-on and felt nothing but deflated.

She looked…well, her hair was wet and straggly, and she looked half-drowned. She didn't look curvy or shimmery or delightful.

This was the problem with tight clothes. They only made her more aware of her curve deficit.

Where the blonde last night had filled her dress out admirably, and in all the right places, on Anna this dress kind of looked like a piece of fabric stretched over an ironing board. Not really all that sexy.

She sighed heavily, trying to ignore the sinking feeling in her stomach.

Chase really was going to have to be a miracle worker in order to pull this off.

She didn't really want to show him. Instead, she found the idea of putting the coveralls back on a lot less reprehensible. At least with the coveralls there would still be some mystery. He wouldn't be confronted with just how big a task lay before him.

"Buck up," she said to herself.

So what was one more moment of feeling inadequate? Honestly, in the broad tapestry of her life it would barely register. She was never quite what was expected. She never quite fit. So why'd she expect that she was going to put on a sexy dress and suddenly be transformed into the kind of sex kitten she didn't even want to be?

She gritted her teeth, throwing open the bedroom door and walking out into the room. "I hope you're happy," she said, flinging her arms wide. "You get what you get."

She caught a movement out of the corner of her eye and turned her head, then recoiled in horror. It was even worse out here. Out here, there was a full-length mirror. Out here, she had the chance to see that while her breasts remained stunningly average, her hips and behind had gotten rather wide. Which was easy to ignore when you wore loose attire most days. "I look like the woman symbol on the door of a public restroom."

She looked over at Chase, who had been completely silent upon her entry into the room, and remained so.

She glared at him. He wasn't saying anything. He was only staring. "Well?"

"It's nice," he said.

His voice sounded rough, and kind of thin.

"You're a liar."

"I'm not a liar. Put the shoes on."

"Do you even know what size I wear?"

"You're a size ten, which I know because you complain about how your big feet make it impossible for you to find anything in your size. And you're better off buying men's work boots. So yes, I know."

His words made her feel suddenly exposed. Well, his words in combination with the dress, she imagined. They knew each other a little bit too well. That was the problem. How could you impress a guy when you had spent a healthy amount of time bitching to him about your big feet?

"Fine. I will put on the shoes." He held them up, and her jaw dropped. "I thought you were taking me out to dinner."

"I am."

"Do I have to pay for it by working the pole at the Naughty Mermaid?"

"These are *nice* shoes."

"If you're a five-foot-two-inch Barbie like that chick you were talking to last night. I'm like…an Amazon in comparison."

"You're not an Amazon."

"I will be in those."

"Maybe that would bother some men. But you want a man who knows how to handle a woman. Any guy with half a brain is going to lose his mind checking out your legs. He's not going to care if you're a little taller than he is."

She tried her best to ignore the compliment about her legs. And tried even harder to keep from blushing.

"I care," she muttered, snatching the shoes from his hand and pondering whether or not there was any truth to her words as she did.

She didn't really date. So it was hard to say. But now that she was thinking about it, yeah. She was self-conscious about the fact that with pretty low heels she was eye level with half the men in town.

She finished putting the shoes on and straightened. It was like standing on a glittery pair of stilts. "Are you satisfied?" she asked.

"I guess you could say that." He was regarding her closely, his jaw tense, a muscle in his cheek ticking.

She noticed that he was still a couple of inches taller than her. Even with the shoes. "I guess you still meet the height requirement to be my dinner date."

"I didn't have any doubt."

"I don't know how to walk in these," she said.

"All right. Practice."

"Are you out of your mind? I have to *practice* walking?"

"You said yourself, you don't know how to walk in heels. So, go on. Walk the length of the room."

She felt completely awash in humiliation. She doubted there was another woman on the planet that Chase had ever had to instruct on walking.

"This is ridiculous."

"It's not," he said.

"All of women's fashion is ridiculous," she maintained. "Do you have to learn how to walk when you put on dress shoes? No, you do not. And yet, a full-scale lesson is required for me to go out if I want to wear something that's considered *feminine*."

"Yeah, it's sexist. And a real pain in the ass, I'm sure. It's also hot. Now walk."

She scowled at him, then took her first step, wobbling a bit. "I don't understand why women do this."

She took another step, then another, wobbling a little less each time. But the shoes did force her hips to sway, much more than they normally would. "Do you have any pointers?" she asked.

"I date women in heels, Anna. *I've* never walked in them."

"What happened to helping me be a woman?"

"You'll get the hang of it. It's like… I don't know, water-skiing maybe?"

"How is this like water-skiing?"

"You have to learn how to do it and there's a good likelihood you'll fall on your face?"

"Well, I take it all back," she said, deadpan. "These shoes aren't silly at all." She took another step, then another. "I feel like a newborn baby deer."

"You look a little like one, too."

She snorted. "You really need to up your game, Chase. If you use these lines on all the women you take out, you're bound to start striking out sooner or later."

"I haven't struck out yet."

"Well, you're still young and pretty. Just wait. Just wait until time starts to claim your muscular forearms and chiseled jawline."

"I figure by then maybe I'll have gotten the ranch back to its former glory. At that point women will sleep with me for my money."

She rolled her eyes. "It's nice to have goals."

In her opinion, Chase should have better goals for himself. But then, who was she to talk? Her current goal was to show her brothers that they were idiots and she could too get a date. Hardly a lofty ambition.

"Yes, it is. And right now my goal is for us not to miss our reservation."

"You made a...reservation?"

"I did."

"It's not like it's Valentine's Day or something. The restaurant isn't going to be full."

"Of course it won't be. But I figured if I made a reservation for the two of us, we could start a rumor, too."

"A rumor?"

"Yeah, because Ellie Matthews works at Beaches, and I believe she has been known to *service* your brother Mark."

Anna winced at the terminology. "True."

"I thought the news of our dining experience might make it back to him. Like I said, the more we can make this look organic, the better."

"No one ever need know that our relationship is in fact grown in a lab. And in no way GMO free," she said.

"Exactly."

"I don't have any makeup on." She frowned. "I don't have any makeup. At all."

"Right," he said. "I didn't really think of that."

She reached out and smacked him on the shoulder. "You're supposed to be my coach. You're failing me."

He laughed, dodging her next blow. "You don't need makeup."

She let out an exasperated sigh. "You're just saying that."

"In fairness, you did threaten to castrate me with your car keys earlier."

"I did."

"And you hit me just now," he pointed out.

"It didn't hurt, you baby."

He took a deep breath, and suddenly his expression turned sharp. "Believe me when I tell you you don't need makeup." He reached out, gripping her chin with his thumb and forefinger. His touch was like a branding iron, hot, altering. "As long as you believe it, everyone else will, too. You have to believe in yourself, Anna."

He released his hold on her, straightening. "Now," he said, his tone getting a little bit rougher, "let's go to dinner."

Chase felt like he had been tipped sideways and left walking on the walls from the moment that Anna had emerged from the bathroom at his house wearing that dress. Once she had put on those shoes, the feeling had only gotten worse.

But who knew that underneath those coveralls his best friend looked like that?

She had been eyeing herself critically, and his brain had barely been working at all. Because he didn't see anything to criticize. All he saw was the kind of figure that would make a man willingly submit to car key castration.

She was long and lean, toned from all the physical labor she did. Her breasts were small, but he imagined they would fit in a man's hand nicely. And her hips…well, using the same measurement used for her breasts, they would be about perfect for holding on to while a man…

*Holy hell.* He was losing his mind.

She was Anna. Anna Brown, his best friend in the entire world. The one woman he had never even considered going there with. He didn't want a relationship with the women he slept with. When your only criteria for being with a woman was orgasm, there were a lot of options available to you. For a little bit of satisfaction he could basically seek out any woman in the room.

Sex was easy. Connections were hard.

And so Anna had been placed firmly off-limits from day one. He'd had a vague awareness of her for most of his life. That was how growing up in a small town worked. You went to the same school from the beginning. But they had separate classes, plus at the time he'd been pretty convinced girls had cooties.

But that had changed their first year of high school. He'd ended up in metal shop with the prickly teen and had liked her right away. There weren't very many girls who cursed as much as the boys and had a more comprehensive understanding of the inner workings of engines than the teachers at the school. But Anna did.

She hadn't fit in with any of the girls, and so Chase and Sam had been quick to bring her into their group. Over the years, people had rotated in and out, moved, gone their separate ways. But Chase and Anna had remained close.

In part because he had kept his dick out of the equation.

As they walked up the path toward Beaches, he considered putting his hand on her lower back. Really, he should. Except it was potentially problematic at the moment. Was he this shallow? Stick her in a tight-fitting dress and suddenly he couldn't control himself? It was a sobering realization, but not really all that surprising.

This was what happened when you spent a lot of time practicing no restraint when it came to sex.

He gritted his teeth, lifting his hand for a moment before placing it gently on her back. Because it was what he would do with any other date, so it was what he needed to do with Anna.

She went stiff beneath his touch. "Relax," he said, keeping his voice low. "This is supposed to look like a date, remember?"

"I should have worn a white tank top and a pair of jeans," she said.

"Why?"

"Because this looks… It looks like I'm trying too hard."

"No, it looks like you put on a nice outfit to please me."

She turned to face him, her brow furrowed. "Which is part of the problem. If I had to do this to please you, we both know that I would tell you to please yourself."

He laughed, the moment so classically Anna, so familiar, it was at odds with the other feelings that were buzzing through his blood. With how soft she felt beneath his touch. With just how much she was affecting him in this figure-hugging dress.

"I have no doubt you would."

They walked up the steps that led into the large white restaurant, and he opened the door, holding it for her. She looked at him like he'd just caught fire. He stared her down, and then she looked away from him, walking through the door.

He moved up next to her once they were inside.
"You're going to have to seem a little more at ease with
this change in our relationship."

"You're being weird."

"I'm not being weird. I'm treating you like a lady."

"What have you been treating me like for the past
fifteen years?" she asked.

"A...bro."

She snorted, shaking her head and walking toward
the front of the restaurant where Ellie Matthews was
standing, waiting for guests. "I believe we have a reservation," Anna said.

He let out a long-suffering sigh. "Yes," he con-
firmed. "Under my name."

Ellie's eyebrow shot upward. "Yes. You do."

"Under Chase McCormack and Anna Brown,"
Chase clarified.

"I know," she said.

Ellie needed to work on her people skills. "It was
difficult for me to tell, since you look so surprised,"
Chase said.

"Well, I knew you were reserving the table for the
two of you, but I didn't realize you were...reserving
the table for *the two of you*." She was looking at Anna's
dress, her expression meaningful.

"Well, I was," he said. "Did. So, is the table ready?"

She looked around the half-full dining area. "Yeah,
I'm pretty sure we can seat you now."

Ellie walked them over to one of the tables by a
side window that looked out over the Skokomish River
where it fed into the ocean. The sun was dipping low
over the water, the rays sparkling off the still surface
of the slow-moving river. There were people milling

along the wooden boardwalk that was bordered by docks on one side and storefronts on the other, before being split by the highway and starting again, leading down to the beach.

He looked away from the scenery, back at Anna. They had shared countless meals together, but this was different. Normally, they didn't sit across from each other at a tiny table complete with a freaking candle in the middle. Mood lighting.

"Your server will be with you shortly," Ellie said as she walked away, leaving them there with menus and each other.

"I want a burger," Anna said, not looking at the menu at all.

"You could get something fancier."

"I'll get it with a cheese I can't pronounce."

"I'm getting salmon."

"Am I paying?" she asked, an impish smile playing around the corners of her lips. "Because if so, you better be putting out at the end of this."

Her words were like a punch in the gut. And he did his best to ignore them. He swallowed hard. "No, *I'm* paying."

"I'll pay you back after. You're doing me a favor."

"The favor's mutual. I want to go to the fund-raiser. It's important to me."

"You still aren't buying my dinner."

"I'm not taking your money."

"Then I'm going to overpay for rent on the shop next month," she said, her tone uncompromising.

"Half of that goes to Sam."

"Then he gets half of it. But I'm not going to let you buy my dinner."

"You're being stubborn."

She leaned back in her chair, crossing her arms and treating him to that hard glare of hers. "Yep."

A few moments later the waiter came over, and Anna ordered her hamburger, and the cheeses she wanted, by pointing at the menu.

"Which cheese did you get?" he asked, attempting to move on from their earlier standoff.

"I don't know." She shrugged. "I can't pronounce it."

They made about ten minutes of awkward conversation while they waited for their dinner to come. Which was weird, because conversation was never awkward with Anna. It was that dress. And those shoes. And his penis. That was part of the problem. Because, suddenly, it was actually interested in his best friend.

*No, it is not. A moment of checking her out does not mean that you want to...do anything with her.*

Exactly. It wasn't a big deal. It wasn't anything to get worked up about. Not at all.

When their dinner was placed in front of them, Anna attacked her sweet potato fries, probably using them as a displacement activity.

"Chase?"

Chase looked up and inwardly groaned when he saw Wendy Maxwell headed toward the table. They'd all gone to high school together. And he had, regrettably, slept with Wendy once or twice over the years after drinking too much at Ace's.

She was hot. But what she had in looks had been deducted from her personality. Which didn't matter when you were only having sex, but mattered later when you had to interact in public.

"Hi, Wendy," he said, taking a bite of his salmon.

Anna had gone very still across from him; she wasn't even eating her fries anymore.

"Are you… Are you on a date?" Wendy asked, tilting her head to the side, her expression incredulous.

Wendy wasn't very smart in addition to being not very nice. A really bad combination.

"Yes," he said, "I am."

"With Anna?"

"Yeah," Anna said, looking up. "The person sitting across from him. Like you do on a date."

"I'm just surprised."

He could see color mounting in Anna's cheeks, could see her losing her hold on her temper.

"Are you here by yourself?" Anna asked.

Wendy laughed, the sound like broken crystal being pushed beneath his skin. "No. Of course not. We're having a girls' night out." She eyed Chase. "Of course, that doesn't mean I'm going home with the girls."

Suddenly, Anna was standing, and he was a little bit afraid she was about to deck Wendy. Who deserved it. But he didn't really want to be at the center of a girl fight in the middle of Beaches.

That only worked in fantasies. Less so in real life.

But it wasn't Wendy whom Anna moved toward.

She took two steps, came to a stop in front of Chase and then leaned forward, grabbing hold of the back of his chair and resting her knee next to his thigh. Then she pressed her hand to his cheek and took a deep breath, making determined eye contact with him just before she let her lids flutter closed. Just before she closed the distance between them and kissed him.

# *Chapter 4*

She was kissing Chase McCormack. Beyond that, she had no idea what the flying f-bomb she was doing. If there was another person in the room, she didn't see them. If there was a reason she'd started this, she didn't remember it.

There was nothing. Nothing more than the hot press of Chase's lips against hers. Nothing more than still, leashed power beneath her touch. She could feel his tension, could feel his strength frozen beneath her.

It was...intoxicating. Empowering.

So damn *hot*.

Like she was about to melt the soles of her shoes hot. About to come without his hands ever touching her body hot.

And that was unheard-of for her.

She'd kissed a couple of guys, and slept with one,

and orgasm had never been in the cards. When it came to climaxes, she was her own hero. But damn if Chase wasn't about to be her hero in under thirty seconds, and with nothing more than a little dry lip-to-lip contact.

Except it didn't stay dry.

Suddenly, he reached up, curling his fingers around the back of her head, angling his own and kissing her hard, deep. With tongue.

She whimpered, the leg that was supporting her body melting, only the firm hold he had on her face, and the support of his chair, keeping her from sliding onto the ground.

The slick glide of his tongue against hers was the single sexiest thing she'd ever experienced in her life. And just like that, every little white lie she'd ever told herself about her attraction to Chase was completely and fully revealed.

It wasn't just a momentary response to an attractive man. Not something any red-blooded female would feel. Not just a passing anomaly.

It was real.

It was deep.

She was so screwed.

Way too screwed to care that they were making out in a fancy restaurant in front of people, and that for him it was just a show, but for her it was a whole cataclysmal, near-orgasmic shift happening in the region of her panties.

Seconds had passed, but they felt like minutes. Hours. Whole days' worth of life-changing moments, all crammed into something that probably hadn't actually lasted longer than the blink of an eye.

Then it was over. She was the one who pulled away and she wasn't quite sure how she managed. But she did.

She wasn't breathing right. Her entire body was shaking, and she was sure her face was red. But still, she turned and faced Wendy, or whichever mean girl it was. There were a ton of them in her nonhalcyon high school years and they all blended together. The who wasn't important. Only the what. The *what* being a kiss she'd just given to the hottest guy in town, right in front of someone who didn't think she was good enough. Pretty enough. Girlie enough.

"Yeah," she said, her voice a little less triumphant and a lot more unsteady than she would like, "we're here on a date. And he's going home with me. So I'd suggest you wiggle on over to a different table if you want to score tonight."

Wendy's face was scrunched into a sour expression. "That's okay, honey, if you want my leftovers, you're welcome to them."

Then she flipped her blond hair and walked back to her table, essentially acting out the cliché of every snotty girl in a teen movie.

Which was not so cute when you were thirty and not fifteen.

But, of course, since Wendy was gone, they'd lost the buffer against the aftermath of the kiss, and the terrible awkwardness that was just sitting there, seething, growing.

"Well, I think that started some rumors," Anna said, sitting back down and shoving a fry into her mouth.

"I bet," Chase said, clearing his throat and turning back toward his plate.

"My mouth has never touched your mouth directly

before," she said, then stuffed another fry straight into her mouth, wishing it wasn't too late to stifle those ridiculous words.

He choked on his beer. "Um. No."

"What I mean is, we've shared drinks before. I've taken bites off your sandwiches. Literally sandwiches, not— I mean, whatever. The point is, we've germ-shared before. We just never did it mouth-to-mouth."

"That wasn't CPR, babe."

She made a face, hoping the disgust in her expression would disguise the twist low and deep in her stomach. "Don't call me babe just because I kissed you."

"We're dating, remember?"

"No one is listening to us talk at the table," she insisted.

"You don't know that."

Her heart was thundering hard like a trapped bird in her chest and she didn't know if she could look at him for another minute without either scurrying from the room like a frightened animal or grabbing him and kissing him again.

She didn't like it. She didn't like any of it.

It all felt too real, too raw and too scary. It all came from a place too deep inside her.

So she decided to do what came easiest. Exactly what she did best.

"I expected better," she told him, before taking a bite of her burger.

"What?"

"You're like a legendary stud," she said, after swallowing her food. "The man who every man wants to be and who every woman wants to be with. Blah, blah." She picked up another sweet potato fry.

"It wasn't good for you?" he asked.

"Six point five from the German judge. Who is me, in this scenario." She was a liar. She was a liar and she was a jerk, and she wanted to punch her own face. But the alternative was to show that she was breaking apart inside. That she had been on the verge of the kind of ecstasy she'd only ever imagined, and that she wanted to kiss him forever, not just for thirty seconds. And that was…damaging. It wasn't something she could admit.

"Six point five."

"Sorry." She lifted her shoulder and shoved the fry into her mouth.

They finished the rest of the dinner in awkward silence, which made her mad because things weren't supposed to be awkward between them. They were friends, dammit. She was starting to think this whole thing was a mistake.

She could bring Chase as her plus one to the charity thing without her brothers buying into it. She could lose the bet. The whole town could suspect she'd brought a friend because she was undatable and who even cared?

If playing this game was going to screw with their friendship, it wasn't worth it.

Chase paid the tab—she was going to pay the bastard back whether he wanted her to or not—and then the two of them walked outside. And that was when she realized her truck was back at his place and he was going to have to give her a ride.

That sucked donkey balls. She needed to get some Chase space. And it wasn't going to happen.

She wanted to go home and put on soft pajamas and watch *Seven Brides for Seven Brothers*. She needed a safe, flannel-lined space and the fuzzy comfort of an old movie. A chance to breathe and be vulnerable for a second where no one would see.

She was afraid Chase might have seen already.

They still didn't talk—all the way back out of town and to the McCormack family ranch, they didn't talk.

"My dirty clothes are in your house," she said at last, when they pulled into the driveway. "You can take me to the house first instead of the shop."

"I can wash them with mine," he said.

Her underwear was in there. That was not happening.

"No, I left them folded in the corner of the bathroom. I'd rather come get them. And put my shoes on before I try to drive home actually. How do people drive in these?" She tapped the precarious shoes against the floor of the pickup.

Chase let out a harsh-sounding breath. "Fine," he said. He sounded aggrieved, but he drove on past the shop to the house. He stopped the truck abruptly, throwing it into Park and killing the engine. "Come on in."

Now he was mad at her. Great. It wasn't like he needed her to stroke his ego. He had countless women to do that. He had just one woman who listened to his bullshit and put up with all his nonsense, and in general stood by him no matter what. That was her. He could have endless praise for his bedroom skills from those other women. He only had friendship from *her*. So he could simmer down a little.

She got out of the truck, then wobbled when her foot hit a loose gravel patch. She clung tightly to the door, a very wussy-sounding squeak escaping her lips.

"You okay there, *babe*?" he asked, just to piss her off.

"Yeah, fine. Jerk," she retorted.

"What the hell, Anna?" he asked, his tone hard.

"Oh, come on, you're being weird. You can't pretend you aren't just because you're layering passivity over your aggression." She stalked past him as fast as her shoes would let her, walked up the porch and stood by the door, her arms crossed.

"It's not locked," he said, taking the stairs two at a time.

"Well, I wasn't going to go in without your permission. I have manners."

"Do you?" he asked.

"If I didn't, I probably would have punched you by now." She opened the door and stomped up the stairs, until her heel rolled inward slightly and she stumbled. Then she stopped stomping and started taking a little more consideration for her joints.

She was mad at him. She was mad at herself for being mad at him, because the situation was mostly her fault. And she was mad at him for being mad at her for being mad at him.

Mad, mad, *mad*.

She walked into the bathroom and picked up her stack of clothes, careful not to hold the greasy articles against her dress. The dress that was the cause of so many of tonight's problems.

*It's not the dress. It's the fact that you kissed him and now you can't deal.*

Rationality was starting to creep in and she was nothing if not completely irritated about that. It was forcing her to confront the fact that she was actually the one being a jerk, not him. That she was the one who was overreacting, and his behavior was all a response to the fact that she'd gone full Anna-pine, with quills out ready to defend herself at all costs.

She took a deep breath and sat down on the edge of his bed, trading the high heels for her sneakers, then collecting her things again and walking back down the stairs, her feet tingling and aching as they got used to resting flat once more.

Chase wasn't inside.

She opened the front door and walked out onto the porch.

He was standing there, the porch light shining on him like a beacon. His broad shoulders, trim waist... oh, Lord, his ass. Wrangler butt was a gift from God in her opinion and Chase's was perfect. Something she'd noticed before, but right now it was physically painful to look at him and not close the space between them. To not touch him.

This was bad. This was why she hadn't ever touched him before. Why it would have been best if she never had.

She had needs. Fuzzy-blanket needs. She needed to get home.

She cleared her throat. "I'm ready," she said. "I just... If you could give me a lift down to the shop, that would be nice. So that I'm not cougar food."

He turned slowly, a strange expression on his face. "Yeah, I wouldn't want you to get eaten by any mangy predators."

"I appreciate that."

He headed down the steps and got back into the truck, and she followed, climbing into the cab beside him. He started the engine and maneuvered the truck onto the gravel road that ran through the property.

She rested her elbow on the armrest, staring outside at the inky black shadows of the pine trees, and the white glitter of stars in the velvet-blue sky. It was a clear night, unusual for their little coastal town.

If only her head was as clear as the sky.

It was full. Full of regret and woe. She didn't like that. As soon as Chase pulled up to the shop, she scrambled out, not waiting for him to put the vehicle in Park. She was heading toward her own vehicle when she heard Chase behind her.

"What are you doing?" she asked, turning to face him.

But her words were cut off by what he did next. He took one step toward her, closing the distance between them as he wrapped his arm around her waist and drew her up against his chest. Then, before she could protest, before she could say anything, he was kissing her again.

This was different than the kiss at the restaurant. This was different than…well, than any kiss in the whole history of the world.

His kiss tasted of the familiarity of Chase and the strangeness of his anger. Of heat and lust and rage all rolled into one.

She knew him better than she knew almost anyone. Knew the shape of his face, knew his scent, knew his voice. But his scent surrounding her like this, the feel of his face beneath her hands, the sound of that voice—transformed into a feral, passionate growl as he continued to ravish her—was an unknown. Was something else entirely.

Then, suddenly—just as suddenly as he had initiated it—the kiss was over. He released his hold on her, pushing her back. There was nothing but air between them now. Air and a whole lot of feelings. He was standing there, his hands planted on his lean hips, his chest rising and falling with each labored breath. "Six point five?" he asked, his tone challenging. "That sure as hell was no six point five, Anna Brown, and if you're honest with yourself, you have to admit that."

She sucked in a harsh, unsteady breath, trying to keep the shock from showing on her face. "I don't have to admit any such thing."

"You're a little liar."

"What does it matter?" she asked, scowling.

"How would you like it if I told you that you were only average compared to other women I've kissed?"

"I'd shut your head in the truck door."

"Exactly." He crossed his arms over his broad chest. "So don't think I'm going to let the same insults stand, honey."

"Don't *babe* me," she spat. "Don't *honey* me."

Triumph glittered in his dark eyes. The smugness so certain it was visible even in the moonlight. "Then don't kiss me again."

"You were the one who kissed me!" she shouted, throwing her arms wide.

"*This* time. But you started it. Don't do it again." He turned around, heading back toward his truck. All she could do was stand there and stare as he drove away.

Something had changed tonight. Something inside of her. She didn't think she liked it at all.

## Chapter 5

"Now, I don't want to be insensitive or hurt your feelings, princess, but why are you being such an asshole today?"

Chase looked over at Sam, who was staring at him from his position by the forge. The fire was going hot and they were pounding out iron, doing some repairs on equipment. By hand. Just the way both of them liked to work.

"I'm not," Chase said.

"Right. Look, there's only room for one of us to be a grumpy cuss, and I pretty much have that position filled. So I would appreciate it if you can get your act together."

"Sorry, Sam, are you unable to take what you dish out every day?"

"What's going on with you and Anna?"

Chase bristled at the mention of the woman he'd kissed last night. Then he winced when he remembered the kiss. Well, *remembered* was the wrong word. He'd never forgotten it. But right now he was mentally replaying it, moment by moment. "What did you hear?"

Sam laughed. An honest-to-God laugh. "Do I look like I'm on the gossip chain? I haven't talked to anybody. It's just that I saw her leaving your house last night wearing a red dress and sneakers, and then saw her this morning when she went into the shop. She was pissier than you are."

"Anna is always pissy." Sam treated his statement to a prolonged stare. "It's not a big deal. It's just that her brothers bet her that she couldn't get a date. I figured I would help her out with that."

"How?"

"Well…" he said, hesitating about telling his brother the whole story. Sam wasn't looking to change the business on the ranch. He didn't care about their family legacy. Not like Chase did. But Chase had made promises to tombstones and he wasn't about to break them.

It was one of their main sources of contention. So he wasn't exactly looking forward to having this conversation with his older brother.

But it wasn't like he could hide it forever. He'd just sort of been hoping he could hide it until he'd shown up with investment money.

"That's an awfully long pause," Sam said. "I'm willing to bet that whatever you're about to say, I'm not going to like it."

"You know me well. Anna got invited to go to the big community charity event that the West family hosts every year. Now I want to make sure that we can extend our contract with them. Plus…doing horseshoes and gates isn't cutting it. We can move into doing details on custom homes. To doing art pieces and selling our work across the country, not just locally. To do that we need investors. And the West fund-raiser's a great place to find them. Plus, if I only have to wear a suit once and can speak to everyone in town that might be interested in a single shot? Well, I can't beat that."

"Dammit, Chase, you know I don't want to commit to something like that."

"Right. You want to continue on the way we always have. You want to shoe horses when we can, pound metal when the opportunity presents itself, build gates, or whatever else might need doing, then go off and work on sculptures and things in your spare time. But that's not going to be enough. Less and less is done by hand, and people aren't willing to pay for hand-crafted materials. Machines can build cheaper stuff than we can.

"But the thing is, you can make it look special. You can turn it into something amazing. Like you did with my house. It's the details that make a house expensive. We can have the sort of clients who don't want work off an assembly line. The kind who will pay for one-of-a-kind pieces. From art on down to the handles on their kitchen cabinets. We could get into some serious custom work. Vacation homes are starting to spring up around here, plus people are renovating to make rentals thanks to the tourism increase. But we need some investors if we're really going to get into this."

"You know I hate this. I don't like the idea of charging a ton of money for a…for a gate with an elk on it."

"You're an artist, Sam," he said, watching his

brother wince as he said the words. "I know you hate that. But it's true."

"I hate that, too."

"You're talented."

"I hit metal with a hammer. Sometimes I shape it into something that looks nice. It's not really all that special."

"You do more than that and you know it. It's what people would be willing to pay for. If you would stop being such a nut job about it."

Sam rubbed the back of his neck, his expression shuttered. "You've gotten off topic," he said finally. "I asked you about Anna, not your schemes for exploiting my talents."

"Not really. The two are connected. I want to go to this thing to talk to the Wests. I want to talk about investment opportunities and expanding contracts with other people deemed worthy of an invite. In case you haven't noticed, we weren't on that list."

"Yeah, I get that. But why would the lately not-so-great McCormacks be invited?"

"That's the problem. This place hasn't been what it was for a couple of generations, and when we lost Mom and Dad…well, we were teenagers trying to keep up a whole industry, and now we work *for* these people, not with them. I aim to change that."

"You didn't think about talking to me?" Sam asked.

"Oh, I did. And I decided I didn't want to have to deal with you."

Sam shot him an evil glare. "So you're going as Anna's date. And helping her win her bet."

"Exactly."

"And you took her out last night, and she went back to your place, and now she's mad at you."

Chase held his hands up. "I don't know what you're getting at—"

"Yes, you do." Sam crossed his arms. "Did you bang her?"

Chase recoiled, trying to look horrified at the thought. He didn't *feel* horrified at the thought. Which actually made him feel kind of horrified. "I did not."

"Is that why you're mad? Because you didn't?"

His brother was way too perceptive for a guy who pounded heavy things with other heavy things for a living.

"No," he said. "Anna is my friend. She's just a friend. We had a slight…altercation last night. But it's not that big a deal."

"Big enough that I'm worried with all your stomping around you're eventually going to fling the wrong thing and hit me with molten metal."

"Safety first," Chase said, "always."

"I bet you say that to your dates, too."

"You would, too, if you had any."

Sam flipped Chase the bird in response.

"Just forget about it," Chase said. "Forget about the stuff with the Wests, and let me deal with it. And forget about Anna."

When it came to that last directive, he was going to try to do the same.

Anna was dreading coming face-to-face with Chase again after last night. But she didn't really have a choice. They were still in this thing. Unless she called it off. But that would be tantamount to admitting that what had happened last night *bothered* her. And she didn't want to do that. More, she was almost incapable of doing it. She was pretty sure her pride would wither up and die if she did.

But Chase was coming by her shop again tonight, with some other kind of lesson in mind. Something he'd written down on that stupid legal pad of his. It was ridiculous. All of it was ridiculous.

Herself most of all.

She looked at the clock, gritting her teeth. Chase would be by any moment, and she was no closer to dealing with the feelings, needs and general restlessness that had hit her with the blunt force of a flying wrench than she had been last night.

Then, right on time, the door opened, and in walked Chase. He was still dirty from work today, his face smudged with ash and soot, his shirt sticking to his muscular frame, showing off all those fine muscles underneath. Yeah, that didn't help.

"How was work?" he asked.

"Fine. Just dealing with putting a new cylinder head on a John Deere. You?"

"Working on a gate."

"Sounds…fun," she said, though she didn't really think it sounded like fun at all.

She liked solving the puzzle when it came to working on engines. Liked that she had the ability to get in there and figure things out. To diagnose the situation.

Standing in front of a hot fire forging metal didn't really sound like her kind of thing.

Though she couldn't deny it did pretty fantastic things for Chase's physique.

"Well, you know it would be fine if Sam wasn't such a pain in the ass."

"Sure," she said, feeling slightly cautious. After last night, she felt like dealing with Chase was like approaching a dog who'd bitten you once. Only, in this case he had kissed her, not bitten her, and he wasn't a dog. That was the problem. He was just much too *much* for his own good. Much too much for her own good.

"So," she said, "what's on the lesson plan for tonight?"

"I sort of thought we should talk about…well, talking."

"What do you mean?"

"There are ways that women talk to men they want to date. I thought I might walk you through flirting."

"You're going to show me how to flirt?"

"Somebody has to."

"I can probably figure it out," she said.

"You think?" he asked, crossing his arms over his chest and rocking back on his heels.

His clear skepticism stoked the flames of her temper, which was lurking very close to the surface after last night. That was kind of her default. Don't know how to handle something? Don't know *what* you feel? Get angry at it.

"Come on. Men and women have engaged in horizontal naked kickboxing for millennia. I'm pretty sure flirting is a natural instinct."

"You're a poet, Anna," he said, his tone deadpan.

"No, I'm a tractor mechanic," she said.

"Yeah, and you talk like one, too. If you want to get an actual date, and not just a quick tumble in the back of a guy's truck, you might want to refine your art of conversation a little."

"Who says I'm opposed to a quick rough tumble in the back of some guy's truck?"

"You're not?" he asked, his eyebrows shooting upward.

"Well, in all honesty I would probably prefer my truck, since it's clean. I know where it's been. But why the hell not? I have needs."

He scowled. "Right. Well, keep that kind of talk to yourself."

"Does it make you uncomfortable to hear about my *needs*, Chase?" she asked, not quite sure why she was poking at him. Maybe because she felt so unsettled. She was kind of enjoying the fact that he seemed to be, as well. Really, it wouldn't be fair if after last night he felt nothing at all. If he had been able to one-up her and then walk away as though nothing had happened.

"It doesn't make me uncomfortable. It's just unnecessary information. Now, talking about your needs is probably something you shouldn't do with a guy, either."

"Unless I want him to fulfill those needs."

"You said you wanted to date. You want the kind of date who can go to these functions with you, right?"

"It's moot. You're going with me."

"This time. But be honest, don't you want to be able to go out with guys who belong in places like that?"

"I don't know," she said, feeling uncomfortable.

Truth be told, she wasn't all that comfortable thinking about her needs. Emotional, physical. Frankly, if it went beyond her need for a cheeseburger, she didn't really know how to deal with it. She hadn't dated in years. And she had been fine with that. But the truth of the matter was the only reason Mark and Daniel had managed to get to her when they had made this bet was that she was beginning to feel dissatisfied with her life.

She was starting a new business. She was assuming a new position in the community. She didn't just want to be Anna Brown, the girl from the wrong side of the tracks. She didn't just want to be the tomboy mechanic for the rest of her life. She wanted…more. It had been fine, avoiding relationships all this time, but she was thirty now. She didn't really want to be by herself. She didn't want to be alone forever.

Dear Lord, she was having an existential crisis.

"Fine," she said, "it might be nice to have somebody to date."

Marriage, family—she had no idea how she felt when it came to those things. But a casual relationship… That might be nice. Yes. That might be nice.

Last night, she had gone home and gotten under a blanket and watched an old movie. Sometimes, Chase watched old movies with her, but he did not get under the blanket with her. It would be nice to have a guy to be under the blanket with. Somebody to go home to. Or at least someone to call to come over when she couldn't sleep. Someone she could talk to, make out with. Have sex with.

"Fine," she said. "I will submit to your flirting lessons."

"All the girls submit to me eventually," he said, winking.

Something about that made her stomach twist into a knot. "Talking about too much information…"

"There," he said, "that was almost flirting."

She wrinkled her nose. "Was it?"

"Yes. We had a little bit of back and forth. There was some innuendo."

"I didn't make innuendo on purpose," she said.

"No. That's the best kind. The kind you sort of walk into. It makes you feel a little dangerous. Like you might say the wrong thing. And if you go too far, they might walk away. But if you don't go far enough, they might not know that you want them."

She let out a long, frustrated growl. "Dating is complicated. I hate it. Is it too late for me to become a nun?"

"You would have to convert," he pointed out.

"That sounds like a lot of work, too."

"You can be pleasant, Anna. You're fun to talk to. So that's all you have to do."

"Natural to me is walking up to a hot guy and saying, 'Do you want to bone or what?'" As if she'd ever done that. As if she ever would. It was just...she didn't really know how to go about getting a guy to hook up with her any other way. She was a direct kind of girl. And nothing between men and women seemed direct.

"Fine. Let's try this," he said, grabbing a chair and pulling it up to her workbench before taking a seat.

She took hold of the back of the other folding chair in the space and moved it across from his, positioning herself so that she was across from him.

"What are you drinking?" he asked.

She laughed. "A mai tai." She had never had one of those. She didn't even know what it was.

"Excellent. I'm having whiskey, straight up."

"That sounds like you."

"You don't know what sounds like me. You don't know me."

Suddenly, she got the game. "Right. Stranger," she said, then winced internally, because that sounded a little bit more Mae West in her head, and just kind of silly when it was out of her mouth.

"You here with anyone?"

"I could be?" she said, placing her elbow on the workbench and tilting her head to the side.

"You should try to toss your hair a little bit. I dated this girl Elizabeth who used to do that. It was cute."

"How does touching my hair accomplish anything?" she asked, feeling irritated that he had brought another woman up. Which was silly, because the only reason he was qualified to give her these lessons was that he had dated a metric ton of women.

So getting mad about the thing that was helping her right now was a little ridiculous. But she was pretty sure they had passed ridiculous a couple of days ago.

"I don't know. It's cute. It looks like you're trying to draw my attention to it. Like you want me to notice."

"Which…lets you know that I want you in my pants?"

He frowned. "I guess. I never broke it down like that before. But that stands to reason."

She reached up, sighing as she flicked a strand of her hair as best she could. It was tied up in a loose bun and had fallen partway thanks to the intensity of the day's physical labor. Still, she had a feeling she did not look alluring. She had a feeling she looked like she'd been caught in a wind turbine and spit out the other end.

"Are you new in town?"

"I'm old in town," she said, mentally kicking herself again for being lame on the return volley.

"That works, too," Chase said, not skipping a beat.

Yeah, there was a reason the man had never struck out before.

She started to chew on her lip, trying to think of what to say next.

"Don't chew a hole through it," he said, smiling and reaching across the space, brushing his thumb over the place her teeth had just grazed.

And everything in her stopped dead. His touch ignited her nerve endings, sending a brush fire down her veins and all through her body.

She hadn't been this ridiculous over Chase since she was sixteen years old. Since then, she had mostly learned to manage it.

She pulled away slightly, her chair scraping against the floor. She laughed, a stilted, unnatural sound. "I won't," she said, her voice too loud.

"If you're going to chew on your lip," he said, "don't freak out when the guy calls attention to it or touches you. It looks like you're doing it on purpose, so you should expect a comment."

"Duh," she said, "I was. That was…normal."

She wanted to crawl under the chair.

"There was this girl Miranda that I—"

"Okay." She cut him off, growing more and more impatient with the comparisons. "I'm old in town, what about you?"

"I've been around."

"I bet you have been," she said.

"I'm not sure how I'm supposed to take that," he said, flashing her a lopsided grin.

"Right," she said, "because I don't know what I'm doing."

"Maybe this was a bad idea," he said. "I think you

actually need to feel some chemistry with somebody if flirting's going to work."

His words were sharp, digging into her chest. *You actually had to feel some chemistry* to be able to flirt.

They had chemistry. She had felt it last night. So had he. This was his revenge for the six-point-five comment. At least, she hoped it was. The alternative was that he had really felt nothing when their lips attached. And that seemed…beyond unfair.

She had all this attraction for Chase that she had spent years tamping down, only to have it come roaring to the surface the moment she had begun to pretend there was more going on between them than just friendship. And then she had kissed him. And far from being a disappointment, he had superseded her every fantasy. The jackass. Then he had kissed her, kissed her because he was angry. Kissed her to get revenge. Kissed her in a way that had kept her awake all night long, aching, burning. And now he was saying he didn't have chemistry with her.

"It's just that usually when I'm with a girl it flows a little easier. The bar to the bedroom is a pretty natural extension. And all those little movements kind of lead into the other. The way they touch their hair, tilt their head, lean in for a kiss…"

Oh, that did it.

"The women that I usually hook up with tend to—"

"Right," she said, her tone hard. "I get it. They flip their hair and scrunch their noses and twitch at all the appropriate times. They're like small woodland creatures who only emerge from their burrows to satisfy your every sexual whim."

"Don't get upset. I'm trying to help you."

She snorted. "I know." Just then, she had no idea what devil possessed her. Only that one most assuredly did. And once it had taken hold, she had no desire to cast it back out again.

She was mad. Mad like Chase had been last night. And she was determined to get her own back.

"Elizabeth was good at flipping her hair. Miranda gave you saucy interplay like so." She stood up, taking a step toward him, meeting his dark gaze with her own. "But how did they do this?" She reached down, placing her hand between his thighs and rubbing her palm over the bulge in his jeans.

Oh, sweet Lord, there was more to Chase Mc-Cormack than met the eye.

And she had a whole handful of him.

Her brain was starting to scream. Not words so much as a high-pitched, panicky whine. She had crossed the line. And there was no turning back.

But her brain wasn't running the show. Her body was on fire, her heart pounding so hard she was afraid it was going to rip a hole straight through the wall of her chest and flop out on the ground in front of him. Show him all its contents. Dammit, *she* didn't even want to see that.

But it was her anger that really pushed things forward. Her anger that truly propelled her on.

"And how," she asked, lowering herself slowly, scraping her fingernails across the line of his zipper, before dropping to her knees in front of him, "did they do this?"

## Chapter 6

For one blinding second, Chase thought that he was engaged in some sort of high-definition hallucination.

Because there was no way that Anna had just put her hand…there. There was no way that she was kneeling down in front of him, looking at him like she was a sultry-eyed seductress rather than his best friend, still dirty from the workday, clad in motor-oil-smudged coveralls.

He blinked. Then he shook his head. She was still there. And so was he.

But he was so hard he could probably pound iron with his dick right about now.

He knew what he should do. And just now he had enough sense left in his skull to do it. But he didn't want to. He knew he should. He knew that at the end of this road there was nothing good. Nothing good at all. But he shut all that down. He didn't think of the road ahead.

He just let his brain go blank. He just sat back and watched as she trailed her fingers up the line of his zipper, grabbing hold of his belt buckle and undoing it, her movements clumsy, speaking of an inexperience he didn't want to examine too closely.

He didn't want to examine any of this too closely, but he was powerless to do anything else.

Because everything around the moment went fuzzy as the present sharpened. Almost painfully.

His eyes were drawn to her fingers as she pulled his zipper down, to the short, no-nonsense fingernails, the specks of dirt embedded in her skin. That should… well, he had the vague idea it should turn him off. It didn't. Though he had a feeling that getting a bucket of water thrown on him while he sat in the middle of an iceberg naked wouldn't turn him off at this point. He was too far gone.

He was holding his breath. Every muscle in his body frozen. He couldn't believe that she would do what it appeared she might be doing. She would stop. She had to stop. He needed her to stop. He needed her to never stop. To keep going.

She pressed her palm flat against his ab muscles before pushing her hand down inside his jeans, reaching beneath his underwear and curling her fingers around him. His breath hissed through his teeth, a shudder racking his frame.

She looked up at him, green eyes glittering in the dim shop light. She had a smudge of dirt on her face that somehow only highlighted her sharp cheekbones, somehow emphasized her beauty in a way he hadn't truly noticed it before. Yes, last night in the red dress she had been beautiful, there was no doubt about that. But for some reason, her femininity was highlighted wrapped in these traditionally masculine things. By the backdrop of the mechanic shop, the evidence of a day's hard work on her soft skin.

She tilted her chin up, her expression one of absolute challenge. She was waiting for him to call it off. Waiting for him to push her away. But he wasn't going to. He reached out, forking his fingers through her hair and tightening them, grabbing ahold of the loose bun that sat high on her head. Her eyes widened, her lips going slack. He didn't pull her away. He didn't draw her closer. He just held on tight, keeping his gaze firmly focused on hers. Then he released her. And he waited.

She licked her lips slowly, an action that would have been almost comically obvious coming from nearly anyone else. Not Anna.

Then she squeezed him gently before drawing her hand back. He should be relieved. He was not.

But her next move was not one he anticipated. She grabbed hold of the waistband of his jeans and underwear, pulling them down slowly, exposing him. She let out a shaky, shuddering breath before leaning in and flicking her tongue over the head of his arousal.

"Hell." He wasn't sure at first if he had spoken it out loud, not until he heard it echoing around him. It was like cursing in a church somehow, wrong considering the beauty of the gift he was about to receive.

Still, he couldn't think of anything else as she drew the tip of her tongue all the way down to the base of his shaft before retracing her path. She shifted, and that was when he noticed her hands were shaking. Fair enough, since he was shaking, too.

She parted her lips, taking him into her mouth completely, her lips sliding over him, the wet, slick friction almost too much for him to handle. He didn't know what was wrong with him. If it was the shock of the moment, if it was just that he was this base. Or if there was some kind of sick, perverted part of him that took extra pleasure in the fact that this was wrong. That he should not be letting his best friend touch him like this.

Because he'd had more skilled blow jobs. There was no question about that. This didn't feel good because Anna was an expert in the art of fellatio. Far from it.

Still, his head was about to blow off. And he was about to lose all of his control. So there was something.

Maybe it was just her.

She tilted her head to the side as she took him in deep, giving him a good view of just what she was doing. And just who was doing it. He was so aware of the fact that it was Anna, and that most definitely added a kick of the forbidden. Because he knew this was bad. Knew it was wrong.

And not many things were off-limits to him. Not many things had an illicit quality to them. He had kind of allowed himself to take anything and everything that had ever seemed vaguely sexy to him.

Except for her.

He shoved that thought in the background. He didn't like to think of Anna that way, and in general he didn't.

Sure, in high school, there had been moments. But he was a guy. And he had spent a lot of time with Anna. Alone in her room, alone in his. He had a feeling that half the people who had known them had imagined they were getting it on behind the scenes. Friends with benefits, et cetera. In reality, the only benefit to their friendship had been the fact that they'd been there for each other. They had never been there for each other in this way.

Maybe that's what was wrong with him.

Of course, nothing felt wrong with him right now. Right now, pleasure was crackling close to the surface of his skin and it was shorting out his brain. All he could do was sit back and ride the high. Embrace the sensations that were boiling through his blood. The magic of her lips and tongue combined with a shocking scrape of her teeth against his delicate skin made him buck his hips against her even as he tried to rein himself in.

But he was reaching the end of his control, the end of himself. He reached down, cupping her cheek as she continued to pleasure him, as she continued to drive him wild, urging him closer to the edge of control he hadn't realized he possessed.

He felt like he lived life with the shackles off, but she was pushing him so much further than he'd been before that he knew he'd been lying to himself all this time.

He'd been in chains, and hadn't even realized it.

Maybe because of her. Maybe to keep himself from touching her.

She gripped him, squeezing as she tasted him, pushing him straight over the edge. He held on to her hair, harder than he should, as a wave of pleasure rode up inside of him. And when it crashed he didn't ride it into shore. Oh, hell no. When it crashed it drove him straight down to the bottom of the sea, the impact leaving him spinning, gasping for breath, battered on the rocks.

But dammit all, it was worth it. Right now, it was worth it.

He knew that any moment the feeling would fade and he would be faced with the stark horror of what he'd just done, of what he'd just allowed to happen. But for now, he was foggy, floating in the kind of mist that always blanketed the ocean on cold mornings in Copper Ridge.

And he would cling to it as long as possible.

Oh, dear God. What had she done? This had gone so far beyond the kiss to prove they had chemistry. It had gone so far past the challenge that Chase had thrown down last night. It had gone straight into Crazy Town, next stop You Messed Up the Only Friendship You Hadville.

In combination with the swirling panic that was wrapping its claws around her and pulling her into a spiral was the fuzzy-headed lingering arousal. Her lips felt swollen, her body tingling, adrenaline still making her shake.

She regretted everything. She also regretted nothing.

The contradictions inside her were so extreme she felt like she was going to be pulled in two.

One thing her mind and body were united on was the desire to go hide underneath a blanket. This was definitely the kind of situation that necessitated hiding.

The problem was, she was still on her knees in front of Chase. Maybe she could hide under his chair.

*What are you doing? Why are you falling apart?*

*This isn't a big deal. He has probably literally had a thousand blow jobs.*

This one didn't have to be that big a deal. Sure, it was the first one she had ever given. But he didn't have to know that, either.

If she didn't treat it like a big deal, it wouldn't be a big deal. They could forget anything had ever happened. They could forget that in a moment of total insanity she had allowed her anger to push her over the edge, had allowed her inability to back down from a challenge to bring them to this place. And that was all it was—the fact that she was absolutely unable to deal with that blow to her pride. It was nothing else. It couldn't be anything else.

She rocked back on her heels, planting her hands flat on the dusty ground before rising to her feet. She felt dizzy. She would go ahead and blame that on the speed at which she had stood up.

"I think it's safe to say we have a little bit more chemistry than you thought," she said, clearing her throat and brushing at the dirt on her pants.

He didn't say anything. He just kept sitting there, looking rocked. And he was still exposed. She did her very best to look at the wall behind him. "I can still see your…"

He scrambled into action, standing and tugging his pants into place, doing up his belt as quickly as possible. "I think we're done for the day."

She nodded. "Yeah. Well, *you* are."

She could feel the distance widening between them. It was what she needed, what she wanted, ultimately. But for some reason, even as she forced the breach, she regretted it.

"I don't… What just happened?"

She laughed, crossing her arms and cocking her hip out to the side. "If you have to ask, maybe I didn't do a very good job." The bolder she got, the more she retreated inside. She could feel herself tearing in two, the soft vulnerable part of her scrambling to get behind the brash, bold outward version that would spare her from any embarrassment or pain.

"You're…okay?"

"Why wouldn't I be okay?"

"Because you just…"

She laughed. Hysterically. "Sure. But let's not be ridiculous about it. It isn't like you punched me in the face."

Chase looked stricken. "Of course not. I would never do that."

"I know. I'm just saying, don't act like you punched me in the face when all I did was—"

"There's no need to get descriptive. I was here. I remember."

She snorted. "You should remember." She turned away from him, clenching her hands into fists, hoping he didn't notice that they were shaking. "And I hope you remember it next time you go talking about us not having chemistry."

"Do you *want* us to have chemistry?"

She whirled around. "No. But I have some pride. You were comparing me to all these other women. Well, compare that."

"I…can't."

She planted her hands on her hips. "Damn straight."

"We can't… We can't do this again," he said, shaking his head and walking away.

For some reason, that made her feel awful. For some reason, it hurt. Stabbed like a rusty knife deep in her gut.

"I don't want to do it again. I mean, you're welcome, but I didn't exactly get anything out of it."

He stopped, turning to face her, his expression tense. "I didn't ask you to do anything."

"I'm aware." She shook her head. "I think we're done for tonight."

"Yeah. I already said that."

"Well," she said, feeling furious now, "now I'm saying it."

She was mad at herself. For taking it this far. For being upset, and raw, and wounded over something that she had chosen to do. Over his reaction, which was nothing more than the completely predictable response. He didn't want her. Not really.

And she knew that. This evening's events weren't going to change it. An orgasm on the floor of the shop she rented from him was hardly going to alter the course of fifteen years of friendship.

An orgasm. Oh, dear Lord, what had she done? She really had to get out of here. There was no amount of bravado left in her that would save her from the meltdown that was pending.

"I have to go."

She was gone before he had a chance to protest. He should be glad she was gone. If she had stayed, there was no telling what he might have done. What other stupid bit of nonsense he might have committed.

He had limited brainpower at the moment. All of his blood was still somewhere south of his belt.

He turned, surveying the empty shop. Then, in a fit of rage, he kicked something metal that was just to the right of the chair. And hurt his foot. And probably broke the thing. He had no idea if it was important or not. He hoped it wasn't. Or maybe he hoped it was. She deserved to have some of her tractor shit get broken. What had she been thinking?

He hadn't been able to think. But it was a well-known fact that if a man's dick was in a woman's mouth, he was not doing much problem solving. Which meant Chase was completely absolved of any wrong-doing here.

Completely.

He gritted his teeth, closing his eyes and taking in a sharp breath. He was going to have to figure out how to get a handle on himself between now and the next time he saw Anna. Because there was no way things could continue on like this. There weren't a whole lot of people who stuck around in his world. There had never been a special woman. After the death of his and Sam's parents, relatives had passed through, but none of them had put down roots. And, well, their parents, they might not have chosen to leave, but they were gone all the same. He couldn't afford to lose anyone else. Sam and Anna were basically all he had.

Which meant when it came to Sam's moods and general crankiness, Chase just dealt with it. And when it came to Anna…no more touching. No more… No more of any of that.

For one second, he allowed himself to replay the moment when she had unzipped his pants. When she had leaned forward and tasted him. When that white-hot streak of release had undone him completely.

He blinked. Yeah, he knew what he had been thinking. That it felt good. Amazing. Too good to stop her. But physical pleasure was cheap. A friendship like theirs represented years of investment. One simply wasn't worth sacrificing the other for. And now that he was thinking clearly he realized that. So that meant no more. No more. Never.

Next time he saw her, he was going to make sure she knew that.

## Chapter 7

Anna was beneath three blankets, and she was starting to swelter. If she hadn't been too lazy to sit up and grab hold of her ice-cream container, she might not be quite so sweaty.

The fact that she was something of a cliché of what it meant to be a woman behind closed doors was not lost on her. Blankets, old movies, Ben & Jerry's. But hey, she spent most of the day up to her elbows in engine grease, so she supposed she was entitled to a few stereotypes.

She reached her spoon out from beneath the blankets and scraped the top of the ice cream in the container, gathering up a modest amount.

"Oklahoma!" she sang, humming the rest of the line while taking the bite of marshmallow and chocolate ice cream and sighing as the sugar did its good work.

Full-fat dairy products were the way to happiness. Or at least the best way she knew to stop from obsessing.

Her phone buzzed and she looked down, cringing when she saw Chase's name. She swiped open the lock screen and read the message.

In your driveway. Didn't want to give you a heart attack.

Why are you in my dr—

She didn't get a chance to finish the message before there was a knock on her front door.

She closed her eyes, groaning. She really didn't want to deal with him right now. In fact, he was the last person on earth she wanted to deal with. He was the reason she was currently baking beneath a stack of blankets, seeking solace in the bosom of old movies.

Still, she couldn't ignore him. That would make things weirder. He was still her best friend, even if she had— Well, she wasn't going to think about what she had. If she ignored him, it would only cater to the weirdness. It would make events from earlier today seem more important than they needed to be. They did not need to be treated as though they were important.

Sure, she had never exactly done *that* with a man. Sure, she hadn't even had sexual contact of any kind with a man for the past several years. And sure, she had never had that kind of contact with Chase. But that was no reason to go assigning meaning. People got ribbons and stickers for their first trips to the dentist. They did not get them for giving their first blow job.

She groaned. Then she rolled off the couch, pushing herself into a standing position before she padded through the small living area to the entryway. She jerked the door open, pushing her hair out of her face and trying to look casual.

Too late, she realized that she was wearing her pajamas. Which were perfectly decent, in that they covered every inch of her body. But they were also baggy, fuzzy and covered in porcupines.

All things considered, it just wasn't the most glorious of moments.

"Hello," she said, keeping her body firmly planted in the center of the doorway.

"Hi," he returned. Then he proceeded to study her pajamas.

"Porcupines," she informed him, just for something to say.

"Good choice. Not an obvious one."

"I guess not. Considering they aren't all that cuddly. But neither am I. So maybe it's a more obvious choice than it originally appears."

"Maybe. We'll have to debate animal-patterned pajama philosophy another time."

"I guess. What exactly did you come here to debate if not that?"

He stuffed his hands in his pockets. "Nothing. I just came to…check on you."

"Sound of body and mind."

"I see that. Except you're in your pajamas at seven o'clock."

"I'm preparing for an evening in," she said, planting her hand on her hip. "So pajamas are logical."

"Okay."

She frowned. "I'm fine."

"Can I come in?"

She was frozen for a moment, not quite sure what to say. If she let him come in…well, she didn't feel entirely comfortable with the idea of letting him in. But if she didn't let him in, then she would be admitting that she was uncomfortable letting him in. Which would betray the fact that she actually wasn't really all that okay. She didn't want to do that, either.

No wonder she had avoided sexual contact for so long. It introduced all manner of things that she really didn't want to deal with.

"Sure," she said finally, stepping to the side and allowing him entry.

He just stood there, filling up the entry. She had never really noticed that before. How large he was in the small space of her home. Because he was Chase, and his presence here shouldn't really be remarkable. It was now.

Because things had changed. She had changed them. She had kissed him the other day, and then…well, she had changed things.

"There. You are in," she said, moving away from him and heading back into the living room. She took a seat on the couch, picking up the remote control and muting the TV.

"Movie night?"

"Every night is movie night with enough popcorn and a can-do attitude."

"I admire your dedication. What's on?"

*"Oklahoma!"*

He raised his brows. "You haven't seen that enough times?"

"There is no such thing as seeing a musical too

many times, Chase. Multiple viewings only enhance the experience."

"Do they?"

"Sing-alongs, of course."

"I should have known."

She smiled, putting a blanket back over her lap, thinking of it as a sort of flannel shield. "You should know these things about me. Really, you should know everything about me."

He cleared his throat, and the sudden awkwardness made her think of all the things he didn't know about her. And the things that he did know. It hit her then—of course, right then, as he was standing in front of her— just how revealing what had happened earlier was.

Giving a guy pleasure like that…well, a woman didn't do that unless she wanted him. It said a lot about how she felt. About how she had felt for an awfully long time. No matter that she had tried to quash it, the fact remained that she did feel attraction for him. Which he was obviously now completely aware of.

Silence fell like a boulder between them. Crushing, deadly.

"Anyway," she said, the transition as subtle as a landslide. "Why exactly are you here?"

"I told you."

"Right. Checking on me. I'm just not really sure why."

"You know why," he said, his tone muted.

"You check on every woman you have…encounters with?"

"You know I don't. But you're not every woman I have encounters with."

"Still. I'm an adult woman. I'm neither shocked nor injured."

She was probably both. Yes, she was definitely perilously close to being both.

He shifted, clearly uncomfortable. Which she hated, because they weren't uncomfortable with each other. Ever. Or they hadn't been before. "It would be rude of me not to make sure we aren't...okay."

She patted herself down. "Yes. Okay. Okay?"

"No," he said.

"No? What the hell, man? I said I'm fine. Do we have to stand around talking about it?"

"I think we might. Because I don't think you're fine."

"That's bullshit, McCormack," she said, rising from the couch and clutching her blanket to her chest. "Straight-up bullshit. Like you stepped in a big-ass pile somewhere out there and now you went and dragged it into my house."

"If you were fine, you wouldn't be acting like this."

"I'm sorry, how did you want me to act?"

"Like an adult, maybe?" he said, his dark brows locking together.

"Um, I am acting like an adult, Chase. I'm pretending that a really embarrassing mistake didn't happen, while I crush my regret and uncertainty beneath the weight of my caloric intake for the evening. What part of that isn't acting like an adult?"

"We're friends. This wasn't some random, forgettable hookup."

"It is so forgettable," she said, her voice taking on that brash, loud quality that hurt her own ears. That she was starting to despise. "I've already forgotten it."

"How?"

"It's a penis, Chase, not the Sistine Chapel. My life was hardly going to be changed by the sight of it."

He reached forward, grabbing hold of her arm and drawing her toward him. "Stop," he bit out, his words hard, his expression focused.

"What are you doing?" she asked, some of her bravado slipping.

"Calling you on *your* bullshit, Anna." He lowered his voice, his tone no less deadly. She'd never seen Chase like this. He didn't get like this. Chase was fun, and light. Well, except for last night when he'd kissed her. But even then, he hadn't been quite this serious. "I've known you for fifteen years. I know when your smile is hiding tears, little girl. I know when you're a whole mess of feelings behind that brick wall you put up to keep yourself separate from the world. And I sure as hell know when you aren't fine. So don't stand there and tell me that it didn't change anything, that it didn't mean anything. Even if you gave out BJs every day with lunch—and I know you don't—that would have still mattered because it's *us*. And we don't do that. It changed something, Anna, and don't you dare pretend it didn't."

No. *No.* Her brain was screaming again, but this time she knew for sure what it was saying. It was all denial. She didn't want him to look at her as if he was searching for something, didn't want him to touch her as if it was only the beginning of something more. Didn't want him to see her. To see how scared she was. To see how unnerved and affected she was. To see how very, very not brave she was beneath the shield she held up to keep the world out.

*He already knows it's a shield. And you're already screwed ten ways, because you can't hide from him and you never could.*

He'd let her believe she could. And now he'd changed his mind. For some reason it was all over now. Well, she knew why. It had started with a dress and high heels and ended with an orgasm in her shop. He was right. It had changed things.

And she had a terrible, horrible feeling more was going to change before they could go back to normal.

If they ever could.

"Well," she said, hearing her voice falter. Pretending she didn't. "I don't think anything needs to change."

"Enough," he said, his tone fierce.

Then, before she knew what was happening, he'd claimed her lips again in a kiss that ground every other kiss that had come before it into dust, before letting them blow away on the wind.

This was angry. Intense. Hot and hard. And it was happening in her house, in spite of the fact that she was holding a blanket and *Oklahoma!* was on mute in the background. It was her safe space, with her safe friend, and it was being wholly, utterly invaded.

By him.

It was confronting and uncomfortable and scary as hell. So she responded the only way she could. She got mad, too.

She grabbed hold of the front of his shirt, clinging to him tightly as she kissed him back. As she forced her tongue between his lips, claiming him before he could stake his claim on her.

She shifted, scraping her teeth lightly over his bottom lip before biting down. Hard.

He growled, wrapping his arms around her waist. She never felt small. Ever. She was a tall girl with a broad frame, but she was engulfed by Chase right now. His scent, his strength. He was all hard muscle against her, his heart thundering beneath her hands, which were pinned between their bodies.

She didn't know what was happening, except that right now, kissing him might be safer than trying to talk to him.

It certainly felt better.

It let her be angry. Let her push back without saying anything. And more than that…he was an amazing kisser. He had taken her from zero to almost-there with one touch of his lips against hers.

He slid his hand down her back, cupping her butt and bringing her up even harder against him so she could feel him. All of him. And just how aroused he was.

He wanted her. Chase wanted her. Yes, he was pissed. Yes, he was…trying to prove a point with his tongue or whatever. But he couldn't fake a hard-on like that.

She was angry, but it was fading. Being blotted out by the arousal that was crackling in her veins like fireworks.

Suddenly, she found herself being lifted off the ground, before she was set down on the couch, Chase coming down over her, his expression hard, his eyes sharp as he looked down at her.

He pressed his hand over her stomach, pushing the hem of her shirt upward.

She should stop him. She didn't.

She watched as his strong, masculine hand pushed

her shirt out of the way, revealing a wedge of skin. The contrast alone was enough to drive her crazy. Man, woman. Innocuous porcupine pajamas and sex.

Above all else, above anything else, there was Chase. Everything he made her feel. All of the things she had spent years trying *not* to feel. Years running from.

She couldn't run. Not now. Not only did she lack the strength, she lacked the desire. Because more than safety, more than sanity, she wanted him. Wanted him naked, over her, under her, *in* her.

He gripped the hem of her top and wrenched it over her head, the movement sudden, swift. As though he had reached the end of his patience and had no reserve to draw upon. That left her in nothing more than those ridiculous baggy pajama pants, resting low on her hips. She didn't have anything sexier underneath them, either.

But Chase didn't look at all disappointed. He didn't look away, either. Didn't have a faraway expression on his face. She wasn't sure why, but she had half expected to look up at him and be able to clearly identify that he was somewhere else in his mind, with someone else. But he was looking at her with a sharp focus, a kind of single-mindedness that no man, no *one*, had ever looked at her with before.

He knew. He knew who she was. And he was still hot for her. Still hard for her.

"You are so hot," he said, pressing his hand flat to her stomach and drawing it down slowly, his finger-tips teasing the sensitive skin beneath the waistband. "And you don't even know it, do you?"

Part of her wanted to protest, wanted to fight back, because that was what she did. Instead, everything inside of her just kind of went limp. Melted into a puddle. "N-no."

"You should know," he said, his voice low, husky. A shot of whiskey that skated along her nerves, warming her, sending a kick of heat and adrenaline firing through her blood. "You should know how damn sexy you are. You're the kind of woman who could make a man lose his mind."

"I could?"

He laughed, but it wasn't full of humor. It sounded tortured. "I'm exhibit A."

He shifted his hips forward, his hard length pressing up against that very aroused part of her that wanted more of him. Needed more of him. She gasped. "Soon," he said, the promise in his words settling a heavy weight in her stomach. Anticipation, terror. Need.

He continued to tease her, his fingertips resting just above the line of her panties, before he began to trail his hand back upward. He rested his palm over her chest, reaching up and tracing her lower lip with his thumb.

She darted her tongue out, sliding the tip of it over his skin, tasting salt, tasting Chase. A flavor that was becoming familiar.

Then she angled her head, taking his thumb into her mouth and sucking hard. His hips arched forward hard, his cock making firm contact, sending a shower of sparks through her body as he did.

"You're going to be the death of me," he said, every word raw, frayed.

"I might say the same about you," she said, her voice thick, unrecognizable. She didn't know who she was right now. This creature who was a complete and total slave to sexual sensation. Who was so lost in it, she could feel nothing else. No sense of self-preservation, no fear kicking into gear and letting her know that she needed to put her walls up. That she needed to go on the defense.

She was reduced. She had none of that. And she didn't even care.

"You're a miracle," he said, tracing the line of her collarbone with the tip of his tongue. "A damn *miracle*, do you know that?"

"What?"

"The other day I told you you didn't look like a miracle. I was a fool. And I was wrong. Every inch of you is a miracle, Anna Brown."

Those words were like being submerged in warm water, feeling it flow over every inch of her, a kind of deep, soul-satisfying comfort that she really, really didn't want. Or rather, she didn't *want* to want it. But she did, bad enough that she couldn't resist.

But it was all a little too heavy. All a little too much. Still, she didn't have the strength to turn him away.

"Kiss me."

She said that instead of *get the hell out of my house*, and instead of *we can't do this*, because it was all she had strength for. Because she needed that kiss. And maybe, just maybe, if they didn't talk, she could make it through.

Chase—gentleman that he was—obliged her.

He angled his head, reaching up to cup her breast as he did, his mouth crashing down on hers just as his palm skimmed her nipple. She gasped, arching up against him, the combination of sensations almost too much to handle.

Yeah, she did not remember sex being like this.

Granted, it had been a million years, but she would have remembered if it had come anywhere close to this. And her conclusion most certainly wouldn't have been that it was vaguely boring and a little bit gross. Not if it had even been in the same ballpark as what she was feeling now.

There was no point in comparing. There was just flat out no comparison.

He kissed her, long, deep and hard; he kissed her until she couldn't breathe. Until she thought she was going to die for wanting more. He kissed her until she was dizzy. And when he abandoned her mouth, she nearly wept. Until he lowered his head and skimmed his tongue over one hardened bud, until he drew it between his lips and sucked hard, before scraping her sensitized flesh with his teeth.

She arched against him, desperate for more. Desperate for satisfaction. Satisfaction he seemed intent on withholding.

"I'm so close," she said, panting. "Just do it now." Then it would be over. Then she would have what she needed, and the howling, yawning ache inside of her would be satisfied.

"No," he said, his tone authoritative.

"What do you mean no?"

"Not yet. You're not allowed to come yet, Anna. I'm not done."

His words, the calm, quiet command, made everything inside of her go still. She wanted to fight him. Wanted to rail against that cruel denial of her needs, but she couldn't.

Not when this part of him was so compelling. Not

when she wanted so badly to see where complying would lead.

"We're not done," he said, tracing her nipple with the tip of his tongue, "until I say we are." He lifted his head so that their eyes met, the prolonged contact touching something deep inside of her. Something that surpassed the physical.

He kissed her again, and as he did, he pulled his T-shirt over his head, exposing his incredible body to her.

Her mouth dried, and other parts of her got wet. Very, very wet.

"Oh, sweet Lord," she said, pressing her hand to his chest and drawing her fingertips down over his muscles, his chest hair tickling her skin as she did.

It was a surreal moment. So strange and fascinating. To touch her best friend like this. To see his body this way, to know that—right now—it wasn't off-limits to her. To know that she could lean forward and kiss that beautiful, perfect dip just next to his hip bone. Suddenly, she was seized with the desire to do just that. And she didn't have to fight it.

She pushed against him, bringing herself into a sitting position, lowering her head and pressing her lips to his heated skin.

"Oh, no, you don't," he said, his voice rough. He took hold of her wrist, drawing her up so that she was on her knees, eye to eye with him on the couch. "We're not finishing it like that," he said.

"Damn straight we aren't," she said. "But that doesn't mean I didn't want to get a little taste."

"You give way too much credit to my self-control, honey."

"You give too much credit to mine. I've never…"
She stared at his chest instead of finishing her sentence.
"It's like walking into a candy store and being told I can
have whatever I want. Restraint is not on the menu."

"Good," he said, leaning in, kissing her, nipping her
lower lip. "Restraint isn't what I want."

He wrapped his arm around her, drawing her up
against him, her bare breasts pressing against his hard
chest, the hair there abrading her nipples in the most
fantastic, delicious way.

And then he was kissing her again, slow and deep
as his hand trailed down beneath the waistband of her
pants, cupping her ass, squeezing her tight. He pushed
her pants down over her hips, taking her panties with
them, leaving her completely naked in front of him.

He stood up, taking his time looking at her as he
put his hands on his belt buckle.

Nerves, excitement, spread through her. She didn't
know where to look. At the harsh, hungry look on his
face, at the beautiful lines of muscle on his perfectly
sculpted torso. At the clear and aggressive arousal visible through his jeans.

So she looked at all of him. Every last bit. And she
didn't have time to feel embarrassed that she was sitting there naked as the day she was born, totally exposed to him for the first time.

She was too fascinated by him in this moment. Too
fascinated to do anything but stare at him.

This was Chase McCormack. The man that women
lost their minds—and their dignity—over on a regular
basis. This was Chase McCormack, the sex god who
could—and often did—have any woman he pleased.

She had known Chase McCormack, loyal friend and

confidant, for a very long time. But she realized that up until now, she had never met *this* Chase McCormack. It was a strange, dizzying realization. Exhilarating.

And she was suddenly seized by the feeling that right now, he was hers. All hers. Because who else knew both sides of him? Did anyone?

She was about to.

"Get your pants off, McCormack," she said, impatience overriding common sense.

"You don't get to make demands here, Anna," he said.

"I just did."

"You want to try giving orders? You have to show me you can follow them." His eyes darkened, and her heart hammered harder, faster. "Spread your legs," he said, his words hard and uncompromising.

She swallowed. There was that embarrassment that she had just been so proud she had bypassed. But this was suddenly way outside her realm of experience. It was one thing to sit there in front of him naked. It was quite another to deliberately expose herself the way he was asking her to. She didn't move. She sat there, frozen.

"Spread your legs for me," he repeated, his voice heavy with that soft, commanding tone. "Or I put my clothes on and leave."

"You wouldn't," she said.

"You don't know what I'm capable of."

That was true. In this scenario, she really didn't know him. He was a stranger, except he wasn't.

Actually, if he had been a stranger, all of this would've been a lot easier. She could have spread her legs and she wouldn't have worried about how she looked. Wouldn't have worried about the consequences. If a stranger saw her do something like that, was somehow unsatisfied and then walked away, well, what did it matter? But this was Chase. And it mattered. It mattered so very much.

His hands paused on his belt buckle. "I'm warning you, Anna. You better do as you're told."

For some reason, that did not make her want to punch him. For some reason, she found herself sitting back on the couch, obeying his command, opening herself to him, as adrenaline skittered through her system.

"Good girl," he said, continuing his movements, pushing his jeans and underwear down his legs and exposing his entire body to her for the first time. And then, it didn't matter so much that she was sitting there with her thighs open for him. Because now she had all of him to look at.

The light in his eyes was intense, hungry, and he kept them trained on her as he reached down and squeezed himself hard. His jaw was tense, the only real sign of just how frayed his control was.

"Beautiful," he said, stroking himself slowly, leisurely, as he continued to gaze at her.

"Are you just going to look? Or are you going to touch?" She wasn't entirely comfortable with this. With him just staring. With this aching silence between them, and this deep, overwhelming connection that she felt.

There were no barriers left. There was no way to hide. She was vulnerable, in every way. And normally she hated it. She kind of hated it now. But that vulnerability was wrapped in arousal, in a sharp, desperate need unlike anything she had ever known. And so it was impossible to try to put distance between them, impossible to try to run away.

"I'm going to do a lot more than look," he said, dropping down to his knees, "and I'm going to do a hell of a lot more than touch." He reached out, sliding his hands around to her ass, drawing her forward, bringing her up toward his mouth.

"Chase," she said, the short, shocked protest about the only thing she managed before the slick heat of his tongue assaulted that sensitive bundle of nerves at the apex of her thighs. "You don't have to…"

He lifted his head, his dark eyes meeting her. "Oh, I know I don't have to. But you got to taste me, and I think turnabout is fair play."

"But that wasn't…"

"What?"

"It's just that men…"

"Expect a lot more than they give. At least some of them. Anyway, as much as I liked what you did for me—and don't get me wrong, I liked it a lot—you have no idea how much pleasure this gives me."

"How?"

He leaned in, resting his cheek on her thigh. "The smell of you." He leaned closer, drawing his tongue through her slick folds. "The taste of you," he said. "You."

And then she couldn't talk anymore. He buried his face between her legs, his tongue and fingers working black magic on her body, pushing her harder, higher, faster than she had imagined possible. Yeah, making out with Chase had been enough to nearly give her an orgasm. This was pushing her somewhere else entirely.

In her world, orgasm had always been a solo project. Surrendering the power to someone else, having her own pleasure not only in someone else's hands but in his complete and utter control, was something she had never even thought possible for her. But Chase was proving her wrong.

He slipped a finger deep inside of her as he continued to torture her with his wicked mouth, then a second, working them in and out of her slick channel while he teased her with the tip of his tongue.

A ball of tension grew in her stomach, expanded until she couldn't breathe. "It's too much," she gasped.

"Obviously it's not enough yet," he said, pushing her harder, higher.

And when the wave broke over her, she thought she was done for. Thought it was going to drag her straight out to sea and leave her to die. She couldn't catch her breath as pleasure assaulted her, going on and on, pounding through her like a merciless tide, battering her against the rocks, leaving her bruised, breathless.

And when it was over, Chase was looming over her, a condom in his hand.

She felt like a creature without its shell. Sensitive, completely unprotected. She wanted to hide from him, hide from this. But she couldn't. How could she? The simple truth was, they still weren't done. They had gone only part of the way. And if they didn't finish this, she would always wonder. He would, too.

She imagined that—whether or not he admitted it— was why he had come here tonight in the first place.

They had opened the lid on Pandora's box. And

they couldn't close it until they had examined every last dirty, filthy sin inside of it.

Even though she thought it might kill her, she knew that they couldn't stop now.

He tore open the condom, positioning the protection over the blunt head of his arousal, rolling it down slowly.

She was transfixed. The sight of his own hand on his shaft so erotic she could hardly stand it.

She would pay good money to watch him shower, to watch his hands slide over all those gorgeous muscles. To watch him take himself in hand and lead himself to completion.

Oh, yeah. That was now her number one fantasy. Which was a problem, because it was a fantasy that would never be fulfilled.

*Don't think about that now. Don't think about it ever.*

He leaned in, kissing her, guiding her so that she was lying down on the couch, then he positioned himself between her legs, testing the entrance to her body before thrusting forward and filling her completely.

She closed her eyes tight, unable to handle the feeling of being invaded by him, both in body and in her soul.

"Look at me," he said.

And once more, she was completely helpless to do anything other than obey.

She opened her eyes, her gaze meeting his, touching her down deep, where his hands never could.

And then he kissed her, soft, gentle. That kind of tenderness that had been missing from her life for so long. The kind that she had always been too embar-

rassed to ask for from anyone. Too embarrassed to
show that she needed. That she desperately craved.

But Chase knew. Because he was Chase. He just
knew.

He flexed his hips again, his pelvis butting up
against her, sending a shower of sparks through her
body. There was no way she was ready to come again.
Except he kept moving, creating new sensations inside
of her, deeper than what had come before.

It shouldn't be possible for her to have another orgasm now. Not after the first one had stripped her so
completely. But apparently tonight, nothing was impossible.

There was something different about this. About the
two of them, working toward pleasure together. This
wasn't just her giving it out to him, or him reciprocat-
ing. This was something they were sharing.

She focused on pieces of him. The intensity in his
eyes. The way the tendons in his neck stood out, evidence of the control he was exerting. She looked at
his hand, up by her head, grabbing hold of one of the
blankets she had been using, clinging tightly to it, as
though it were his lifeline.

She looked down at his throat, at the pulse beating there.

All these close, intimate snapshots of this man that
she knew better than anyone else.

Her chest felt heavy, swollen, and then it began to
expand. She was convinced that she was going to break
apart. All of these feelings, all of this pleasure. It was
just too much. She couldn't handle it.

"Please," she begged. "Please."

He released his grip on the blanket to grasp her

hips, holding her steady as he pounded harder into her, as he pounded them both toward release. Toward salvation. It was too much. It needed to end. It was all she could think. She was begging him inside. *End it, Chase. Please, end it.*

Orgasm latched on to her throat like a wild beast, gripping her hard, violently, shaking her, pleasure exploding over her. Ugly. Completely and totally beyond control.

And then Chase let out a hoarse cry, freezing above her as he thrust inside her one last time, shivering, shaking as his own release took hold.

They were captive to it together. Powerless to do anything but wait until the savage beast was finished having its way. Until it was ready to move on.

And when it was over, only the two of them were left.

Just the two of them. Chase and Anna. No clothes, no shields.

She remembered the real reason she hadn't had sex since that first time. It had nothing to do with how good or bad it had felt. Nothing to do with what a jerk she'd been after.

It had been this. This feeling of being unable to hide. But with the other guy, it had been easy to regroup. Easy to pretend she felt nothing.

She couldn't do that with Chase. She was defenseless.

And for the first time in longer than she could remember, a tear slid down her cheek.

# Chapter 8

He couldn't swear creatively enough. He had just screwed his best friend's brains out on a couch in her living room. On top of what might be the world's friendliest, most non-sexual-looking blanket. With a Rodgers and Hammerstein musical on the TV in the background.

And then she had started crying. She had started crying, and she had wiggled out from beneath him and gone into the bathroom. Leaving him alone.

He had been sitting there by himself for a full thirty seconds attempting to reconcile all of these things.

And then he sprang into action.

He got up—still bare-ass naked—and walked down the hall. "Anna!" He didn't hear anything. And so he pounded on the bathroom door. "Anna!"

"I'm in the bathroom, dumbass!" came the terse, watery reply.

"I know. That's why I'm knocking on the bathroom door."

"Go away."

"No. I'm not going to go away. You need to talk to me."

"I don't want to talk."

"Anna, dammit, did I hurt you?"

He got nothing in return but silence. Then he heard the lock rattle, and the door opened a crack. One green eye looked up at him, accusing. "No."

"Why are you hiding?" He studied the eye more closely. It was red-rimmed. Definitely still weeping a little bit.

"I don't know," she said.

"Well…you had me convinced that I… Anna, it happened really fast."

"Not *that* fast. Believe me, I've had faster."

"You wanted all of that…? I mean…"

She laughed. Actually laughed, pushing the door open a little bit wider. "After my emphatic… After all the *yes-ing*… You can honestly ask whether or not I wanted it?"

"I have a lot of sex," he said. "I don't see any point in beating around the bush there. And women have had a lot of reactions to the sex. But I can honestly say none of them have ever run away crying. So, yeah, I'm feeling a little bit shaky right now."

"You're shaky? I'm the one that's crying."

"And if I was alone in this…if I pushed you further than you wanted to go… I'm going to have to ask Sam to fire up the forge and prepare you a red-hot poker so you can have your way with me in an entirely different manner."

"I wanted it, Chase." Her tone was muted.

"Then why are you crying?"

"I'm not very experienced," she said.

"Well, I mean, I know you don't really hook up."

"I've had sex once. One other time."

He was stunned. Stunned enough that he was pretty sure Anna could have put her index finger on his chest, given a light push and knocked him flat on his ass. "Once."

"Sure. You remember Corbin. And that whole fiasco. Where I kind of made fun of his…lack of…attributes and staying power in the hall at school. And…basically ensured that no guy would ever touch me ever again."

"Right." He remembered that.

"Well, I didn't really get what the fuss was about."

"But you… I mean, you've had…"

"Orgasms? Yes. Almost every day of my life. Because I am industrious and red-blooded and self-sufficient."

He cleared his throat, trying to ignore the shot of heat that image sent straight through his blood. Anna. Touching herself.

What the hell was happening to him? Well, there was nothing happening. It had damn well *happened*. On the couch in Anna's living room.

He could never look at her again without seeing her there, obeying his orders. Spreading her thighs for him so that he could get a good look at her. Yeah, he could never unsee that. Wasn't sure if he wanted to. But where the hell did he go from here? Where did they go?

There were a lot of women he could have sex with, worry-free. Anna wasn't one of them. She was a rare, precious thing in his life. Someone who knew him.

Who knew all about how affected he and Sam had been by the loss of their parents.

Someone he never had to explain it to because she'd been there.

He didn't like explaining all that. So the solution was keep the friends that were there when it happened, and make sure everyone else was temporary.

Which meant Anna couldn't be temporary. She was part of him. Part of his life. A load-bearing wall on the structure that was Chase McCormack. Remove her, and he would crumble.

That was why she had always stayed a friend. Why he had never done anything like this with her before. It wasn't because of her coveralls, or her don't-step-on-the-grass demeanor. Or even because she'd neatly neutered the reputation of the guy she'd slept with in high school.

It was because he needed her friendship, not her body.

But the problem was now he knew what she looked like naked.

He couldn't get that image out of his head. And he didn't even want to.

Same with the image of all her self-administered, industrious climaxes.

Damn his dirty mind.

"Okay," he said, taking a step away from the door. "Why don't you come out?"

"I'm naked."

"So am I."

She looked down. "So you are."

"We need to talk."

"Isn't it women who are supposed to require conversation after basic things like sex?"

"I don't know. Because I never stick around long enough to find out. But this is different. This is you and me, Anna, and I will be damned if I let things get messed up over a couple of orgasms."

She chewed her lower lip. She looked...well, she looked young. And she didn't look too tough. It made him ache. "They were pretty good ones."

"Are you all right?"

"I'm fine. It's just that all of this is a little bit weird. And I'm not really experienced enough to pretend that it isn't."

"Right." The whole thing about her having been with only one guy kind of freaked him out. Made him feel like he was responsible for some things. Big things, like what she would think of sex from this day forward. And then there was the bone-deep possessiveness. That he was the first one in all this time... He should hate it. It should scare him. It should not make him feel...triumph.

He was triumphant, dammit. "Why haven't you slept with anyone else?"

She lifted a shoulder. "I told you. I didn't really think my first experience was that great."

"So you just never..."

"I'm also emotionally dysfunctional, in case you hadn't noticed."

A shocked laugh escaped his lips. "Right. Same goes."

"I don't know. Sex kind of weirds me out. It's a lot of closeness."

"It doesn't have to be," he pointed out. It felt like a

weird thing to say, though, because what they'd done just now had been the epitome of closeness.

"It just all feels…raw. And…it was good. But I think that's kind of why it bothered me."

"I don't want it to bother you."

"Well, the other thing is it was *you*. You and me, like you said. We don't do things like this. We hang out, we drink beer. We don't screw."

"Turns out we're pretty compatible when it comes to the screwing." He wasn't entirely sure this was the time to make light of what had just happened. But he was at sea here. So he had to figure out some way to talk to her. He figured he would make his best effort to treat her like he always did.

"Yeah," she said, finally pushing her way out of the bathroom. "But I'm not really sure there's much we can do with that."

He felt like he was losing his grip on something, something essential, important. Like he was on a rope precariously strung across the canyon, trying to hang on and not fall to his doom. Not fall to *their* doom, since she was right there with him.

What she was saying should feel like safety. It didn't. It felt like the bottom of the damn canyon.

"I don't know if that's the way to handle it."

"You don't?" she asked, blinking.

Apparently. He hadn't thought that statement through before it had come out of his mouth. "Yeah. Look, you kissed me yesterday. You gave me…oral pleasure earlier. And now we've had sex. Obviously, this isn't going away. Obviously, there's some attraction between us that we've never really acknowledged before."

"Or," she said, "someone cast a spell on us. Yeah, we drank some kind of sex potion. Makes you horny for twenty-four hours and then goes away."

"Sex potion?"

"It's either that or years of repressed lust, Chase. Pick whichever one makes you most comfortable."

"I would go with sex potion if I thought such a thing existed." He took a deep breath. "You know there's a lot of people that think men and women can't just be friends. And I've always thought that was stupid. Maybe this is why. Maybe it's because eventually, something happens. Eventually, the connection can't just be platonic. Not when you've spent so long in each other's company. Not when you're both reasonably attractive and single."

She snorted. "*Reasonably* attractive. What happened to me being a *damn miracle*?"

"I was referring to myself when I·said reasonably. I'd hate to sound egotistical."

"Honestly, Chase, after thirty years of accomplished egotism, why worry about it now?"

He looked down at her. She was stark naked, standing in front of him, and he felt like he was in front of the pastry display case at Pie in the Sky. He wanted to sample everything, and he didn't know where to start.

But he couldn't do anything about that now. He was trying to make amends. Dropping to his knees in front of her and burying his face between her legs probably wouldn't help with that.

He could feel his dick starting to wake up again. And since he was naked he might as well just go ahead and shout his intentions at her, because he wouldn't be able to hide them.

He couldn't look at her and not get hard, though. A new development in their relationship. But then, so was standing in front of each other without clothes.

"You're beautiful," he said, unable to help himself.

She wasn't as curvy as the women he usually gravitated toward. Her curves were restrained, her waist slim, with no dramatic sweep inward, just a slow build down to those wide, gorgeous hips that he now had fantasies about grabbing hold of while he pumped into her from behind. Her breasts were small but perfection in his mind. More would just be more.

He couldn't really imagine how he had ever looked at her face and found it plain. He had to kick his own ass mentally for that. He had been blind. Someone with unrefined, cheap taste. Who thought that if you stuck rhinestones and glitter on something, that meant it was prettier. But that wasn't Anna. She was simple, refined beauty. Something that only a connoisseur might appreciate. She was like a sunset over the ocean in comparison to a gaudy ballroom chandelier. Both had their strong points. But one was real, deep. Priceless instead of expensive.

That was Anna.

Something about those thoughts made a tightening sensation start in his gut and work its way up to his chest.

"Maybe what happened was just inevitable," he said, looking at her again.

"I can't really disprove that," she said, shifting uncomfortably. "You know, since it happened. I really need to put my clothes on."

"Do you have to?"

She frowned. "Yes. And you do, too. Because if we don't…"

"We'll have sex again."

The words stood between them, stark and far too true for either of their liking.

"Probably not," she said, sounding wholly unconvinced.

"Definitely yes."

She sighed heavily. "Chase, you can have sex with anyone you want. I'm definitely hard up. If you keep walking around flashing that thing, I'm probably going to hop on for a ride, I'll just be honest with you. But I understand if I'm not half as irresistible to you as you are to me."

Anger roared through him, suddenly, swiftly. And just like earlier, when she'd thrown her walls up and tried to drive a wedge between them, he found himself moving toward her. Moving to break through. He growled, backing her up against the wall, almost sighing in relief when his hardening cock met up with her soft skin, when her small breasts pressed against his chest. He grabbed hold of her hands, drawing them together and lifting them up over her head. "Let's get one thing straight, Anna," he said. "You are irresistible to me. If you weren't irresistible to me, I would still be at home. I never would have come here. I never would have kissed you. I never would have touched you. Don't you dare put yourself down. If this is because of your brothers, because of your dad…"

She closed her eyes, looking away from him. "Don't. It's not that."

"Then what is it? Why don't you think you can have this?"

"There's nothing to have. It's just sex. You mean the world to me. And just because I'm…suddenly unable to handle my hormones, I'm not going to compromise our friendship."

"It doesn't have to compromise it," he said, lowering his voice.

"What are you suggesting? We can't have a relationship with each other. We don't have those kinds of feelings for each other. A relationship is more than sex. It's romance and all kinds of stuff that I'm not even sure I want."

"I don't want it, either," he said. "But we're going to see each other. Pretty much every day. Not just because of the stupid bet. Not just because of the charity event. I'd call all that off right now if I thought it was going to ruin our friendship. But the horse has left the stable, Anna, well and truly. It's not going back in." He rolled his hips forward, and she gasped. "See what I mean? And if you were resistible? Then sure, I would tell you that we could just be done. We could pretend it didn't happen. But you're not. So I can't."

She opened her eyes again, looking up at him. "Then what are we doing?"

"You've heard of friends with benefits. Why can't we do that? I mean, I would never have set out to have that relationship. Because I don't think it's very smart. But…it's a little bit late for smart."

"Friends with benefits. As in…we stay friends by day and we screw each other senseless by night?"

*Gah.* That about sent him over the edge. "Yeah."

"Until what? Until…"

"Until you get that other date. Until the charity thing. As long as we're both single, why not? You're working toward the relationship stuff. You said you didn't want to be alone anymore. So, maybe this is good in the meantime. I know you're both industrious and red-blooded, and can get those orgasms all by yourself." He rolled his hips again and, much to his satisfaction, a small moan of pleasure escaped her lips. "But are they this good?"

"No," she said, her tone hushed.

"This is possibly the worst idea in the history of the world. But hell, you wanted to get some more experience… I'm offering to give it to you." The moment he said the words he wanted to bite his tongue off. The idea of giving Anna more experience just so she could go and do things with other men? That made him see red. Made him feel violent. Jealous. Things he never felt.

But what other option was there? He couldn't keep her. Not like this. But he couldn't let her go now.

He was messed up. *This* was messed up.

"I guess… I guess that makes sense. You know, until earlier today I'd never even given a guy a blow job."

"You're killing me," he said, closing his eyes.

"Well, I don't want you to die. You just offered me your penis for carnal usage. I want you alive."

"So that's it? My penis has now become the star of the show. Wow, how quickly our friendship has eroded."

"Our friendship is still solid. I think it just goes to prove how solid your dick is."

"With romantic praise like that, how are you still single?"

"I have no idea. I spout sonnets effortlessly."

He leaned forward, kissing her, a strange, warm

sensation washing over him. He was kissing Anna. And it didn't feel quite as rushed and desperate as all the other times before it. A decision had been made. This wasn't a hasty race against sanity. This wasn't trying to get as much satisfaction as possible squeezed into a moment before reality kicked in. This was...well, in the new world order, it was sanctioned.

Instantly, he was rock hard again, ready to go, even though it'd been only a few minutes since his last orgasm. But there was one problem. "I don't have a condom," he said, cursing and pushing himself away from her. "I don't suppose the woman who has been celibate for the past thirteen years has one?"

"No," she said, sagging against the wall. "You only carry one on you?"

"Yeah. I'm not superhuman. I don't usually expect to get it on more than once in a couple of hours."

"But you were going to with me?"

He looked down at his very erect cock. "Does this answer your question?"

"Yeah."

"Well, then." He let out a heavy sigh.

"You could stay and watch...*Oklahoma!* with me."

He nodded slowly. He should stay and watch *Oklahoma!* with her. If he didn't, it kind of made a mockery of the whole friends-with-benefits thing. Because, before the sex, he would have stayed with her to watch a movie, of course. To hang out, because she was one of his favorite people on earth to spend time with. Even if her taste in movies was deeply suspect.

Of course, he didn't particularly want to stay now, because she presented the temptation that he could not give in to.

"Unless you have to work early tomorrow."

"I really do," he said.

"Thank God."

His eyebrows shot up. "You want to get rid of me?"

"I don't really want to hang out with you when I know I can't have you."

"I felt the same way, but I didn't want to say it. I thought it seemed kind of offensive."

Strangely, she smiled. "I'm not offended. I'm not offended at all. I kind of like being irresistible."

Instead of leaving, he knew that he could drive down to the store and buy a box of condoms. And he seriously considered it. The problem with that was there had to be some boundaries. Some limits. He was pretty sure being so horny and desperate that you needed to buy condoms right away instead of just waiting until you had protection on hand probably didn't fit within the boundaries of friends with benefits.

"I'll see you tomorrow, then."

She nodded. "See you tomorrow."

# Chapter 9

By the time Anna swung by the grocery store in the afternoon, she was feeling very mature, and very proud of herself. She was having a no-strings sexual relationship with her friend. And she was going to buy milk, cheese and condoms. Because she was mature and adult and completely fine with the whole situation. Also, mature.

She grabbed a cart and began to slowly walk up and down the aisles. She was not making sure that no one she knew was around. Because, of course, she wasn't at all embarrassed to be in the store looking for milk, cheese and—incidentally—prophylactics. She was *thirty*. She was entitled to a little bit of sexual release. Anyway, no one was actually watching her.

She swallowed hard, trying to remember exactly which aisle the condoms were in. She had never bought any. Ever. In her entire life.

She had been extremely tempted to make a dash to the store last night when Chase had discovered he didn't have any more protection, but she had imagined that was just a little bit too desperate. She was going to be nondesperate about this. Very chill. And not like a woman who was a near virgin. Or like someone who was so desperate to jump her best friend's bones it might seem like there were deeper emotions at play. There were not.

The strong feelings she had were just…in her pants. Pants feelings. That's it.

Last night's breakdown had been purely because she was unaccustomed to sex. Just a little postorgasmic release. That's all it was. The whole thing was a release. Postorgasmic tears weren't really all that strange.

She felt bolstered by that thought.

She turned down the aisle labeled Family Planning and made her way toward the condoms. Lubricated. Extra-thin. Ribbed. There were options. She had to stand there and seriously ponder ribbed. She should have asked Chase what he had used last night. Because whatever that had been had been perfect.

"Anna." The masculine voice coming from her left startled her.

She turned and—to her utter horror—saw her brother Mark standing there.

"Hi," she said, taking two steps away from the condom shelf, as though that would make it less obvious why she was in the aisle. Whatever. They were adults. Neither of them were virgins and they were both aware of that.

Still, she needed some distance between herself and

anything that said "ribbed for her pleasure" when she was standing there talking to her brother.

"Haven't seen you in a couple days."

"Well, you pissed me off last time I saw you."

He lifted a shoulder. "Sorry."

He probably was, too.

"Hey, whatever. I win your bet."

His brows shot up. "I heard a rumor about you and Chase McCormack kissing at Beaches, but I was pretty sure that..." His eyes drifted toward the condoms. *"Really?"*

Dying of embarrassment was a serious risk at the moment, but she was caught. Completely and totally caught. And as long as she was drowning in a sea of horror...well, she might as well ride the tide.

If he needed proof her date with Chase was real, she imagined proof of sex was about the best there was.

She took a fortifying breath. "Really," she said, crossing her arms beneath her breasts. "It's happening. I have a date. I have more than a date. I have a whole future full of dates because I have a relationship. With Chase. You lose."

"I'm supposed to believe that you and McCormack are suddenly—" his eyes drifted back to the condoms again *"—that."*

"You don't have to believe it. It's true. He's also going to be my date to the charity gala that I'm invited to. I will take my payment in small or large bills. Thank you."

"I'm not convinced."

"You're not convinced?" She moved closer to the shelf and grabbed a box of condoms. "I am caught in the act."

"Convenient," he said, grabbing his own box.

She made a face. "It's not convenient. It happened."

"You're in love with him?"

The question felt like a punch to the stomach. She did not like it. She didn't like it at all. More than that, she had no idea what to say. *No* seemed...wrong. *Yes* seemed worse. And she wasn't really sure either answer was true.

*You can't love Chase.*

She couldn't not love him, either. He was her friend, after all. Of course she wasn't in love with him.

Her stomach twisted tight. No. She did not love him. She didn't do love. At all. Especially not with him. Because he would never...

"You look like you just got slapped with a fish," Mark said, and, to his credit, he looked somewhat concerned.

"I... Of course I love him," she said. That was a safe answer. It was also true. She did love him. As a friend. And...she loved his body. And everything about him as a human being. Except for the fact that he was a man slut who would never settle down with any woman, much less her.

*Why not you?*

No. She was not thinking about this. She wasn't thinking about any of this.

"Tell you what. If you're still together at the gala, you get your money."

"That isn't fair. That isn't what we agreed on."

He lifted a shoulder. "I know. But I also didn't expect you to grab your best friend and have him be your date. That still seems suspicious to me, regardless of... purchases."

"You didn't put any specifications on the bet, Mark. You can't change the rules now."

"We didn't put any specifications on it saying I couldn't."

"Why do you care?"

He snorted. "Why do you care?"

"I have pride, jackass."

"And I don't trust Chase McCormack. If you're still together at the gala, you get your money. And if he hurts you in any way, I will break his neck. After I pull his balls off and feed them to the sharks."

It wasn't very often that Mark's protective side was on display. Usually, he was too busy tormenting her. Their childhood had been rough. Their father didn't have any idea how to show affection to them, and as a result none of them were very good at it, either. Still, she never doubted that—even when he was a jerk— Mark cared about her.

"That's not necessary. Chase is my best friend. And now…he's more. He isn't going to hurt me."

"Sounds to me like he has the potential to hurt you worse than just about anybody."

His words settled heavily in the pit of her stomach. She should be able to brush them off. Because she and Chase were in a relationship. She and Chase were friends with benefits. And nothing about that would hurt at all.

"I'll be fine."

"If you need anything, just let me know."

"I will."

He lifted the condom box. "We'll pretend this didn't happen." Then he turned and started to walk away.

"Pretend what didn't happen?" She pulled her own

box of condoms up against her chest and held it tightly. "See? I've already forgotten. Mostly because I can't afford therapy. At least not until you pay me the big bucks at the gala."

"We'll see," he said, walking out of sight.

She turned, chucking the box into her cart and making her way quickly down to the milk aisle. Chase wasn't going to hurt her, because Mark was wrong. They were only friends, and she quashed the traitorous flame in her stomach that tried to grow, tried to convince her otherwise.

She wasn't going to get hurt. She was just going to have a few orgasms and then move on.

That was her story, and she was sticking to it.

"I'm taking you dancing tonight," Chase said as soon as Anna picked up the phone.

"Did you bump your head on an anvil today?"

He supposed he shouldn't be that surprised to hear Anna's sarcasm. After last night—vulnerability, tears—he'd had a feeling that she wasn't going to be overly friendly today. In fact, he'd guessed that she would have transformed into one of the little porcupines that were on her pajamas. He had been right.

"No," he said. "I'm just following the lesson plan. I said I was taking you out, and so I am."

"You know," she said, her voice getting husky, "I'm curious about whether or not making me scream was anywhere on the lesson plan."

His body jolted, heat rushing through his veins. He looked over his shoulder at Sam, who was working steadily on something in the back of the shop. It was Anna's day off, so she wasn't on the property. But he and Sam were in the middle of a big custom job. A gate with a lot of intricate detail, with matching work for the deck and interior staircase of the home. Which meant they didn't get real time off right now.

"No," he returned, satisfied his brother wasn't paying attention, "that wasn't on the lesson plan. But I'm a big believer in improvisation."

"That was improvisation? In that case, it seems to be your strength."

The sarcasm he had expected. This innuendo, he had not. They'd both pulled away hard last night, no denying it. It would have been simple to go out and get more protection and neither of them had.

But damn, this new dynamic between them was a lot to get used to. Still, for all that it was kind of crazy, he knew what he wanted. "I'd like to show you more of my strengths tonight."

"You're welcome to improvise your way on over to my bed anytime." There was a pause. "Was that flirting? Was that *good* flirting?"

He laughed, tension exiting his body in a big gust. He should have known. He wasn't sure how he felt about this being part of the lesson. Not when he had been on the verge of initiating phone sex in the middle of a workday with his brother looming in the background. But keeping it part of the lesson was for the best. He didn't need to lose his head. This was Anna, after all. He was walking a very fine line here.

On the one hand, he knew keeping a clear line drawn in the sand was the right thing to do. They weren't just going to be able to slide right back into their normal relationship. Not after what had happened. On the other hand, Anna was…Anna. She was essential to him. And she wasn't jaded when it came to sexual relationships. Wasn't experienced. That meant he needed to handle her with care. And it would benefit him to remember that he couldn't play with her the way he did women with a little more experience. Women who understood that this was sex and nothing more.

It could never be meaningless sex with Anna. He couldn't have a meaningless conversation with her. That meant that whatever happened between them physically would change things, build things, tear things down. That was a fact. A scary one. Taking control, trying to harness it, label it, was the only solution he had. Otherwise, things would keep happening when they weren't prepared. That would be worse.

Maybe.

He cleared his throat. "Very good flirting. You got me all excited."

"Excellent," she said, sounding cheerful. "Also, I bought condoms."

He choked. "Did you?"

"They aren't ribbed. I wasn't sure if the one you used last night was."

"No," he said, rubbing the back of his neck and casting a side eye at his brother. "It wasn't."

"Good. I was looking for a repeat performance. I didn't want to get the wrong thing. Though maybe sometime we should try ribbed."

Sometime. Because there would be more than once. More than last night. More than tonight. "We can try it if you want."

"I feel like we might as well try everything. I have a lot of catching up to do."

"Dancing," he said, trying to wage a battle with the

heat that was threatening to take over his skull. "Do you want to go dancing tonight?"

"Not really. But I can see the benefit. Seeing as there will be dancing at the fund-raiser. And I bet I'm terrible at dancing."

"Great. I'm going to pick you up at seven. We're going to Ace's."

"Then I'll be ready."

He hung up the phone and suddenly realized he was at the center of Sam's keen focus. That bastard had been listening in the entire time. "Hot date tonight?" he asked.

"Dancing. With Anna," he said meaningfully. The meaning being *with Anna and not with you.*

"Well, then, you wouldn't mind if I tagged along." Jerkface was ignoring his meaning.

"I would mind."

"I thought this was just about some bet."

"It is," he lied.

"Uh-huh."

"You don't want to go out. You want to stay home and eat a TV dinner. You're just harassing me."

Sam shrugged. "I have to get my kicks somewhere."

"Get your own. Get laid."

"Nope."

"You're a weirdo."

"I'm selective."

Maybe Sam was, maybe he wasn't. Chase could honestly say that his brother's sex life was a mystery to him. Which was fine. Really, more than fine. Chase had a reputation, Sam…did not. Well, unless that reputation centered around being grumpy and antisocial.

"Right. Well, you enjoy that. I'm going to go out."

"Chase," Sam said, his tone taking on a note of steel. "Don't hurt her."

Those words poked him right in the temper. "Really?"

"She's the best thing you have," Sam said, his voice serious. "You find a woman like that, you keep her. In whatever capacity you can."

"She's my best friend. I'm not going to hurt her."

"Not on purpose."

"I don't think you're in any position to stand there and lecture me on interpersonal relationships, since you pretty much don't have any."

"I have you," Sam said.

"Right. I'm not sure that counts."

"I have Anna. But if you messed things up with her, I won't have her, either."

Chase frowned. "You don't have feelings for her, do you?" He would really hate to have to punch his brother in the face. But he would.

"No. Not like you mean. But I know her, and I care about her. And I know you."

"What does that mean?"

Sam pondered that for a second. "You're not her speed."

"I'm not trying to be." He was getting ready to punch his brother in the face anyway.

"I'm just saying."

"You're just saying," he muttered. "Go *just say* somewhere else. A guy whose only friends are his younger brother and that brother's friend maybe shouldn't stand there and make commentary on relationships."

"I'm quiet. I'm perceptive. As you mentioned, I am an artist."

"You can't pull that out when it suits you and put it away when it doesn't."

"Sure I can. Artists are temperamental."

"Stop beating around the bush. Say what you want to say."

Sam sighed. "If she offers you more than friendship, take it, dumbass."

"Why would you think that she would ever offer that? Why would you think that I want it?"

He felt defensive. And more than a little bit annoyed. "She will. I'm not blind. Actually, being antisocial has its benefits. It means that I get to sit back and watch other people interact. She likes you. She always has. And she's the kind of good... Chase, we don't get good like that. We don't deserve it."

"Gee. Thanks, Sam."

"I'm not trying to insult you. I'm just saying that she's better than either of us. Figure out how to make it work if she wants to."

Everything in Chase recoiled. "She doesn't want to. And neither do I." He turned away from Sam, heading toward the door.

"Are you sleeping with her yet?"

Chase froze. "That isn't any of your business."

"Right. You are."

"Still not your business."

"Chase, we both have a lot of crap to wade through. Which is pretty obvious. But if she's standing there willing to pull you out, I'm just saying you need to take her up on her offer."

"She has enough crap of her own that she's hip deep in, Sam. I don't need her taking on mine."

Sam rubbed his hand over his forehead. "Yeah, that's always the thing."

"Anyway, she doesn't want me. Not like that. I mean, not forever. This is just a…physical thing." Which was way more information than his brother deserved.

"Keep telling yourself that if it helps you sleep at night."

"I sleep like a baby, Sam." He continued out the door, heading toward his truck. He had to get back to the house and get showered and dressed so that he could pick up Anna. And he was not going to think about anything his brother had said.

Anna didn't want forever with him.

That thought immobilized him, forced him to imagine a future with Anna, stretching on and on into the distance. Holding her, kissing her. Sleeping beside her every night and waking up with her every morning.

Seeing her grow round with his child.

He shut it down immediately. That was a fantasy. One he didn't want. One he couldn't have.

He would have Anna as a friend forever, but the "benefits" portion of their relationship was finite.

So, he would just enjoy this while it lasted.

## Chapter 10

She looked like a cliché. A really slutty one. She wasn't sure she cared. But in her very short denim skirt and plaid shirt knotted above the waistline she painted quite the picture.

One of a woman looking to get lucky.

"Well," she said to her reflection—her made-up reflection, compliments of her trip to the store in Tolowa today, as was everything else. "You *are* looking to get lucky."

Fair. That was fair.

She heard the sound of a truck engine and tires on the gravel in her short little driveway. She was renting a house in an older neighborhood in town—not right in the armpit of town where she'd grown up, but still sort of on the fringe—and the yard was a little bit…rustic.

She wondered if Chase would honk. Or if he would come to the door.

Him coming to the door would feel much more like a date. A real date.

A *date* date.

Oh, Lord, what were they doing?

She had flirted with him on the phone, and she'd enjoyed it. Had wanted—very much—to push him even harder. Trading innuendo with him was…well, it was a lot more fun than she'd imagined.

There was a heavy knock on the door and she squeaked, hopping a little bit before catching her breath. Then she grabbed her purse and started to walk to the entry, trying to calm her nerves. He'd come to the door. That felt like A Thing.

*You're being crazy. Friends with benefits. Not boyfriend.*

The word *boyfriend* made her stomach lurch, and she did her best to ignore it. She jerked the door open, watching his face intently for his response to her new look. And she was not disappointed.

"Damn," he said, leaning forward, resting his forearm on the doorjamb. "I didn't realize you would be showing up dressed as Country Girl from My Dirtiest Dreams."

She shouldn't feel flattered by that. But she positively glowed. "It seemed fair, since you're basically the centerfold of *Blacksmith Magazine*."

He laughed. "Really? How would that photo shoot go?"

"You posing strategically in front of the forge with a bellows over your junk."

"I am not getting my *junk* near the forge. The last thing I need is sensitive body parts going up in flames."

"I know I don't want them going up in flames." She

cleared her throat, suddenly aware of a thick blanket of awkwardness settling over them. She didn't know what to do with him now. Did she...not touch him unless they were going to have sex? Did she kiss him if she wanted to or did she need permission?

She needed a friends-with-benefits handbook.

"Um," she began, rather unsuccessfully. "What exactly are my benefits?"

"Meaning?"

"My benefits additional to this friendship. Do I... kiss you when I see you? Or..."

"Do you want to kiss me?"

She looked up at him, all sexy and delicious looking in his tight black T-shirt, cowboy hat and late-in-the-day stubble. "Is that a trick question? Because the only answer to 'Do I want to kiss a very hot guy?' is yes. But not if you don't want to kiss me."

He wrapped his arm around her waist, drawing her up against him before bending down to kiss her slowly, thoroughly. "Does that help?"

She let out a long, slow breath, the tension that had been strangling her since he'd arrived at her house leaving her body slowly. "Yes," she said, sighing. "It does."

"All right," he said, extending his hand. "Let's go."

She took hold of his hand, the warmth of his touch flooding her, making her stomach flip. She let him lead her to the truck, open her door for her. All manner of date-type stuff. The additional benefits were getting bound up in the dating lessons and at the moment she wasn't sure what was for her and what was for the Making Her Datable mission.

Then she decided it didn't matter.

She just clung to the good feelings the whole drive to Ace's.

When they got there, she felt the true weight of the spectacle they were creating in the community. Beaches was one thing. Them being together there had certainly caused a ripple. But everyone in Copper Ridge hung out at Ace's.

Sierra West, whose family was a client of both her and Chase, was in the corner with some other friends who were involved with local rodeo events. Sheriff Eli Garrett was over by the bar, along with his brother, Connor, and their wives, Sadie and Liss.

She looked the other direction and saw Holly and Ryan Masters sitting in the corner, looking ridiculously happy. Holly and Ryan had both grown up in foster care in Copper Ridge and so had been part of the town-charity-case section at school. Though Holly was younger and Ryan a little older, so she'd never been close friends with them. Behind them was Jonathan Bear, looking broody and unapproachable as usual.

She officially knew too many damn people.

"This town is the size of a postage stamp," she muttered as she followed Chase to a table where they could deposit their coats and her purse.

"That's good," he said. "Men are seeing you attached. It's all part of changing your reputation. That's what you want."

She grunted. "I guess." It didn't feel like what she wanted. She mostly just wanted to be alone with Chase now. No performance art required.

But she was currently a dancing monkey for all of Copper Ridge, so performance art was the order of the evening.

She also suddenly felt self-conscious about her wardrobe choice. Wearing this outfit for Chase hadn't seemed bad at all. Wearing it in front of everyone was a little much.

The jukebox was blaring, and Luke Bryan was demanding all the country girls shake it for him, so Anna figured—regardless of how uncomfortable she was feeling—it was as good a time as any for them to get out on the dance floor.

The music was fast, so people weren't touching. They were just sort of, well, *shaking it* near each other.

She was just standing there, looking at him and not shaking it, because she didn't know what to do next. It felt weird to be here in front of everyone in a skirt. It felt weird to be dancing with Chase. It felt weird to not touch him. But it would be weirder to touch him.

Hell if she knew what she was doing here.

Then he reached out, brushing his fingers down her arm. That touch, that connection, rooted her to the earth. To the moment. To him. Suddenly, it didn't matter so much what other people around them were doing. She moved in slightly, and he put his hand on her hip.

Then, before she was ready, the song ended, slowing things down. And now she really didn't know what to do. It seemed that Chase did, though. He wrapped his arm around her waist, drawing her in close, taking hold of her hand with his free one.

Her heart was pounding hard. And she was pretty sure her face was bright red. She looked up at Chase, his expression unreadable. He was not bright red. Of course he wasn't. Because even if this relationship was new for him, this kind of situation was not. He knew how to handle women. He knew how to handle sex feelings. Meanwhile, she was completely unsure of what to do. Like a buoy floating out in the middle of the ocean, just bobbing there on her own.

Her breathing got shorter, harder. Matching her heartbeat. She couldn't just dance with him like this. She needed to not be in front of people when she felt these things. She felt like her arousal was written all over her skin. Well, it was. She was blushing like a beacon. She could probably guide ships in from the sea.

She looked at Chase's face again. There was no way to tell what he was thinking. His dark gaze was shielded by the dim lighting, his jaw set, hard, his mouth in a firm line. That brief moment of connection that she'd felt was gone now. He was touching her still, but she had no idea what he was feeling.

She looked over to her left and noticed that people were staring. Of course they were. She and Chase were dancing and that was different. And, of course, a great many of the stares were coming from women. Women who probably felt like they should be in her position. Like she didn't belong there.

And they could all see how much she wanted it. That she wanted him more than he wanted her. That she was the one who was completely and totally out of control. Needing him so much she couldn't even hide it.

And they all knew she didn't deserve it.

She pulled away from him, looking around, breathing hard. "I think...I just need a break."

She crossed the room and went back to their table, grabbing her purse and making her way over to the bar.

Chase joined her only a few moments later. "What's up?"

She shook her head. "Nothing."

"We were dancing, and then you freaked out."

"I don't like everybody watching us."

"That's the point, though."

That simple statement stabbed her straight through the heart. "Yeah. I know." That was the problem. He was so conscious of why they were doing this. This whole thing. And she could so easily forget. Could so easily let down all the walls and shields that she had put in place to protect her heart. And just let herself want.

She hated that. Hated craving things she couldn't have. Affection she could never hope to earn.

Her mother had left. And no amount of wishing that she would come back, no amount of crying over that lost love, would do anything to fix it. No amount of hoping her father would drop that crusty exterior and give her a hug when she needed it would make it happen. So she just didn't want. Or at least, she never let people see how much she wanted.

"I know," she said, her tone a little bit stiffer than she would like.

She was bombing out here. Failing completely at remaining cool, calm and unaffected. She was standing here in public, hemorrhaging needs all over the place.

"What's wrong?"

"I need a drink."

"Why don't we leave?"

She blinked. "Just…leave?"

"If you aren't having fun, then there's no point. Let's go."

"Where are we going?"

He grabbed her hand and started to lead her through the bar. "Somewhere fun."

She followed him out into the night, laughing helplessly when they climbed into the truck. "People are going to talk. That was all a little weird."

"Let them talk. They need something to do."

He started the engine and backed out of the parking lot, turning sharply and heading down the road, out of town.

"Where are we going?"

"Somewhere I bet you've never been."

"You don't know my life, Chase McCormack. You don't know where I've been."

"I do know your life, Anna Brown."

She gritted her teeth, because, of course, he did. She said nothing as they continued to drive up the road. And still said nothing when he turned onto a dirt road that forked into a narrower dirt road as it went up the mountain.

"What are we doing?" she asked again.

Just then, they came to a flat, clear area. She couldn't see anything; there were no lights except for the headlights on the truck, illuminating nothing but the side of another mountain, thick with evergreens.

"I want to make out with you. This is where you go do that."

"We're adults," she said, ignoring the giddy fluttering in her stomach. "We have our own bedrooms. And beds. We don't need to go make out in a car."

"*Need* is not the operative word here. We're expanding experiences and stuff." He flicked the radio on, country music filling the cab of the truck. "Actually, I think before we make out—" he opened the driver's-side door "—we should dance."

Now there was nobody here. Which meant there was no excuse. Actually, this made her a lot more emotional. She did not like that. She didn't like the super-power that Chase seemed to have of reaching down inside of her, past all the defenses, and grabbing hold of tender, emotional things.

But she wasn't going to refuse, either.

It was dark out here. At least there was that.

Before she had a chance to move, Chase was at her side of the truck, opening her door. He extended his hand. "Dance with me?"

She was having a strange out-of-body experience. She wasn't sure who this woman was, up in the woods with only a gorgeous man for company. A man who wanted to dance with her. A man who wanted to make out with her.

She unbuckled, accepting his offered hand and popping out of the truck. He spun her over to the front of the vehicle, the headlights serving as spotlights as the music played over the radio. "I'm kind of a crappy dancer," he said, pulling her in close.

"You don't seem like a crappy dancer to me."

"How many men have you danced with?"

She laughed. "Um, counting now?"

"Yeah."

"One."

He chuckled, his breath fanning over her cheekbone. So intimate to share the air with him like this. Shocking. "Well, then, you don't have much to compare it to."

"I guess not. But I don't think I would compare either way."

"Oh, yeah? Why is that?"

"You're in a league of your own, Chase McCormack, don't you know?"

"Hmm. I have heard that a time or two. When teachers told me I was a unique sort of devil, sent there to make their lives miserable. Or all the times I used to get into it with my old man."

"Well, you did raise a lot of hell."

"Yeah. I did. I continue to raise hell, in some fashion. But I need people to see a different side of me," he said, drawing her even tighter up against him. "I need for them to see that Sam and I can handle our business. That we can make the McCormack name big again."

"Can you?" she asked, tilting her head up, her lips brushing his chin. The stubble there was prickly, masculine. Irresistible. So she bit him. Just lightly. Scraping her teeth over his skin.

He gripped her hair, pulling her head back. The sudden rush of danger in the movements sending a shot of adrenaline through her blood. This was so strange. Being in his arms and feeling like she was home. Like he was everything comforting and familiar. A warm blanket, a hot chocolate and a musical she'd seen a hundred times.

Then things would shift, and he would become something else entirely. A stranger. Sex, sin and all the things she'd never taken the time to explore. She liked that, too.

She was starting to get addicted to both.

"Oh, I can handle myself just fine," he said, his tone hard.

"Can you handle me?" she asked.

He slid his hand down to cup her ass, his eyes never leaving hers as they swayed to the music. "I can handle you. However you want it."

"Hard," she said, her throat going dry, her words

slightly unsteady. She wasn't sure what had possessed her to say that.

"You want it hard?" he asked, his words sounding strangled.

"Yes," she said.

"How else do you want it?" he asked, holding her against him, moving in time with the beat. She could feel his cock getting hard against her hip.

"Aren't you the one with the lesson plan?"

"You're the one in need of the education," he said.

"I don't want tonight to be about that," she said, and she was as sure about that as she'd been about wanting it hard and equally unsure about how she knew it.

"What do you want it to be about?"

"You," she said, tracing the sharp line of his jaw. "Me. That's about it."

"What do you want from me?" he asked.

*Only everything.* She shied away from that thought. "Show me what the fuss is about."

"I did that already."

Something hot and possessive spiked in her blood. Something she never could have anticipated, because she hadn't even realized that it lived inside of her. "No. Something you don't give other women, Chase. You're my friend. You're...more to me than one night and an orgasm. You're right. I could have gotten that from a lot of guys. Well, maybe not the orgasm. But sex for sure. My coveralls aren't that much of a turnoff. And you could have any woman. So give me you. And I'll give you me. Don't hold back."

"You're...not very experienced."

She stretched up on tiptoes, pressing her lips to his. "Did I ask for a gentleman? Or did I ask for hard?"

He tightened his grip on her hair, and this time when she looked up at his face, she didn't see a stranger. She saw Chase. The man. The whole man. Not divided up into parts. Not Her Friend Chase or Her Lover Chase, but just…Chase.

He was all of these things. Fun and laid-back, intense and deeply sexual. She wanted it all. She craved it all. As hard as he could. As much as he could. And still, it would never, ever be enough.

"Go ahead," she said, "take me, cowboy."

She didn't have to ask twice.

He propelled them both backward, pressing her up against the truck, kissing her deeply, a no-holds-barred possession of her mouth. She hadn't even realized kissing like this existed. She wasn't entirely sure what she had thought kissing was for. Affection. A prelude to sex. This was something else entirely. This was a language all its own. Words that didn't exist in English. Words that she knew Chase would never be able to say.

And her body knew that. Understood it. Responded. As surely as it would have if he had spoken.

She was drowning. In this, in him. She hadn't expected emotion to be this…fierce. She hadn't really expected emotion at all. She hadn't understood. She really had not understood.

But then she didn't have the time to think about it. Or the brainpower. He tugged on her hair, drawing her head to the side before he pressed his lips to her tender neck, his teeth scraping along the sensitive skin before he closed his lips around her and sucked hard.

"You want it hard?" he asked, his voice rough. "Then we're going to do it my way."

He grabbed hold of her hips, turning her so that she

was facing the truck. "Scoot just a little bit." He guided her down to where the cab of the truck ended and the bed began. "Grab on." She curved her fingers around the cold metal, a shiver running down her spine. "You ever do it like this?" he asked.

She laughed, more because she was nervous than because she thought the question was funny. "Chase, before you I had never even given a guy a blow job. Do you think I've ever done this before?"

"Good," he said, his tone hard, very definitely him. "I like that. I'm a sick bastard. I like the fact that no other man has ever done this to you before. I should feel guilty." He reached around and undid the top button on her top. "But I'm just enjoying corrupting you."

He undid another button, then another. She wasn't wearing a bra underneath the top. Because, frankly, when you were as underendowed as she was, there really wasn't any point. Also, it made things a little bit more easy access. Though that wasn't something she had thought about until just now. Until Chase undid the last button and left her completely bare to the cool night air.

"I'm kind of enjoying being corrupted."

"I didn't tell you you could talk."

She shut her mouth, surprised at the commanding tone he was taking. Not entirely displeased about it. He cupped her breasts, squeezing them gently before moving his hands down her stomach, bringing them around her hips. Then he tugged her skirt down, leaving her in nothing but her boots and her underwear.

"We'll leave the boots on. I wouldn't want you to step on anything sharp."

She didn't say anything. She bit her lip, eagerly anticipating what he might do next. He slipped his hand down between her thighs, his fingertips edging beneath her panties. He stroked his fingers through her folds, a harsh growl escaping his lips. "You're wet for me," he said—not a question.

She nodded, closing her eyes, trying to keep from hurtling over the edge as soon as his fingertips brushed over her. But it was a pretty difficult battle she was waging. Just the thought of being with Chase again was enough to take her to the precipice. His touch nearly pushed her over immediately.

He gripped her tightly with his other hand, drawing her ass back up against his cock as he teased her between her legs with his clever fingers. He slipped one deep inside of her, continuing to toy with her with the edge of his thumb while he thrust in and out of her slowly. He added a second finger, then another. And she was shaking. Trembling with the effort of holding back her climax.

But she didn't want it to end like this. Didn't want it to end so quickly. Mostly, she just didn't want him to know that with one flick of his fingertip over her sensitized flesh he could make her come so hard she wouldn't be able to see straight. Because at the end of the day it didn't matter how much she wanted him; she still had her pride. She still rebelled against the idea of revealing herself quite so easily.

She probably already had. Here she was, mostly naked, out underneath the stars. Here she was, telling him she wanted just the two of them, that she wanted it hard. Probably there were no secrets left. Not really. There were all sorts of unspoken truths filling in the silences between them, but she felt like they were easy enough to read, if he wanted to look at them.

He might not. She didn't really want to. Yet it didn't make them go away.

But she could ignore them. She could focus on this. On his touch. On the dark magic he was working on her body, the spell that was taking her over completely.

He swept her hair to the side, pressing a hot kiss to the back of her neck. And then there was no holding back. Climax washed over her like a wave as she shuddered out her release.

"Good girl," he whispered, kissing her again before moving away for a moment. He pushed her panties down her legs, helping her step out of them, then he kissed her thigh before straightening.

She heard him moving behind her. But she didn't change her position. She stood there, gripping the back of the truck. Dimly, she was aware the radio was still on. That they had a sound track to this illicit encounter in the woods. It added to the surreal, out-of-body quality.

But then he was back with her, touching her, kissing her, and it didn't feel so surreal anymore. It was too raw. Too real. His voice, his scent, his touch. He was there. There was no denying it. This wasn't fantasy. Fantasy was gauzy, distant. This was sharp, so sharp she was afraid it would cut right into her. Dangerous. She wanted it. All of it. And she was afraid that in the end there would be nothing of her left. At least nothing that she recognized. That his friendship wouldn't be something that she recognized. But they'd gone too far to turn back, and she didn't even want to anymore. She wanted to see what was on the other side of this. Needed to see what was on the other side.

He reached up, bracing his hand on the back of her neck, holding her hip with the other as he positioned himself at the entrance to her body. He pressed the blunt head of his erection against her, sliding in easily, thrusting hard up inside her. She gasped as he went deeper than he had before. This was almost overwhelming. But she needed it. Embraced it.

His hold was possessive, all-encompassing. She felt like she was being consumed by him completely. By her desire for him. Warmth bloomed from where he held her, bled down beneath the surface of her skin, hemorrhaged in her chest.

"I fantasized about this," he said, the words seeming to scrape along his throat. Rough, raw. "Holding you like this. Holding on to your hips as I did this to you."

She couldn't respond. She couldn't say anything. His words had grabbed ahold of her, squeezing her throat tight, making it impossible for her to speak. He had fantasized about her. About this.

This position should feel less personal. More distant. But it didn't. That made it... It made it exactly what she had asked for. This was for her. And this was him. What he wanted, not just the next item on a list of things she needed to learn. Not just a set routine that he had with women he slept with.

He slid his hand down along the line of her spine, pressing firmly, the impression of his possession lingering on her skin. Then he held both of her hips tight, his blunt fingertips digging into her skin. He thrust harder into her, his skin slapping against hers, the sound echoing in the darkness. She gripped the truck hard, lowering her head, a moan escaping her lips.

"You wanted hard, baby," he ground out. "I'll give it to you hard."

"Yes," she whispered.

"Who are you saying yes to?" There was an edge to his words, a desperation she hadn't imagined he would feel, not with her. Not over this.

"Chase," she said, closing her eyes tight. "Yes, Chase. Please. I need this. I need you."

She needed all of him. And she suddenly realized why those thoughts about having someone to spend her nights with had seemed wrong. Because at the end of the day when she thought of sharing evenings with someone, when she thought of curling up under a blanket with someone, of watching *Oklahoma!* with someone for the hundredth time, it was Chase. It was always Chase. And that meant no other man had ever been able to get close enough to her. Because he was the fantasy. And as long as he was the fantasy, no one else had a place.

And now, now after this, she was ruined forever. Because she would never be able to do this with another man. Ever. It would always be Chase's hand she imagined on her skin. That firm grip of his that she craved.

He flexed his hips, going harder into her, then slipped his fingers around between her thighs again, stroking her as he continued to fill her. Then he leaned forward, biting her neck as he slammed into her one last time, sending them both over the edge. He growled, pulsing inside of her as he found his release. The pain from his teeth mingled with the all-consuming pleasure rolling through her in never-ending waves, pounding over her so hard she didn't think it would ever end. She didn't think she could survive it.

And when it passed, it was Chase who held her in his arms.

There was no denying it. No escaping it. And she was scraped raw. As stripped as she'd been after their first encounter, she was even more exposed now. Because she had read into all those empty, unspoken things. Because she had finally realized what everything meant.

Her asking him for help. Her kissing him. Her going down on him.

Her not having another man in her life in any capacity.

It was because she wanted Chase. All of Chase. It was why everything had come together for her tonight. Why she'd realized she couldn't compartmentalize him.

She wasn't ready to think the words yet, though. She couldn't. She did her very best to hold them at bay. To stop herself from thinking the things that would crumble her defenses once and for all.

Instead, she released her hold on the truck and turned to face him, looping her arms around his neck, pressing her bare body against his, luxuriating in him.

"That was quite the dance lesson," she said finally.

"A lot more fun than it would have been in Ace's." He slid his hand down to her butt, holding her casually. She loved that. So much more than she should.

"Yeah, we would have gotten thrown out for that."

"But can you imagine the rumors?"

"Are they really rumors if everyone has actually seen you screw?"

"Good question," he said, leaning forward and nipping her lower lip.

"You're bitey," she said.

"And you like to be bitten."

She couldn't deny it. "I guess I should… I mean, I have to work tomorrow."

"Me, too," he said, sounding regretful.

She wanted so badly to ask him to stay with her. But he wasn't bringing it up. And she didn't know if the almighty Chase McCormack actually *slept* with the women he was sleeping with.

So she didn't ask.

And when he dropped her off at her house, leaving her at her doorstep, she tried very, very hard not to regret that.

She didn't succeed.

# Chapter 11

The best thing about having her own shop was working alone. Some people might find it lonely; Anna found it a great opportunity to run through every musical number she knew. She had already gone through the entirety of *Oklahoma!* and was working her way through *Seven Brides for Seven Brothers*.

Admittedly, she wasn't the best singer in the world, but in her own shop she was the best singer around.

And if the music helped drown out all of the neuroses that were scampering around inside of her, asking her to deal with her Chase feelings, then so much the better. She didn't want to deal with Chase feelings.

"When you're in love, when you're in love, there is no way on earth to hide it," she sang operatically, the words echoing off the walls.

She snapped her mouth shut. That was a bad song.

A very bad song for this moment. She was not… She just wasn't going to think about it.

She turned her focus back to the tractor engine she currently had in a million little pieces. At least an engine was concrete. A puzzle she could solve. It was tactile, and most of the time, if she could just get the right parts, find the source of the problem, she could fix it. That wasn't true with much of anything else in life. That was one reason she found a certain sort of calm in the garage.

Plus, it was something her father knew how to do. He was his own mechanic, and weekends were often spent laboring over his pickup truck, getting it in working order so that he could drive it to work Monday. So she had watched, she had helped. It was about the only way she had been able to connect with her gruff old man. It was still about the only way she could connect with him.

It certainly wasn't through musicals. It could never have been a desire to be seen differently by other kids at school. A need to look prettier for a boy that she liked.

So she had chosen carburetors.

"But it can't be carburetors forever." Well, it could be. In that she imagined she would do this sort of work for the rest of her life. She loved it. She was successful at it. She filled a niche in the community that needed to be filled. But…it couldn't be the only thing she was. She needed to do more than fill. She needed to…be filled.

And right now everything was all kind of turned on its head. Or bent over the back of a pickup truck. Her cheeks heated at the memory.

Yeah, Chase had definitely come by his reputation honestly. It wasn't difficult to see why women lost their ever-loving minds over him.

That made her frown. Because she didn't like to think that she was just one of the many women losing their minds over him because he had a hot ass and skilled hands. She had known about the hot ass for years. It hadn't made her lose her mind. In fact, she didn't really think she had lost her mind now. She knew exactly what she was doing. She frowned even more deeply.

Did she know what she was doing? They had stopped and had discussions, made conscious decisions to do this friends-with-benefits thing. Tricked themselves into thinking that they were in control of this. Or at least that's what she had been doing. But as she had been carried away on a wave of emotion last night, she had known for an absolute fact that she wasn't in control of any of this.

"Doesn't mean I'm going to stop."

That, at least, was the absolute truth. He would have to be the one to call it off.

Just the thought made her heart crumple up into a little ball.

"Quitting time yet?"

She turned to see Chase standing in the doorway. This was a routine she could get used to. She wanted to cross the space between them and kiss him. And why not? She wasn't hiding her attraction to him. They weren't hiding their association.

She dropped her ratchet, wiped her hands on her coveralls and took two quick steps, flinging herself into his arms and kissing him on the lips. She wasn't embarrassed until about midway through the kiss, when she realized she had been completely and totally enthusiastic and hadn't hidden any of it. But he was holding on to her, and he was kissing her back, so maybe it didn't matter. Maybe it was okay.

When they parted, he was smiling.

Her heart felt tender, exposed. But warm, like it was being bathed in sunlight. Something to do with that smile of his. With that easy acceptance of what she had offered. "I think it's about time to quit," she said.

"I like your look," he said, gesturing to her white tank top, completely smeared with grease and dirt, and her coveralls, which were unbuttoned and tied around her waist.

"Really?"

"Last night you were my dirty country girl fantasy and today you're a sexy mechanic fantasy. Do you take requests? Around Christmas you could go for Naughty Mrs. Claus."

She rolled her eyes, grabbing the end of her tank top and knotting it up just under her breasts. "Maybe more like this? Though I think I'm missing the breast implants."

His smile turned wicked. "Baby, you aren't missing a damn thing."

Her heart thundered harder, a rush of adrenaline flowing through her. "I didn't think this was your type. Remember? You had to give me a makeover."

"Yeah, that was stupid. I actually think I just needed to get knocked upside the head."

"Did I…knock you upside the head?"

"Yeah." He wrapped his arms around her bare waist, his fingertips playing over her skin. "You're pretty perfect the way you are. You never needed a dress or high heels. I mean, you're welcome to wear them if you want. I'm not going to complain about that outfit you wore last night. But all that stuff we talked about in the beginning, about you needing to change so that people would believe we were together... I guess everyone is just going to have to believe that I changed a little bit."

"Have you changed?" she asked, brushing her thumb over his lower lip. A little thrill skittered down her spine. That she could touch him like this. Be so close to him. Share this kind of intimacy with a man she had had a certain level of emotional intimacy with for years and years.

It was wonderful. It also made her ache. Made her feel like her insides were being broken apart with a chisel. And she was willingly submitting to it. She didn't know quite what was happening to her.

*Are you sure you don't?*

"Something did," he said, his dark eyes boring into hers.

"You know," she said, trying to tamp down the fluttering that was happening in her chest, "I think it's only fair that I give you a few lessons."

"What kind of lessons?" he asked, his gaze sharpening.

"I'm not sure you know your way around an engine quite the way you should," she said, smiling as she wiggled out of his hold.

"Oh, really?"

She nodded, grabbing hold of a rag and slinging it over her shoulder before picking up her ratchet again. "Really."

"Is this euphemistic engine talk?"

"Do you think I'm expressing dissatisfaction with the way you work under my hood?"

He chuckled. "You're really getting good at this flirting thing."

"I am. That was good. And dirty."

"I noticed." He moved behind her, sweeping her hair to the side and kissing her neck. "But if you're implying that I didn't do a very good job...I would have to clear my good name."

"I was talking about literal engines, Chase. But if you really want to try to up your game, I'm not going to stop you."

"What's that?" he asked, reaching past her and pointing to one of the parts that were spread out on the worktable in front of her.

"A cylinder head. I'm replacing that and the head gasket on the engine. And I had to take a lot of things apart to get to it."

"When do you need to have it done?"

"Not until tomorrow."

"So you don't need me to play the part of lovely assistant while you finish up tonight?"

"I would like you to assist me with a few things," she said, planting her hand at the center of his chest and pushing him lightly. The backs of his knees butted up against the chair that was behind him and he sat down, looking up at her, a predatory smile curving his lips.

"Is this going to be a part of my lesson?"

"Yeah," she said, "I thought it might be."

Last night had been incredible. Last night, he had given her something that felt special. Personal. Now she wanted to give him something. To show him what was happening inside of her, because she could hardly bring herself to think it. She wanted… She just wanted. In ways that she hadn't allowed herself to want in a long time. More. Everything.

"What exactly are you going to teach me?"

"Well, I could teach you all the parts of the tractor engine. But we would be here all night. And it would just slow me down. Someday, we can trade. You can give me some welding secrets. Teach me how to pound steel."

"That sounds dirty, too."

"Lucky me," she said, stretching her arms up over her head, her shirt riding up a little higher. She knew what she wanted to do. But she also felt almost petrified. This was…well, this was the opposite of protecting herself. This was putting herself out there. Risking humiliation. Risking doing something wrong while revealing how desperately she wanted to get it right.

But she wanted to give him something. And honestly, there was no bigger gift she could give him than vulnerability. To show him just how much she wanted him.

She swayed her hips to the right, then moved them back toward the left in a slow circle. She watched his face, watched the tension in his jaw increase, the sharpness in his eyes get positively lethal. And that was all the encouragement she needed. She'd seen enough movies with lap dances that she had a vague idea of how this should go. Maybe her idea was the PG-13-rated version, but she could improvise.

He moved his hand over the outline of his erection, squeezing himself through the denim as she continued to move. Maybe it wasn't rhinestones and a miniskirt, but he didn't seem to mind her white tank top and coveralls. He was still watching her with avid interest as she untied the sleeves from around her waist and let the garment drop down around her feet. She kicked it off to the side, revealing her denim cutoff shorts underneath it.

"Come here," he said, his voice hard.

"I'm not taking orders from you. You have to be patient."

"I'm not feeling very patient, honey."

"What's my name?"

"Anna," he ground out. "Anna, I'm not feeling very patient."

"Not enough women have made you wait. You're getting spoiled."

She slid her hand up her midsection, her own fingertips combined with the electric look on Chase's face sending heat skittering along her veins. She let her fingers skim over her breast, gratified when his breath hissed through his teeth.

"Anna…"

"You know me pretty well, don't you? But you didn't know all this." She moved her hand back down, over her stomach, her belly button, sliding her fingers down beneath the waistband of her shorts, stroking herself where she was wet and aching for him. His fingers curled around the edge of the chair, his knuckles white, the cords on his neck standing out, the strength it was taking him to remain seated clear and incredibly compelling.

"Take them off," he said.

"Didn't I just tell you that you're not in charge?"

"Don't play games with me."

"Maybe patience is the lesson you need to learn."

"I damn well don't," he growled.

She turned around, facing away from him, taking a deep breath as she unsnapped her shorts and pushed them down her hips, revealing the other purchase she had made at the store yesterday. A black, lacy thong, quite unlike any other pair of underwear she had ever owned. And she had slipped it on this morning hoping that this would be the end of her day.

"Holy hell," he said.

She knew that she was not the first woman to take her clothes off for him. Much less the first woman to reveal sexy underwear. But that only made his appreciation for hers that much sweeter. She swayed her hips back and forth before dropping down low, and sweeping back up. It felt so cheesy, and at the same time she was pretty proud of herself for pulling it off.

When she turned to face him, his expression was positively feral.

Her shirt was still knotted beneath her breasts, and now she was wearing work boots, a thong and the top. If Chase thought the outfit was a little bit silly, he certainly didn't show it.

She moved over to the chair, straddling him, leaning in and kissing him on the lips. "I want you," she said.

She had said it before. But this was more. Deeper. This was the truth. Her truth, the truest thing inside of her. She wanted Chase. In every way. Forever. She swallowed hard, grabbing hold of his T-shirt and tugging it up over his head. She licked her lips, looking at his body, at his chest, speckled with just the right amount of dark hair, at his abs, so perfectly defined and tempting.

She reached between them, undoing his belt and

jerking it through the loops, before tugging his pants and underwear down low on his hips. He put his hand on her backside, holding her steady as she maneuvered herself so that she was over him, rubbing up against his arousal. "I would never have considered doing something like this before last week. Not with anyone. It's just you," she said, leaning in and kissing his lips lightly. "You do this to me."

He shuddered beneath her, her words having the exact effect she hoped they would. He liked feeling special, too.

He took hold of her hand, drawing it between them, curving her fingers around him. "And you do this to me. You make me so hard, it hurts. I've never wanted a woman like this before. Ever."

She flexed her hips, squeezed him tighter, trapping him between her palm and the apex of her thighs. "Why? Why do you want me like this?"

It was important to know. Essential.

"Because it's you, Anna. There's this idea that having sex with a stranger is supposed to be exciting. Because it's dirty. Because it's wrong. Maybe because it's unknown? But I've done that. And this is… You're right. I know you. Knowing you like this… Your face is so familiar to me, your voice. Knowing what it looks like when I make you come, how you sound when I push you over the edge, baby, there's nothing hotter than that."

His words washed over her, everything she had never known she needed. This full, complete acceptance of who she was. Right here in her garage. The mechanic, the woman. The friend, the lover. He wanted her. And everything that meant.

She didn't even try to keep herself from feeling it now. Didn't try to keep herself from thinking it.

She loved him. So much. Every part of him, with every part of her. Her friend. The only man she really wanted. The only person she could imagine sharing her days and nights and blankets and musicals with.

And that realization didn't even make her want to pull away from him. Didn't make her want to hide. Instead, she wanted to finish this. She wanted to feel connected to him. Now that she was in, she was in all the way. Ready to expose herself completely, scrape herself raw, all for him.

She rose up so that she was on her knees, tugged her panties down her hips and maneuvered herself so that she was able to dispense with them completely before settling over him, grabbing hold of his broad shoulders as she sank down onto his hardened length.

He swore, the harsh word echoing in the empty space. "Anna, I need to get a condom."

She pulled away from him quickly, hovering over him as he lifted his hips, grabbing his wallet and pulling out a condom with shaking hands, taking care of the practicalities quickly. She was trembling, both with the adrenaline rush that accompanied the stupidity of her mistake and with need. With regret because she wished that he was still inside of her even though it wouldn't be responsible at all.

Soon, he was guiding her back onto him, having protected them both. Thankfully, he was a little more with it than she was.

He gripped her tightly, guiding her movements at first, helping her establish a rhythm that worked for them both.

He moved his hands around, brushing his fingertips along the seam of her ass before teasing her right where their bodies were joined. She gasped, grabbing hold of the back of the chair, flexing her hips, chasing her own release as he continued to touch her. To push her higher.

She slid her hands up, cupping his face, holding him steady. She met his gaze, a thrill shooting down her spine. "Anna," he rasped, the words skating over her skin like a caress, touching her everywhere.

Pleasure gripped her, low and tight, sending her over the edge. She held his face as she shuddered out her orgasm and chanted his name, endlessly. Over and over again. And when it was over, he held her to him, kissing her lips, whispering words against her mouth that she could barely understand. She didn't need to. The only words she understood were the ones she most needed to hear.

"Stay with me tonight."

## Chapter 12

They dressed and drove across the property in Chase's truck. His heart was still hammering like crazy, and he had no idea what the hell he was doing. But then, it was Anna. She wasn't some random hookup. He wanted her again, and having her spend the night seemed like the best way to accomplish that.

He ignored the little terror claws that wrapped themselves around his heart and squeezed, and focused instead on the heavy sensation in his gut. In his dick. He wanted her, and dammit, he was going to have her.

The image of her dancing in front of him in the shop…that would haunt him forever. And it was his goal to collect a few more images that would make his life miserable when their physical relationship ended.

That was normal.

He parked the truck, then got out, following Anna

mutely up the steps. When they got to the door, Anna paused.

"I don't...have anything with me. No porcupine pajamas."

Some of the tension in his chest eased. "You won't need pajamas in my bed," he said, his voice low, almost unrecognizable even to himself.

Which was fair enough, since this whole damn situation was unrecognizable. Saying this kind of stuff to Anna. Seeing her like this. Wanting her like this.

She was a constant. She was stability. And he felt shaky as hell right now.

"I've never spent the night with anyone," she blurted.

The words hit him hard in the chest. Along with the realization that this was a first for him, too. He knew it, logically. But for some reason it hadn't seemed momentous when he'd issued the invitation. Because it was Anna and sleeping with her had seemed like the most natural thing on earth. He liked talking to her, liked kissing her, liked having sex with her, and he didn't want her to leave. So the obvious choice was to ask her to stay the night.

Now it was hitting him, though. What that usually meant. Why he didn't do it.

But it was too late to take the invitation back, and anyway, he didn't know if he wanted to.

"I haven't, either," he said.

She blinked. "You...haven't? I mean, I had a ten-minute roll in the hay—literally—with a loser in high school, so I know why I've never spent the night with anyone. But you...you do this a lot."

"Are you calling me a slut?"

"Yes," she said, deadpan. "No judgment, but yeah, you're kind of slutty."

"Well, you don't have to spend the night with someone when you're done with them. I guess that's why I haven't. Because I am kind of slutty, and it has nothing to do with liking the person I'm with. Just…"

Oblivion. The easiest, most painless connection on earth with no risk involved whatsoever.

But he wasn't going to say that.

Anna wasn't oblivion. Being with her was like… being inside his own skin, really in it, and feeling it, for the first time since he was sixteen.

Like driving eighty miles per hour on the same winding road that had killed his parents, daring it to come for him, too. He'd felt alive then. Alive and pushing up against the edge of mortality as hard as he could.

Then he'd backed way off the gas. And he'd backed way off ever since.

This was the closest thing to tasting that surge of adrenaline, that rush he'd felt since the day he'd basically begged the road to take him, too.

*You're a head case.*

Yes, he was. But he'd always known that. Anna hadn't, though.

"Just?" she asked, eyebrows shooting up. She wasn't going to let that go, apparently.

"It's just sex."

"And what is this?" she asked, gesturing between the two of them.

"Friendship," he said honestly. "With some more to it."

"Those benefits."

"Yeah," he said. "Those."

He shoved his hands in his pockets, feeling like he'd just failed at something, and he couldn't quite figure out what. But his words were flat in the evening air. Just sort of dull and resting between them, wrong and weird, but he didn't know what to do about it.

Because he didn't know what else to say, either.

"Want to come inside?" he asked finally.

"That is where your bed is," she said.

"It is."

They made their way to the bedroom, and somehow it all felt different. He could easily remember when she'd been up here just last week, walking in those heels and that dress. When he'd been overwhelmed with the need to touch her, but wouldn't allow himself to do so.

He could also remember being in here with her plenty of times before. Innocuous as sharing the space with any friend.

*How?* How had they ever existed in silences that weren't loaded? In moments that weren't wrapped in tension. In isolation that didn't present the very tempting possibility of chasing pleasure together. Again and again.

This wasn't friendship plus benefits. That implied the friendship remained untouched and the benefits were an add-on. Easy to stick there, easy to remove. But that wasn't the case.

Everything was different. The air around them had changed. How the hell could he pretend the friendship was the same?

"I'm just—" She smiled sheepishly and pulled her shirt up over her head. "Sorry." Then she unhooked her bra, tossing it onto the floor. He hadn't had a chance to look at her breasts the last time they'd had sex. She'd kept them covered. Something that had added nicely to the tease back in the shop. But he was ready to drop to his knees and give thanks for their perfection now.

"Why are you apologizing for flashing me?"

"Because. In the absence of pajamas I need to get comfortable now." She stripped her shorts off, and her underwear—those shocking black panties that he simply hadn't seen coming, much like the rest of her—and then she flopped down onto his bed. He didn't often bring women back here.

*Sometimes*, depending on the circumstances, but if they had a hotel room, or their own place available, that was his preference. So it was a pretty unusual sight in general. A naked woman in his room. Anna, in this familiar place—naked and warm and about as inviting as anything had ever been—was enough to make his head explode.

His head, and other places.

"You never have to apologize for being naked." He stripped his shirt off, then continued to follow her lead, until he was wearing nothing.

He lay down beside her, not touching her, just looking at her. This was hella weird. If a woman was naked, he was usually having sex with her, bottom line. He didn't lie next to one, simply looking at her. Right now, Anna was something like art and he just wanted to admire her. Well, that wasn't *all* he wanted. But it was what he wanted right now. To watch the soft lamplight cast a warm glow over her curves, to examine every dip and hollow on the map of her figure. To memorize the rosy color of her nipples, the dark hair at the apex of her thighs. The sweet flare of her hips and the slight roundness of her stomach. She was incredible. She was Anna. Right now, she was his.

That thought made his stomach tighten. How long had it been since something was his?

This place would always be McCormack, through and through. The foundation of the forge and the business…it was built on his great-grandfather's back, carried down by his grandfather, handed to their father.

And he and Sam carried it now.

This ranch would always be something they were bound to by blood, not by choice. Even if given the choice, he could probably never leave. Their family… It didn't feel like their family anymore. It hadn't for a lot of years.

It was two of them, him and Sam. Two of them trying so damn hard to push this legacy back to where it had been. To make their family extend beyond these walls, beyond these borders. To fulfill all of the promises he'd made to his dad, even though the old man had never actually heard them.

Even though Chase had made them too late.

And so there was something about that. Anna, this moment, being for him. Something that he chose, instead of something that he'd inherited.

"I like when you look at me like that," she said, her voice hushed.

"I like when you take control like you did back in the shop. I like seeing you realize how beautiful you are," he said. It was true. He was glad that she knew now. And pissed that she was going to take that knowledge and work her magic on some other man with her newfound power. He wanted to kill that man.

But he could never hope to take his place, so he wouldn't.

"You're the first person who has made me feel like it all fit. And maybe it's because you're my friend. Maybe it's because you know me," she said.

"I don't follow."

"I had to be tough," she said, her tone demonstrating just that. "All my life I've had to be tough. My brothers raised me, and they did a damn good job, and I know you think they're jerks, and honestly a lot of the time they are. But they were young boys who were put in charge of taking care of their kid sister. So they took care of me, but they tortured me in that way only brothers can. Probably because I tortured them in ways that most little sisters could never dream. They didn't go out in high school. They had to make sure I was taken care of. They didn't trust my dad to do it. He wasn't stable enough. He would go out to the bar and get drunk, and he would call needing a ride home. They handled things so that I didn't have to. And I never felt like I could make their lives more difficult by showing how hard it was for me."

She shifted, sighing heavily before she continued. "And then there was my dad. He didn't know what to do with a daughter. As pissed as he was that his wife left, I think in some ways he was relieved, because he didn't have to figure out how to fit a woman into his life anymore. But then I kind of started becoming a woman. And he really didn't know what to do. So I learned how to work on cars. I learned how to talk about sports. I learned how to fit. Even though it pushed me right out of fitting when it came to school. When it came to making friends."

He knew these things about Anna. Knew them because he'd absorbed them by being in her house, being near her, for fifteen years. But he'd never heard her say them. There was something different about that.

"You've always fit with me, Anna," he said, his voice rough.

"I know. And even though we've never talked about this, I'm pretty sure somehow you knew all of it. You always have. Because you know me. And you accept me. Not very many people know about the musicals. Because it always embarrassed me. Kind of a girlie thing."

"I guess so," he said, the words feeling inadequate.

"Also, it was my thing. And…I never like anyone to know how much I care about things. I… My mom loved old musicals," she said, her voice soft. "Sometimes I wonder what it would be like to watch them with her."

"Anna…"

"I remember sneaking out of my room at night, seeing the TV flickering in the living room. She would be watching *The Sound of Music* or *Cinderella. Oklahoma!* of course. And I would just hang there in the hall. But I didn't want to interrupt. Because by the end of the day she was always out of patience, and I knew she didn't want any of the kids to talk to her. But it was kind of like watching them with her." Anna's eyes filled with tears. "But now I just wish I had. I wish I had gone in and sat next to her. I wish I had risked her being upset with me. I never got the chance. She left, and that was it. So, maybe she would've been mad at me, or maybe she wouldn't have let me watch them with her. But at least I would've had the answer. Now I just wonder. I just remember that space between us.

Me hiding in the hall, and her sitting on the couch. She never knew I was there. Maybe if I'd done a better job of connecting with her, she wouldn't have left."

"That's not true, Anna."

"She didn't have anyone to watch the movies with, Chase. And my dad was so… I doubt he ever gave her a damn scrap of tenderness. But maybe I could have. I think… I think that's what I was always trying to do with my dad. To make up for that. It was too late to make her stay, but I thought maybe I could hang on to him."

Chase tried to breathe past the tightness in his chest, but it was nearly impossible. "Anna," he said, "any parent that chooses to leave their child…the issue is with them. It was your parents' marriage. It was your mom. I don't know. But it was never you. It wasn't you not watching a movie with her, or irritating her, or making her angry. There was never anything you could do."

She nodded, a tear tracking down her pale cheek. "I do know that."

"But you still beat yourself up for it."

"Of course I do."

He didn't have a response to that. She said it so matter-of-factly, as though there was nothing else but to blame herself, even if it made no sense. He had no response because he understood. Because he knew what it was like to twist a tragedy in a thousand different ways to figure out how you could take it on yourself. He knew what it was like to live your life with a gaping hole where someone you loved should be. To try to figure out how you could have stopped the loss from happening.

In the years since his parents' accident he had

moved beyond blame. Not because he was stronger than Anna, just because you could only twist death in so many different directions. It was final. And it didn't ask you. It just was. Blaming himself would have been a step too far into martyrdom.

Still, he knew about lingering scars and responses to those scars that didn't make much sense.

But he didn't know what it was like to have a parent choose to leave you. God knew his parents never would have chosen to abandon their sons.

As if she'd read his mind, Anna continued. "She's still out there. I mean, as far as I know. She could have come back. Anytime. I just feel like if I had given her even a small thing…well, then, maybe she would have missed me enough at some point. If she'd had anything back here waiting for her, she could have called. Just once."

"You were you," he said. "If that wasn't enough for her…fuck her."

She laughed and wiped another tear from her face. Then she shifted, moving closer to him. "I appreciate that." She paused for a moment, kissing his shoulder, then she continued. "It's amazing. I've never told you that before. I've never told anyone that before. It's just kind of crazy that we could know each other for so long and…there's still more we don't know."

He wanted to tell her then. About the day his parents died. About the complete and total hole it had torn in his life. She knew to a degree. They had been friends when it happened. He had been sixteen, and Sam had been eighteen, and the loss of everything they knew had hit so hard and fast that it had taken them out at the knees.

He wanted to tell her about his nightmares. Wanted to tell her about the last conversation he'd had with his dad.

But he didn't.

"Amazing" was all he said instead.

Then he leaned over and kissed her, because he couldn't think of anything else to do, couldn't think of anything else to say.

*Liar.*

A thousand things he wanted to tell her swirled around inside of him. A thousand different things she didn't know. That he had never told anybody. But he didn't want to open himself up like that. He just… He just couldn't.

So instead, he kissed her, because that he could do. Because of all the changes that existed between them, that was the one he was most comfortable with. Holding her, touching her. Everything else was too big, too unknown to unpack. He couldn't do it. Didn't want to do it.

But he wanted to kiss her. Wanted to run his hands over her bare curves. So he did.

He touched her, tasted her, made her scream. Because of all the things that were happening in his life, that felt right.

This was…well, it was a detour. The best one he'd ever taken, but a detour all the same. He was building the family business, like he had promised his dad he would do. Or like he should have promised him when he'd had the chance. He might never have been able to tell the old man to his face, but he'd promised it to his grave. A hundred times, a thousand times since he'd died.

That was what he had to do. That was on the other side of making love with Anna. Going to that benefit with her all dressed up, trying to help her get the kind of reputation she wanted. To send her off with all her newfound skills so that she could be with another man after.

To knuckle down and take the McCormack family ranch back to where it had been. Beyond. To make sure that Sam used his talents, to make sure that the forge and all the work their father had done to build the business didn't go to waste.

To prove that the fight he'd had with his father right before he died was all angry words and teenage bluster. That what he'd said to his old man wasn't real.

He didn't hate the ranch. He didn't hate the business. He didn't hate their name. He was their name, and damn him for being too young and stupid to see it then.

He was proving it now by pouring all of his blood, all of his sweat, all of his tears into it. By taking the little bit of business acumen he had once imagined might get him out of Copper Ridge and applying it to this place. To try to make it something bigger, something better. To honor all the work their parents had invested all those years.

To finish what they started.

He might not have ever made a commitment to a woman, but this ranch, McCormack Iron Works…was his life. That was forever.

It was the only forever he would ever have.

He closed those thoughts out, shut them down completely and focused on Anna. On the sweet scent of her as he lowered his head between her thighs and lapped at her, on the feel of her tight channel pulsing around his fingers as he stroked them in and out. And finally, on the tight, wet clasp of her around him as he slid home.

*Home.* That's really what it was.

In a way that nowhere else had ever been. The ranch was a memorial to people long dead. A monument that he would spend the rest of his life building.

But she was home. She was his.

If he let her, she could become everything.

*No.*

That denial echoed in his mind, pushed against him as he continued to pound into her, hard, deep, seeking the oblivion that he had always associated with sex before her. But it wasn't there. Instead, it was like a veil had been torn away and he could see all of his life, spreading out before him. Like he was standing on a ridge high in the mountains, able to survey everything. The past, the present, the future. So clear, so sharp it almost didn't seem real.

Anna was in all of it. A part of everything.

And if she was ever taken away…

He closed his eyes, shutting out that thought, a wave of pleasure rolling over him, drowning out everything. He threw himself in. Harder than he ever had. Grateful as hell that Anna had found her own release, because he'd been too wrapped up in himself to consider her first.

Then he wrapped his arms around her, wrapped her up against him. Wrapped himself up in her. And he pushed every thought out of his mind and focused on the feeling of her body against his, the scent of her skin. Feminine and sweet with a faint trace of hay and engine grease.

No other woman smelled like Anna.

He pressed his face against her breasts and she sighed, a sound he didn't think he'd ever get tired of. He let everything go blank. Because there was nothing in his past, or his future, that was as good as this.

## Chapter 13

Chase woke in a cold sweat, his heart pounding so heavily he thought it would burst through his bone and flesh and straight out into the open. His bed was empty. He sat up, rubbing his hand over his face, then forking his fingers through his hair.

It felt wrong to have the bed empty. After spending only one night wrapped around Anna, it already felt wrong. Not having her... Waking up in the morning to find that she wasn't there was... He hated it. It was unsettling. It reminded him of the holes that people left behind, of how devastating it was when you lost someone unexpectedly.

He banished the thought. She might still be here. But then, she didn't have any clean clothes or anything, so if she had gone home, he couldn't necessarily blame her. He went straight into the bathroom, took a shower, took care of all other morning practicalities. He resisted the urge to look at his phone, to call Anna's phone or to go downstairs and see if maybe she was still around. He was going to get through all this, dammit, and he was not going to behave as though he were affected.

As though the past night had changed something fundamental, not just between them, but in him.

He scowled, throwing open the bedroom door and heading down the stairs.

He stopped dead when he saw her standing there in the kitchen. She was wearing his T-shirt, her long, slim legs bare. And he wondered if she was bare all the way up. His mouth dried, his heart squeezing tight.

She wasn't missing. She wasn't gone. She was cooking him breakfast. Like she belonged here. Like she belonged in his life. In his house. In his bed.

For one second it made him feel like he belonged. Like she'd been the missing piece to making this his, to making it more than McCormack.

He felt like he was standing in the middle of a dream. Standing there looking at somebody else's life. At some wild, potential scenario that in reality he would never get to have.

Right in front of him was everything. And in the same moment he saw that, he imagined the hole that would be left behind if it was ever taken away. If he ever believed in this, fully, completely. If he reached out and embraced her now, there would be no words for how empty his arms would feel if he ever lost her.

"Don't you have work?" he asked, leaning against the doorjamb.

She turned around and smiled, the kind of smile that lit him up inside, from his head, down to his toes.

He did his very best not to return the gesture. Did his best not to encourage it in any way.

And he cursed himself when the glow leached out of her face. "Good morning to you, too," she said.

"You didn't need to make breakfast."

"*Au contraire.* I was hungry. So breakfast was needed."

"You could've gone home."

"Yes, Grumpy-Pants, I could have. But I decided to stay here and make you food. Which seemed like an adequate thank-you for the multiple orgasms I received yesterday."

"Bacon? You're trying to pay for your orgasms with bacon?"

"It seemed like a good idea at the time." She crossed her arms beneath her breasts and revealed that she did not, in fact, have anything on beneath the shirt. "Bacon is a borderline orgasmic experience."

"I have work. I don't have time to eat breakfast."

"Maybe if you had gotten up at a decent hour."

"I don't need you to lecture me on my sleeping habits," he bit out. "Is there coffee?"

"It's like you don't know me at all." She crossed the room and lifted a thermos off the counter. "I didn't want to leave it sitting on the burner. That makes it taste gross."

"I don't really care how it tastes. That's not the point."

She rested her hand on the counter, then rapped her knuckles against the surface. "What's going on?"

"Nothing."

"Stop it, Chase. Maybe you can BS the other bimbos that you sleep with, but you can't do it to me. I know you too well. This has nothing to do with waking up late."

"This is a bad idea," he said.

"What's a bad idea? Eating bacon and drinking coffee with one of your oldest friends?"

"Sleeping with one of my oldest friends. It was stupid. We never should've done it."

She just stood there, her expression growing waxen, and as the color drained from her face, he felt something even more critical being scraped from his chest, like he was being hollowed out.

"It's a little late for that," she pointed out.

"Well, it isn't too late to start over."

"Chase…"

"It was fun. But, honestly, we accomplished everything we needed to. There's no reason to get dramatic about it. We agreed that we weren't going to let it affect our friendship. And it…it just isn't working for me."

"It was working fine for you last night."

"Well, that was last night, Anna. Don't be so needy."

She drew back as though she had been slapped and he wanted to punch his own face for saying such a thing. For hitting her where he knew it would hurt. And he waited. Waited for her to grow prickly. For her to retreat behind the walls. For her to get angry and start insulting him. For her to end all of this in fire and brimstone as she scorched the earth in an attempt to disguise the naked pain that was radiating from her right now.

He knew she would. Because that was how it went. If he pushed far enough, then she would retreat.

She closed the distance between them, cupping his face, meeting his eyes directly. And he waited for the blow. "But I feel needy. So what am I going to do about that?"

He couldn't have been more shocked than if she had reached up and slapped him. "What?"

"I'm needy. Or maybe…wanty? I'm both." She took a deep breath. "Yes, I'm both. I want more. Not less. And this is… This is the moment where we make decisions, right? Well, I've decided that I want to move forward with this. I don't want to go back. I can't go back."

"Anna," he said, her name scraping his throat raw.

"Chase," she said, her own voice a whisper in response.

"We can't do this," he said.

He needed the Anna he knew to come to his rescue now. To laugh it all off. To break this tension. To say that it didn't matter. To wave her hand and say it was all whatever and they could forget it. But she wasn't doing that. She was looking at him, her green eyes completely earnest, vulnerability radiating from her face. "We need to do this. Because I love you."

Anna could tell that her words had completely stunned Chase. Fair enough, they had shocked her just as much. She didn't know where all of this was coming from. This strength. This bravery.

Except that last night's conversation kept echoing in her mind. When she had told him about her mother. When she had told him about how she always regretted not closing the distance between them. Always regretted not taking the chance.

That was the story of her entire life. She had, from the time she was a child, refused to make herself vulnerable. Refused to open herself up to injury. To pain. So she pretended she didn't care. She pretended nothing mattered. She did that every time her father ignored her, every time he forgot an important milestone in her life. She had done it the first time she'd ever had sex with a guy and it had made her feel something. Rather than copping to that, rather than dealing with it, she had mocked him.

All of her inner workings were a series of walls and shields, carefully designed to keep the world from hitting the terrible, needy things inside of her. Designed to keep herself from realizing they were there. But she couldn't do it anymore. She didn't want to do it anymore. Not with Chase. She didn't want to look back and wonder what could have been.

She wanted more. She needed more. Pride be damned.

"I do," she said, nodding. "I love you."

"You can't."

"I'm pretty sure I can. Since I do."

"No," he said, the word almost desperate.

"No, Chase, I really do. I mean, I have loved you since I was fifteen years old. And intermittently thought you were hot. But mostly, I just loved you. You've been my friend, my best friend. I needed you. You've been my emotional support for a long time. We do that for each other. But things changed in the past few days. You're my…everything." Her voice broke on that last word. "This isn't sex and friendship, it isn't two different things, this is all the things, combined together to make something so big that it fills me completely. And I don't have room inside my chest for shields and protection anymore. Not when all that I am just loves you."

"I can't do this," he bit out, stepping away from her.

"I didn't ask if you could do this. This isn't about

you, not right now. Yes, I would like you to love me, too, but right now this is just about me saying that I love you. Telling you. Because I don't ever want to look back and think that maybe you didn't know. That maybe if I had said something, it could have been different." She swallowed hard, battling tears. "I don't know what's wrong with me. Unless it's a movie, I almost never cry, but you're making me cry a lot lately."

"I'm only going to make you cry more," he said. "Because I don't know how to do this. I don't know how to love somebody."

"Bull. You've loved me perfectly, just the way I needed you to for fifteen years. The way that you take care of this place, the way that you care for Sam… Don't tell me that you can't love."

"Not this kind. Not this… Not this."

"I'm closing the gap," she said, pressing on, even though she could see that this was a losing battle. She was charging in anyway, sword held high, chest exposed. She was giving it her all, fighting even though she knew she wasn't going to walk away unscathed. "I'm not going to wonder what would've happened if I'd just been brave enough to do it. I would rather cut myself open and bleed out. I would rather risk my heart than wonder. So I'm just going to say it. Stop being such a coward and love me."

He took another step back from her and she felt that gap she was so desperate to close widening. Watched as her greatest fear started to play out right before her eyes. "I just… I don't."

"You don't or you won't?"

"At the end of the day, the distinction doesn't really matter. The result is the same."

She felt like she was having an out-of-body experience. Like she was floating up above, watching herself get rejected. There was nothing she could do. She couldn't stop it. Couldn't change it. Couldn't shield herself.

It was…horrible. Gut-wrenching. Destructive. Freeing.

Like watching a tsunami racing to shore and deciding to surrender to the wave rather than fight it. Yeah, it would hurt like hell. But it was a strange, quiet space. Past fear, past hope. All she could hear was the sound of her heart beating.

"I'm going to go," she said, turning away from him. "You can have the bacon."

She had been willing to risk herself, but she wouldn't stand there and fall apart in front of him. She would fall apart, but dammit, it would be on her own time.

"Stay and eat," he said.

She shook her head. "No. I can't stay."

"Are we going to… Are we going to go to the gala together still?"

"No!" She nearly shouted the word. "We are not going to go together. I need to… I need to think. I need to figure this out. But I don't think things can be the same anymore."

It was his turn to close the distance between them. He grabbed hold of her arms, drawing her toward him, his expression fierce. "That was not part of the deal. It was friends plus benefits, remember? And then in the end we could just stop with the benefits and go back to the friendship."

"We can't," she said, tears falling down her cheeks. "I'm sorry. But we can't."

"What the hell?" he ground out.

"We can't because I'm all in. I'm not going to sit back and pretend that it didn't really matter. I'm not going to go and hide these feelings. I'm not going to shrug and say it doesn't really matter if you love me or not. Because it does. It's everything. I have spent so many years not wanting. Not trying. Hiding how much I wanted to be accepted, hiding how desperately I wanted to try to look beautiful, how badly I wanted to be able to be both a mechanic and a woman. Hiding how afraid I was of ending up alone. Hiding under a blanket and watching old movies. Well, I'm done. I'm not hiding any of it anymore. And you know what? Nothing's going to hurt after this." She jerked out of his hold and started to walk toward the front door.

"You're not leaving in that."

She'd forgotten she wasn't exactly dressed. "Sure I am. I'm just going to drive straight home. Anyway, it's not your concern. Because I'm not your concern anymore."

The terror that she felt screaming through her chest was reflected on his face. Good. He should be afraid. This was the most terrifying experience of her life. She knew how horrible it was to lose a person you cared for. Knew what kind of void that left. And she knew that after years it didn't heal. She knew, too, you always felt the absence. She knew that she would always feel his. But she needed more. And she wasn't afraid to put it all on the line. Not now. Not after everything they had been through. Not after everything she had learned about herself. Chase was the one who had told her she needed more confidence.

Well, she had found it. But there was a cost.

Or maybe this was just the cost of loving. Of caring, deeply and with everything she had, for the first time in so many years.

She strode across the property, not caring that she was wearing nothing more than his T-shirt, rage pouring through her. And when she arrived back at the shop she grabbed her purse and her keys, making her way to the truck. When she got there, Chase was standing against the driver's-side door. "Don't leave like this."

"Do you love me yet?"

He looked stricken. "What do you want me to say?"

"You know what I want you to say."

"You want me to lie?"

She felt like he had taken a knife and stabbed her directly through the heart. She could barely breathe. Could barely stand straight. This was… This was her worst fear come true. To open herself up so completely, to make herself so entirely vulnerable and to have it all thrown back in her face.

But in that moment, she recognized that she was untouchable from here on out. Because there was nothing that could ever, ever come close to this pain. Nothing that could ever come close to this risk.

How had she missed this before? How had she missed that failure could be such a beautiful, terrible, freeing experience?

It was the worst. Absolutely the worst. But it also broke chains that had been binding her for years. Because if someone had asked her what she was so afraid of, this would have been the answer. And she was in it. Living it. Surviving it.

"I love you," she repeated. "This is your chance. Listen to me, Chase McCormack, I am giving you a

chance. I'm giving you a chance to stop being so afraid.
A chance to walk out of the darkness. We've walked
through it together for a long time. So I'm asking you
now to walk out of it with me. Please."

He backed away from the truck, his jaw tense, a
muscle there twitching.

"Coward," she spat as he turned and walked away
from her. Walked away from them. Walked back into
the damned darkness.

And she got in her truck and started the engine,
driving away from him, driving away from the things
she wanted most in the entire world.

She didn't cry until she got home. But then, once
she did, she was afraid she wouldn't stop.

# Chapter 14

She was going to lose the bet. That was the safest thought in Anna's head as she stood in her bedroom the night of the charity event staring at the dress that was laid across her bed.

She was going to have to go there by herself. And thanks to the elaborate community theater production of their relationship everyone would know that they had broken up, since Chase wouldn't be with her. She almost laughed.

She was facing her fears all over the place, whether she wanted to or not.

Facing fears and making choices.

She wasn't going to be with Chase at the gala tonight. Wasn't going to win her money. But she had bought an incredibly slinky dress, and some more makeup. Including red lipstick. She had done all of that for him. Though in many ways it was for her, too. She had wanted that experience. To go, to prove that she was grown-up. To prove that she had transcended her upbringing and all of that.

She frowned. Was she really considering dressing differently just because she wasn't going to be with Chase?

Screw that. He might have filleted her heart and cooked it like those hideous charred Brussels sprouts cafés tries to pass off as a fancy appetizer, but he *wasn't* going to take his lessons from her. She had learned confidence. She had learned that she was stronger than she thought. She had learned that she was beautiful. And how to care. Like everything inside her had been opened up, for better or for worse. But she would never go back. No matter how bad it hurt, she wouldn't go back.

So she wouldn't go back now, either.

As she slipped the black dress over her curves, laboring over the makeup on her face and experimenting with the hairstyle she had seen online, she could only think how much harder it was to care about things. All of these things. It had been so much easier to embrace little pieces of herself. To play the part of another son for her father and throw herself into activities that made him proud, ignoring her femininity so that she never made him uncomfortable.

All of these moments of effort came at a cost. Each minute invested revealing more and more of her needs. To be seen. To be approved of.

But there were so many other reasons she had avoided this. Because this—she couldn't help but think as she looked in the mirror—looked a lot like trying. It looked a lot like caring. That was scary. It was hard.

Being rejected when you had given your best effort was so much worse than being rejected when you hadn't tried at all.

This whole being-a-woman thing—a whole woman who wanted to be with a man, who loved a man—it was hard. And it hurt.

She looked at her reflection, her eyes widening. Thanks to the smoky eye shadow her green eyes glowed, her lips looking extra pouty with the dark red color on them. She looked like one of the old screen legends she loved so much. Very Elizabeth Taylor, really.

This was her best effort. And yes, it was only a dress, and this was just looks, but it was symbolic.

She was going to lay it all on the line, and maybe people would laugh. Because the tractor mechanic in a ball gown was too ridiculous for words. But she would take the risk. And she would take it alone.

She picked up the little clutch purse that was sitting on her table. The kind of purse she'd always thought was impractical, because who wanted a bag you had to hold in your hand all night? But the salesperson at the department store had told her it went with her dress, and that altogether she looked flawless, and Anna had been in desperate need of flattery. So here she was with a clutch.

It *was* impractical. But she *did* look great.

Of course, Chase wouldn't be there to see it. She felt her eyes starting to fill with tears and she blinked, doing her best to hold it all back. She was not going to smear her makeup. She had already put it all out there for him. She would be damned if she undid all this hard work for him, too.

With that in mind, Anna got into her truck and drove herself to the ball.

"Hey, jackass," Sam shouted from across the shop. "Are you going to finish with work anytime today?"

Okay, so maybe Chase had thrown himself into work with a little more vehemence than was strictly necessary since Anna had walked out of his life.

*Anna.* Anna had walked out of his life. Over something as stupid as love.

*If love was so stupid, it wouldn't make your insides tremble like you were staring down a black bear.*

He ignored his snarky internal monologue. He had been doing a lot of that lately. So many arguments with himself as he pounded iron at the forge. That was, when he wasn't arguing with Sam. Who was getting a little bit tired of him, all things considered.

"Do I look like I'm finished?" he shouted back.

"It's nine o'clock at night."

"That's amazing. When did you learn to tell time?"

"I counted on my fingers," Sam said, wandering deeper into the room. "So, are we just going to pretend that Anna didn't run out of your house wearing only a T-shirt the other morning?"

"I'm going to pretend that my older brother doesn't Peeping Tom everything that happens in my house."

"We live on the same property. It's bound to happen. I was on my way here when I saw her leaving. And you chasing after her. So I'm assuming you did the stupid thing."

"I told her that I couldn't be in a relationship with

her." That was a lie. He had done so much more than that. He had torn both of their hearts out and stomped them into the ground. Because Sam was right, he was an idiot. But he had made a concerted effort to be a safe idiot.

*How's that working for you?*

"Right. Why exactly?"

"Look, the sage hermit thing is a little bit tired. You don't have a social life, I don't see you with a wife and children, so maybe you don't hang out and lecture me."

"Isn't tonight that thing?" Sam seemed undeterred by Chase's rudeness.

"What thing?"

"The charity thing that you were so intent on using to get investors. Because the two of us growing our family business and restoring the former glory of our hallowed ancestors is so important to you. And exploiting my artistic ability for your financial gain."

"Change of plans." He grunted, moving a big slab of iron that would eventually be a gate to the side. "I'm just going to keep working. We'll figure this out without schmoozing."

"Who are you and what have you done with my brother?"

"Just shut up. If you can't do anything other than stand there looking vaguely amused at the fact that I'm going through a personal crisis, then you can go straight to hell without passing Go or collecting two hundred dollars."

"I'm not going to be able to afford Park Place anyway, because you aren't out there getting new investors."

"I'm serious, Sam," Chase shouted, throwing his

hammer down on the ground. "It's all fine for you because you hold everyone at a distance."

Sam laughed. The bastard. "*I* hold everyone at a distance. What do you think you do? What do you think your endless string of one-night stands is?"

"You think I don't know? You think I don't know that it's an easy way to get some without ever having to have a conversation? I'm well aware. But I don't need you standing over there so entertained by the fact that…"

"That you actually got your heart broken?"

Chase didn't have anything to say to that. Every single word in his head evaporated like water against molten metal. He had nothing to say to that because his heart was broken. But Anna wasn't responsible. It was his own fault.

And the only reason his heart was broken was because he…

"Do you know what I said to Dad the day that he died?"

Sam froze. "No."

No, he didn't. Because they had never talked about it. "The last thing I ever said to him was that I couldn't wait to get away from here. I told him I wasn't going to pound iron for the rest of my life. I was going to get away and go to college. Make something real out of myself. Like this wasn't real."

"I didn't realize."

"No. Because I didn't tell you. Because I never told anybody. But that's why I needed to fix this. It's why I wanted to expand this place."

"So it isn't really to harness my incredible talent?"

"I don't even know what it's for anymore. To what?

To make up for what I said to a dead man. And for promises that I made at his grave… He can't hear me. That's the worst thing."

Sam stuffed his hands in his pockets. "Is that the only reason you're still here?"

"No. I love it here. I really do. I had to get older. I had to put some of my own sweat into this place. But now… I get it. I do. And I care about it because I care about it, not just because they cared about it. Not just because it's a legacy, but because it's worth saving. But…"

"I still remember that day. I mean, I don't just remember it," Sam said, "it's like it just happened yesterday. That feeling… The whole world changing. Everything falling right down around us. That's as strong in my head now as it was then."

"How many times can you lose everything?" Chase asked, making eye contact with his brother. "Anna is everything. Or she could be. It was easy when she was just a friend. But…I saw her in my house the other morning cooking me breakfast, wearing my T-shirt. For a second she made me feel like…like that house was our house, and she could be my…my everything."

"I wouldn't even know what that looked like for me, Chase. If you find that…grab it."

"And if I lose it?"

"You'll have no one to blame but yourself."

Chase thought back to the day his parents died. That was a kind of pain he hadn't even known existed. But, as guilty as he had felt, as many promises as he had made at his father's grave site, he couldn't blame himself for their death. It had been an accident. That was the simple truth.

But if he lost Anna now… Pushing her away hadn't been an accident. It was in his control. Fully and absolutely. And if he lost her, then it was on him.

He thought of her face as she had turned away from him, as she had gotten into her truck.

She had trusted him. His prickly Anna had trusted him with her feelings. Her vulnerability. A gift that he had never known her to give to anybody. And he had rejected it. He was no better than he had been as an angry sixteen-year-old, hurtling around the curves of the road that had destroyed his family, daring it to take him, too.

Anna, who had already endured the rejection of a mother, the silent rejection of who she was from her father, had dared to look him in the face and risk his rejection, too.

"I'll do it," Sam said, his voice rough.

"What?"

"I'm going to start…pursuing the art thing to a greater degree. I want to help. You missed this party tonight and I know it mattered to you…"

"But you hate change," Chase reminded him.

"Yeah," Sam said. "But I hate a lot of things. I have to do them anyway."

"We're still going to have to meet with investors."

"Yeah," Sam replied, stuffing his hands in his pockets. "I can help with that. You're right. This is why you're the brains and I'm the talent."

"You're a glorified blacksmith, Sam," Chase said, trying to keep the tone light because if he went too deep now he might just fall apart.

"With talent. Beyond measure," Sam said. "At least my brother has been telling me that for years."

"Your brother is smart." Though he currently felt anything but.

Sam shrugged. "Eh. Sometimes." He cleared his throat. "You discovered you cared about this place too late to ever let Dad know. That's sad. But at least Dad knew you cared about him. You know he never doubted that," Sam said. "But, damn, bro, don't leave it too late to let Anna know you care about her."

Chase looked at his brother, who was usually more cynical than he was wise, and couldn't ignore the truth ringing in his words.

Anna was the best he'd ever had. And had been for the past fifteen years of his life. Losing her...well, that was just a stupid thing to allow.

But the thing that scared him most right now was that it might already be too late. That he might have broken things beyond repair.

"And if it is too late?" he asked.

"Chase, you of all people know that when something is forged in fire it comes out the other side that much stronger." His brother's expression was hard, his dark eyes dead serious. "This is your fire. You're in it now. If you let it cool, you lose your chance. So I suggest you get your ass to wherever Anna is right now and you work at fixing this. It's either that or spend your life as a cold, useless hunk of metal that never became a damn thing."

It had not gone as badly as she'd feared. It hadn't gone perfectly, of course, but she had survived. The lowest point had been when Wendy Maxwell, who was still angry with Anna over the whole Chase thing, had wandered over to her and made disparaging comments

about last season's colors and cuts, all the while implying that Anna's dress was somehow below the height of
fashion. Which, whatever. She had gotten the dress on
clearance, so it probably was. Anna might care about
looking nice, but she didn't give a rat's ass about fashion.

She gave a couple of rat's asses about what had happened next.

*Where's Chase?*

Her newfound commitment to honesty and emotions
had compelled her to answer honestly.

*We broke up. I'm pretty upset about it.*

The other woman had been in no way sympathetic
and had in fact proceeded to smug all over the rest
of the conversation. But she wasn't going to focus on
the low.

The highs had included talking to several people
whom she was going to be working with in the future.
And getting two different phone numbers. She had
made conversation. She had felt…like she belonged.
And she didn't really think it had anything to do with
the dress. Just with her. When you had already put everything out there and had it rejected, what was there
to fear beyond that?

She sighed as she pulled into her driveway, straightening when she saw that there was a truck already
there.

Chase's truck.

She put her own into Park, killing the engine and
getting out. "What are you doing here, McCormack?"
She was furious now. She was all dressed up, wearing her gorgeous dress, and she had just weathered

that party on her own, and now he was here. She was going to punch his face.

Chase was sitting on her porch, wearing well-worn jeans and a tight black T-shirt, his cowboy hat firmly in place. He stood up, and as he began to walk toward her, Anna felt a raindrop fall from the sky. Because of course. He was here to kick her while she was down, almost certainly, and it was going to rain.

*Thanks, Oregon.*

"I came to see you." He stopped, looking her over, his jaw slightly slack. "I'm really glad that I did."

"Stop checking me out. You don't get to look at me like that. I did not put this dress on for you."

"I know."

"No, you don't know. I put this dress on for me. Because I wanted to look beautiful. Because I didn't care if anybody thought I was pretty enough, or if I'm not fashionable enough for Wendy the mule-faced ex-cheerleader. I did it because I cared. I do that now. I care. For me. Not for you."

She started to storm past him, the raindrops beginning to fall harder, thicker. He grabbed her arm and stopped her, twirling her toward him. "Don't walk away. Please."

"Give me a reason to stop walking."

"I've been doing a lot of thinking. And hammering."

"Real hammering, or is this some kind of a euphemism to let me know you're lonely?"

"Actual hammering. I didn't feel like I deserved anything else. Not after what happened."

"You don't. You don't deserve to masturbate ever again."

"Anna…"

"No," she said. "I can't do this. I can't just have a little taste of you. Not when I know what we can have. We can be everything. At first it was like you were my friend, but also we were sleeping together. And I looked at you as two different men. Chase, my friend. And Chase, the guy who was really good with his hands. And his mouth, and his tongue. You get the idea." She swallowed hard, her throat getting tight. "But at some point…it all blended together. And I can't separate it anymore. I just can't. I can't pull the love that I feel for you out of my chest and keep the friendship. Because they're all wrapped up in each other. And they've become the same thing."

"It's all or nothing," he said, his voice rough.

"Exactly."

He sighed heavily. "That's what I was afraid of."

"I'm sorry if you came over for a musical and a look at my porcupine pajamas. But I can't do it."

He tightened his hold on her, pulling her closer. "I knew it was going to be all or nothing."

"I can even understand why you think that might not be fair—"

"No. When you told me you loved me, I knew it was everything. Or nothing. That was what scared me so much. I have known… For a lot of years, I've realized that you were one of the main supports of my entire life. I knew you were one of the things that kept me together after my parents died. One of the only things. And I knew that if I ever lost you…it might finish me off completely."

"I'm sorry. But I can't live my life as your support."

"I know. I'm not suggesting that you do. It's just… when we started sleeping together, I had the same realization. That we weren't going to be able to separate the physical from the emotional, from our friendship. That it wasn't as simple as we pretended it could be. When I came downstairs and saw you in my kitchen... I saw the potential for something I never thought I could have."

"Why didn't you think you could have that?"

"I was too afraid. Tragedy happens to other people, Anna. Until it happens to you. And then it's like... the safety net is just gone. And everything you never thought you could be touched by is suddenly around every corner. You realize you aren't special. You aren't safe. If I could lose both my parents like that... I could lose anybody."

"You can't live that way," she said, her heart crumpling. "How in the world can you live that way?"

"You live halfway," he said. "You let yourself have a little bit of things, and not all of them. You pour your commitment into a place. Your passion into a job, into a goal of restoring a family name when your family is already gone. So you can't disappoint them even if you do fail." He took a deep breath. "You keep the best woman you know as a friend, because if she ever became more, your feelings for her could consume you. Anna... If I lost you...I would lose everything."

She could only stand there, looking at him, feeling like the earth was breaking to pieces beneath her feet. "Why did you—"

"I wanted to at least see it coming." He lowered his head, shaking it slowly. "I was such an idiot. For a long time. And afraid. I think it's impossible to go through tragedy like I did, like we did, and not have it change you. I'm not sure it's even possible to escape it doing so much as defining you. But you can choose how. It was so easy for me to see how you protected yourself. How you shielded yourself. But I didn't see that I was doing the same thing."

"I didn't know," she said, feeling stupid. Feeling blind.

"Because I didn't tell you." He reached up, drawing his thumb over her cheekbone, his expression so empty, so sad. Another side of Chase she hadn't seen very often. But it was there. It had always been there, she realized that now. "But I'm telling you now. I'm scared. I've been scared for a long time. And I've made a lot of promises to ghosts to try to atone for stupid things I said when my parents were alive. But I've been too afraid to make promises to the people that are actually still in my life. Too afraid to love the people that are still here. It's easier to make promises to ghosts, Anna. I'm done with that.

"You are here," he said, cupping her face now, holding her steady. "You're with me. And I can have you as long as I'm not too big an idiot. As long as you still want to have me. You put yourself out there for me, and I rejected you. I'm so sorry. I know what that cost you, Anna, because I know you. And please understand I didn't reject you because it wasn't enough. Because you weren't enough. It's because you were too much, and I wasn't enough. But I'm going to do my best to be enough for you now. Now and forever."

She could hardly believe what she was hearing, could hardly believe that Chase was standing there making declarations to her. The kind that sounded an awful lot like love. The kind that sounded an awful lot like exactly what she wanted to hear. "Is this because I'm wearing a dress?"

"No." He chuckled. "You could be wearing coveralls. You could be wearing nothing. Actually, I think I like you best in nothing. But whatever you're wearing, it wouldn't change this. It wouldn't change how I feel. Because I love you in every possible way. As my friend, as my lover. I love you in whatever you wear, a ball gown or engine grease. I love you working on tractors and trying to explain to me how an engine works and watching musicals."

"But do you love my porcupine pajamas?" she asked, her voice breaking.

"I'm pretty ambivalent about your porcupine pajamas, I'm not going to lie. But if they're a nonnegotiable part of the deal, then I can adjust."

She shook her head. "They aren't nonnegotiable. But I probably will irritate you with them." Then she sobbed, unable to hold her emotions back any longer. She wrapped her arms around his neck, burying her face in his skin, breathing his scent in. "Chase, I love you so much. Look what we were protecting ourselves from."

He laughed. "When you put it that way, it seems like we were being pretty stupid."

"Fear is stupid. And it's strong."

He tightened his hold on her. "It isn't stronger than this."

Not stronger than fifteen years of friendship, than holding each other through grief and pleasure, laughter and pain.

When she had pulled up and seen his truck here,

Anna Brown had murder on her mind. And now, everything was different.

"Remember when you promised you were going to make me a woman?" she asked.

"Right. I do. You laughed at me."

"Yes, I did." She stretched up on her toes and kissed his lips. "Chase McCormack, I'm pretty sure you did make me a woman. Maybe not in the way you meant. But you made me feel…like a whole person. Like I could finally put together all the parts of me and just be me. Not hide any of it anymore."

He closed his eyes, pressing his forehead against hers. "I'm glad, Anna. Because you sure as hell made me a man. The man that I want to be, the man that I need to be. I can't change the past, and I can't live in it anymore, either."

"Good. Then I think we should go ahead and make ourselves a future."

"Works for me." He smiled. "I love you. You're everything."

"I love you, too." It felt so good to say that. To say it and not be afraid. To show her whole heart and not hold anything back.

"I bet that I can make you say you love me at least a hundred more times tonight. I bet I can get you to say it every day for the rest of our lives."

She smiled, taking his hand and walking toward the house, not caring about the rain. "I bet you can."

He led her inside, leaving a trail of clothes in the hall behind them, leaving her beautiful dress on the floor. She didn't care at all.

"And I bet—" he wrapped his arm around her waist,

then laid her down on the bed "—tonight I can make you scream."

"I'll take that bet," she said, wrapping her legs around his hips.

And that was a bet they both won.

\* \* \* \* \*

We hope you enjoyed reading

**MAN IN CONTROL**

by *New York Times* bestselling author

**DIANA PALMER**

and

**TAKE ME, COWBOY**

by *New York Times* bestselling author

**MAISEY YATES**

Both were originally Harlequin® Desire stories!

**HARLEQUIN®**

*Desire*

**Powerful heroes…scandalous secrets…burning desires.**

From passionate, suspenseful and dramatic
love stories to inspirational or historical,
Harlequin offers different lines to
satisfy every romance reader.
Up to eight new books in each line
are available every month.

www.Harlequin.com

# Get 2 Free Books,
## <u>Plus</u> 2 Free Gifts –
### just for trying the *Reader Service!*

STRS17R2

She wandered out of the kitchen and into the living room just
as the door to the guest bedroom opened and Knox walked out,
pulling his T-shirt over his head—but not quickly enough. She
caught a flash of muscled, tanned skin and...

She was completely immobilized by the sight of her best
friend's muscles.

It wasn't like she had never seen Knox shirtless before.
But it had been a long time. And the last time, he had most
definitely been married.

Not that she had forgotten he was hot when he was married
to Cassandra. It was just that...he had been a married man. And
that meant something to Selena. Because it meant something
to him.

It had been a barrier, an insurmountable one, even bigger
than that whole long-term friendship thing. And now it wasn't
there. It just wasn't. He was walking out of the guest bedroom
looking sleep rumpled and entirely too lickable. And there was

just…nothing stopping them from doing what men and women did.

She'd had a million excuses for not doing that. For a long time. She didn't want to risk entanglements, didn't want to compromise her focus. Didn't want to risk pregnancy. Didn't have time for a relationship.

But she was in a place where those things were less of a concern. This house was symbolic of that change in her life. She was making a home. And making a home made her want to fill it. With art, with warmth, with knickknacks that spoke to her.

With people.

She wondered, then. What it would be like to actually live with a man? To have one in her life? In her home? In her bed?

And just like that she was fantasizing about Knox in her bed…

*Don't miss*
*THE RANCHER'S BABY*
*by* New York Times *bestselling author Maisey Yates,*
*the first book in the* **TEXAS CATTLEMAN'S CLUB:**
**THE IMPOSTOR** *series! Available January 2018*
*wherever Harlequin® Desire books and ebooks are sold.*

*And then follow the whole saga—*
*Will the scandal of the century lead to love for these rich ranchers?*
*The Rancher's Baby by* New York Times *bestselling author Maisey Yates*
*Rich Rancher's Redemption by* USA TODAY *bestselling author Maureen Child*
*A Convenient Texas Wedding by Sheri WhiteFeather*
*Expecting a Scandal by Joanne Rock*
*Reunited…with Baby by* USA TODAY *bestselling author Sara Orwig*
*The Nanny Proposal by Joss Wood*
*Secret Twins for the Texan by Karen Booth*
*Lone Star Secrets by Cat Schield*

www.Harlequin.com

## HARLEQUIN Desire

**Powerful heroes…scandalous secrets…burning desires.**

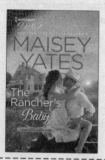

Save **$1.00**

on the purchase of ANY
Harlequin® Desire book.

Available wherever books are sold,
including most bookstores, supermarkets,
drugstores and discount stores.

---

# Save $1.00

## on the purchase of any Harlequin® Desire book.

Coupon valid until March 31, 2018.
Redeemable at participating outlets in the U.S. and Canada only.
Not redeemable at Barnes & Noble stores. Limit one coupon per customer.

**52615418**

5  65373 00076  2   (8100)0 12333

® and ™ are trademarks owned and used by the trademark owner and/or its licensee.

© 2018 Harlequin Enterprises Limited

NYTCOUP0118

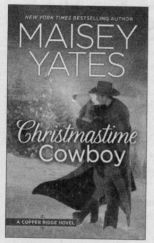

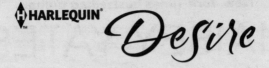